# One Spoon
# on This Earth

LIBRARY OF KOREAN LITERATURE

2

# One Spoon on This Earth

## Hyun Ki Young

*Translated by*
Jennifer M. Lee

DALKEY ARCHIVE PRESS
CHAMPAIGN / LONDON / DUBLIN

Originally published in Korean as *Chisang e sutkarak hana* by Silch'ŏn Munhaksa, Seoul, 1999

Library of Congress Cataloging-in-Publication Data

Hyon, Ki-yong, 1941-
[Chisang e sutkarak hana. English]
One spoon on this earth / Hyun Ki-young ; translated by Jennifer M Lee. -- First edition.
pages cm
ISBN 978-1-56478-915-0 (alk. paper)
1. Autobiographical memory--Fiction. 2. Cheju Island (Korea)--Fiction. 3. Korea--Fiction. 4. Psychological fiction. I. Lee, Jennifer M. (Jennifer Myunghee), translator. II. Title.
PL992.3.K5C4513 2013
895.7'34--dc23
2013027135

Partially funded by a grant from the Illinois Arts Council, a state agency

Library of Korean Literature
Published in collaboration with the Literature Translation Institute of Korea

www.dalkeyarchive.com

Cover: design and composition by Mikhail Iliatov

Printed on permanent/durable acid-free paper

*Father*

My father, who led an ill-fated life, must have known that he would obediently resign himself to the hands of death. Without showing any trace of that fate on his face, he lost his appetite all of a sudden and within fifteen days he had laid down his spoon once and for all. During the last three days of his life he was unconscious. The doctor said the deterioration of his lungs caused his fast decline in health. I tried to feed him rice gruel by trickling portions of it into his mouth but his stomach could not handle it; he had diarrhea every time. Even though my father was unconscious, he was still obsessive about cleanliness so much so that whenever there was any indication of diarrhea coming on he woke up startled and frantically looked for the bedpan. This happened several times and eventually he even rejected the rice gruel and calmly prepared himself to meet death.

Even though he was moaning lowly in his attempt to breathe life into his body, his faced looked calm and serene. The low lull of his moaning sounded like the fading ashes of a bonfire settling to the ground ash by ash. As I witnessed the ever-so-natural progression of his death, I was reminded of my father's gruesome car accident six years ago. My father almost died from excessive hemorrhaging; the suffering he had experienced, until he had shriveled up into the sad figure of a cripple because of a severely fractured right femur, was the cruelest pain of all. Was he so at peace with himself because he had already experienced the sufferings of death? Above all else, he who had a life of turmoil looked like someone who was reconciled with death. Wasn't this the final victory of a loser?

Overwhelmed by the emotions of gratitude and regret, I put my hand inside the covers and started massaging the bottom of my father's feet. When I was in junior high school, I used to massage my father's feet so he could fall asleep. What started out as an act of love later became a loathsome act of obligation. I used to be an obedient junior high school student, but I became a rebellious high school punk who clashed with my father in reckless conflicts. In other words, at the center of my father's life of turmoil was my share of unfilial acts.

On the day my father breathed his last breath, my younger siblings and I purified our father's body with scented water before shrouding him in his last garment. At this moment, I realized with every ounce of my being that his body was doomed to return to matter like a chopped up stump, stiff and spiritless. He was emaciated and bony. His skin had lost its luster like a dried-up fish scale, and the leg that had suffered the fracture was severely warped. I was cleaning his pitiful body with scented water and when my hand finally went to his crotch area, I was so overwhelmed with uncontrollable emotions that tears just rolled down my face.

For the first time in my life, I saw my father's genitals. The tension I felt when I was cleaning that area, and the touch of his skin, evoked emotions I could still feel even after three years had passed. The fact that my very being originated from here was so self-evident that it seemed rather illusory, to such a great extent, that it felt like an enormous burden that overpowered me at that very moment. It was one seed of existence, the place where the existence called "I" originated by chance, but the origin of life is now returning to ruins. That ruin was my father's death, and his eternal absence was confirmed in me as a sharp pain. His death made me realize that the reality of my death would find me sooner or later.

I've seen many deaths in my life, but I never felt the reality of death so vividly as I did at that time. I can still distinctly feel the sharp pain I felt when I came face to face with death—a death which originally hovered from a distance like a hazy form of illusion, then one day made a surprise attack on my father and penetrated his body. The sorrow and fear of seeing one's own death too soon were probably embedded in the tears I cried as the eldest son before the spirit of my departed father. Now that my father has passed away, it's my turn to go; this rude awakening pierced the innermost part of my heart. Birth is an accident but death is an unavoidable necessity.

However, death does not mean the complete extinction of life. Death does not completely destroy human individuality. This is evidenced by the fact that my father's image still lives on in my heart and soul, even though he has died. Even after his death, my father has been in and out of my consciousness, making me feel as if he had moved into my heart. Actually, isn't my father none other than myself? I am beginning to look more and more like my father. My father's life did not cease. It lives on in me, his son. The end is not a discontinuation but a beginning. Likewise my existence is not a separate entity but it signifies the blood ties of one connected link of collective lives.

My father was laid to rest in the family burial plot at the base of Mt. Halla. My uncle was already buried at that graveyard prepared by my cousins and me. Next to him, one grave site away, a second burial mound was created for my father. I took a few measured steps and stood on the plot where I too will be buried. At that moment my thoughts naturally went to the image of my eldest son in his first year of college. Touched by this strange sentiment, I laughed out loud.

The grave site had a good view. In one glance, I was able to see the breathtaking scene of the vast sky and the ocean meeting at the horizon and vying for the blue light, the wide and level green fields, the ascent of the soft ridgelines, and the cloud, like white silken fabrics, that floated low at the foot of the mountain. I would never tire of looking at this wonder of nature. In no time my sorrow evaporated and I became lighthearted. Why would anyone get depressed by the thought of death, with such a luxurious grave site? As I thought about my father's spirit, which left his physical body and lightly floated nestled inside that cloud like a white funeral streamer, I accepted not only my father's death but my own death with ease.

Across the path there was one tall cedar tree that obstructed the open view of the family burial plot. I climbed and tried to chop off the top portion of the tree but such a minor task turned out to be so physically taxing that I almost vomited. I could not ignore the fact that I was getting old. On that day, my whole body accepted the grim reality that at the age of fifty, I had fewer days ahead of me than days gone by.

This is how my father's death made a great impact on my psyche; it changed my way of thinking permanently. I picked up a habit of getting lost in absentmindedness and now and then groping around in the memory of my past, and my feet brought me to my hometown more frequently than before. On an island surrounded by water, the boy who dreamed of entering the world by piercing through the horizon and the boy who left by kicking aside his father who was standing like an obstacle at the threshold, has now become a middle aged man in need of a balm for body and soul, desiring to regress into his mother's womb. There is no purpose for writing this story other than to relive my long forgotten days of youth through the telling of this story.

Now only my hometown memories of my childhood and youth shine gloriously in my mind when I think about my past, and the rest of time and tide is a meaningless succession of days. While I am on the subject, let me throw in another silly idea. If we live each day like it is no different from any other, then can we really claim that we have lived a whole lifetime? Doesn't it come down to only one day of living? If we remember what we remember from our past as the true past, then we only really remember today. The past fades by today's glaring sunlight; today we only remember half of yesterday, and we remember two days ago as half of yesterday, three days ago as half of two days ago. If this is the only way we remember the past, through this endless formula, then the calculation we come up with is a little over a day and a half of time that we spend living the past. My dear readers, do not ridicule me for my absurd sophism. This sophism can also be interpreted to mean that today's sun is the most important one in the midst of infinite time. But more than today's bright sun, my long forgotten past is more important to me now.

These days when I go to my hometown, I wander here and there around the land and by the sea trying to piece together all the fragments buried in the darkness of my past. Now I walk around searching for paths of the wayfarer's footprints that have suddenly stopped in their tracks leading to nowhere in the forest. I shout out with joy when I find a banyan tree dangling with many fruits hidden behind an old hackberry tree nearby a shrine. I try to search for my younger self amid all the objects found in nature that remind me of my childhood and youth. People are not the only ones who raised me. I was weaned only a few months after birth but I grew up being nurtured from the breast milk of nature. Watching a newborn calf that just came out of his mother's womb suddenly rise up and stand on his legs after touching the ground for the first time gave me the impression that the calf was born through an eruption of the earth. Anyway it's clear to me that in my hometown, nature played an important role in forming my identity. It was a time of innocence, void of all shame and guilt since nature was a part of my life. It feels like only that period of my life was the truth and the rest was one big lie.

However, the reality is that on that island, Hambagigul Village, which no longer exists on the map, is where my umbilical cord was buried after birth. It may be because I am a writer who is used to seeing the world through metaphors, but since the village had been destroyed by fire during the suppression of 1948, it has been carved out in my consciousness as mere black ashes of ruins. Since that time, I visited that place to confirm that the black ashes of ruins had transformed into green fields of grain. But the only thing that truly stood out in my mind was the bamboo grove that stood at one side of the lot which became someone's barley field and a crape myrtle tree at the entryway of an alley. Didn't the sound of the bamboo thicket swaying with the wind, as if muttering some words, and the pile of bright flowers of a splendid crape myrtle tree, which bloomed defiantly, actually emphasize the scorched ruins of that place all the more?

Therefore, I don't know what to do about this feeling of loss, as if a part of my being had also burned up in flames together with the horrifying fire that scorched that place in 1948. It feels like the first six years of my life spent there—that place of only desolate darkness—had been erased with smeared ink. My perception of this darkness is the sincere truth, but without a doubt it is mostly the exaggerated work of a physiological lapse of memory. Since it was only a short period of time after my birth, my ability to think was not fully developed. In any case, I must simultaneously penetrate the darkness of the black burnt wasteland and the darkness of my lapse of memory, revive the dead village, and confront my forgotten childhood.

### Hambagigul, the Origin

The vast solitary darkness of my hometown—perhaps this darkness was related to the darkness of the origin. A gigantic shooting star fell at one point along a line tracing back to hundreds of years of boundless darkness. A meteorite mass of flames, brightening up the darkness like broad daylight, collided with the earth making a grand roaring sound and created a gigantic crater on that very spot. Later water welled up in the crater and it came to be called a "thunder pool" and a man in search of water began to settle around it. This man was my forefather. The "thunder pool,"— the place where existence began—was where my ancestors, who vanished into darkness after glowing like fireflies for a short while, lived.

In the vast darkness, I felt a new life stirring. And that was me. I was a fruit of that darkness. After I came out of my mother's womb, I was dying even before I let out my first cry. I was slapped in the cheek and my entire body was shaken but I was dying, turning charcoal black. Did I wish to return to that darkness? Birth is a pure accident. Life is nothing but a light as faint as the glow of a firefly so it is not worth desiring. In this moment of life and death my grandmother, who was frantically rubbing my stomach, felt something the size of a chestnut. She pressed hard thinking this might be it. As if she had pressed the button of an automated doll, at that moment my windpipe opened up and I cried out my first cry so loud that it hurt everyone's eardrums.

My existence came about by pure accident, and my family wondered how I would turn out since my beginning was so precarious. About three years after I was born, I was nothing but a piece of soft dough, not a human being. Since I had just come out of darkness I was still vulnerable to the influence of the dark shadow —death. There was a saying that children's mortality rates were equivalent to yielding only half the crops because it was common for children to die of smallpox, measles, and even a cold. At the slightest provocation, I was on the verge of returning to darkness. I almost had an older brother but he too withered and died after a year.

In this state of uncertain, soft-dough existence I was funneled into darkness. I had the smallpox and the measles, spending more time sleeping than staying awake. One day I opened my eyes due to the sensation of something touching my face. After four long years of slumber, I finally opened my eyes. I vividly remember this moment even now as if this is my first memory. It was saliva that came out of my great grandfather's mouth. Great grandfather had me on his lap and he was dozing off. A stream of saliva trickled down on his long beard and like a sticky spider web it touched my face. He was very old at the time.

I had been weaned but my mental capacity remained underdeveloped so that I just remember a few fragments of sensational memories, like the distinct feeling of my great grandfather's saliva. Several months before liberation, Japanese fighter planes were shot down not too far from Maemul, a village on a hill. I remember the enormous explosion but I don't remember at all about the five skirts that were made from partially burnt parachute cloth, one of which my mother wore for herself, and children who were older than me picking up scraps of metal frames, making slides out of them, and playing on the grass.

*Pig's Nose*
But I do remember a pig's nose. The pig's nose hung on my neck like a pendant. I must've been a premature child because I drooled until I was four years old. Like a cow, sticky saliva slobbered endlessly all over me so wearing a bib was useless as it soon got completely soaked like a damp kitchen towel. One corner of my mouth where I drooled and underneath my neck were always wet to the skin.

My mother and grandmother fed me frogs and grasshoppers they caught and roasted. I was even fed roasted insect cocoons. They always called me into the kitchen whenever they found cocoons on dry wood used for firewood. Was it because of a lack of protein due to the year of the bad harvest? Since I drooled for so long, perhaps it wasn't simply a lack of protein but rather a curse of some sort.

My drooling must have been severe as they resorted to cutting and hanging a pig's nose around my neck. Unlike cows, horses or dogs, pigs don't drool so that's why they had done this as an amulet. It would've been better if it were a pig's cuspid or toenail. Imagine a child drooling endlessly with a shriveled up pig's nose hung on a string through its nostrils around his neck! Since I was such a hopeless child, my family was gravely concerned about how I would turn out.

If I were to use the year of liberation (I was four years old at the time) as a basis around which my life is ordered then I could say that I don't have distinct memories before the liberation, as if they were erased. But I do remember certain things that happened three years before I left my hometown.

My father wandered outside because he was ill, and my mother took my baby brother and went to her parents' place. I was being raised in a house where grandparents often quarreled and loneliness began to infiltrate deep inside my body.

*Home*

After liberation, people who had been living a life of hell toiling in the coal mines returned. There were some who came back dead as pulverized bones of ashes. For a while my village was wrapped in violent emotions—some rejoiced for the survivors and some grieved for the dead. But what I remember most is the unfamiliar face of my grandfather whom I met for the first time. Grandfather returned after having worked in Osaka as a peddler for several years and he wore his tale of bravery, knocking down a Japanese laborer with bare hands who attacked him with a dagger, like a medal of honor.

The country was liberated but joy was short lived. The grain quota delivery to the government remained unchanged and the people's grievances mounted all over the island due to the bad harvest. I remember the poverty of that time, inferred from the memory that remained in my palate. I think it's because for the longest time I was deprived of any fish. I remember a piece of scabbard fish covered with cinders that was grilled on a barley straw fire. It was so delicious that my tongue still remembers that intense savory sensation. I don't remember much about various events and happenings at the time, but I vividly remember the taste of that scabbard fish which stimulated my taste buds momentarily then disappeared quickly.

Isn't it odd that the sense of taste and smell that fades away first still remains in my memory when other events and happenings have vanished? During such times of poverty it was unlikely that scabbard fish could be bought with money or traded with grains, so perhaps it was exchanged for a bowl of cold rice. Due to the severe drought even a handful of millet was precious. A woman from the seaside carrying a bamboo basket went around the small alleys of the village yelling out "Scabbard fish! Scabbard fish!" until her voice became hoarse but I guess no one bought her fish. Because she was hungry and tired, she must have entered my house asking for a bowl of leftover rice and in return she left one scabbard fish.

One day of idleness during the summer season meant ten days of no food in winter, so grandmother and mother were always busy working in the field; needless to say there was no time for them to take care of me. Furthermore, mother had to attend to my baby brother who was two years younger than me. Between working in the field and taking care of the baby, how was it possible for me to experience the loving touch of my mother's hands? She even had to lay the baby down in the shade in order to work. Later mother told me while badmouthing grandmother that the reason I had less than three months of breast milk was entirely due to grandmother's nagging. She insisted that if my mother breastfed me for a long time, I would turn out to be a spoiled child and not so smart. She added that one of the shellfish divers began feeding her baby rice seven days after his birth. During the busy farming season even a corpse stirred and worked, so it was not easy for my mother to carry the baby on her back and breastfeed often.

Anyway, I had to let go this sensual and physical pleasure of suckling early on, and my mother had to give up the joy of breastfeeding. Since she was so busy tilling the soil, the only person who could look after me was my great grandfather. That's why the image of my great grandfather appears as my first memory. Even that consisted of a few fragments of tangible sensational memories—his white ramie-like beard, the smell of tobacco, and the smell of urine from a chamber pot in the corner of the room. Despite the stench, even now it's a heart-rending memory for me, as if I could still reach out and touch the warmth of his body.

In a house filled with madness and discord, the only place I could find comfort as a child was in his arms. Father was suffering from a mental disorder. He had his first fit the year I turned three years old, so it was the year before the liberation. His illness turned out to be a blessing in disguise at that time when the Pacific War was coming to an end. Father, who was a graduating senior in the agricultural school, was able to get exempted from conscription thanks to his mental illness. His illness could not be attributed to any traumatic event though. The symptoms of his illness included endlessly murmuring to himself and wandering around aimlessly. He was suspected of feigning madness, so he was taken by the Japanese MP and tortured. Fortunately he wasn't dragged into the battlefield, but he suffered severely for close to three years, until a year after the liberation. He was fine one minute, then he had a fit the next; he left the house after he had a fit and roamed all over the place for several days. When he became tired, he just plopped down and slept, so one cheek was normal but the other side got dark and tanned.

Even when he regained consciousness he couldn't remember what he did or where he went. One time he took me for a bicycle ride and left me behind at a relative's house in a different village. My family frantically looked for me. Mother must have suffered the most from his madness. I guess she couldn't endure it any longer, so she ran off to her parents' place with my baby brother. Thinking back on it now, my father's illness might have been hereditary. Could it be the blood that had been transmitted for generations which might have caused the problems? Headstrong and extremely temperamental dispositions of my blood kin—this strong temperamental blood was manifested as madness in my father's time. My grandfather was notorious for picking fights for he was also hot tempered. Even I caused several commotions, seized by destructive passion when I was young. When my fierce temperament flared up, my mind turned completely blank and I was consumed with reckless impulses. Thinking back on those moments, even now I shudder.

*Great Grandfather*

My great grandfather spent most of his time lying down due to his old age. From his throat came a ceaseless wheezing sound as if nicotine was burning from the bowl of a tobacco pipe. After my grandparents left for work, the entire house sank deep in solitude all day long, making my loneliness even more intense. I wanted to go outside and play, but my buddy Kyesŏng had small-pox. So crawling insects scattered about on the courtyard became my friends. I gazed at the ants' procession absentmindedly and played with the cast-off shell of a cicada on the bottom of a citron tree and a mole cricket that couldn't fly even though it had wings. I even baited a bagworm inside a hole with barley ear and pulled out an earthworm going into a hole after spitting dirt outside and cutting it off at its waist. That kind of mischief was a matter of life and death for those insects but it was fun for me. I caught a beetle bug and broke off its four legs and laid it upside down and enjoyed watching it flapping violently, grazing the ground, turning round and round. I peed inside the hole of an old and decayed persimmon tree trunk swarming with ant larva. I caught a bee inside a pumpkin flower and took out its sting and killed it. But I was scared and disgusted by a centipede the size of the span of a hand and a mushy snail dragging its white slime.

It was not only insects that lived in the house. There was also a yellow-spotted serpent the size of an adult's arm living in the ceiling. Sometimes it leisurely crawled up the crossbeam. One time I saw the serpent dangling at the edge of the eaves. It swung back and forth for a while then, as if it could not hold up its own weight, it went plop and fell to the ground. The serpent didn't stir for a while, as though it had been knocked out, then it slowly raised its head. I was so scared that I ran gasping to the room where my great grandfather was lying down.

"Grandpa, that serpent came out again! It fell from the roof!"

Great grandfather raised his body halfway and clicked his tongue, staring at the serpent turning the corner,

"That 'old man' must have fallen trying to go around the eaves to eat sparrows' eggs. Those sparrows live in a hole in the eaves. He must be getting old if he didn't make it there."

Great grandfather called the disgusting, creepy serpent "an old man." This idea of regarding the house serpent as sacred, a protector of wealth, must have generated mixed feelings of gratitude and fear, like being in a god's presence. The house serpent was an object of appreciation for getting rid of rats that were eating away grains on the one hand and an unapproachable object of fear on the other.

*Night*

What I feared more than the serpent was the wild cat. I went to a bamboo forest in the back of the house by chance and was shocked out of my mind when I found bones scattered about on top of the fallen leaves. I was told that this wild animal came down at night and attacked chicken coops. Didn't grandmother say that it not only attacked chickens but snatched away crying babies? It happened before I was born, but one time this wild cat even came into the room. Everyone was frightened and so was the animal. In the pitch-dark room, the wild cat clung to the wall, frantically jumping from this wall to that wall; after a while it finally found the door and left. So every night I was scared to death that the wild cat had snuck into the room. Night, in fact, came during daytime, too. I burst out crying when my eyes were temporarily blinded by the abrupt change in light to dark from being outside in the sunlight and then suddenly entering the dark room. Because of this, I knew that even during the day darkness loomed large.

When the nighttime drew near, the sunlight receded into darkness and the inside of the house got even darker and loneliness arose like goose bumps. I felt dejected and went to the sunny spot of the courtyard where soy sauce crocks were placed. I rubbed my back against the jars, trying to find warmth and went further and further in between the jars. Since the crocks had been exposed to the sun all day long, my chest and back became warm when I rubbed my body against them. The smell of savory bean paste and salted anchovies grazed the tip of my nose. The faint warmth of mother's body heat . . . mother's been long gone to her parents' place . . . the courtyard was getting darker and darker. The dark of night that had retreated during the daytime slowly crawled out to reclaim its place in the house. From the dark ceiling the serpent crawled out and the wild cat crept into the dark bamboo forest. My heart froze. Mother was at her parents' house with my baby brother and no one knew where father was . . . tears rolled down my cheeks silently.

In the desolate and vast darkness of my hometown, a speck of light was turned on. It was the tiny bean-sized flame of an oil lamp. The shadows of my grandparents and me having a late dinner emerged in that light. Everything was traced in the shadows—bowls of barley rice on the table and the people who were eating. I felt my grandfather's gaze and I shoved barley rice into my mouth with my head down. I think my cheeks had traces of tears.

"Crying again? *Tsk-tsk*! Tears come out as easily as peeing. I wonder if you're going to be okay when you grow up. . . . Go to sleep!" said grandfather and blew out the lamp.

The light only stayed on briefly when we ate dinner and the room was once again buried in complete darkness. I tossed and turned next to grandmother who had her back to me fast asleep from fatigue. From the next room I heard great grandfather's breathing filled with phlegm in his throat, and the sound of wind rising from the bamboo forest where the wild cat lived. Tears welled up again as I thought about my mother at her parents' house with the baby and father

*Grandparents*

I would've been less lonely if I had received love and attention from my grandmother in lieu of my mother's love, but grandmother was also always busy so she couldn't really take care of me. Grandmother knew nothing but work. After a busy farming season ended, she didn't even have time to catch her breath because she immediately set out to peddle grains. She took a cow to the slash and burn farming villages of Mudŭngiwat and Mŏngul located to the east of the distant Mt. Halla to buy buckwheat and sold it at the town market. She was a stickler, for she did not even throw away one grain of rice, so her personality clashed with my mother who was a bit slower and more generous. My grandmother always looked around in search of any barley ear on the ground as she went about her business. She couldn't even pass a useless piece of cloth the size of a fingernail without picking it up. The reason why my father and uncle could graduate from the only agricultural school in town was solely due to my grandmother's diligence. But my grandfather grumbled terribly saying that grandmother was like a cow who knew nothing but work. He said he could live with a fox but not a cow.

I was afraid of my grandfather. Because he had just returned from doing hard labor in Osaka, he had a foul mouth. He got angry at even trivial things and hit grandmother. Every time he hit her I would go to one corner of the kitchen and cry silently. I think my embarrassing habit of crying started around this time.

I was a crybaby until I entered junior high school. The fact that I cried over nothing was extremely embarrassing. Even when I tried hard not to cry, I couldn't stop my tears from welling up uncontrollably. How many times did I cry over trivial matters? All those bland tears . . . Even now when I encounter a slightly sad part reading a novel or watching a movie, tears just roll down as easily as if I'm peeing, like my grandfather used to say. Is this called a mechanical inertia or conditional reflex? Or maybe it happened because I cried so often that my lachrymal glands became overdeveloped compared to my other organs and that is why even the slightest stimulation triggered a conditional reflex to secrete tears.

### Father

Father's whereabouts and what he was doing were still unknown. Even when he dropped by once in a while, he didn't stay longer than a day. And he only snuck into the room that grandmother and I shared so my grandfather never knew about his visits. Then he suddenly disappeared again. Because my father was such a mysterious figure, I was not happy to see him, rather I was afraid.

One time he showed up with a kite in his hand and I accepted it with great joy. But it soon became evident that it was someone else's kite that got its line cut off because it was tangled. If the kite owner showed up while I was flying it around outside, I would've felt humiliated. I was so disappointed in my father. Isn't a father supposed to stay home and do things for his children like making a kite and carving a top? Why can't he get it through his head that he must decide once and for all that he has to stay home and think about bringing back mother?

I have this image of my father as a gust of wind that suddenly rises and falls because of the speed of his bicycle. Even now I can clearly visualize my father riding a bicycle with only his upper body bobbing up and down, quickly fading away through the barley field.

One time he had me ride on the back of his bicycle and took me into town in the middle of the night. It was my first time—getting a bicycle ride and going into town—but there was no time for sightseeing. We stopped by my uncle's house briefly and came back home that same night. What I experienced going and coming back was nothing but darkness. In darkness, we rode the bicycle on a pebbled path so my butt hurt badly feeling every bump on the road. On top of that, I was so afraid that I was going to catapult out of the seat that I wasn't in my right mind. My father kept mumbling something but I couldn't hear a thing because of the headwind. I found out later that his senseless mumbling was due to his mental illness. He found a position as a driver in the livestock sector of the county office but had to let it go even though it was a long awaited opportunity.

*Maternal Grandparents' Home*
For several months my body was utterly consumed in loneli-

ness and I was suffering so much from solitude that even my strict grandfather took pity on me and allowed me to go to my maternal grandparents' house. I couldn't go whenever I wanted to; but I was permitted to go once in ten days and sleep over for only one night.

I was tormented by darkness and loneliness for so long that my maternal grandparents' home seemed like a totally different world. It was a bright and sunny place where cheerful laughter, lively gestures, and tender voices pervaded. The first day I went, I was so awe-struck by the bright and warm atmosphere that I stood in the courtyard like I had just been dropped out of the sky.

My maternal grandparents had three daughters so I, the first grandson, was really adorable in their eyes. Whenever I went there, my grandparents fought over me, trying to hold me in their arms, so my mother was pushed aside and had no chance of even getting close to me.

My maternal grandparents were kind-hearted people; they resembled each other like siblings. They worried themselves sick, fretting over the fact that they couldn't prepare something tasty for me during the bad harvest season. Every childish move I made became a source of sheer fascination in their eyes. My true nature, which had been suppressed, came alive whenever I went there, jumping and running around all over the house to my heart's content without any inhibitions. I was so agile that I ran here and there but I fell after stumbling on a rock or tripping over someone's foot. My grandparents felt bad that they couldn't feed me well so one time my grandfather let me drink rice wine made out of hulled millet. One drop of wine made me so drunk that I staggered here and there and everywhere. I finally fell on a pile of straw and fell asleep.

Unlike my paternal grandparents who automatically turned off the light after dinner, my maternal grandparents had the light on until late hours. It wasn't just a tiny bean size flame; it was a lamplight that couldn't even be compared. My maternal grandparents were better off compared to other villagers, but they weren't wasteful. After dinner, my mother, grandmother, and three or four other women from the neighborhood sat around the lamplight and made horsehair hats. Since it ate up a lot of oil, the neighbors brought some to help out.

I liked that lamplight. For someone like me who was used to inhaling black soot, smelling its sickening odor and only seeing the dim light of the lantern, the bright light that emanated from the lamp felt like it was illuminating the insides of my heart. I also liked the warm body heat that came from my mother's back. I didn't want to miss out on the light and comfort so I stayed up late, wetting my heavy drowsy eyes with horsehair water. There were moments when tears rolled down while looking at the flame flickering like a moth flapping its wings. When the night was over, I had to return to my father's home in the upper village. Mother immediately noticed and turned to look at me with sympathetic eyes and asked, "Are you crying again?" At that moment I was afraid I might see tears in my mother's eyes, so I replied, "No, it's not that. I was sleepy so I dabbed my eyes with water."

I dreaded going home so there were several occasions when I stayed a few more days. But my paternal grandmother usually came without fail to get me and got angry at my maternal grandmother, asking her why she didn't send me home on time.

### Cholera

I went back and forth to my maternal grandparents' home and spent about half a year there without any problems, but all of a sudden that summer when I turned five years old the road was completely blocked off. There is a saying that cholera strikes during the bad harvest years. Sure enough, cholera broke out on the entire island. It was an extremely contagious disease with a high mortality rate. Roads that connected from village to village were cut off and houses with cholera victims had "no-trespassing" rope hung at the entrance of the houses. As cholera spread rampantly, mistrust from village to village, town to town, and neighbor to neighbor intensified. Any friendly sentiment that had existed before soon vanished and fear loomed large. People who returned from the mainland and those who left home for a while had to set up a dugout in the corner of a field because they couldn't enter the village.

In my village, young men guarded the stone walls that were built to block the road to the village. Nŏbŭnŭrŭ was where my maternal grandparents lived and wasn't far, but no one was allowed to enter unless it was an urgent matter. Inside the village, I could move around freely and carry on as before. Even when children were playing, rolling on the ground and getting themselves all entangled and covered with mud, no one tried to pull them apart in fear of cholera. The disease seemed like a distant rumor, but there was a cholera victim in our village as well.

I remember a Black Kite that appeared from time to time circling around slowly, creating large circles high up in the sky in Hambagigul Village as if that was the only thing to do. One day the harmless and carefree Black Kite plunged in a flash with its huge wings spread out to reveal its true color. What the Black Kite pounced upon were chicks that were playing in the neighbor's yard. Like the Black Kite floating up high in the sky, the feeling of cholera terror that seemed vague and distant suddenly became real and immediate when the first victim appeared.

The comings and goings of the neighbors were less frequent and children playing outside were all called back into their homes. Since the mortality rate was high especially among the children, households with children were extremely fearful. My grandmother was overly anxious about me, so she kept reciting the "Goddess of Mercy." One time I ate something that made me have diarrhea all day long, and it scared my grandmother out of her wits. She thought I had cholera so she poured boiled soy sauce into my anus. Afraid that my rectum might fall out, she seared it with a burnt straw sandal. It was so piping hot that even now thinking about that day makes my rectum get stiff with dull pain. When afflicted with cholera, I was told that my rectum would fall out and pus-like feces would run like water.

The epidemic spread so quickly that within a short period of time the rest of the neighbors were infected. When one member of the family caught cholera almost the entire family became afflicted. Houses with cholera infected people were blocked with stone walls built at the front entrance to keep them inside. Drinking water was provided by the next door neighbors. Even in the alley where I lived, cholera crawled in like a tiger, biting and tearing apart five family members of my friend Yŏngjae. She was a pretty girl. As if they were sitting across from a wide-mouthed tiger, the neighbors were fearful whenever infected people stepped onto our alleyway. Even grandfather was reluctant to pass by Yŏngjae's house, so he locked the entrance door. Instead he demolished the stone walls in the back to create a passageway. From time to time, I heard the footsteps of young men patrolling the alleyway. One time a young girl's desperate cry for water was heard from Yŏngjae's house, so grandmother started chanting the "Goddess of Mercy" and ran quickly outside with a water jar.

One day when I was playing in the yard, I heard crowds of people running in the alleyway. I quickly ran and peeked through the hole in the stone walls. I was terrified! I couldn't make out whether they were ghosts or people! All four of them looked ghastly, completely covered in white cloth except for their eyes and their hands, which were also wrapped in cloth, were holding what looked like rakes and rags.

Grandmother ran out quickly when she heard me scream, and then she shoved me into the house. She then threw a handful of salt to the stonewall hole where I peeked out and spat on it. She made me drink water, and then she dabbed the crown of my head with the rest of the water as she chanted, "Oh, return spirit! Return spirit!" She was chanting because she was worried that I would lose my mind in shock, and the salt was used to drive the bad spirits away; even a kid like me knew that much. *Were what I just saw ghosts, and not humans?*

"My child, don't be scared. They went there to sterilize the house. They wrapped their faces like that in fear of infection," explained my grandmother.

They weren't there to sterilize, but to clean up the dead bodies. I found out after a few days had passed. This conversation came up between grandmother and a neighbor. I was startled to hear that two people died from Yŏngjae's house so I asked, "What about Yŏngjae? Not Yŏngjae, right?" Grandmother's answer was rather silly.

"Oh, yes, yes, that Yŏngjae. She was a good girl. Pretty face. Yes, that's right!"

Her way of announcing death was so unfamiliar to me that I was confused. Rather than burst out crying, I only shed a few tears.

"She hurt her hand . . . she hurt her hand when we tried to crack open a peach pit with a stone," I said.

Her death didn't seem real. It felt as though she was still living at home like my other friends whom I couldn't meet because of cholera. I didn't know what death meant at the time. How could a child who killed insects for meaningless fun understand death?

That summer, cholera lasted three months. In the small village of fifty households, more than ten lives were taken away, mostly children. The shadow of death must have hovered over me, too. Since I was immature and childish, I didn't fear death but felt really lonely, having been cooped up in the house for so long. I stole out of the house through an opening of the stone walls while grandfather was out, but I got into big trouble when he found out. I avoided a tiger then met a wolf; I didn't get infected with cholera, but I almost died from a fall.

*Horseshoe Scar*

Behind our house there was a field and in the middle of the fenced wall there stood a bead-tree. I was afraid that I would be caught by the village elders, so instead of going into the village I played under the tree. I caught a yellow horsefly sucking tree sap and made a marble out of a clump of tree sap. Many droning cicadas sounded like a sudden rain shower pouring down, deafening my ears. I really wanted to catch a cicada at least once, but it was stuck so high up that at first I didn't dare. But I succumbed to temptation.

Since it was my first time climbing a tree, I was overwhelmed with an incredible fear. After moving to the tree branch by using the wall as a stepping stone, I felt a sudden chill. I thought about going down, but when I grabbed and pulled the branch above my head, my body moved up quite easily. Full of nerves, I cautiously stretched out my trembling arm toward the cicada after I climbed up the second branch. I could barely reach the cicada. I held my breath and swooped on it with my hand. At that moment my hand felt like it had caught fire. The cicada thrashed violently inside my hand. I was so frightened by the violent struggle that my foot slipped and I fell head first down from the tree. I hit my head on the stone wall. And I fell inside the foxtail millet field and lost consciousness. I would've been in a more serious condition if the person who was tilling the field hadn't come immediately.

My injury was near fatal to the point where my brain was showing through a crack in the skull. Due to the road blockade, going to the town hospital was impossible so my life was left in the hands of fate. Even antiseptic couldn't be found easily. As an emergency measure, hair around the injured part was removed by searing it with a burning cotton ball. The torn-up red flesh with tattered piece of skin was washed with urine. A dark green millet leaf was taken out of the deep open cuts and my brain was clearly exposed. It remains fresh in my memory as if I had seen that white brain with my own eyes.

In any case, I was a resilient kid. After that, the only hospital medicine used on my injury was antiseptic that was obtained with much difficulty, but luckily the wound healed without any infection. More than anything, I was happy to see my mother again because of this accident. Having my mother next to me was so comforting that I wished that my wound wouldn't heal too quickly. My mother had this worried look on her face as she fanned the wound, fearing that flies might settle to lay eggs and hatch into maggots.

My mother returned to her home after my wound healed. Even if she insisted on taking me with her, it would have been utterly impossible because my grandparents wouldn't permit it. My mother, too, had no intention of coming back to live with my grandparents unless my father's illness was cured. So like before, mother went to her parents' house with my infant brother and father's whereabouts were still unknown. I became lonely again.

Later my grandmother confessed to me that she was so scared after the fall that she thought about putting me up for adoption at a shaman's house for a year or so. Since I almost died when I was born, she thought I had an ominous fate.

The wound hadn't been stitched properly and looked hideous when I saw it in the mirror. The size and shape looked like a horse-shoe imprinted on mud. That's why 'Horseshoe Head' became my nickname. Since I spent my childhood and adolescent years walking around with the ghastly looking wound on my bald head, it played an important role in the formation of my personality. When the kids called me by my nickname, they teased me re-lentlessly saying, "Look at that head, horseshoe head." I had two inferiority complexes during my adolescent years—one was math and the other was my scar. I wished so much to graduate from school, not to study math and grow my hair long to cover up the scar.

Now that I'm in my fifties and have a receding hairline, I notice the scar that has long been forgotten. With the reappearance of the scar, my cowardly tendencies resurfaced from the bygone days of 'Horseshoe Head' and I found my hands going to my head trying to cover the scar with the little hair that remained. My childhood scar resurfaced as I aged and once again the lost memories of the past come alive.

That summer, the sweltering heat and cholera that raged for three months retreated around mid-August when it was cool in the mornings and evenings. The number of deaths throughout the island reached three hundred and fifty in total. The villages had already been devastated by the epidemic, and the drought led to another bad millet harvest. They didn't have time to recuperate from the physical and mental distress caused by cholera because they were thrown into the abyss of famine.

The three years after the liberation marked a vicious cycle of bad harvest, epidemic, and bad harvest again. The country was liberated after the severe suffering at the end of the colonial period, but life was a quagmire. For the islanders, liberation didn't mean true liberation. The notorious rice delivery during the colonial period continued even after the liberation. So how could you call it liberation when the two foreign countries divided up the nation and occupied one each? The following year on March 1, 1947, twenty thousand citizens gathered to demonstrate. This protest signified the painful outcries of people who were pushed to their limits. The American military forces responded with indiscriminate shooting at the people who were gathered to express their sorrow and grievances. Six innocent civilians were killed.

*School*

Around this time father had returned home. His expression was bright as if he had woken up from a nightmare, and his mental state had returned to normal. On the morning of a major gathering at the town, the road to the entrance of the village was crowded with people who came from different villages to attend the meeting. My father was also among the crowd. It was the first time in my life that I saw such an enormous crowd of people. It was quite a sight to see them passing by with straw mat banners on top of their heads bobbing up and down. Watching that spectacle, I was all excited but, most of all, I was delighted that my father was there.

Father returned home from the gathering around dusk all smiling and he untied a small bundle in front of me. To my surprise I found a pencil, a notebook, and a pair of rubber shoes inside the bundle. I was so happy that I cried. It was the first time I got a "real" present from my father. I thought perhaps my father was thinking of an even greater present by bringing back mother from her parents' house.

The next day I entered Hambag School, a provisional elementary school in the village. I wore the rubber shoes and carried the notebook and pencil. As if I had entered a whole new world, I went from one exciting day to the next. I was a student carrying a pencil and a notebook, and I stepped out into the unknown world of letters. My rubber shoes made every step I took really worthwhile. What softness that snuggled my bare feet! When twisted, the rubber shoes shrank and distorted but when let go, the shoes quickly transformed back into their original shape, like a living creature. So whenever I got bored, I had them face each other for a cockfight.

But my excitement soon ended. A week after I entered school, a demonstration took place on the entire island in protest against the March 1st massacre, so the school closed down for an endless vacation.

In order to break up the general strike, a large number of police and youth groups from the mainland came to the island. From the sweeping roundup, five hundred people were arrested and they were severly tortured. Half of them were remanded pending a trial, but the torture was so severe that two of them died. The American military put down the general strike and exercised brutal violence once again. They demanded the delivery of barley, thus infuriating the islanders. The entire island was filled with resentment. In every village and work place, secret meetings were held and handbills were passed out.

*Torchlight*

I understood the situation as something similar to cholera since I was only a child and knew nothing better. It was around the time of the barley harvest. The young men of the village built stone walls at the entrance of the village like the time of cholera and blockaded the road. It was done to prohibit the entry of the police cars, but the villagers were free to come and go. The young men watched from afar and whenever they spotted a police car, they yelled out "Cholera! Cholera!" alerting everyone. They hid themselves in the field and told even the children to yell out "Cholera!" whenever strangers were spotted. The young men didn't just take refuge; they came back with firewood when they returned from hiding on the mountain. On those days, they tried to incite fighting spirit by displaying torchlight from early evening.

But the situation didn't settle; it only became worse. I only went to school for three or four days. Even after several months had passed Hambag School was still shut down with no signs of reopening. I started to hear rumors that so and so working in the field or so and so running errands were taken by the police. Some young men ran away because they were afraid to stay home. And father left home again. When the traffic at the entrance of the village became visibly scarce, once again grandfather declared home confinement so that I couldn't go to my maternal grandparents' house. The village was gripped by fear like the time when cholera broke out.

It was around that time a lump appeared on my neck. It was scrofula, a chronic mass that didn't go away easily. My grandmother called the process of the pus filling the lump and rupturing as "picking when it's ripe." The swelling became worse and worse and it turned into a large mass. I was suffering from depression and on top of that I had scrofula so I was filled with grief and wept endlessly. My head was always tilted because my neck was pulled to one side. Even talking was painful, so I stopped speaking altogether. I couldn't even play with other kids so I sat around and watched them despairingly. Even my best friend Kyesŏng hung out with his other friends, so I was alone all summer long. Because of the scrofula, I sporadically had chills in the middle of sweltering heat. The children were cheerfully running around the myrtle tree that had mounds of bright pink flowers on its top at the village entrance and the honeybees that Kyesŏng's family harvested busily buzzed around. But I became weak hearted to the point where it pained me to even watch the pink flowers.

My grandfather had a dubious look. He was doubtful as to whether I could grow up to be a man since I almost died twice. I must have looked like a despicable, shabby looking colt with this chronic scrofula. It was understandable that he questioned whether I could survive in this world. I became a great disappointment to my grandfather when I was struck with scrofula.

My depression became worse but there was one exciting thing. It was the torchlight demonstrations that took place from time to time. When I heard the noise of the demonstrations in early evening, I was compelled to slip out of the house because of uncontrollable impulses. Watching the wavering and burning torchlight that kindled the darkness and hearing the resounding shouts of people while stomping their feet made my young blood boil, so I found myself following the tail end of the demonstrators. I forgot all about the pain in my neck. The torchlight had a strange power and it took me by storm. During that gloomy period of my life, I was easily attracted to fire but the torchlight was quite different. The flame represented something very powerful, and I desired to possess it.

One night when I heard the sound of the torchlight from outside, I entered the kitchen wanting to make my own. I poured gasoline inside a bamboo tube that I had prepared earlier and stuffed cotton at the mouth and struck a match light. Alas! The fire that had caught on the cotton spread quickly to the bamboo tube I was holding. The outside of the bamboo tube was smeared with gasoline. I dropped the tube quickly and I fell on my behind. The fire quickly caught on the barley straws and spread to the clay walls. At that moment my grandfather ran in. I must have screamed for help. After my grandfather put out the fire with a broomstick, he caught me by the back of my collar with his coarse hand and threw me out of the kitchen. He did not beat me up because I was sick but he was furious. My grandfather yelled out saying that I was an ingrate. He had saved my life twice and I was returning his gratitude by burning down the house.

More than anything else, he was furious because I was trying to make torchlight. At the time, the young men pursued by the police entered the mountains and the torchlight strike became more frequent, worrying the elders. My grandfather considered the young men's torchlight strike as exceedingly dangerous.

I was not allowed to even step outside as a punishment for almost burning down the house. There were frequent arguments between grandmother and grandfather regarding what my father should do. It was not possible to abandon one's home and leave the village so grandmother insisted that one of their sons had to side with the mountain people. My uncle at the time was a civil servant, working at the provincial government office. Kyesŏng's older brother came together with my second uncle and asked about my father's whereabouts and expressed their anger saying, "How can he flee when he needs to fight with us?"

Every time an argument broke out between my grandmother and grandfather, they hurled abuse at each other. I shut myself in the kitchen and cried silently. My great grandfather was in a coma due to old age. There was nothing I could do about the infinite sadness. It was during the monsoon season, and my sad soul was deeply lost in the rain. Fortunately when the rain poured down hard, I was able to cry louder because my grandfather in the room couldn't hear me.

*Leaving Hometown*

My great grandfather passed away at last. I don't know how my father knew but he came home in time for the funeral. The funeral was carried out in fear that the police might rush in and disturb the ceremony to question the mourners. Those young men who went into the mountains couldn't come down to the village, so they had to make a condolence visit at the burial ground and took care of all the tomb work. But my father disappeared again after the funeral. What did my father talk about with them at the burial ground? He probably made an excuse for himself by saying that he was not in his right mind.

Father was always out, and mother was at her parents' house. I kept crying because I was utterly discouraged and afraid of my strict grandfather. Even now when I watch the rain pouring down really hard during the monsoon season, I remember the dreary, tear-filled sadness of my childhood.

In the fall of that year, something unexpected happened. It was as though my heart had been drenched with pouring rain, but suddenly a ray of warm sunlight entered. My maternal grandmother's second son-in-law was a notorious leftist, and her youngest son-in-law became a policeman. My grandfather, who didn't know where to stand between left and right wing, finally decided to move into town, and at the time my mother took me with her. I had no idea that would be my last time in my hometown! The following year, Hambagigul was reduced to ashes and it disappeared from the map forever. At the time of the Cheju Massacre, Nohyŏngri together with Hambagigul suffered tremendous damages.

*Ill Omen*

That year in May when I left my hometown, something extraordinary happened around the pool that was used for drinking water. Out of the blue, several water snakes appeared in the pool. Of course there were water snakes before, but only one appeared once in a while. When I got thirsty while playing with other kids, I stuck my head inside the pool and drank the water like a horse. Even though the water snake was swimming there inside the pool, I wasn't afraid. I felt a bit uneasy when I drank the water too fast fearing that I might inhale water snake eggs on the bottom. But after seeing several water snakes violently cutting across the water, I was even afraid to drink the water that was drawn from the pool at home. Drinking the water would not just mean swallowing snake eggs but an entire snake. The number of snakes increased due to the presence of many tadpoles in the pool, and they would disappear after eating all the tadpoles.

It was unknown why so many tadpoles were there. Right above the pool, a small pond, the size of a grinding stone, was filled with tadpoles like black ink water. It was a hideous sight! The crowded tadpoles looked like red bean porridge boiling in a pot. What was even stranger was that after a little while all the tadpoles died even before the snakes swallowed them up. Dead tadpoles with their white stomachs up in the air filled the surface of the water.

As if that wasn't enough, the dead tadpoles overflowed to the water's edge. What an appalling sight! *Can something like this happen for real?* I thought the tadpoles all died because they caught cholera. I sensed fear in the adults as they whispered to each other, "This is unusual. Isn't this a sign of death?"

Their suspicion came true the following year. The decimation of the tadpoles transformed into the mass slaughter in the Cheju Massacre. Since I didn't witness the Cheju Massacre with my own eyes, I only guessed it through the ominous symbol of the destruction of the tadpoles. The catastrophe of the tadpoles was a phenomenon that could be explained ecologically, not caused by black magic. I accidentally came across a section in a book that explained that when the natural enemies of the tadpoles disappear, due to an unknown reason in a small pond it causes the tadpoles to flourish, filling up the water; but they all die due to the lack of oxygen supply. Science explained the pond's mystery but I still could not get over the idea of supernatural phenomenon. I was reminded of the pond full of dead tadpoles when I heard that many corpses were piled up vertically and horizontally using each other like pillows and heard a witness saying that ten bodies were buried in a small ditch like sardines.

*Mukŭnsŏng Village*

The distance from Hambagigul to town was about two miles. People who went to the town market to peddle often rested midway in Toryŏngmaru, so it was called "*t'uch'am* way" or halfway. The day we moved into town, I was happy and excited as I walked down the town road for the first time in my life. I followed my mother who was carrying a heavy rice sack on her head. The year before I came to town with my father on a bicycle, but since it was at night, all I could remember was pitch black darkness. I saw the ocean for the first time. I was only as tall as the wall surrounding the field so I had a narrow view. Upon climbing Toryŏngmaru, I caught a glimpse of what looked like a blue band far on the north side, and as this band became bigger and bigger, turning into the vast ocean, my eyes opened wide at the spectacular sight of the azure ocean.

When I reached the main street after walking on small country roads, I became frightened by trucks that sped away with an explosive sound, kicking up huge clouds of dust and rocks. What was even scarier was crossing the bridge over a huge stream at the entrance of the village. It was Han Stream that I'd heard so much about. It was a sturdy concrete bridge with proper railings, but I felt dizzy looking down the deep valley below. I could not take a step forward because I felt as if my body was floating up in the air. So I literally crawled with my nose touching my mother's heel and crossed the bridge. There is a saying that when people from the country went to Seoul they started crawling from the outskirts because they felt so small and overwhelmed. I was like that. I was scared of the electric poles standing tall and the shop windows glaring in the sunlight. I was even scared of a hoop that children were rolling around so I held on to the hem of my mother's skirt. Everything was new so I looked around with my eyes wide open and after a while I came across another bridge that caused much distress. I do not know why I was so scared of crossing bridges. Thinking back now, since I almost died from falling off a tree, I developed a fear of heights.

I trembled while I was crossing Pyŏngmun Stream and after that I walked down along the stream. The ocean, which I had only caught a glimpse of at Toryŏngmaru, revealed its deep blue hue at the mouth of the river right before my eyes. The moment I confronted the ocean that swelled up threatening to overflow at the mouth, the ocean that later became the cradle of my childhood and youth, I exclaimed, "Wow! Look at all this water!" Later my mother told me, laughing, that I was such a country boy who only knew water in a small pond near my old home. One of my relatives had moved a month earlier, and my female cousin who was two years younger than me playing outside the gate, greeting me happily and calling me brother, "*Oppa!*" as soon as she saw me. She had grown so tall since the last time I had seen her that I felt a bit awkward.

From that day on, we lived off my maternal grandparents and our destitute existence began. There were two extra rooms. One of the rooms was rented out to a young couple, and we lived in the other.

The village was called Mugŭnsŏng because it was located where the old castle used to stand. By the riverside, small thatched houses, similar to the one my grandparents' lived in, clustered together where the eaves touched each other, but further into the center of village, there were many big and fancy houses. There were several antique style Chosŏn houses, Western style houses with ceramic tiles on walls, Japanese style houses, and houses with coal tar galvanized roofs. Even in the thatched roof houses, glass windows were installed to block out the wind and the rain instead of wood. The stone walls outside the houses were nicely sealed with cement instead of soil and the patterns at the joints were quite stylish.

Two days after we moved in, my mother and I went around the entire village to look and to say hello to our relatives. My cousins from my father's side lived in a galvanized roof house with tall pillars, and my cousins from my mother's side lived in a thatched roof house with glass windows. They lived in big houses but they were hard-pressed for money. My uncle could not support his big family of six children with his salary as a clerk working at the provincial government, so he raised and sold horses on the side. Since the horse drawn mills were replaced by electric machines, there were several that were no longer in use. He raised the horses by using one of the old mills as a stable. My uncle had a knack for turning a mean horse into a healthy one. Once I saw him force-feeding a horse from a soda bottle filled with sesame oil mixed in with eggs. I wonder if that was his secret to raising a healthy horse? One time I happened to pass by the mill at night and was startled when I saw the horses' eyes glittering in the darkness.

After I moved into town, everything I saw and experienced was new and wonderful, but what shocked me the most was the house search in the middle of the night. Several days after we moved in, a house search took place in our neighborhood. A man wearing army boots came into the room where three of us slept and flipped over the blanket with the muzzle of a gun and asked, "Where's your husband?" From the unfamiliar northern accent, it was clear that he was one of those notorious Sŏch'ŏng police. It happened so fast and unexpectedly in the middle of the night that my mother couldn't think straight. But fortunately he was after someone else so he didn't wait for her to answer and left abruptly the same way he came in.

I saw my cousin Namsu who was a year older, and he said he was not scared at all. He was quite smug and said, "You idiot! You're such a scaredy cat. To me, it's nothing. This is my third time. Do you know what happened during the March 1st demonstration? It was quite a scene. You can't pay money to see something like that. There were so many people that the roads were packed, the stone walls collapsed, and the store windows shattered to pieces. It sure was something." He also told me that he almost died in a stampede when he watched the demonstration outside the gate and the people who were running away from the shooting ran inside the gate like a swarm of bees. He proudly showed a faint scar on his forehead.

*Entering School*

My father, who was hiding not knowing whether to side with the left or the right, enlisted for the national defense guards at the insistence of my mother's father and her brother a month after our move. He was twenty-seven years old at the time. After he joined the national defense guards, he hardly came home. He was posted at the end of the west side of the island in Mosŭlp'o, which was very far. Later he was in the mainland for training, so he continued to remain absent and I was fatherless.

Then father appeared on the day when I entered Puk Elementary School the following spring. Father had just returned from the training and showed up late for the opening ceremony. Entering an elementary school meant having a new set of family. In other words, it was like having an even stricter father and even more selfish brothers and sisters. I was extremely scared since I was nothing but a country boy, so my father's presence was comforting and I felt secure. Father had transformed into a stylish Chief MP, wearing a military uniform with nice sharp creases and an armband. He had always trodden in darkness and that was the reason why I suffered depression, sodden with tears. But when I saw my father beaming with smiles, I felt my depressed heart filling with the light of hope.

Together with the memory of my father appearing at the ceremony, I remember my math class. There were many students who had studied the basic numbers before entering school so I felt stupid. In particular, I had a hard time writing the number eight. I was scared of my homeroom teacher who had dark eyebrows and really big eyes. "What is this? Is this a worm? Get it right. If you can't write eight, your life will be ruined. Understand?" My teacher said this because the number 8 sounds similar to the word fate in Korean. I advanced to an upper class, but I continued to have difficulty writing eight in Chinese characters. Perhaps that's why I became an ill-fated foolish writer. Since I survived a politically dangerous and volatile period when living and dying was purely determined by chance, perhaps my fate isn't so bad after all.

## Signal Fire and Arson

It's widely known that for a year after what happened during the March 1st massacre, the brutal suppression from the police and right wing youth groups from the mainland generated a desperate resistance calling forth, "Either you die sitting down or stand up and fight!" The April 3rd insurrection led to boycotting of the May 10th election, but the unfolding of these events meant nothing more than rumors to me; they simply weren't real. As my maternal grandfather had said, our town was completely dominated by the government authority and was protected like a well, so the people weren't easily shaken up. The village people participated in the general election as well. *How could I possibly see anything clearly and understand the rumors that were floating around when I was only a child as tall as the wall surrounding the field?* I only heard half of what was being said.

However, I could clearly see the signal fires that rose at night. After the uprising, the fire rose often from the direction of the faraway ascending ridges of Mt. Halla. Every time I saw the signal fire, my heart pounded with strange excitement. Once, the signal fire flared up close by in Toryŏngmaru, and I was surprised that the fire I saw at Hambagigul had advanced there.

Around this time, the Cheju regiment of defense guards launched a full-scale military action. Until then, the defense guards adopted the middle stance as the national army, advocating neither the left nor right wing and understanding the insurrection as a conflict arising between the police and the people. However, the defense guards were crushed when the American government killed the chief leaders in the central military. Immediately after the replacement of the commander, the defense guards were ordered to get involved in the counterinsurgency operation called "suppressing the riot." That's what they called it, but in reality it was more like massacring ordinary citizens. Among the men in the counterinsurgency operation, there were Cheju natives who were caught in between. They became the target of the police because they were young men, so they had to take shelter joining the defense guards to survive. However, as the defense guards they were in the position of aiming their guns at their own family members. They were outraged at their fate, leading to massive desertion and heading to the mountains. In the end, this led to the assassination of the commander. After this incident, Cheju Island natives were under suspicion. Their guns were taken away and the people were kept in isolation. Those Cheju natives were vexed and troubled with the reality of having to kill their own brothers, but as for my father who was in charge of a clerical work as an MP, he probably was under less stress.

Around that time, he was transferred to the office in town from Mosŭlp'o. My father often went to Seoul as a courier, and he usually took ten days or more. Even though he was working in town, he lived in the barracks, so he rarely came home. We only saw him briefly when he stopped by during his rounds at night. I hovered around the military base hoping that I would run into my father. Then one day I saw him standing guard and I was utterly disappointed. I thought three stripes meant he was high in ranking, but he was nothing but a guard. After that, he was guarding the governor's residence, which was located near my school. I was in despair, so I used the back street to get to school to avoid him. That was about the time the governor's life was threatened by the rioters.

The gap between my father and I could not easily be bridged due to different things that happened to us. It was not my father's fault entirely. I was not a likeable child. I cried a lot and didn't talk much; I only answered his questions curtly. So how could he find me likeable? And for no apparent reason, I was afraid of him.

One time my father, who showed no particular interest in me, took me to a theater. We entered for free since he was working as an inspector that day. He sat in the inspector's seat in the back of the theater and had me sit on his lap. It was my first time watching a movie at a movie theater and my first time sitting on his lap. Actually, sitting on his lap felt like I was on pins and needles. What was projected on the movie screen was an old film of an image of pouring rain, so I had no idea what the movie was about. On top of that, I didn't like being in such close contact with my father, so I fidgeted the whole time.

By the autumn, the situation had taken a turn for the worse. Taking advantage of the commander's assassination, indiscriminate hostility toward the villagers spread throughout the island, reeking of murderous intent.

My grandparents stayed on in Hambagigul, and my mother went back and forth to tend to the fields. After the millet harvest, it was no longer safe to go home. My mother could not possibly find a way to transport the millet she harvested, so she left it with a relative who lived across from our house. She stayed for two or three days to sow barley seeds. Then the terrible disaster fell upon us. About one hundred and thirty houses in the village were set on fire and the massacre had begun.

One early evening, the glow of the setting sun on the western horizon was unusually bright red. My mother murmured to herself nervously and said something wasn't right. Then all of a sudden she screamed, "Oh my god!" It wasn't the glow of the setting sun. As the night drew near, the red glow intensified, covering the entire sky and coloring the town with crimson red. My mother's shocked face was tinged with a red glow as well. The night fire was difficult to contain and unpredictable, so I was told, and it looked as if the fire was burning close by, right below the bridge over Han Stream. But the fire was burning two and a half miles outside where we were. It was the fire that was burning down Hambagigul and Nohyŏngri, the places where I was born and grew up.

The fire, which began in the middle of the slopes, spread from one place to the next. The crimson clouds floated here and there. I couldn't see the fire since it was too far and couldn't hear the sound of gunshots. The only thing I could see was the uncanny smoke that filled between the sky and the earth, writhing together with the clouds.

The fire that burnt down Nohyŏngri was not put out even the following morning, so the western sky was filled with smoke. This incident made my father realize his powerlessness. My grandmother was safe because she had come to my uncle's house a few days before. But we were worried about grandfather who was left alone in the old house. People fled to the mountains in herds. And after the commander's assassination, my father could not move about freely since he was an MP. Those who were in the defense guards were suspected of having connections with the mountain people. He told his superior that he needed two hours to go back to his hometown to bring back his father, begging and crying. Rather than being sympathetic, his superior looked at him with suspicion and said, "What are you saying? Your father is in that village where the rioters are rampaging? Isn't it strange that he stayed behind when he should've been in town already? Anyway, the counterinsurgency operation is beyond our defense guards' control. Since they're going to work on that village all day today, no one is allowed to enter."

This "work" was none other than finding survivors from the incineration and killing them off. Then they were ordered to transport foods to the seashore. We were worried to death about grandfather's safety. My father was busy doing his rounds and my uncle, using his position as a civil servant, was able to go to the seashore village Todu. Before my uncle even had the chance to look for my grandfather among the refugees, he was under suspicion and was dragged around with a bridle on his neck.

The next day after the "work" was completed my father was

granted permission to enter the village. We thought my grandfather was dead, but fortunately he hid himself behind the bamboo forest and was safe. He came out when my father called out his name, and he had the family ancestral tablet tightly held against his chest. I was told that he plopped down in front of a citron tree, unable to take even a few steps soon after he came out. All the tension was released at once. The images of the ruins described by my father—a half burnt old citron tree, scorched branches with no leaves, a chicken in shock perched on the branch dozing off, my grandfather squatted down underneath the branch holding the ancestral tablet to his chest, his eyes unfocused and clouded with fear—left a vivid memory like a charcoal sketch in a perfect composition in my consciousness.

The millet that my mother left with my relatives disappeared in the flames, too. That would've been our family's provisions for half a year. One hundred and thirty households situated between Mt. Halla and the seashore villages were engulfed in the flames. With the fiery holocaust, a large-scale massacre had begun. Half of the people who fled to the mountain were labeled as rioters and became the target of shooting, and the other half, mostly old people and women, were ordered to move to the seaside and were executed because they were the rioters' family members. In addition to the people, cows and horses were also indiscriminately slaughtered.

I did not know what was going on because I was only a child at the time. I did not know the true meaning of the terrifying flames that engulfed the entire sky. My friends didn't know either so they called it "arson." I too called it arson. The fire that rose in the beginning of the massacre on top of the mountain was a signal fire and the fire set by the counterinsurgency forces was arson. I later understood the differences in meaning when I became an adult.

I still don't understand the true meaning of the monstrous fire.

I understand the torchlight, and that several torchlights became a signal fire, but I just can't comprehend the holocaust that engulfed the entire sky. The flames soared into the sky and humans and animals were destroyed en masse. The sky was filled with screaming and moaning, but even the gods were confused and didn't understand. Heaven was idiotically indifferent as usual. It was even more difficult to comprehend because it was a manmade calamity, not a natural disaster. How can anyone possibly explain that outrageous massacre? It just doesn't do justice describing the atrocity with words like merciless or inhuman cruelty.

*Survivors*

After Nohyŏngri was completely burnt down, my maternal grandparents' place was crowded with relatives who fled from the disaster. My grandfather had two cows and put them out to pasture but lost them in the fire. People even occupied the empty stable. They were mostly my mother's aunts from both her maternal and paternal side and her brother's family, who barely escaped death when their village was on fire. They also lost their family members in the shooting.

My maternal grandparents' misfortune did not stop there but fell onto my two aunts. When the family members of those who entered the mountain were executed, my two aunts barely escaped death by concealing their identity. When they came to town, they were taken away by the police. And we received an urgent message informing us that my youngest uncle who drove a police car died in a car accident.

The youngest aunt who had been married for a year had a baby girl. She cried and wailed, rolling around the floor, and I sobbed next to her. She was pretty, so I liked her a lot. She was crying her heart out when the door was flung open, and my grandfather angrily said, "Stop crying! You're not the only one. Everyone in the village and everyone on this island is going through the same thing. You ought to be ashamed of yourself crying like that in front of all your relatives!"

I was told that people cry when they are not completely heart-broken. I had never seen my other relatives cry out loud. They only sighed heavily. My uncle's family all died except for their young daughter and most of my mother's aunts' families died, too. I was also told that people cry when they are not terror stricken. The reason why they didn't cry was because they were utterly ter-rified. Their family members were killed because they were re-lated to the rioters, so they lived in fear for their own immanent death. They were afraid that if they cried out loud they were ex-posing themselves as the family of one of the rioters. The reason my youngest aunt was able to cry her heart out was because her husband was a police officer.

My family was comprised of a military family, a police family, and a rioters' family. My grandfather had sons-in-law who were an MP, a police officer, and a rioter. To prepare for house-to-house searches, he decorated his police officer son-in-law's por-trait with flowers and placed it on a dais that everyone could see easily. And he asked his soldier son-in-law to stop by frequently whenever possible. I still remember the portrait of my youngest uncle who had on the black uniform with double breasted brass buttons. Placing his portrait on the dais was effective because we had two house searches but passed without any problems.

My father's powerlessness was once again apparent because he could not help get my aunt out when she was taken in for questioning. After severe torture for ten days, my aunt was re-leased when the police confirmed my uncle's death. She was a student at the village night school. She surpassed her fellow male classmates and was top of her class. Later she married the hand-some night school teacher, who was also an eloquent speaker, and she became the object of everyone's envy. But everything came to naught. After she returned home, she suffered from the aftereffects of torture and was bedridden for several days. Her face was bruised but the bluish shade underneath her eyes strangely remained even after all her bruises disappeared. I did not know at the time, but apparently she was born with the bluish birthmark. Seeing my aunt unable to overcome her traumatic experience for a long time, I thought of the bluish shade as the bruise she got from the torture.

My other relatives and my friend Kyesŏng and his brother took shelter at my uncle's house. My father was doing the rounds trying to find relatives among the refugees when he found Kyesŏng and his brother and brought them home. Kyesŏng had turned into a gloomy person. He rolled his hollowed eyes and refused to answer any questions. He looked as if he was still in shock. The day the village was on fire, Kyesŏng and his brother said goodbye to their parents and came down to the seaside. Their parents went into the mountain and, before they separated, their mother said, "You two go down to the seaside. They're not going to kill children." Their mother cried and literally pushed them to go down. Who knew that was going to be their final farewell? Once people went to the mountain, they didn't return. Kyesŏng's parents and his older brother never came back.

There was a story about a honey jar Kyesŏng hid underneath the compost. A police officer came unexpectedly right before setting the village on fire trying to look for his older brother. He poked everywhere with a bayonet and found the jar and took it with him. Kyesŏng's family was well off because his parents were engaged in bee farming. Every time I think of their tragic downfall, I think of the honey jar in the compost. Some times I think what was inside the jar was not honey but Kyesŏng's older brother.

*First Class MP Sergeant*
What I remember in connection with Kyesŏng is the image of

my father in his eyes. Once Kyesŏng passed by the MP head-
quarters and bowed in delight when he saw my father guarding
in front of the building. But he told me that my father had said
something strange in a low voice. "Why did you come here? Pretend you don't know me and get the hell out!" After my father
said this, he completely changed his expression and talked to him
as if he was giving directions to a stranger. "Cheil Pharmacy? Go
past Kwandŏk Pavilion and walk just a little more. It's in front of
the town office. OK?" My father even spoke in the standard Seoul
dialect and gave him instructions to the place he didn't even ask
for. I couldn't believe what he said, but looking at Kyesŏng's puz-
zled look on his face, I didn't think he was making up the story. I
thought perhaps my father's mental illness had relapsed.

Now I understand perfectly why my father did what he did.
As a native islander he was treated unfairly and had an inferiority complex. I think my father wanted to hide his background. I
understand that he was flustered and was at a loss as what to do
when Kyesŏng, the brother of a well-known leftist, showed up
unexpectedly.

When my father was transferred out of the island to Mokp'o
on the mainland, I'm sure he felt as if he were being freed from
prison. I have a photo we took with my uncle's family before my
father left which was around mid-December. Everyone in the
picture was male and I could recall a few memorable moments.

A young and handsome First Class MP Sergeant looked
straight into the camera and smiled. With his hat off, his expression was as vivid as if he were about to smile brightly, showing his
white teeth. A white scarf shown inside the collar of the military
uniform looked fresh and clean. On one side of the collar, a pair
of pistols which are the emblem of the MP was placed like an
insect on a leaf. The man in the picture was enviously young. He
was twenty-eight years old which is my son's age. Contrary to his
bright face, the boy sitting on his lap on the left looked stubborn

and sullen. The boy looked absurdly stiff, and it was obvious he didn't want to sit on his father's lap. Like that time at the movie theater, the boy was eager to come down from his father's lap.

My father was always away. He returned home after becoming an MP, but he rarely stayed in the house even though we lived in the same town. He had a fiery personality, so even when I saw him after a long absence I couldn't easily talk to him. What was most disappointing about my father was that he was nothing but an insignificant and powerless soldier. I said goodbye to my father and saw him off to the mainland before I even had a chance to get to know him well. At the time, I had no idea, not even in my dreams, that he would be gone for such a long time. I saw him off at the harbor without shedding a single tear.

*Snow Covered Mt. Halla*

Since half a year's worth of millet was burnt down, we ended up freeloading off my maternal grandparents. Actually we weren't the only ones. My two aunts and other relatives who fled from the fire had to rely on my grandparents as well. So we never had enough food. It was around this time I saw wheat bran on the table. I was always hungry. Enduring hunger was sad and pitiful, but what was even more difficult to tolerate was the heavy and somber atmosphere at home. I went outside because I couldn't stand their whispering voices and sighs of despair and fear. But I felt even more suffocated when I saw low hanging gray clouds outside.

There were many dreary days during winter on the island where thick gray clouds hung low in the sky. Even now, when I return to the island in the wintertime, dark and sullen memories weigh down on me. And I feel compelled to drink. The clouds that hung low silhouetted the rolling fields. The fire that covered the entire sky, burning down the villages, metamorphosed into an appalling sight resembling bloody entrails. I felt dejected looking at the clouds that hung low at the foot of Mt. Halla. The vast and flat grassland that sprawled out covered in snow because the scenery resembled those chaotic days. Looking at the landscape, I shiver at the wintry cold that bites the skin and my heart shrinks at the sound of rustling leaves. What were the dead leaves trying to tell me, rustling loudly in the wind?

At one point six thousand people were hiding underneath the snowfield of Mt. Halla. Once I refused to eat wheat bran and my mother told me to think about my friends Chiye and Wansik, starving underneath the snow. I felt a pang of conscience when she scolded me like that. Chiye was the daughter of my father's maternal aunt and Wansik was my neighbor who had left for the mountain. After my friends and relatives went to Mt. Halla to take refuge, the mountain had turned into something more than mere backdrop to landscape. I often looked over to the Mt. Halla side while playing with my friends, and every time I looked it was buried in clouds as if it was in deep sorrow.

Since I lived by the warm seaside, I had never seen snow piled up high so I could not imagine the biting cold fierce winds and piles of snow on Mt. Halla. The only snow I saw was the kind that melted as soon as it hit the ground or snow covered dirt swept by the wind in the ditch. It was more like sleet rather than snow. Since there wasn't enough snow, I didn't even know what a snowman was. In my math class, there was a chart where numbers were reconfigured into objects. For example, number 2 was written in the shape of a duck and 4 was a sailboat. But I had a difficult time understanding 8 since I had no idea what a snowman looked like. I had never seen an icicle either. There was a nursery rhyme, "Icicle, icicle, crystal icicle," which I sang without even understanding what it meant. Whenever the snow fell, the neighbors' dogs were startled and started barking, and the chickens pecked at the snow thinking it was grain.

That winter, the warm and peaceful town was reduced to

charcoal by indiscriminate arson. Those people who left for the mountain in fear of their lives from the counterinsurgency forces were buried deep in the snow. Since they had no reason to go to the mountain during winter, it was their first time experiencing the severe cold and snow. At first the children jumped up and down with joy like puppies and the people admired the beautiful snow landscape, not knowing how dreadful it could be. The scenery of beautiful white snow flowers on bare tree branches in the forest must have been breathtaking.

The people in the mountain dug the ground deep enough to sit in and made roofs with bamboos. In the underground bunker they ate like birds to save food, barely making ends meet each day. After a month passed, the counterinsurgency forces' attacks grew more frequent so they were driven out of their shelters and ran here and there in the snow chased by them. The attackers might have enjoyed the feeling of rabbit hunting, running after the people scattered in all directions in the snowfield. Mostly the old people, the children, and the women with small children who couldn't run fast enough were targeted victims. Mothers who beat their small children for not walking fast enough were shot, and their children were mercilessly bayoneted as if they were being skewered. I was told that the blood spattered on the snow was monstrously red. Mt. Halla was buried in the sullen clouds all winter long.

*King Crows*
The sky was gloomy with no trace of kites in the air. The political situation was so unstable that even the children didn't dare to fly their kites. A flock of insidious crows often appeared and circled around in place of children's playful kites. An ominous aerial show put on by hundreds of prairie king crows or drongos left a vivid image in the minds of the villagers. These king crows pecked on the human bodies strewn about in the mountain, so they were

regarded as dreadful and treacherous. After I heard that a flying crow dropped a piece of human flesh with hair intact, whenever I saw crows perched on a bead-tree rubbing their beaks I threw rocks at them. The frenzied dancing of the hundreds of crows in the sky was inauspicious as if they became insane after eating human flesh. The crows swayed in the wind, as if they were riding the waves, then suddenly they shot up high in the sky like a whirlpool of black smoke and nosedived quickly. The whirring wind sound the crows made and their cawing sickened my heart.

## Political Speeches

Many government and public offices lined the street around Kwandŏk Pavilion. The atmosphere around the pavilion was always solemn. The adults avoided walking on the main street in fear of getting into trouble, so they used the back streets instead. The main street was always busy with the comings and goings of military trucks and three wheeled trucks. Soldiers wore helmets with white stripes around them and on their chests the hand grenades hung like testicles. The counterinsurgency police forces, on the other hand, had on dog fur hats and wore ammunition belts and blankets on their shoulders in a crisscross manner. All day long at home I could hear the noise of the vehicles driving by and the singing and shouting of the military songs and slogans.

From time to time the villagers who were busy trying to make ends meet were forced to gather around the pavilion square to listen to speeches. They couldn't sit on the cold ground, so they squatted and listened. Children always sat in the front. The speakers displayed new weapons such as artillery guns and trench mortars to openly intimidate people. They called it a speech but it was nothing more than a threat. Perhaps we felt it as a threat because the speakers were speaking in the unfamiliar standard language. There were several island natives, but what they said was something like "It's our loss if we hate the mainlanders." I was too young to understand what they were saying, so I just sat among other children like an imbecile.

However, there was room to breathe despite the threatening atmosphere. We couldn't dare burst out laughing whenever a high-ranking officer with a gun and a horsewhip or a chief police made blunders, stammering, stumbling and fumbling for words. But there was no way we could suppress our giggles when a civilian with a straw hat made a mistake. There were many occasions to laugh during the speeches. For example, once a speaker screamed so loudly that his face turned completely red. He was foaming at the mouth and was asking for a glass of water all choked up. It was utterly ridiculous. Another time a speech paper flew away in the wind, but the wind was so strong in Cheju that the paper flew up high in the air. So the speaker had to stop abruptly midway through. The result was the same when a rock was placed on top of the paper. Once a speaker was talking about the treacherous communist party and the rioters, and he hit the podium with his fist. I was so startled, and the rock placed on top of the paper flung up, making the paper fly away. For us children we didn't care about the speeches; it was fun to look at the speakers' expressions as they changed from pale to red and their ridiculously high-pitched voices. We especially enjoyed it when the speakers made mistakes, which made us laugh out loud.

### Mountain People, Mountain Rioters

We laughed at their hideous speeches, but we were interested and amused by them. The fact that we showed interest meant that we slowly got used to them. Also, we were curious about the activities of the people on the mountain, too. We called them the "mountain people." Their leader, Yi Tŏkku, was thought to possess special powers, like dodging bullets, jumping over roofs as if his knees were elastic springs, and appearing here and there and everywhere. The image of Yi Tŏkku fighting vigorously was a source of great vitality in the hearts of all children, but it was short lived—only two months while he was engaged in battles.

Now that I think about it, the children adapted to a new environment faster than the adults. The situation had already turned to the point of no return. The town and the small seaside villages were lumped together with the citizens' organization and were forced to be hostile toward the people on Mt. Halla. These people were utterly in despair. What a fate, having to follow the counterinsurgency forces with bamboo spears to kill their own brothers and family members!

Unlike the adults who were guilt-ridden for committing atrocities, the way in which children cut off ties with the past was simple and cruel as if it was in their nature. The children actively adapted to the new environment whereas the adults passively accepted the changes. They intuitively followed and gravitated toward the strong, shifting their allegiances without any reservations. Perhaps these town children were quick to make their move because they did not experience the bloodshed. Similar to fascists, the only acceptable code of conduct in the children's world was conformity. In order to win the confidence of the people, the fascists who seized power with weapons needed to curry favor with the children first and use them to promote and appeal to the general public.

Among the children, the "mountain army" and "mountain people" soon changed and came to be called "mountain rioters." In the children's world, thinking and acting differently were unacceptable, and those who did not conform to the norm were completely ostracized. So it was necessary to keep it a secret if a family member was killed by the counterinsurgency forces. I did not want to call my relatives and neighbors "mountain rioters."

The children's quick adjustment to the situation was shocking to the adults. One of the kids made a gun out of wood and pretended he was shooting. He yelled out, "Come out, you rebel!

Come out, you commie!" I can still remember the shocked and terrified look on the faces of the adults.

I also remember an incident where a female police officer was embarrassed because of the mischievous children. It happened after the winter break, shortly after school began. My homeroom teacher and the female police officer walked in to the classroom during a recess. All the children who were laughing and playing around quickly took their seats and the entire room became dead silent. *What's going on? Why did a policewoman come to the classroom?* It was something extraordinary. *Is she here to take away someone whose father's a mountain rioter?* Perhaps the other kids in the classroom thought the same.

To everyone's surprise the police officer was the mother of our class vice-president. She had come to pick up her ill son. After the teacher's brief introduction, everyone in the classroom screamed in delight and surprise. There were only one or two female police officers in town. I couldn't believe one of them was my classmate's mother. It was incredible. She had the black uniform on, and she was pretty, too. Everyone clapped their hands, and she replied with a smile.

I clapped, too. I think I was more excited than any of my classmates. I was proud of the fact that my friend's mother was one of the police officers, but there was another reason why I was overwhelmed with excitement. I heard that one of my relatives escaped death thanks to a female police officer. I knew for sure that my friend's mother was the one who had helped my relative the day when the village had been burnt down and the villagers were driven to the seaside. The counterinsurgency forces were hunting down the family members of the mountain rioters, and both the adults and children cried not knowing what to do. In the midst of this chaos, the female police officer patrolling the traffic helped them get away.

In any case everyone in the classroom was excited, and we

frantically clapped, but our excitement got out of hand. All of a sudden, the entire class sang a song about annihilating communist guerrillas. One classmate started it and soon everyone sang in unison.

> *Destroy the communist traitors*
> *Destroy the mountain rioters*
> *Sing the national anthem and march forward!*

Our teacher and the police officer wore baffled expressions on their faces. The policewoman's face turned red, and she grabbed her son and darted out of the room even before the song was finished.

While the communist guerrilla annihilation song was resonating throughout, ghastly things happened. Instead of holding speech assemblies at the Kwandŏk Pavilion, a temporary court was set up. Several shabby-looking young men went up to the platform one after another and they repeated their crimes—how they attacked and blocked the streets and cut off the power lines— as ordered by an official. Then the young men were dragged to the execution ground. Later the heads of those young men appeared in the square. A piece of flesh flapping on the truncated head was pierced through a spear like a pumpkin. One of the heads was hung on a soldier's waist by the hair, dangling in the air. Then he yelled out, "Look at the last days of the rioters!" They marched proudly through the village in all four directions. The king crows saw the truncated heads bobbing up and down in the air as the counterinsurgency forces marched on, and they circled right above, cawing frighteningly.

The heads were displayed on several occasions at the five-way crossing of the entrance to the pavilion. There was a head with long hair and a pale face with all the blood drained out. Also there was a black head with no hair or eyebrows that looked like a half-burnt tree trunk. Each head was labeled as so and so from such and such village. The pavilion square was on the way to school so every time I passed by I felt suffocated by fear. I unconsciously touched my neck because I felt something cold and sharp grazing the back of my neck. I was scared to death to look, but for some odd reason I kept gazing at the heads. The kids next to me, huffing and puffing in fear, said "Look! Rioters! They look like burnt pigs' faces."

One time Kyesŏng's father's name was attached to one of the burnt charcoal heads. I didn't know his father's name so I passed it not knowing it was my friend's father. I found out when I stopped by at my uncle's place. My uncle went first to see the head, and then he took Kyesŏng thinking that his own flesh and blood would recognize it. However, the head was so severely burnt that Kyesŏng couldn't recognize the face. Later the head was strewn about on the crossroads on a straw mat, but it was verified as someone else's head—one of our relatives who lived in the same town.

I learned the true account of the cruel atrocities after I became an adult. Actually you couldn't even call it "true account." Not because it was concealed or complicated, but because it was so simple that my blood froze. Without a word of exaggeration, all witnesses said the same thing and explained it thus:

"The authority handed the order down to finish the Cheju insurrection as quickly as possible. Since the counterinsurgency forces were running out of time, they forced their subordinates to kill their own family members and neighbors, baiting them with a special promotion in rank. At first they asked them to bring back one ear per body they killed, but some of them cut off both ears to double their rewards. There were some who cut off elders' and women's ears as well. Many dead bodies of old people and women with their ears cut off were found on the mountain. That's why they asked to bring back the heads."

"Then what about those burnt heads?"

"There's a story behind it. You know there was a civilian group called "*minbodan*" who followed the counterinsurgency forces with bamboo spears. The counterinsurgency forces captured the rioters alive, and often ordered the civilian group members to kill them off. It was an order issued by the authority, but the reason was to make "*minbodan*" accomplices by having them kill their own kin. The people in the civilian organization group were threatened with a gun aimed at their heads, so they had no choice but to succumb and stab them with bamboo spears. But people didn't die immediately after being stabbed, so they resorted to setting them on fire. It was truly atrocious."

Later visitors who traveled to that part of the island during wintertime said the red camellias blossoming in the snow were beautiful. I'm certain that red fallen blossoms strewn about on the white snowfield were sublime. It's normal to regard it as beautiful. When I was a little boy I used to suck the nectar from fallen flower blossoms and was extremely happy. However, since that atrocity, my aesthetic sensibility had been warped. I longer think of the fallen flowers as flowers but as blood sprayed all over the snow. It's truly terrifying. When an entire flower falls off rather than a single petal at a time, I am reminded of the severed human heads rolling and tumbling on the ground.

That winter and early spring when the massacre was rampant, camellia flowers fell endlessly on Mt. Halla. Was that why the mountain and the sky hid their faces behind the clouds, grieving and lamenting? The gray clouds always hung low, and under the sullen sky the stage was set to massacre tens of thousands of people while king crows danced in frenzy in the air. An equal number of domestic animals were slaughtered, too. I was told that survivors could cry if they weren't quite sad or terrified. Even after twenty some years have passed, they still cannot cry out loud. They said no words can possibly express what they went through. It was beyond what any words can describe.

### White Flag of Surrender

After taking so many lives indiscriminately, the ruthless conquerors sought peace extending their blood-soaked hands. A song spread among children to encourage people in the mountain to surrender, guaranteeing their safety and livelihood.

> *Return! Return to our warm embrace*
> *Look at our national flag flying*
> *And let us rejoice our land!*

Those people who survived the cruel winter descended the mountain waving a white flag. They were skeptical thinking that it was a trick, but even if it meant death they wanted to die by the warm seaside. They wanted to walk the streets lavished in sunlight one last time before getting shot and killed. For three months they had lived on the mountain, never taking off their clothes or shoes. They endured the severe cold, extreme hunger, and fear of death.

Once or twice I saw the mountain people passing by the pavilion square in a group of ten under the supervision of the counterinsurgency forces. I couldn't believe people could look so wretched. There were hardly any young men but mostly old people, women and children. Some had bruises on their faces from the blows of gun butts. Their eyes and cheeks were caved in from extreme hunger, and their faces and clothes were filthy. They were rained on when they were coming down from the mountain, so they were walking shivering in cold.

Thinking back now it was a ridiculous and hideous sight. There was a white flag made from a stained, dirty woman's headband attached to a wooden stick flapping in front of them. I still remember a kid next to me yelling out, "Look! Rioters! They stink!" It was true. The wretched looking weak old men, women, and children were all "rioters." The mountain people were massacred and were forced to hold the white flag because they were rioters. After they came down, they were taken in for questioning for several days. Chiye's family came to my uncle's house to stay after they were released from the interrogation. She had turned into a gloomy and quiet person.

After a month the stream of people descending from the mountain stopped. And soon after, Syngman Rhee, the center of the new power, arrived on the island. He saw those survivors who had escaped death from the fire and massacre prostrate before him. They had their heads bowed low and didn't move at all, but it was difficult not to whisper to each other. "That old man gained fortune by marrying an American woman, right? He became President because of his wife." My mother and her friends talked about him. Although what they had said was an ignorant remark, mistaking Former Lady Francesca as an American, they were absolutely right.

### Great Leader's Final Day

The pavilion square where Syngman Rhee's welcoming ceremony was held was also the place where the dead body of Yi Tŏkku, the head of the mountain raid unit, was displayed.

There are myths and legends about several generals and important figures with extraordinary power who faced tragic deaths after putting up a fight against the central government. These leaders had indomitable spirits to save the people from the despotic government officials. Thus they were called the "great leaders." They led the people and took over the main fortress to overthrow the government authority. They gladly offered their lives as martyrs to help the people. Centering around Kwandŏk Pavilion, the people gathered like clouds inside and outside the fortress and shouted out so loudly that their screaming and wailing travelled to the mainland. When their lamentation reached the king's ears, he was alarmed and tried to appease them by saying, "I had no idea you were suffering so much."

However, in 1948 and 1949, the central government openly declared that the sacrifice of half of the Cheju people was inevitable if they wanted to fulfill their political ambitions. Unlike those great leaders who gave up their lives to save the people, the great leader Yi Tŏkku was a tragic hero who was killed. His death was inevitable because everything was already on the decline. One of his subordinates betrayed him and exposed his hideout, and he was killed in action. However, the official statement was that he was captured and shot to death. Most people wanted to believe that he took his own life.

His dead body was displayed in the pavilion square, and he had the old tattered military uniform on. Whether or not it was intentional to ridicule him, the executioner hung his body on the cross like the symbol of Christ's suffering. Perhaps that was one of the reasons why the onlookers had mixed feelings and wore disturbed looks on their faces. He had his arms stretched out and his head drooped to the side. From one side of his mouth and one of his ears, dripping blood had coagulated. His face looked peaceful as if he were sleeping. The executioner had stuck a spoon in the jacket pocket to mock the dead man, but no one laughed.

That day the legend ended, leaving only the trace of martyrdom. The rise of the great leaders from the ordinary people and the tradition of their resistance had forever come to an end.

I jumped on the bus to Mt. Halla and arrived at the foot of the mountain. I could always listen to the beginning of the words spoken by the rough wind and wild grass undulating in the strong wind. Walking here and there in the field with reeds that came up to my waist, the strong smell of wild grass pierced through my soul. I became fully aware of my existence and became indulgent about my own death. My father and my ancestors were buried in the field. This grassland was the mother's womb where all island people were born and eventually return to when they die. But what about those who died in the massacres of 1948 and 1949? Full of resentment and hatred, they also returned to the field to rest, but they could never forgive and forget.

Mt. Halla was right in front of my eyes. The gorge that stretched out from the top of the mountain in the steep slope was so close that it looked magnified. The movement of the small clouds was clearly visible, too. I saw the clouds that appeared and disappeared in the valley. The valley truly looked like a mother's womb. From the deep womb where the water originated, the clouds rose up and vanished. Looking at the womb that bore children and swallowed them back up, I thought about the pig that ate its young. So I called Mt. Halla an evil mountain, expressing hatred to my heart's content. But how is Mt. Halla responsible for all those dead bodies?

As twilight deepens across the grassy plain, the evening glow sets the entire west sky on fire, enveloping the dark forest in the surging fire and reminding me of that time.

*Rice*

After several months of blood bath, a great famine followed. Among the refugees, the ones who had no family members living by the seaside had the hardest time. The counterinsurgency forces had taken half burnt grains from the burnt down villages and sold them in town and made the people feel even more devastated. The villagers were the true owners of the grains, yet they had to buy back their supply with money they didn't have.

Dried sweet potatoes, radish, barley husks, and wheat bran were used as fodder before, but they became the main staple food for the people, including the weeds horses and cows liked to eat. The people later reminisced that they weren't humans back then. They were lucky that so many horses and cows died during the fire. Otherwise, people and animals would have had to fight over the weeds. How could they take a dump after eating what animals ate? They struggled to relieve themselves and when they failed, they stuck a finger up their anus to dig it out. "Now even the pigs get nutritious fodder so their dung makes good fertilizer."

My mother, my brother, and I were better off compared to the others since we relied on our maternal grandparents. We ate the wild vegetables and weeds the horses and cows used to eat. Since we didn't have soy sauce, we reused salt used on salted mackerel. As for our rice, one fifth was wheat bran and the rest was foxtail millet. From time to time in foxtail millet we found burnt grains and every time my mother found them, she thought about the grains that were burnt and grumbled, "Those bastards!"

We each had our own soup bowl but all of us shared rice from one large bowl. Having our own rice bowl was unthinkable since we were freeloading and living in a single cramped room. We didn't even use a table; it was shoved in one corner of the kitchen. Even though the rice was mixed with barley husks and wheat bran, I was never full. I was greedy and tried to eat more than my mother and my sister. Yellowish foxtail millet among the brownish wheat bran looked like golden grains. I tried to scoop out the part where millets were concentrated the most; I guess I looked like a chicken pecking at grains. My mother could not stand seeing me doing that, so she ended up dividing up the rice in three ways. One time I was about to spit out wild vegetables because I could not swallow and my mother scolded me and said, "Swallow it. You won't die."

One day I was eating breakfast, and a boy came begging for food with a two year old girl on his back. He wore an old student cap without a badge, but he looked like he was three or four years older than me. As soon as the girl saw the food, she fidgeted and swung her arms, crying out, "Rice! Rice!" The boy's eyes were filled with tears.

"My sister's hungry. Please give her something to eat. Please."

My mother murmured under her breath, "We beg for food ourselves . . ." She hesitated for a minute, but then she took away my sister's and my spoons and invited the boy and his sister to come into the room.

"You poor thing! You must've been so hungry. She must've weaned not so long ago. *Tut-tut!* Come on in and eat. You, too!"

When the spoon was handed to the boy, his face lit up. About half of the rice was left in the bowl, but the boy and his sister gobbled it up in the blink of an eye. Hunger was a frightening thing. After he finished eating, he was finally able to see us in the room and expressed his gratitude and apology toward me with a nod.

*Young Paulownia Tree*

The refugees living by the seaside returned to their ruined villages at the end of April. But they were isolated like prisoners of war since they were still under the suspicion of the police and couldn't return to their own homes. The stone walls were built around them like a pigsty, and their cramped, concentration camp-like living began. They were allowed to leave in the daytime, but the gate was shut when the sun went down.

When the stone walls were built, my grandfather and mother went to help out for several days. How could they possibly have any strength when they were starving? The women fell into the ditches carrying heavy stones but there was a rumor that so and so's wife was strong enough to carry the heavy stones.

Life in the concentration camp was deplorable. They labored for half a month to build the stone walls on empty stomachs. Soon after, a fire broke out and one hut after another got caught on fire and burnt down more than twenty huts. After the fire, cholera broke out, driving people to another wave of fear. Fortunately, the cholera outbreak ended taking away only three lives.

My grandmother and I visited the concentration camp in early June before cholera broke out. It was our first time going home in two years. After the massacre, the road was blocked for a long time and was extremely dangerous, but once again people started using the road. Yet the road was still covered with overgrown weeds and rutted with the tire tracks of military trucks since it was not often walked on by human feet. Even the fields along the road were covered in weeds creating an eerie atmosphere. It was creepy, as if someone was going to jump out at any minute. Also, many fields had been burned during the massacre. Even the barley field that had been plowed was full of weeds. The most frightening part was crossing over the Toryŏngmaru pass. At one point dead bodies were scattered all over the pine grove. My grandmother told me in a low voice not to look, and she grabbed my hand and walked by really fast.

Our field was located on the big roadside right before the concentration camp. The barley field that was to feed everyone in my family was only so in name because it was full of weeds as if pigs would be raised. That year the barley harvest was only half the usual crop, and most were empty husks. That was why the three of us had to endure hunger until the millet harvest in late autumn. Without the stone walls, the weed-covered barley field looked even more wretched. It was not just our field—all the other fields were the same. All the stones were used to build the walls around the concentration camp.

I entered inside the dark and dreary stone walls and found huts as big as a pigsty lying low at an arm's length apart. An indescribable stench pierced through my nose. That day was the day of the memorial service for my great grandmother. The roof and the walls of the hut were plastered with weaved arrowroots.

The ceiling was so low that one could only sit or lie down. Even the floor was covered with arrowroots, so every time I moved, it made a rustling sound. I hadn't seen Chiye for a long time but couldn't get one word out of my mouth after seeing the wretched living conditions.

My grandmother brought a small folding table, a set of brass rice and soup bowls, a handful of rice, sweet rice wine in a cider bottle, one apple and one egg, which she took out carefully one by one. That night my great grandmother's memorial service was held with only rice, wine, one apple and an egg. When the sun went down, the hut turned completely dark like the inside of a cave. In the darkness, the adults whispered lowly in the midst of the rustling sound of the arrowroots. The night deepened and it was time for the memorial service. I felt so relieved and happy when a speck of light was lit in the middle of the suffocating darkness. A small folding table was used instead of the usual ceremony table and a small plate of oil was placed on top. It was my first time seeing such a light. Inside the small plate of vegetable oil a piece of paper was twisted and used as a wick, creating a small flame. The single flame glowed in the darkness reflecting off of Chiye's eyes, staring at me quietly.

I woke up the following morning and went to my old burnt down home with my grandmother and saw the paulownia tree. The young paulownia tree was standing strongly in the midst of the burnt debris like a fountain. Everything inside the stone walls was covered with black soot and was ruined. The rusted black nails squirmed like worms in the heaps of charcoals. In the middle of black debris, the paulownia tree stood green and powerful.

The images of the small plate that illuminated the dark hut, Chiye's big glittering eyes, and the paulownia tree standing in the middle of the debris were etched in my mind like the powerful symbols of life. Children grow up no matter what happens. Children are not held back by their past. That's why children who were born without fathers because of the Cheju Massacre grew up to cover the dark ruins of the past with verdant grass.

### Dead Without a Funeral Bier

My grandfather passed away that June. He survived the massacre and the deadly fire, but he passed away four days after he had a bad case of diarrhea.

I don't remember much about his funeral. Since I was so scared of him, I wasn't particularly sad about his death. My father who was in the mainland received the notice late, but he made it in time for the funeral. After two days of greeting the visitors, he left the island again. I only saw my father from afar in his funeral garment. The memory of meeting my father again is vague.

The funeral was shabby and pathetic since it was during the extreme famine season, so there wasn't even a bowl of red bean porridge to go around for the visitors. But the wailing and loud lamentations did not stop. Unlike other things that are vague in my memory, I can still hear their cries, clearly ringing in my ears. I thought it was strange that my distant relatives were lamenting more than the immediate mourners unlike other funerals. I was too scared to go in, so I hung outside with my cousin Namsu. The women's wailing came from the room behind the kitchen and was endless. A strange atmosphere hovered in the air as the mourners' and visitors' roles were reversed.

I found out later that those women cried to lament their own fate and misfortune, not to grieve my grandfather's death. In their eyes, my grandfather's death was a blessing even though it was a shabby funeral with no food. How could people not be envious when there were mourners and visitors grieving for the deceased? When their family members died, there were no mourners and they couldn't even cry out loud because they were afraid they would be labeled as rioters.

Young and unmarried men died with no children to grieve

their deaths. Some of the temporarily buried bodies were decayed because they had been merely covered with straw mats and tree branches with dirt sprinkled on top. There were so many bodies that hadn't been recovered from ditches and caves. It wasn't the right time for the survivors to cry over the deceased. Once again they were struck with another calamity. For close to a year nothing happened, but the following summer, the Korean War broke out. With the outbreak of the war, a primary inspection for returnees, those who came down from the mountain, took place. Several hundred of them were killed and the rest were drafted to fight in the war.

Now that I've reached this point, I think I should refrain from talking about the Cheju Massacre. Thinking about that time makes me want to throw up, so I don't have the strength to continue writing about it. Let's not talk about that anymore. This narrative is about a boy growing up. It is true that this cruel event is deeply ingrained in my mind, unable to erase dark and deadly images, causing my depression to grow deeper and deeper. As a result of the depression, I had been stuttering for a long time and a trace of stammer continued to remain on my tongue. Children instinctively avoid things that are harmful. Sadness and loneliness are detrimental for growing children. Children don't hold things back; they cry one minute and laugh the next. They think and act simply. Even in the saddest moment, they fly up lightly like a feather toward the land of happiness.

My old home Nohyŏngri left a deep scar in my mind. For the longest time, my heart sank just hearing the name. The name Nohyŏngri was synonymous with misfortune or namelessness. After I witnessed the ruins during my great grandmother's memorial service, I didn't visit home until much later. Most of my relatives had moved to town, so I didn't have to go to my old home for memorial services. But I visited the villages near my old home often. Since I was a fourth grader, I helped my mother till the fields. So I went close to my old home but had not set foot in the village. For some odd reason, I was afraid to run into my friends Kyesŏng and Wansik, but I never ran into them on the street.

Even now after so many years have passed, I only recall my hometown in the image of complete ruin. I feel like everything had died in the midst of that darkness except for two children who were the sole survivors, squirming and wriggling. My friends Kyesŏng and Wansik, whom I hadn't seen since we separated, remain in my memory as forever children, not aged at all.

### Child of Pyŏngmun Stream

I came out of my shell of sadness and loneliness and became one of the town kids in every respect. I made new friends and hung out with them all the time, and they became the source of my happiness. We were like a flock of small sparrows chatting away and hugging each other, kicking, tickling, laughing without stopping . . . not being able to differentiate myself from the other children, I had no idea time was passing by so quickly.

As if my entire body was drenched in honey, I was intoxicated by the sweetness of time. I was so engrossed in playing that one time I ran around the stream naked and got into trouble. My mother came out looking for me to send me on an errand. She was furious when I didn't respond to her yelling and screaming because I was in the water having fun; so she took my clothes I left near the stream. I couldn't go home completely naked when there were people walking on the street. I felt so embarrassed, like a snail without its shell. I picked up some leaves and covered my private area and ran home. Passersby giggled and laughed. That evening I cried and cried saying that I was so embarrassed and tried to boycott eating dinner. But that was my mother's way of disciplining, so what could I say? That wasn't the only time she humiliated me. One time I touched some poison ivy and broke out in rashes. My mother made me stand at the entrance of the town completely naked and she chanted, "Make the rashes go away! Hurry! Hurry!" while rubbing salt all over my body and brushing it off with a broom.

When I wet my bed, I was humiliated in the same fashion. Those who had wet their blankets as a child would remember the strange sensation of warmth spreading down your legs as you relieve yourself. You wake up startled when you feel the cold wetness and the overwhelming feeling of despair that follows. The morning came but I could not go out, so I hesitated for a long time. As a punishment I had to go to a neighbor's house and beg for salt. The first time I wet my bed I didn't know getting salt from the neighbor's was a punishment, so I took a huge stainless bowl and was utterly humiliated. The neighbor's grandma was sitting in the kitchen, and she smirked when she saw me. She pretended that she was getting salt, but then ran toward me with a straw basket, covering my head and beating me with a broom stick. She said, "You wet your bed! You wet your bed!" laughing out loud, so I was startled and embarrassed at the same time. After that I passed by her without saying anything because I was upset about what she had done; then I got beaten by my mother for not saying hello.

### Tears Come Down and Spoons Go Up

Whenever I did something wrong, my mother first went for a whip. It wasn't her style to talk to me to make me understand what I did wrong. Even if she wanted to be a warm loving mother, she simply didn't have the time or patience. In those days I was so forgetful that I lost things often. I was beaten because I kept losing my school shoe bag. It was a difficult time and material things were rare; even a piece of cloth was valuable to mend worn out clothes. I deserved to be beaten for losing my shoe bag so often.

As my mother said I must have left out all my senses and hung them on my tailbone because I was too busy playing around. If I had tied my shoe bag around my waist, I wouldn't have lost it.

My mother always struck me twice—she took an iron rod and struck the ground several times to make me scared and to psyche me out, then she hit my calves a few times which turned out to be not so bad. What was unbearable was the moment of anticipation, the time between the iron rod hitting the ground and attacking my calves all of sudden.

I don't know what got into me that day, but after I got beaten I expressed my anger. I was upset at being struck with the iron rod, but I was angrier at myself for losing my shoe bag again. I was so upset that when the dinner table was brought in, I blurted out, "I'm not eating," and turned my back against the dinner table. My mother's not the type to beg me to eat at a time like that. Instead she sneered and said, "Why? Does your stomach hurt? It's good to skip a meal then."

I was irritated by what she had said, so I blew my nose hard. Then all of a sudden my mother grabbed me by the collar of my neck like a falcon's talons.

"Are you itching for a beating? How dare you express your anger at me? Turn around."

"Brother, hurry up and eat." My younger sister tugged at my sleeve.

This was my chance. *Should I turn around? Lunch wasn't great so if I skip dinner I'm only losing out . . .* The sweet smell of potatoes wafted through the room gently tickling my nose. Then I shook off my mother's grip and jumped up like a spring.

"I'm not eating. I won't eat," I yelled out. As I stepped out of the room, my mother came behind me and grabbed me by the neck again.

"Where do you think you're going?" I held on to the pillar to avoid getting dragged into the room. My mother held me by my shoulders and pulled me. With all my strength, I held onto the pillar. In that moment I said something I shouldn't have said. I meant to say "I'm not eating" but I ended up blurting out, "I'm not eating that kind food. That's not rice, it's only sweet potatoes. You always feed me that kind of food."

My eyes widened as I was surprised at what came out of my mouth. I must have hit the most vulnerable part because my mother became so angry that her eyes looked like they were sizzling.

"What did you say? Only sweet potatoes? You ingrate, being picky about food. If you knew how hard I worked, you couldn't possibly say that to me."

I cried holding onto the pillar and got hit four or five times. Then I was dragged into the room and was forced to sit down in front of the table. Sweet potatoes tasted even better after going through an ordeal. I had three sweet potatoes and three slices of kimchi. Hunger sure whets the appetite. I sobbed while eating my share of sweet potatoes. My mother gazed at me gently and even though eating sweet potatoes did not require a spoon, she talked about a spoon theory.

"See. Tears come down and spoons go up. That's why eating is the most important thing."

My mother's way of dealing with her children was very straightforward and to the point. It was an intense game like sudden showers, pelting down for a short period of time and stopping all of a sudden. My mother seemed to relish this kind of game. It was a match that I was bound to lose, but I certainly was not an easy opponent. I cried hard so that the entire neighborhood could hear me and in order to bring me under control, she had to muster every ounce of energy she had. After we went through a hellish battle, we felt something that we couldn't feel before—a sense of comfort and peace. Like the blue sky after the storm, my mother's expression was as bright as the blue sky. *How refreshing a sudden shower is on a hot scorching summer day!* All that commotion that she caused to teach her children contained an entertainment value as well. The time of death had passed, but hunger continued on. We couldn't straighten our backs because we were always searching for food like ants. There was no such thing as entertainment and there was no time to have fun. Our neighborhood, which was dead silent during the day, became lively around the time when people returned home from work—people cursing out loud and children crying as they got hit. For poor parents, hitting was their way of educating their children as well as a source of entertainment.

### Shit Crab "Ttonggingi"

My mother was not the only person who nurtured and raised me. My friends helped me grow and mature, and the ground that I ran on and played in was the cradle of my growth, too. I was an extension of my mother, and at the same time I belonged to my friends and to this great land.

Whenever I did something endearing, my maternal grandmother said things like, "You're so adorable! Where did you spring from?" Listening to her, I felt strange—as if I hadn't come out of my mother's womb but had somehow sprung out of the ground. Now people rarely use this expression "spring forth," but when I was young, people in my hometown said it to express how adorable children were. Rather than saying "born" or "come into being," they said children either "gushed forth" or "sprung forth." I'm not sure why they used that expression though. I could only guess that the family names of Ko, Yang, and Pu all came from the ground, so that might have been how it was originated. My maternal grandparents were the Cheju Yang clan.

In any case, I was my mother's son and nature's offspring. When I was young, I was under the complete control of both my mother and nature. But what had I become by the time I reached adulthood? The people I knew shaped me into who I am today, but nature also played a big part. My parents, all those people I knew and the vast land made me who I am today.

Pyŏngmun Stream, like most streams on the island, was a dried out stream. The water flowed only after the big rains. After the pouring rain, the reddish muddy water overflowed and rushed toward the sea, making loud rumbling noises. The rocks on the lower part of the stream were nice and clean, glittering in the sunlight after three or four days of gushing water. The water in the ditch was clean, too; then the stream turned into the children's playground. All summer long the stream area became noisy with naked children swimming.

I went swimming even when it was cloudy. When I came out of the water after a long time, I shivered from the cold. Imagine a boy shivering with teeth chattering whose lips turned bluish purple as if he had mulberries, his eyes turned red like rabbit eyes, his fingers and toes all wrinkly like beans soaked in water, and his shrunken penis!

"You're in trouble. Your penis is gone."

Five year old boys thought it was really true and burst out crying.

There were so many kinds of shellfish in the water where we swam. They showed off their excellent swimming skills and played with us. Damselflies hovered above the water and kept dunking their tails in the water, trying to have their share of fun; the flowers on the waterside swayed and danced every time we jumped in as the water rippled. Even not-so-courageous sparrows kept veering from the shallow water and flew up immediately after getting their wings wet. They perched on a tree branch and plumed themselves.

We caught insects and played with them, too. We split the end of a bamboo stick and had a spider web around it and used it as a net to catch dragonflies. When we caught a male dragonfly we smeared red mud on its tail to make it look like a female and lured other male dragonflies. There were many grasshoppers by the stream. It was easy to catch grasshoppers, so we had a string full of them in a short time. Crabgrass was used to string the grasshoppers. I could still vaguely feel the sensation in my fingers when the crabgrass pierced through the soft body of the grasshoppers. The grasshoppers didn't die even though they were pierced, and they tried to fly up, kicking off very hard. They were truly resilient. Sometimes I got bitten by a grasshopper; I didn't bleed or anything but it sure was painful. I could have easily killed the grasshopper that would not let go of the bite immediately, but instead I endured the pain and slowly pulled its tail to rip the body apart. I didn't feel sorry for the grasshopper because it felt so natural. I could even kill a repulsive looking centipede with my bare hands. I quickly pressed the head of the centipede crawling on the ground with the tip of my finger and didn't care when the centipede bit the top of my hand, curling up backward. In a rage, I twisted it and snapped it into pieces. I did terrible things back then which seemed natural but now I could not even possibly fathom. I think I was a different species back then. Perhaps I was able to do those cruel things because I was so close to nature.

It was useless to catch dragonflies, grasshoppers and centipedes because we were renting a room so we had no chickens to feed them to. It was so sad when I had to give away my prizes. Sometimes I pulled out the tail of the dragonfly and stuck barley reed in its place and set it free rather than giving it away.

But I never caught the small crabs called "ttonggingi" which was my nickname. In Cheju dialect "kingi" was sea crab but somehow other children twisted my name and called me Shit Crab and that upset me. Sea crabs looked ridiculously gross with hairy legs, and they lived in dark holes so their color was blackish. People called them "shit crabs" to indicate they were inedible. Since I complained so much about the lean years, readers might ask why we didn't eat those sea crabs to help alleviate hunger. But there were so many different kinds of shellfish to eat other than gross-looking sea crabs. They were good side dishes but they could not ease my hunger like rice.

I had two nicknames—Shit Crab and Ttaemt'ong or Scar. My friends caught sea crabs to feed the chickens they raised, but I never touched them, not even as a joke. After two years of swimming in Pyŏngmun Stream, I moved to fresh water then ventured out to the ocean to swim. Even after a fresh water crab had transformed into a sea crab, my nickname stuck with me for a very long time.

### Lefty "Wengingi"

I wasn't the only one with nicknames. Most of the kids around me also went by their nicknames. Our given names were used in school on attendance sheets only. I was called Shit Crab and Wŏngyŏng was known as Lefty since he was left-handed and Chunyŏng was called Centipede. Other nicknames were Sling, Cow Dung, and Chicken Butt since the way he puckered his lips looked like a chicken's butt. There was a boy who used to live in Japan and came to Cheju and joined our group late. He spoke with a lisp so words didn't come out quite right. For example, he pronounced words like *yangmal* as *anmal*, *kongbu* as *konbu*, and *ŏngdŏngi* as *ŏndŏni*. So his nickname was *ŏndŏn* or Butt. He saw the ocean for the first time, so while he was playing in the water catching crabs, the tide began to ebb and the water was pushed back. When he saw this, he screamed in a pleasant surprise and said, "*Padang's* disappeared!" And all of us burst out into laughter. Instead of saying *pada*, meaning ocean he said *padang*, so his other nickname was "*padang* disappeared."

Lefty was the son of a blacksmith. He was always the leader because he was strong and quick and he was also good at fighting. He was a few years older than the rest of us, so no one dared to

challenge him. When he called me by my nickname Shit Crab, I
didn't dare say anything.

Between us children we called each other by our nicknames
so it wasn't a big deal but when my mother called me by my
nickname I hated it. Lefty and Chicken Butt got their nicknames
because their mothers started calling them, so between mothers
and sons they often had fights. And they quarreled like this.

We were playing with marbles and heard someone yelling,
"Lefty! Lefty!" But he pretended he didn't hear and continued
to play. Even when his mother kept calling he didn't budge, not
batting an eye. As he remained calm, the rest of us became very
uncomfortable and wanted to run away, but he glared at us in a
threatening way.

"Don't move! Pretend you didn't hear."

Lefty's angry mother approached us. She grabbed him by the
ear and dragged him away, and he screamed in pain.

"Why didn't you answer me? Did you stick a donkey's penis
in your ear?"

"When did you call me? I heard someone calling 'Lefty' but
didn't hear anyone calling my name."

Lefty's mother was speechless at her son's playing innocence.

"You think you can fool me because I'm stupid or something?"

"Well, you don't know my name. My name is not Lefty but
Wŏngyŏng. It's Kim Wŏngyŏng. OK?"

"Kim Wengingi . . . It's the same thing, there's no difference."

Lefty was a great prankster. For example, I was trying out the
dirt marbles I had just made at the entrance of the village, and he
appeared out of nowhere. He snuck up from behind and swung
his leg over my head since I was squatted down. He teased me
saying, "You're not going to grow anymore!" and that was his way
of saying hello. One time it was after the rain had stopped, but
I felt the water drops. When I looked up he was up on the tree

shaking the branches. I had no idea when he had climbed up the tree. I was so angry that I stood up. Then he grabbed all my marbles and ran off. He was really quick and agile. He barely escaped from getting caught and climbed up the tree again. He was great at climbing trees so his other nickname was "monkey." Even boys who were bigger than him could not do anything once he was up in the tree. That was the end of their chase, and he stood up like a prince and giggled as he looked down below.

"Oh, you poor thing! If you come up here, I'll give your marbles back."

I was even more upset at him because he knew my weak spot. Since I almost died falling from the tree trying to catch a cicada, I hated climbing up trees. I was so angry that I gave him the finger.

"Hey! Lefty, you Monkey Butt! Take this. Lefty's butt is red." Lefty hated being called Lefty the Monkey Butt.

"Hey, you Shit Crab. Shit Shit Crab. Come on let's have it." Lefty opened his eyes wide and stood up. He started jumping up and down on the branches and shaking off all the disgusting insects from the tree to fall on my head. There was nothing I could do to beat him. While I was shivering in disgust and busy brushing the insects from my hair, he came down from the tree and smirked.

"Let me see how well you made the marbles. I'm going to inspect them."

He took out my marbles from his pocket and put them on his palm and he frowned.

"Hey, Shit Crab, you can't call these marbles! They're rabbit dung. You didn't do as I said, did you?"

"I did. I let them dry in the shade for three days and put them in the kitchen fire."

"Kitchen fire? You stupid idiot. That's why these are not done right. You need to put them in a cow dung fire or a horse dung fire. You moron! How embarrassing trying to play marble games with these!"

As Lefty said, my marbles weren't strong enough, so they crumbled easily. Lefty took out what we called an "iron marble," a big, hard ball bearing, from his pocket and dropped it from the eye-level of our sitting position. My marble cracked miserably at such height. Those of us who were too poor to buy glass marbles had to settle for marbles made with dirt. What I learned from Lefty was that marbles made out of dirt needed to be baked like glazed earthenware, hard and shiny, so that they can be played against glass marbles.

*Bead-tree*

Now that I have mentioned the bead-tree that stood at the entrance of the village I need to clear my head and think for a moment. That tree was long gone with the road expansion but the image of the tree had been replanted in my mind. In my vague memory the tree stands tall and green in the midst of gray landscape. The tree was hundreds of years old, and its trunk was thicker than a man could encircle with his arms. One side was all worn out due to cruel winter winds and the branches rested on top of the wall in the shape of a capital L turned upside down and stretched out pointing in the southern direction. The spread of its branches made the tree as big as one's front yard. In spring, purplish flower clouds appeared on the tree and in summer, the lush and thick leaves created cool shade. It was brilliant when it bore clusters of yellow fruit.

My friends and I always played in the tree's shade. The tree bark was smooth and shiny after many years of children's rubbing and touching. I experienced so many things under that tree. What made me feel dizzy in spring when I felt weak from hunger was the strong flower scent and the swarm of bees buzzing. The droning of the cicadas rang in my ears like rain pouring down in the middle of lush foliage in summertime. On autumn days, birds flew over to peck at the fruit and I got hit by bird poop. These are some of the things that happened in different seasons simplified into several images. But the bead-tree had more than bees, cicadas, and birds as its family members.

The bead-tree offered its sap to feed many insignificant animals such as yellow flies, caterpillars, beetles, ladybugs, ants, aphids, snails, and spiders. Especially in summer, because of its abundance of sap, even more insects flocked to the tree. I was told that if I collected and shaped tree sap into a ball and bury it underground, the following year it would turn into a hard and golden marble like a yellow fly. What a beautiful lie!

I dug the ground to bury the tree sap ball but I was completely disgusted when I found its rotten roots were entangled with *kumbengi*. A year or two later I learned in class that *kumbengi* were cicada larvae, but I couldn't understand how *kumbengi* could become cicadas. I liked insects but hated caterpillars. At the base of the tree there were lots of caterpillars. Inside a hollowed tree there was a hole rotting away and ant larvae wriggled under the dried leaves. Whenever I got bored, I peed in the hole. Not only was the old bead-tree nourishing numerous insects but caterpillars as well.

That wasn't all. The tree created a nice cool shade that in sweltering heat attracted many insects to gather around. The children always played under the shade, so just like all those insects the children were nurtured by the tree, too. We liked to play by ourselves, but we also liked playing with insects. We even loved snails because their skin color was pink resembling a baby's, so they looked like a naked baby crawling. When the snails went into their shells, we sang a song "Open the window. Want to see your soft skin," pleading with them to come out of their shells. We liked disgusting looking spiders, so we tried to entice them to come out and play with dog and cow dung. They were smart so when our eyes met, they quickly went up again.

To children, insects were also part of their family but they were fussy tyrants at times. They pulled out centipede's teeth, broke the ladybug's legs and placed it upside down to see it flapping its wings. We chased after a mole cricket and peed on it, took away food the ants were transporting. We observed an inchworm squirming in amusement but when we got bored we flicked it really hard and killed it.

There were other insects that died after being harassed because we were too rough on them. When we caught grasshoppers we held on to their hind legs and made them dance. We caught cicadas and tied a thread around their necks and let them go. We often caught golden colored yellow flies with sheer wings because they were pretty but we only let them go when they were on the verge of dying. Our games became life and death for those insects. Numerous insects died due to our "excessive love" for them, but what can we do, that's how children are!

Nevertheless, those insects were like one big bead-tree family. One time I was practically on the ground rolling my dirt marble and saw a dung beetle passing by rolling a dung ball. When I saw this I couldn't stop laughing because it looked as if it wanted to play marbles with me. The winter arrived when all the leftover nuts that birds had pecked and the ones that children didn't pick fell down and the strong wind followed. The tree stood alone naked after it shook off everything it had. All the insects were gone and only the children were left under the tree. Stick tossing and kite flying were difficult in the severe wind, because the kites often blew headlong to the top of the tree. It snowed occasionally but the strong wind it blew horizontally and it clung to the branches.

I can't forget the dignified look the tree had, withstanding the harsh winter wind. All the branches up in the air were tangled densely like fishing nets and my stingray kite was caught in them as well as dead leaves that flew up when the strong wind blew. Every time a gust of wind swept through, all those branches shook like roaring waves. When those young branches were bruised and broken by the strong wind, the tree stood with dignity bearing all those eggs and larvae. The tree sap ball I buried under the ground together with the cicadas' larvae that were preparing for the coming winter months.

When I recall that tree, the first thing that comes to mind is the sound of roaring waves the branches used to make and it still rings in my ear. The sound of the waves was the highlight of all those different recollections the tree inspired. It withstood great hardships to prepare for the lush summer season so that the cicadas could dwell in it and sing, resembling the sound of rain pouring down, the praises of abundance in the midst of that thick and well-shaded tree. In winter it sounded like the roaring ocean waves and in summer the pouring rain . . . in the midst of it, I grew up. I knew, without even digging up the ground, that the tree sap ball had turned into nothing.

*Lumber Mill*

The droning sound of cicadas in summer was extremely noisy to the point where my ear drums felt like they were going to burst. From afar, it sounded very similar to the sound of an electric saw coming from the lumber mill. The lumber mill was located not too far from where the bead-tree was. Outside the mill there was a pile of pine tree timber. When the new batch of timber came in, it was the children's job to peel off the bark with a sickle. And we took the bark home for firewood.

The lumber mill was a place where incredible power could be witnessed. Between the two thick woods, there was a filthy black thing covered in oil crouched down like a toad; this monster was the motor, and it possessed incredible power.

It was fun watching the motor getting started. The black

monster was as temperamental and ferocious in disposition as it looked, so it never started on the first try. It slowly started after putting half a dozen people through hell. One of the workers clung to the machine and turned the wheel really fast with all his strength. He spun the wheel so fast that it looked as if the person and the wheel were spinning together. The man's face was distorted and puffed up as if he was about to explode while struggling to fight a monster hissing and emitting fire through its nose. I let out a gasp as I watched him. After he poured out all his strength desperately trying to get the motor running, at that critical moment it let out a roaring sound signaling it finally worked. Then all of us burst into cheers.

The engine with the incredible energy shook vigorously, bursting with power ready to jump up. And that strength was linked to the electric saw and made the saw spin. The work was to saw the logs into planks and the power and the incredible sound generated from the saw was overwhelming. Two people struggled to carry a log and placed it on the work table, and the saw cut the huge log into planks as quickly as if it was a piece of cake, exhibiting its incredible physical strength. With a roaring sound, the sharp and stern-looking blades cut up the log without any hesitation, spewing out sawdust in the air like a water fountain. The lumber mill was covered with sawdust and it reeked of pine resin. All the workers were covered in sawdust and the power that dominated the lumber mill pierced through my small body. What kind of profound influence did this strength and this smell have on my personal growth? The roaring sound of the electric saw shook the plank walls of the lumber mill. When I was inside the lumber mill, I was so captivated by the noise that it was more like the enormous power of violence. Once I stepped outside, I was able to return to reality. My deafened ears became unplugged, and I could hear things clearly again. It was strange, but the sawing sure sounded like the droning of cicadas.

I could faintly hear the sound coming from the lumber mill during class at school. And there was another sound that travelled as far—the metal pounding sound from the blacksmith shop.

*Blacksmith Shop*

Lefty's blacksmith shop was located near the bridge in Pyŏngmun Stream. Whenever I heard the sound of iron pounding while doing my homework, I was compelled to run over there. There was magnificent power hovering in the blacksmith shop, too; compared to the lumber mill, there was so much more to see. Perhaps I felt small in front of Lefty because he was the son of blacksmith. I must have thought he was greater than he really was in terms of strength and courage because of the mythical power the blacksmith shop possessed.

The blacksmith shop was located nearby the stream and it was nothing but a small shabby looking hut. But once the furnace was ablaze with fire, the entire place was filled with power and light. All three members of his family, except Lefty, worked at the shop. Lefty's mother worked at the bellows and his oldest brother handled the red hot heated iron, and his other brother was in charge of forging the iron on an anvil with a large and heavy sledgehammer. His oldest brother came down from the mountain after hiding and had his leg amputated from the knee down because he had frostbite.

It was always fun watching the bellows expel air into the furnace, turning the mud wall red while making a rough breathing sound; a piece of iron slowly heated up in the blazing charcoal fire. It was a stunning metamorphosis of the cold and heavy iron. When the heated piece of iron was removed from the blazing fire and placed on the black anvil that resembled a giant's hoof, it glowed with dazzling brilliance. It was the beauty of white heat that could not be touched. The red hot iron had converted into the unapproachable mass of light, and it looked as if it would soar lightly into space, escaping from the tongs and the anvil. The sledgehammer lost no time and smashed down on the iron. The iron was held by the tongs and the sledgehammer precisely hammered the iron as it was turned over like a pancake. *Ding. Ding.* The heated metal was hammered over and over again into the shape of a tool and lastly it was thrown into the water bucket. In the tempering process, it lost the red luster and returned again to its heavy and depressed iron state.

It was clear from the way in which Lefty's brother handled the sledgehammer that he truly was strong. His shirtless upper body was red from the heat and was shiny with sweat; his small and big muscles bulged out, constantly moving up and down. When he raised the sledgehammer, his muscles twisted like a rope and bulged out. Then he hit the heated iron and his muscles trembled at the shock of hammering. He exerted so much strength that his mouth was severely twisted and his eyes turned goggle-eyed, and the children's mouths were twisted, too.

It was a spectacle not only for kids but for the adults; they liked to watch, too. The adults came to buy something and ended up watching for a long time. When the shop became busy with customers, Lefty quickly came out to help. His job was to ask his mother for the price of an item a customer picked out and receive money and give the item to the customer. Usually customers took their sweet old time when choosing a sickle. They checked to make sure the tempering was done well. They tried to flick the blade with their fingernails and sometimes they brought it to their tongue and tasted the blade. I wondered what it tasted like, so out of curiosity I put a blade on my tongue, too. It had a frightening yet stinging sensation and tasted somewhat smoky. I wonder if it was the taste of the iron or the taste of fire. Perhaps I imagined that taste because I was worried about whether my tongue would get cut.

From time to time they set up an outdoor blacksmith shop

next to the place where I swam. There was a job where they had to cover the steel on a horse drawn cart. It sure was an entertaining spectacle.

There was a pile of more than ten round steel frames and several steps away near the water the same number of wooden wheels was piled up. Also there was a stack of firewood the size of a cow. Everything was in abundance. The fire was built with a heap of firewood and at first I could not see the flame because of the sunlight. But when the blue smoke covered the entire stream like fog, the flame revealed its brilliant beauty even in broad daylight. Another impressive thing, apart from the burning fire in the background, was the wooden wheels that just came out of the lumber mill a snow white color. Since it was a big job, there were many workers as well as children watching. We were watching from afar, but the smell of pine resin burning and the heat wave overwhelmed us.

After the firewood was all burnt and became embers, settling at the bottom, revealing the red hot iron frames, that was when the real work began. The workers, shirtless upper bodies turned red from the heat, were quick and strong. As soon as the heated iron frame was taken out of the fire using the long tongs, its color changed from red to a bluish color in the sunlight. The three workers held the iron frame with the tongs and moved a few steps to place it carefully on the wooden wheel. The other two workers who were waiting immediately hammered with the heavy sledgehammers. Every time they hammered, the cold bluish iron frame flitted right into the wooden wheel. After the iron frame was mounted quickly, one person raised the wheel lifting a spoke and rolled the wheel that was spewing bluish smoke with all his strength toward the pool. The fire shrieked when it touched the water. It made a hissing sound, and blew off water vapor as the water boiled, then the fire slowly died.

When the fire and water fought, the fire wasn't the only thing that died. After ten or so iron wheels had been tempered in the pool, the pool also died and a rotten smell remained. After that I could no longer play in the water because it was infested with fleas and mosquitoes.

*Scar Tissue*

One day in that open-air blacksmith shop, I hurt my finger on a steel-rimmed wheel. It was a cool autumn day so I sat very close to the work area and ended up getting hurt. The workers had been taking the wheels, one at a time, out of the water. My hand was resting on a rock, and in the blink of an eye, one of the wheels rolled toward me and fell on my hand. My left hand was crushed and was covered in blood. I was in so much pain that it felt as though my hand had been torn from the wrist. Unable to endure the pain, I lost consciousness. I was hospitalized for the second time. The first time was when I had my scrofula surgery.

Lefty's brother carried me on his back and ran to the hospital. Fortunately it was not serious. All my fingers were swollen but the bones were not crushed, except the pinkie joint. The pinkie joint was dislocated and had a severe cut. The doctor stitched up the wound without anesthesia, so it was excruciatingly painful. I could not handle the pain, so I fainted again.

I skipped school and went to the hospital for follow-up treatment. I had a relapse of depression while I was away from school and my friends; I cried for no apparent reason. I was looking forward to the fall school excursion, and I couldn't even go to that. In the year and a half since I entered school, because of the Cheju Massacre all school excursions had been cancelled. On the day of the excursion, I waited for my turn in the hospital waiting room. When I saw the excursion procession, children chatting away happily outside the window, I turned my head and cried silently.

An illusion is a strange thing. Even now whenever I see my pinkie, the stitch mark looks remarkably prominent and ugly. The scar certainly is not a burn mark but strangely I am under the impression that my finger was scorched with a hot iron. *I wonder why?* Is it because the hot steel rim left a strong impression on me? I believe this idea has been imprinted in my memory since the time of that accident.

My mother was concerned that the injured finger might get infected, so she didn't send me to school until after it was completely healed and the bandage came off. I missed my friends very much while I stayed home for two weeks. I still feel the painful loneliness I experienced during that time. I cried secretly when my mother wasn't present. I must have felt closer to my friends than to my mother.

I was surprised at the warm welcome I received from my friends after half a month of absence. They looked surprised—as if they could not believe that my pinkie was sewn up like a torn glove. The injured area was pink because new skin had formed, and my friends were amazed even at that. Some even touched my finger. I felt elated as if I were a brave warrior with a medal. Without realizing it, I began to exaggerate the story. I told them about how I fainted twice and from there my story went in a completely different direction. The story became that the piping hot steel rim rolled over my hand. Lefty had witnessed the accident, but he didn't say anything. In order to make them believe my story, I even told them that the pink skin was caused by the burning steel rim.

"That's why this finger still has that burning smell. When I put my tongue to it I can taste the metal."

I gently closed my eyes and tried to lick the scar, like those blacksmiths at Lefty's shop, tasting the sickle with their tongues. I didn't taste anything, but I lied.

"Wow, this tastes great! This certainly is the taste of a metal. I can smell the skin burning. Do you want to try licking my finger?"

After I lied to my friends, I myself began to believe that the scar really had resulted from the burn. If a lie was told to make others believe it to be true, isn't it possible to deceive oneself that the lie wasn't a lie? Perhaps I'm not a good writer, but I'm under the illusion that the stories of mine which readers find interesting are those based on my experience, not the fabricated ones.

I don't know whether it was an animal instinct, but I got in the habit of licking the injured area at the time. My hometown is known for rocks, so it was common to trip over rocks and fall down if you ran around recklessly. There weren't many days where my knees were without bruises. When my knee started to bleed I would lick the area and sprinkle dirt over it to stop the bleeding which was enough to get the injured area to heal without getting it infected. Occasionally I had an inflammatory swelling of a lymphatic gland in the groin, so I couldn't walk easily but it wasn't serious.

One minute I was running around excitedly chasing after and being chased by my friends, the next minute I was tripping over a rock. That was the moment when everything came to a halt. I saw sparks, felt dizzy, and experienced a sharp biting pain. I was a crybaby but I never cried because I was in pain. On this occasion I was more worried about my pants. Every time I came home with holes in my pants and shirts, my mother punished me. I only had a pair of faded black school uniforms, so I wore them day and night at school and home. Thus, it was natural that my clothes wore out faster, but my mother scolded me and said, "Is your body made of blades?" She said the same thing when I broke the lamp-light glass while cleaning. "Are your hands made of blades?"

*Boils*

This interesting expression of "blades growing out of the body" alluded to the fact that my skin was particularly bad. Boils erupted like sharp blades quite frequently on my body. Since I was born with an extremely undesirable skin condition, I suffered from boils until I graduated from elementary school. My nervous temperament might have developed from this painful experience. I still have hideous looking scars from surgery, Chinese cupping treatment, and mercury burn marks. These scars truly testified to my nickname Scar. Other children had boils too but never as bad as mine. When one boil erupted, three or four formed around it. I had the shivers running down my entire body when the area was infected, as if I had a severe case of fever. I was like green vegetables suffering from greenflies.

For small boils I just needed to wait until they were ready to be discharged and pop them. However, the big boils were different; I felt a throbbing pain around the area so in an attempt to alleviate the pain, I even licked the area gently. My mother said it was no use when she saw me licking and she was right. To make the boils discharge faster, she caught a house spider and rubbed it on the area. She even put salted anchovy on a piece of gauze and wrapped this around the inflamed area. After the area was rubbed in the strong salted anchovy liquid, it became unbearably itchy. I felt as if not only the infected area but my perfectly fine skin was getting "pickled" as well. At the touch of my mother's hands, the unbearable itchiness turned into an excruciating pain. After the boils burst, the area felt pleasantly ticklish and scar tissue started to form. I put my tongue on the pinkish skin because I found it pretty.

Like plants, weak people suffer the most from disease. At the time many children were born with weak immune systems. There was a time when whooping cough, small pox, and even flu took infants' lives. Then a horrible cholera epidemic and the tragic massacre followed. The children my age who barely escaped death grew up with a high tolerance for disease. Nevertheless, the boils were chronic and did not go away easily. The children's soft skin was an excellent place for boils to inhabit. There were differences in degrees of seriousness but almost every child suffered from boils. Boils were the most common infection closely associated with the children.

My skin was exceptionally sensitive so until I entered junior high, I had to endure the pain of constantly erupting boils. Those boils disappeared around the time when I entered puberty. My mother said it was because of my awful skin condition. I suffered from lice, mite, and mosquito bites more than the others. Perhaps it wasn't because my skin was disagreeable but because my blood was sweeter and my skin softer that I got all those bites. I'm sure this is like drawing water to one's own mill, interpreting to my advantage. In any case, like Mt. Halla, the mother of all mountains, that commanded a countless number of small volcanic mountains, the boils erupted one after another. I still remember the unbearable itchiness right before the boils discharged and the pain and feeling of relief when they burst open at the hands of my mother's vigorous scratching. Once I helped squeeze my sister's boil that was on her calf. She endured the pain when the yellow pus came out, but when she saw the hole that was left in its place, she burst out crying. She accused me of making a hole in her perfectly healthy leg.

*Piece of Pork Meat*

I believe the cause of the boils was lack of nutrition. We lacked fatty foods and protein. Even a pound of pork meat was served as medicine.

I think I was in third grade. There was an occasion where my mother was in such great shock that she almost lost her mind. It happened during a busy season tilling the ground. She went to draw water at the well before dawn when it was still dark. Whe thought she would get breakfast ready and head out to work in the field. When she got to the well, she set down her water jar and groped for a bucket in the darkness. Then she felt something under her feet. She was startled and looked down and she found a man sprawled on the ground. In a moment of shock, she retreated backward and her feet got caught in the bucket rope and fell. When she heard the loud noise of the bucket smashing into pieces, she became even more shocked. She ran home terrified. She thought it was a dead body. Later we found out that he was a drunkard. The man was sprawled on the ground by the water well and slept through the morning reeking of alcohol until the women's comings and goings became frequent. It sure was a pitiful sight! There was no rice to make rice wine at the time. So, who could be stupid enough to drink until getting wasted and pass out when there wasn't even enough rice to feed people? Who else could it be other than the right wing youth group? My mother was furious saying that those right wing youth group bastards were the only ones who could behave in such a dirty and insolent manner.

My mother was bedridden because of the shock and what was used to cure her illness was a pound of pork. Since her stomach was empty, she was physically weak and led to her illness. There is a saying that when one is extremely hungry, he or she is subject to hallucination. My maternal grandfather sent one pound of pork, saying that my mother needed to eat well to get on her feet again. He instructed her to eat the meat alone. Since it was medicine there was no need for her to feel guilty. However, my mother could not possibly eat it alone. I believe half of that pork went into the mouths of my sister and myself. Boiled pork was sliced and was lightly brushed with honey. Was there another medicine as sweet as this? It literally melted in my mouth. It was so delicious!

We were destitute. A pound of pork was like medicine. Pregnant women, especially, went through difficult times because they didn't have enough to eat. So they even pulled the hair out of a pig in the outhouse to burn and sniff it.

Some readers might wonder what the pig was doing in the

outhouse. At the time, each household raised pigs in the out-house. Please don't say this is filthy! Thanks to the pigs, the out-house was clean and did not smell. After I graduated from high school, I started living in Seoul, but one of the things I hated was the toilet. I detested a small, dark, and enclosed space that reeked with stench. I hated crouching down to take a dump, looking down a deep, dark, bottomless hole. The stench that came from the opened space below was unbearable. I felt claustrophobic. Compared to this, the island's outhouse was safe and comforting. It was called the outhouse but there were no walls and roof; it was made of several stepping stones and rocks were built to cover the front side. It was wonderful taking care of business while gazing at the moving clouds in daylight.

If you can't relate to this, try to recall a time when you had to relieve yourself behind the bushes out in the field somewhere. I call this "field shitting" and I love doing it in the open field. It's so refreshing taking a dump crouching under the bright sunlight while smelling the grass. Even dung looks beautiful. One of two bluebottle flies flew in out of nowhere hovering over a coil of fresh yellowish dung on the green grass. Instead of toilet paper, I grabbed and pulled out a handful of grass to wipe my bottom. Or, I used a smooth rock that had been nicely warmed by the sun. I'm sure you all know what it feels like.

If taking a dump in the field was called "field shitting," taking a dump at night it was called "night shitting." When I was young, my bowel movements were irregular so I often had to go at night. But I was scared and dreaded going to the pitch dark outhouse. In the outhouse, there was a toilet ghost. I had to spit continuously in order to ward off the toilet ghost and the pig in the outhouse was the one that helped me keep the ghost at bay. When the pig crawled out after hearing me spit, I was no longer scared.

In any case, pigs were good and important livestock. They cleaned the outhouse, gave good fertilizer, and their meat tasted really good. Their meat tasted exceptionally good because they were fed human feces. The pigs had less fat, so the meat was juicy and tasty. Those who had had tasted the juicy and tender meat would still remember that flavor on the tip of their tongue. Perhaps I remember it vividly because it was during extremely difficult times. A soup made out of pig's intestines was another special treat.

During weddings and funerals, pigs were slaughtered and the meat and intestines were boiled in a big cauldron pot. The soup was made from the water the meat was boiled along with gulf-weeds; that was called pig's intestine soup. Several years ago I paid a visit to someone I knew from my hometown who was hospitalized after a car accident. He was unconscious and did not even recognize who I was, but he kept going on and on about the soup, licking his lips vigorously. Seeing him like that I became all teary eyed. The taste that had been long forgotten came back to him. Why did he remember this out of all his other memories? So many memories that had been stored became blurred as if they had been lightly erased. At that moment of danger, of losing memories, he unexpectedly remembered the past. The vivid remembrance of the taste was like a hand of salvation which he was holding dearly for his life. The soup signified something good and it could help him live.

When we are hungry we realize fully what it means to live. At the time when we hadn't enough to eat, we were desperate to survive. A piece of fat or a bowl of intestine soup was heavenly. When the thick soup entered the body, I was in a state of bliss. It was the joy of life. That was why pregnant women pulled out pig's hair and smelled the burnt hair.

Ah, that savory smell! On New Year's Eve the entire neighborhood got together and contributed whatever they could to buy a pig. I can still remember the heavenly smell of pig's hair burning. Not only the taste but the smell left a profound impression on me. There are so many things from the past, events, and people I met that I had long forgotten. However, my sense of smell from the starving days remains vivid in my memory. To put it more accurately the smell is related to a piece of pork. How much I wanted to eat even a small piece of pork then. The only time I could have any meat was on New Year's or ancestral memorial service days.

I liked August the best in the lunar calendar because most memorial services fell in this month. The Full Moon Harvest together with my great grandfather and grandfather's memorial services were held in August. I got a bowl of rice with a plate of side dishes after the memorial service, and it was a special treat and was really delicious. Especially the taste of pork was unforgettable. Ah, the taste of fat melting in my mouth! One piece, no more and no less, was my share. I had a piece of pork, fish, one rice cake, two slices of *muk* or "mung bean jelly," and one piece of apple and tangerine. The food was equally divided regardless of age; even the adults had the same portion. Even my grandmother, the eldest in the family, had the exact same portion. However, she only had one piece of mung bean jelly and gave the rest to her grandchildren. She was a devout Buddhist so she did not touch pork.

My sister and I were better off because of my father. Even though my father was in the mainland, he got the same portion of food, so his share was split between my sister and me. I was reminded of the existence of my long forgotten father only at that time.

It was my uncle who taught me how to bow. Traditional folding rice paper screens were set up behind the ceremonial table. One corner was burnt from the fire. My grandfather salvaged the screens from the fire along with the ancestral tablet. His plaque was placed on the table, too. When I was bowing, my uncle solemnly said, "Make sure your butt is not up! Keep your feet together and gently place your butt on top of your feet. That's right."

*Paternal Grandmother*

After my paternal grandfather passed away, my paternal grandmother relied on my uncle and lived with his family. As usual she went to a five-day open market to sell grain. She was a devout Buddhist so she did not eat meat and refused to kill any living creatures; she even let a family of rats live in her room. She had a habit of looking down when she was walking, trying to find if there was anything on the ground. Pieces of cloth and grains she had gleaned from the ground piled up high in one corner of the room, which became a haven for the rats. My grandmother did not mind that her gleanings became the rats' food. Thinking back, my grandmother picked up those fallen grains to take home for the rats.

Rather than chasing the rats out of the room, she considered them her roommates. Perhaps the mother rat felt safe and that was why she had her baby rats. Once I was called in to her musty room and was horrified when I saw pinkish baby rats squirming on a heap of straw rubbish and cloth scraps. I tried to sweep up the disgusting rat babies in a dustpan, but my grandmother stopped me and said, "These are living creatures, too. We can't let them freeze to death out in the cold. When spring comes they'll leave on their own."

Her way of thinking naturally isolated her from the rest of the family. Her daughters-in-law talked behind her back, and we grandchildren refused to go into her room because of the smell of the rat dung. She was illiterate, but she was good at numbers, adding and subtracting in her head. She even memorized Buddhist sutras such as "Prajnaparamita" or "The Heart Sutra" and was able to recite them without difficulty. She was the smartest in the family. The fact that she was able to live with the rats showed her extraordinariness.

*Pig's Bladder*

Even in the worst lean years, a piece of meat was offered at the ancestral memorial service. So when New Year's drew near, all the neighbors pooled their money together to buy a pig. I disliked seeing frog or rabbit specimens in glass bottles in formaldehyde displayed in the school hallway cabinet, but it was fun watching a pig getting dissected. It was raw and real. One time shortly before New Year's day, I heard a pig squealing from out of nowhere. At the sound, all the children rejoiced and ran to see.

The pig had a noose around its neck. It struggled as the butcher and the owner of the pig hoisted up on the bead-tree. They sat next to the tree and smoked, taking a little rest. The pig was gasping for its life, no longer able to squeal. It had been kicking its hind legs in the air, but they finally drooped down. Even the gasping sound stopped; from its opened mouth white foam formed like bubbles rising. But the pig wasn't dead yet. If someone had ventured to loosen the noose at that time, thinking that it was dead, the pig would have run away. We swallowed our saliva and quietly waited a little longer, puffing and gasping. The butcher started to sharpen his knife on a grindstone. At last from the pig's butt, feces came out. After the hard dung soft dung followed, and at this moment all the children flocked to the pig like gnats and started pulling out the pig's hair. The pig's hair was used to make a cloth brush and a shoe shining brush, so a taffy vendor gladly took the pig's hair in exchange for taffy. I grabbed several strands of hair and pulled them out with all my strength. But I couldn't beat those with pincers. With the pincers, they could easily pull out a handful of hair like pulling out grass. Where hair had been pulled out, the skin was red.

"Hey kids, get lost! Go away!"

The pig's owner and the butcher drove the children away. Then they untied the pig, placing it on the ground where the straw mat had been rolled out. Then they started to scorch the pig. The smell of the burning hair was savory. We remembered the long forgotten taste of pork when the pleasant smell wafted by, and our nostrils flared up. The only time we could taste a piece of meat was on the day of the ancestral memorial service. I was excited that I would be able to taste the savory fatty meat! On top of the pig, straw was set on fire and left to burn vigorously. The burning straw was shoved inside the ears, and on the legs, and the crotch to scorch the hair. After all the hair was burnt, the toe nails were pulled out using bare hands like taking socks off. The next step required a knife. The butcher scraped off the ashes that covered the pig's body with the knife as if he was shaving it and doused it with water. The pig's clean white body was revealed after the dirty outer skin had all been scraped off. It was tinged with bluish shade like when sideburns were just shaved off. After the butcher nicely cleaned off its ears, front and hind legs, and the crotch, he began dividing the pig's carcass.

First, he cut off one of the front legs. Then he held the pig upside down holding onto its hind legs. The clotted blood poured out, and its owner caught the blood in a big earthenware pot. The butcher's hand was quick with the knife and was moving faster and faster. In the blink of an eye, he cut off all three legs then he cut off its head. He carefully made cuts in the middle of the stomach so that its entrails didn't get damaged. Then the steam arose and its fresh entrails poured out of the stomach. The butcher put his hand inside the stomach to scrape out the rest. Together with the entrails, the pig's liver and bladder came out. The butcher and the owner were the only ones who got to taste the fresh liver. What was given to the children was the stinking bladder. The butcher and the pig's owner said, "The liver tastes better when it's hot." Stopping what they were doing they sliced the liver and ate it, savoring every bite of it. All the children salivated and gazed at them enviously, then the butcher cut the bladder and threw it toward us and said, "Here. Play with this."

The pig's bladder became our soccer ball. Even the bladder was useful in those days. When the pig was slaughtered, except for squealing and shitting, nothing was wasted. The soccer ball made out of the pig's bladder stunk, but it was fun to kick it around and play. Perhaps it was fun because of the fresh urine and blood stench. It was like kicking a live animal so it was more thrilling than kicking a plastic ball.

First we rubbed the bladder gently with our feet to get all the piss out. Every time we rubbed it, the bladder squirted out piss as if it was startled. It was fun looking at it so we all laughed. "Pee! Poop! You ugly thing!" We sang a song that ridiculed the kids who wet their beds at night. The mixture of bloody smell and urine stench was offensive. The piss filled bladder was covered in dirt when all the children rubbed it with their feet. When it squirted out everything and became deflated, everyone stomped on the bladder to get rid of the stench. But the stench didn't go away easily. Either Lefty or Chicken Butt would insert a reed and blow air into the bladder to make a ball, enduring the stench. I couldn't believe anyone would put the bladder close to their nose. Lefty sure was one tough cookie! The deflated bladder was inflated and the opening was tied tightly with thread. The stench faded a bit, but the bloody smell was still raw and strong. The children flocked toward it and kicked it around. But when the bladder went up in the air and landed on their faces or hands, they screamed in disgust. The stinking and fleshy bladder under my foot felt like a live animal moving. It was resilient and tough; even though we stepped on it again and again, it didn't burst open. When I stepped on the bladder it flattened like a mouse stuck under a wheel, but it quickly returned to its original shape when my foot was removed. The pig's bladder rolled about here and there, and the children chased after it, kicking it around and singing, "Pee! Poop! You ugly thing."

*Snot*

Another characteristic of the children at that time was that many children had runny noses. I drooled until I was four years old but did not really have a runny nose.

Nowadays children have a runny nose when they have a cold, so it might be difficult to imagine thick sticky snot hanging from a child's nose. Some snots were whitish, some bluish, and some yellowish. The best was the yellowish snot. It was more like discharged pus rather than a runny nose, so those children were ostracized from their peers.

My classmate Pangu comes to mind when I think of snot. He was smart so he could avoid being ostracized but he had a severe chronic runny nose problem. Two strands of snivel that looked like squirming worms went in and out of his nostrils. He blew his nose using his thumb and index finger alternately. After he blew out his nose using his index finger, he wiped his nose swiftly. It makes me laugh thinking about his quick action. From time to time he used his sleeve to wipe his nose instead of his index finger. So his right index finger and right side sleeve were always shiny with dried up snot.

The way in which his nose ran was disgusting, but it was amusing at the same time. When two strands of yellowish snot came out of his nostrils, I was afraid that it would go into his mouth. But he knew exactly when he needed to suck in the snot even when he was completely engrossed in playing. Two strands of snot slowly crawled out of his nostrils like two worms and reached his upper lips but without fail those two strands were quickly sucked in with a slurping sound. It almost looked as if two strands of noodles were inhaled. Depending on the condition of his nostrils, sometimes it made a noise like a flapping piece of paper. If that was the case, the sticky liquid turned into a bubble and popped when he exhaled. Slurping, flapping, and popping—it sure was a disgusting and strange sound.

That runny nose Pangu now lives in Pusan and holds an executive position at a large corporation. The way in which he talks and carries himself is perfectly well mannered. It's great when he smiles and touches under his nose with his index finger. I'm certain that no one in the company knows that his habit of touching and wiping under his nose comes from wiping his runny nose in childhood.

It was all because we didn't have enough to eat. We often had sty in our eyes and had warts on top of our hands. When we had sty, a barleycorn and briar thorn was used to get the pus out, and for warts we wrapped spider web around to smother them. If we couldn't get rid of them by smothering with the spider web, we caught a mantis and made it bite into them.

*Electric Light*

I'm not saying that everyone around me was dirt poor. There is a day when the sun comes out even during monsoon season, meaning that even in the most destitute situation, there are people who are better off. There were some people living in the city who knew no poverty during the most difficult times. You could guess someone's financial situation just by looking at a child's school cap. A cap worn by a child from a poor family, like myself, was all faded, crumpled and out of shape, similar to the ones that had been worn for several years by our seniors.

I wore a faded cap like those of my seniors when I entered elementary school. My cap got rained on once and got washed out after that. The dirty rain water dripped from the drenched cap and covered my face and my white shirt. My mother was so upset when I returned home from school looking like that. My drenched cap was as good as a dirty mop. I still remember the angry look my mom had when she was squeezing the dirty water out of the cap and rinsing it a few times.

I was not timid because my family was poor. I wasn't the only one; about half of my classmates were in the same situation. That was why I didn't know exactly what poverty meant. When I saw some classmates who were rich, I just considered them to be different. There were several classmates who were not that well-off but their houses had electricity which was a drastic difference in living standards compared to my house where we had just changed from using an oil lamp to a gas lamp.

One of my classmates even had a record player. When I went to his home and saw a deformed arm looking thing on a turntable producing music, I was so surprised. I was in state of shock because I saw something I had not seen before. But I wasn't envious because I knew it was something I could not easily attain with a little effort. The only things I could get my hands on were old discarded and broken records or light bulbs with broken filaments. The broken records were melted to make marbles, and my mother used discarded light bulbs to help mend socks.

The house was brightly lit with electric lights and the rooms were covered in white powder-like wallpapers, and many picture frames hung on those walls; and I heard the family's bright and happy laughter. I was not envious because these things were completely foreign and unfamiliar to me. In a house like that, a father was always present—the warm and loving father like the electric light in the middle of the room. In my family's cramped single room, poverty pervaded and dominated, instead of my father. My family was poor, but I had more freedom than other children because of my father's absence.

*Worms*

I was always hungry when I was a kid. Even though I had three meals a day, I was still hungry. I was at that age where I could not sit still; I ran around all the time so the food must have digested very fast. But I think I was hungry because I had a "beggar in my stomach." I truly felt like there was a beggar sitting inside my stomach. I never ate to my heart's content in those days, and the worms inside me were eating away at the food I had consumed. I shoved down the food to share with the worms.

I don't know if I had done it when I was little, but I often saw two-year old babies crawling on the ground and eating dirt. Thinking back now, I'm certain that it was deliberate because our bodies craved it. Did we eat dirt because we lacked iron? When Lefty ran his magnet through dirt on the ground, dust-like iron particles stuck on the magnet. Or, did the worms inside my stomach cry for dirt? In Cheju dialect, roundworms are called earthworms; I don't know whether the worms like dirt, but children with roundworms ate dirt.

One time I was relieving myself in the outhouse and saw a worm hanging halfway down from my rectum. I was so shocked that I felt shivers running down my spine and broke out in a cold sweat. I tried very hard to shake it off but it wouldn't budge. I did not know what to do. I could not call my mother because I felt so embarrassed and it was something that should be kept secret. I was hoping the pig inside the outhouse would take care of it; the pig kept jumping up to get the worm. I was worried to death that the pig might miss the worm and bite off my balls, so I had no choice but to use my hand to pull it out. I shuddered in fear, but I grabbed some straws and rolled them up; then I pulled out the disgusting worm.

When I had a stomachache, my mother fed me two spoonfuls of oil. As soon as the oil went inside, I felt a burning sensation so I equated the oil with fire. But what I had actually swallowed was not scorching fire but hot pepper. This is the gist of what happened.

We usually had a bowl of cold barley rice mixed in with water for lunch in the summertime. The one and only side dish was green peppers or cucumbers dipped in extremely salty, soy bean paste. The soy sauce and bean paste tended to be saltier than usual because beans were rare during those years of famine. The soy bean paste was so salty that it was like chewing on hard rock salt and actually it tasted more bitter than salty; and cucumbers that shriveled up in the drought also tasted extremely bitter. The green peppers beaten by the drought were burning hot, too. When I complained to my mother that everything was salty, bitter, and hot, my mother simply said I should eat everything. She added that the reason why adults did not have stomach problems was because they ate salty, bitter, and hot foods.

I nearly fainted several times after eating fiery hot peppers. Hot peppers were like burning fire. I groaned in excruciating pain because my lips, the inside of my mouth, and stomach felt like they were caught on fire. My nose was running and tears poured down, mixing in with my runny nose. My mouth was wide open and thick and sticky saliva drooled endlessly. The worms were on fire as well and stirred frantically in my stomach. I had to run to the outhouse and shit everything out. After I was finished, the fire had transferred over to my rectum and I felt the burning sensation.

The side dishes were always the same, so when a piece of grilled salted mackerel was placed on the table, I went crazy. My chopsticks kept going to get the fish, and my younger sister complained that I was eating her share of the fish; then my mother's scolding soon followed.

"Mom, look at him! He keeps eating fish and not his rice," said my sister.

"Why do you keep eating that salty fish? Are you trying to make pickled fish inside your stomach?" my mother asked.

"What's wrong with making pickled fish? I'm going to kill the worms with it," I replied.

Santonin was the free medicine the school handed out to get rid of the worms. I still remember how shocked I was when I saw all the worms that came out of my body after taking the medicine on an empty stomach and feeling dizzy all day long. My mother who followed me to the outhouse said, "Oh my! There are so many. All dead. You shouldn't kill the big worm."

Big worm. What she meant was I should've left one worm inside my stomach. Like the serpent in the old house that protected the food storage, the big worm was in each of our stomachs to ensure that we had food to eat. I was not certain whether this old saying came from Confucius or Mencius. A few worms were needed to get our appetite going but then . . . There must be something more meaningful behind keeping worms. Even though they are good-for-nothing gluttons, when my mother said don't get rid of them entirely but save the seed, it meant that these worms had nowhere else to go but to dwell in human stomachs. I think she meant we should treat them as a part of our body.

*Hunger*

It was true. Hunger descended upon us because the auspicious serpent was burned during the Cheju Massacre. How could we expect a good harvest when all those gods protecting the poor farmers' food were burned? And how could the living eat well when there were many spirits who died prematurely during the massacre, not even eating half of what a normal person would eat in his or her lifetime?

Did famine continue year after year because of those spirits? Did those thousands and thousands of souls who could not rest in peace dry up the fields? If that wasn't it, then how could one explain not just one year but six years of famine? It lasted my entire elementary school years. There wasn't one year where we had enough food; either there was a bad barley harvest in the summer or a bad millet harvest in the fall. When I was in fifth grade both barley and millet harvests were poor. For three months in spring, we only had barley husks to live on which were leftovers from the time of the massacre. It was common to go without lunch for one month out of the year. All through elementary school, I was malnourished.

When the grains in the jar almost hit rock bottom, my mother measured again and again to see how much was left. Her sad and weak hands took them out of the jar and put them back in. She sighed as if the ground was going to sink and said, "From now on, we need to skip at least one meal a day."

For a growing child skipping a meal for over a month was excruciatingly painful. At first, my mother suggested that I leave half a bowl of rice from breakfast and have the rest for lunch. But then I was more hungry, so I decided to skip lunch altogether. One bowl of rice for breakfast was needed to put an end to that frightening hunger and get me through the day. Hunger truly was dreadful. It was an instinctual fear that reminded me intensely of my flesh slowing eroding.

The gnawing sensation of hunger was so traumatic that I could not erase it from my memory. Even now I fear skipping a meal. When I do, I become exceedingly agitated.

During the years of famine even crabs and a *kodong* type of small shellfish were completely depleted. Every single rock had been turned over so the seaside had transformed into an unfamiliar desolate landscape. I went to the seaside at low tides to look for something to eat. I looked for crabs and shellfish underneath the rocks. I thought I found the *kodong* but it was an empty shell and a *chipge* was inside it. Even though I was extremely hungry, I did not eat *chipge*. A *chipge*'s tail was gross-looking like a caterpillar, but I did not like its nickname which literally meant "living in someone else's house." I lived in a rented room, living in someone else's house, so I found the *chipge* to be brazen and wicked, taking over a *kodong*'s house while it left its shell.

I sigh when I think of the small naked boy looking for fish alone on summer days by the seaside where the water was gently undulating. The boy's empty stomach in his transparent body had a tinge of sad blue color as if it had absorbed the ocean's intense hue of azure blue. Poor starving soul . . .

When I caught a crab, I put the live crab in my mouth and ate it. In Cheju dialect "*kingi*" means "crab" which is also my nickname. It is ironic that a Crab ate a crab. I cracked open different kinds of shellfish and washed them in the water and ate them. Crabs, shellfish, and fish weren't enough to make my stomach content and full, but how could I have endured all those severe lean years without them?

*Sea Crab "*Kingi*"*
The sea cured the boils on my body. I went in and out of the ocean playing in the water and searching for crabs and shellfish. The water and the sun cleansed the children's bodies. We squeezed each other's boils for fun and the holes that were made after the pus came out went all wrinkly in the salty ocean water.

Going in and out of the ocean made scabs come off easily, too. Like most children I did not wash my face very well, only a few dabs of water on my nose like a cat. So, I often had scabs on my head. But it was difficult to get rid of the dirt that settled on the skin. In wintertime, I suffered from sore skin because head lice spread and caused intense itching. Every time my mother washed my hair, she shoved my head into a basin and rubbed my head with all her fingers like she would scrub the bottom of an iron pot. It was so painful! In the ocean, the scabs came off easily. In and out of the ocean repeatedly wetting the head and drying it made the scabs disappear. One time the scorching sunlight was so intense that I scratched my head. I felt something disgusting and it fell to the ground. It was about the size of my palm and it was black. I was so shocked thinking that my entire scalp had come off.

As soon as I got out of the water, my body dried off quickly but was left with white salt residue. The sun didn't feel intense because the ocean breeze cooled my body. The ocean breeze cooled the heat adequately so that I didn't get sunburnt but my translucent body that looked as if it could reflect the ocean water gradually became nicely tanned. What exactly was happening underneath my skin? Perhaps a photosynthesis of the sunlight, salt, and breeze was taking place. I'm not talking about the synthesis of calcium, strengthening bones in young children. The sunlight, salt, and breeze were in harmony, working together with the sky and the ocean. This photosynthesis took place inside my body, too. But in what way or how did this photosynthesis influence my mental well-being?

I can see a child squirming at the bottom of the blue ocean. The water stretched out from where the boy was standing all the way to the horizon—between the sky and the ocean, the expansive space and the burning sun. I, as a minute form of life, crawled under the water. I was like a crab, a small creature. I was dark and tanned except the whites of my eyes and pink around the places where pus had once been squeezed.

The boy was completely lost in time, busy hunting for crabs going round and round. He used a seaweed stalk as a bait to catch crabs between the rocks. Two crabs slowly crawled out of the water following the bait. As soon as one of the crabs grabbed the bait, he snatched it and covered it with his hand. It was a nice shiny looking crab. He salivated even before he put the crab in his mouth. The crab raised its claws and opened its eyes in full alert. In anger, the white foam formed in its mouth. But for the strong boy the foam, resembling that seen when cooking rice, was amusing rather than threatening. The boy sang in excitement. The crab spewed out more foam, almost like soapsuds which glittered in various colors under the sunlight. The boy thought enough foam was produced so the crab was ready to be eaten.

The boy held up the live crab that was struggling. First he put the vicious looking claw in his mouth. Trying not to get bitten by its claw he opened his mouth wide and chewed on it. After he finished eating one, he popped the second claw in his mouth, finally finishing off the rest. He quickly chewed on the body part, fearing that the legs might cut into his tongue. When he bit into the crab's body, the juice squirted out. It was delicious.

The boy lost track of time because he was too engrossed in catching crabs that he didn't realize the high tide had begun a while ago. He saw more and more crabs. What he didn't realize was that all those crabs appeared because the high tide was at its peak. He had just graduated from playing in the shallow water and did not know much about the ocean. While he was busy catching the crabs the water gradually rose over the rocks. On the opposite side of the harbor one of the boats departing blew its boat whistle warning the boy, but he did not hear. He was alone. There was no one to tell him to get out of the water. The water had crept to the middle of the rocks and the clams that were stuck on the rocks opened their mouths.

Fortunately around this time, I realized what was happening. The clouds had covered the sun and the surrounding area suddenly became dark. I stood up startled as if I woke up from a dream and found the water covering more than half of the land. I was completely surrounded by the water. I was scared. I can vividly recall the light silvery color of the water. Perhaps it was that color because the sun was shrouded in thick gray clouds. The silvery water undulated gently in the breeze, as if the white cotton fabric was spread out endlessly. I finally stretched out my stiff legs and jumped into the water thinking that I needed to get out fast. I had my head in the water and swam as fast as I could. I was not quite myself because I was gripped with fear that the water spirits would follow me and grab me by my ankle.

However, I was faced with a problem after I came out of the water. There was no trace of my clothes. Had my mother taken my clothes again like last year? Was Lefty playing a joke on me? I ran here and there looking, but my clothes were nowhere to be found. I was certain that my clothes were swept away by the tide. I went out until the water came up to my waist, but there was no trace of them. All of a sudden tears ran down. The silvery water increased more and more, and I thought of my black shorts and white sleeveless shirt floating somewhere sinking lower to the bottom of the ocean. The ocean had taken my clothes instead of my life.

My close brush with death was a prelude to my friend Changsu's death. One windy day Changsu and I were riding on high waves, but he was swept up and never came back. My experience of losing clothes at the age of ten was so deeply etched in my consciousness that it appeared in my dreams over and over again . . . the images of the white cotton fabric spread out endlessly and a naked child fidgeting with his feet bound.

That summer when I lost my clothes at the beach, the Korean War broke out in the mainland. Since the island was isolated, the islanders thought it was a rumor when the news of the war arrived. They thought it was happening in a remote place and it had nothing to do with them. Then one day martial law was declared and several thousand people who surrendered and came down from the mountain were arrested for detention. The temporary respite of peace and stability that was restored after the Cheju Massacre, was disturbed and a dark atmosphere had returned to the island. Another ordeal had fallen upon its shores.

The war was not going favorably on the mainland and a deluge of refugees came to the island. The young men who survived the Cheju Massacre were sent to the war front. The first three thousand middle school students were recruited as Marine Corps and left the island, then army recruits followed suit. Those who did not pass the primary inspection were incarcerated for a month. Several hundreds were killed and the rest were sent to the front lines. (I detest myself writing this right now. I am only mentioning in passing that several hundreds of people were killed at the time. I am doing an injustice to their wrongful deaths and I hate myself for it. However, the nature of this work prevents me from delving into that event.)

*Sweet Potato Storage*

Those people who did not pass the primary inspection were incarcerated in a small tightly-enclosed room, some at the police station and some at the sweet potato storage barn. I heard that it was like a month of living hell. Instead of sweet potatoes people were stored in the potato storage. They weren't killed right away but were thrown inside the storage for a month. As if they were sweet potatoes in a sack, they were literally on top of each other. They couldn't lie down or stretch their legs, so they sat up with their knees hugged against their chest. They slept in an upright position, leaning against each other. When the temperature went up, the airtight room with no ventilation was like an oven. The body odor was intense, and they hurled curses at each other the moment their arms or legs brushed against each other.

Sitting in the storage room suffering from the heat and not knowing what to expect, they thought they were going to lose their minds. After a while they became delirious and could not determine whether they were better off dying or living. Similar to the fate of sweet potatoes, their use was determined by their quality and several thousand people underwent a similar process. First, several hundred of them were discarded because they were deemed useless in helping rebuild the country. The so-called "quality" was not good. The dead bodies were either buried in the ground or thrown in the middle of the ocean so the exact number was unknown. The rest of them, excluding the old people, were deemed as dispensable war supplies.

After the junior high school student Marine Corps left the island, I witnessed a strange training session taking place when I passed by Ohyŏn Junior High. The reason why I still remember this is the young men's ghastly appearance. For some reason, everyone looked so sick. They looked pale with swollen faces, and they were dragging their legs. Those pitiful men were on their stomachs in the mud puddle, so they were completely caked in mud. Thinking back now, they were the ones who got freed from a month of incarceration and became the war recruits.

*Refugees*

The situation took a turn for the worse. I was scared of the bloodthirsty atmosphere. I could imagine what it was like at the war front. I was worried about my father who was in the midst of the war. It was difficult for me to listen to my mother's endless sighs. She kept saying, "My son, this is a very dangerous time. Don't use the main road. You need to use the back road and stay in the neighborhood."

We heard a rumor that many people were arrested for preliminary detention. The police station detention room and judo room were packed with people and the sound of people screaming from beatings and torture was heard all day long. So I avoided walking in front of the police station when I went to school. Then shortly afterward we had our summer vacation. Around this time, refugees came from the mainland and used the empty school as an internment camp.

The islanders were afraid of the mainlander refugees. They knew it was their duty to take pity and take good care of them, but the islanders didn't have any energy to help out. In truth, they suffered more than the refugees. The islanders were nearly starving themselves, so how could they be hospitable when they had to share what little they had?

The town had turned into one huge hungry mouth. The LST (Landing Ship Tank) was known as the "mouth" where the refugees spewed out endlessly. There were ten thousand of them and this number was enough to overpower the entire island. The atrocity of the Cheju Massacre was still fresh in the minds of the islanders, and they identified themselves as victims. They feared the refugees together with the counterinsurgency forces and the policemen from the mainland. With the influx of the mainland people, the situation looked as if the guests had moved in permanently to dominate the island. The so-called "sympathizer incident" took place, trying to frame communists. Twelve local influential people including a town leader, judge, prosecutor, attorney, principal, chief doctor, and other right wing important figures were arrested as communist sympathizers. This incident was recorded to have taken place before the student soldiers left for the war front.

*Departure Song*

Many young men died. And as if this were not enough, any young men who survived the burning of the island were drafted to fight in the war.

The first group, the Marine Corps Third Class, was composed of middle school students. The recruitment was carried out hastily, so most of them were young boys, fifteen years old or in their late teens. Perhaps they were considered adults then. Two years ago during the massacre, fifteen year old boys were at the crossroads of life and death. They lied about their age and tried to make themselves look shorter to avoid the danger. Those who barely escaped death because they were thirteen or fourteen were now the main target of recruitment. Even fourteen-year-old boys who were tall enough and able to carry a gun were enlisted.

The departure signified an eternal farewell to those who were massacred in the name of insurgents and traitors, opposing the establishment of the South Korean government. The young boys had no choice but to accept the harsh reality. I cannot forget the day they left the island. Everyone had the Korean flag wrapped around their chest and the procession was solemn and emotional.

The islanders who had been gripped by fear of death came out of their victim mentality and shouted to their hearts' content. The only way to open their lips, sealed tightly out of fear, was to go to the war front risking their lives. Their pent up emotions, fear of death, contempt, and disgrace were all unleashed while they were singing. They decided to fight at the front out of desperation because they thought it would be better to die in the battle than be incarcerated on the hellish island. The only way to clear their names as "insurgents" was to participate in the war. Their loud singing shook the entire village. Their uncontrollable anger and uncertainty, not knowing what was right or wrong, were manifested in song.

> *Life is fleeting and*
> *Five hundred years of Yi Dynasty is boundless*
> *If my death can bring the country to rise*
> *I will gladly sacrifice*

The Third Class and Fourth Class were created like this and they participated in the Inch'ŏn Landing. Since then, they led successful battles under the worst circumstances and their reputation became well-known inside and outside of South Korea.

I took big steps trying to catch up with the procession heading toward the pier. Ten years later when I joined the Marine Corps, I confirmed the myth during the basic and educational training of the new recruits. Hearing about the heroic exploits of the Mt. Tosol Battle, "the roll of thunder, the sea of fire on land howling in blood," gave me the shivers, a weak soldier at the time of peace. The marines were called the "ghost-catching marines" or "brutal soldiers." What made them such indomitable warriors? Was it the indiscriminate torture they went through, turning them into aggressive soldiers? I pity those young teenagers who jumped into the fire like tiger moths . . . what cruel fate awaited them? They had served ten years in the Marine Corps, but they were only older by five years. But the five year difference changed the course of our lives. I volunteered to join the army as a result of the pain and failure of my foolish love, whereas they did it to survive. What an extravagant despair!

The recruits circled the pavilion once then headed toward the pier. They each had the Korean flag with writings by their family members praying for their victory and safe return. The pier was crowded with family members crying for their loved ones. The elderly mothers gave their sons rice wine to comfort them, and for many of them it was their first time tasting alcohol so their faces turned red with just one sip. When the ship was about to sail, all the recruits untied the flags from their chests and waved them. With the flags flapping in the air, the ship looked like a flower-covered funeral bier and sailed further and further into the ocean. My older cousin and Lefty's brother were on the ship, too.

> Goodbye mother and father
> I am leaving for the war front
> When the Korean flag flutters at the top of Mt. Paektu
> I shall return home in white ashes

Most of the young men had crossed the ocean as recruits following the Third and Fourth Class, but from the mainland came new recruits to be trained at a training camp set up on the island. It was then that we first saw the LST, known as the "mouth." Watching the big mouth swallow and spit out a large number of people, I caught a glimpse of the cruelty of war.

*Glass Marbles*

I was surprised to see my father on that "mouth" ship. He came to the island, leading the recruits from the mainland. The image of my father I had in my mind was that of the wind. He came like the wind and went away as he pleased. That was the reason why I didn't like my father and I feared him. I accepted my father's absence as something natural, so even when he left for the mainland I did not miss him very much. In fact, I was relieved that my father was not home. However, it was the war that taught me the importance of my father. I was worried to death about him when we lost contact. I cried when my father appeared before my eyes healthy as ever. It was the first time that I felt this warmth toward him.

He was on duty so he could not stay home for very long. He only stayed with us for about four days but it sure was memorable. I was happy that my father had been promoted to First Class Sergeant holstering a gun. The three seagulls and three bars on the insignia around his arm looked even more impressive.

He even brought presents. Glass marbles and candies were the things I wanted most in those days. These were the items only rich kids possessed. I was always so jealous of those children who had a hard rock candy in their mouth and played with the marbles.

Like the wind, my father disappeared once again. I was in a daze as if I had met my father in my dream. I thought I ate the rock candy in my dream, too. Every time I felt this way, I opened the drawer to make sure I had the glass marbles. The glass marbles were incredibly lovely. They were hard and smooth on the surface, but the insides were beautiful and transparent. Different colors ran and mixed splendidly as if drops of oil paints were dripped in clear water. They resembled many things such as a swathe of thick cloud, the earth's equator or meridian . . . The marbles were the evidence of my father's affection. It was around this time I started writing letters to him.

*Female Marine Corps*

Two months before I started writing this, I was startled by something I happened to see on TV. Three women in their sixties ridiculously dressed in camouflage army fatigues were on TV. I watched wondering what kind of ludicrous show they were putting on by having the elderly ladies dressed in camouflage fatigues but when I watched closely it was nothing like that. During the war these women were in the marines. Were there female marines? I was in the marines but never heard of female marines. What was more surprising was that the three elderly ladies were from my hometown.

For the first time, they publicly revealed their sad stories. They were extremely emotional and their voices trembled. When the war broke out many young men were recruited as marines and left the island, and among them there were about twenty young women. They were comprised of high school students and elementary school teachers who were all under twenty years of age. Recruiting of the young women was in direct violation of the military law, but this showed how powerful the authorities were at the time. Perhaps their reasoning was that in order to clear their name as insurgents, women and men equally needed to join and fight the red communists.

Twenty young female marines, the symbol of anti-communism, left the island together with the young men. Fortunately they were not placed on the battle front. After the intensive training was over, the young men begged the military authority to send the young women back home. They pleaded crying and promised that they would fight twice as hard. The military had to let the female marine recruits go before assigning them military numbers because it was illegal not because the young men pleaded, so the twenty female marines ended up as a mere episode. They were placed in a training camp for almost a month and underwent severe training. Their voices trembled as they recalled those days as if they were trying to suppress their anger.

My surprise did not end there. I stared at the TV screen holding my breath and I realized that one of the elderly ladies was my homeroom teacher. She said that she was an elementary school teacher and when I saw her name, I was in utter shock. After forty five years, her name came back to me as quick as a flash. Her face was wrinkled but all of a sudden, she turned into the beautiful teacher I knew, the young woman in her late teens. I could not express how I felt at the time. What is gratifying about writing this is that all my forgotten memories have been miraculously resurrected. Writing this is like digging deep into the unconscious, unearthing the painful memories of my past with a pickax. But every time a piece of those memories surfaces, I feel elated as if I am reliving that very moment.

She was my first female teacher and perhaps through her my eyes were opened to the opposite sex. She often wore a black skirt and a white top. I remember the white collar in particular, and I have this image of her as beautiful yet elegant because of the whiteness of the collar and her big round eyes.

She played the organ very well. At that time not that many female teachers could play the organ so she was a rarity and it made her stand out from the other teachers. My male homeroom teachers during first and second grade could not play the organ. They did not even know how to read the notes so the music class was useless. So I thought that music was only for girls just like sewing was. To an ignorant child, her existence was something mysterious and wonderful. She was an object of admiration not only for me but for the rest of the class as well.

She had a lovely voice, too. When I sang with her I felt as if I had become a girl. It was strange. I felt embarrassed, ticklish, and my heart throbbed. Perhaps my dormant feminine side had surfaced or opened its eyes through singing. My mother often complained how she found no pleasure raising a stubborn and quiet child. Well, my mother likewise was extremely blunt and curt. Maybe I tried to find the soft feminine side in my teacher that was lacking in my mother. To make my voice come out pretty, I opened my mouth wide and even twisted my body, doing everything possible. I had wished that I was a girl like my teacher.

I must have found comfort in her at a time when my mood swings were severe. I was so emotional that I went from being sad to happy several times a day. Once she came over to my desk, giving off a sweet smell of powder and stroked my head complimenting me that I was good at dictation. I was so thrilled that I couldn't breathe. I still cannot forget her soft touch that made me feel like I was floating in the air. What encouragements can do to a growing child! Every time a warm encouragement touches the head of a child, he or she grows that much more.

In that turbulent time, even young female teachers were no exception. When I returned to school after vacation was over, she had already joined the marines. She only taught us for one semester. Even in the sweltering summer heat, I felt the chill of fear.

*Geography Class*

Many single male teachers were also drafted so after the summer school ended, many classes had to be combined. Half of the classrooms were occupied by the refugees so we had to carry the heavy blackboard to the playground or somewhere outside to have our lessons in the dust and the wind. Classes were divided into morning and afternoon sessions. I lost my homeroom teacher so my classmates and I had to go to a different class. We felt like stepchildren so we were discouraged and dispirited, and we could not possibly study in those circumstances. But I enjoyed the geography class.

Around the time when the Inch'on Landing was in full force, numerous leaflets were distributed explaining the war front situation. Those leaflets were collected and used in my geography class. The war situation was shown on the map with arrows, indicating the battle grounds. The arrows from the South were dark and full of energy, but the arrows from the North were small and broken and they looked as if they were retreating. The leaflets plainly showed that the South, which was once in a precarious position along the defensive line to the south of Naktong River, was forcefully expanding and advancing toward the North. One giant arrow swung around the Yellow Sea and struck a blow at Inch'on, and on the other side, several arrows crossed Naktong River, spreading out like a folding fan.

We felt uneasy when we saw the giant arrows in the Inch'on area. The arrows meant that the young men from the island who left singing the departure song a month ago were all assembled there, and they were marching toward the enemy lines. I wondered about their fate.

On the next leaflet the arrow had transformed into a pair of giant scissors. It was the giant scissors crossing the areas of Seoul and Inch'ŏn, cutting deeply into the enemy's waistline. I was so proud of all those young men. While I was busy studying geography, I drew in mountains, rivers, borders, railroads and cities . . . the battlefront was moving towards the North.

*Newsreels*
Shortly after the news of the South marching toward the North was heard, the government propaganda news was shown at the Kwandok Pavilion square. "Liberty News by the United States Public Information" was written in Korean subtitles. For hundreds of years the pavilion was the symbol of the island's regional power, but it was turned over to the U.S. government for their use. The U.S. military gathered people in the pavilion to watch their newsreels.

The spectators were mostly children. It looked as if every single child in the town had gathered to watch the news. The children in the back kept yelling that they could not see the screen so they pushed forward, and those in the front had to get up because they were being squashed. They pushed and shoved each other and yelling and screaming continued. The bottom of the screen was covered with heads bobbing up and down. Every time someone's head covered the screen, curses were shouted and we laughed when we saw the shadow of someone hitting someone's head. Due to electrical problems, the projector often stopped in the middle and when this happened we jumped up and down impatiently. We heckled and some middle school students were bold enough to hurl curses at the person handling the projector. "Hey, why don't you do it properly?" "Did you leave to take a shit?" "Go home! Boo!" The atmosphere was truly chaotic. So much dust rose from the ground that people were coughing and sneezing everywhere. The dust was so dense that even the emission of the intense stream of light from the projector looked as if the dust was part of the image projected onto the screen.

I tried hard not to miss anything in the midst of all that commotion so I craned my neck to watch a shocking depiction of an imminent battle projected onto the screen. Unlike a simple leaflet, the newsreel revealed something shocking about the war. I saw for the first time the monsters—bombers, battleships, tanks, and cannons—rampaging in disarray and the black fumes mushrooming like clouds. The most fearful thing was the bombers dropping black balls. My heart was struck with terror every time I heard the roaring sound of the balls and saw the fumes and the fire. Cities and small towns, I wrote on a leaflet during the geography class, were mercilessly demolished by the bombers.

It was around this time I became acquainted with a refugee boy who became blind after his face got burned trying to flee to the South. Many classrooms were occupied by the refugees and so lessons were held out in the playground. I remember the boy who groped his way along and listened from the back, just a few feet away. If he had not been blind he would be in the same class with me. He said he lost his parents while dodging an air raid and lost his eyesight. And he was good at massaging since he was being trained to become a masseur. When I was in the eighth and ninth grade I used to massage my father's feet and that I learned from him.

*Australian Rice Cake*

It only lasted very briefly but the country Australia became the talk of the town when it was featured as a cover story. Australia did participate in the war as a member of the UN, but for some reason even the U.S. bombers were called Australian fighter bombers. How was that possible? Back then, the islanders actually believed that the Australians came to help President Syngman Rhee, their son-in-law's country because his wife was Australian. There was no way of winning an argument with stubborn people. This ludicrous rumor must have started by some ignorant people who couldn't distinguish between Australia and Austria. Two years before the provisional government was established, people believed Syngman Rhee's wife was an American and that was why the United States was helping him. In an attempt to correct this mistake people started saying his wife's home was Australia not Austria.

After the Cheju Massacre, the literate stratum of society was killed and this episode showed one example of that repercussion. The saying "Ignorance is bliss" did not apply here. First Lady Francesca had been called an "American bride" or "American wife" but now she was referred to as an "Australian bride" or "Australian wife." "Australian wife" in Korean sounded like a rice cake so people laughed whenever they heard it. There weren't that many people who knew that America was behind the massacre on the island two years before.

The news provided by the United States Public Information

Bureau attracted the children's attention. The "Freedom Friend" pamphlet was handed out for free. This pamphlet put an end to the Australia fiasco. The "Freedom Friend" was the United States and she was the only powerful country in the world. So the people's understanding of the world started via the United States Public Information Bureau, and that was also the beginning of materialism on the island.

*Red Team and White Team*

During the annual fall sport day, the entire school was divided into red and white teams. In my third year the team colors changed from red and white to blue and white. Each team yelled "Go Red!" or "Go White!" I could still hear everyone yelling and rooting for their own team. I had a headband sewed with two strips of cloth, red on one side and white on the other. But the red headband was banned, so my mother took out the red strip and sewed on a blue cloth dyed in ink. Red and white was a simple way to divide teams, but the color red took on political and ideological meaning. In other words, red meant danger. After the Russian Revolution, red and white signified the left wing and the right wing.

I only wore the red headband once in my life. It was considered subversive so it was strictly forbidden and soon it disappeared all together. Nearly forty years later, I was shocked when I saw a group of protestors wearing red headbands. The color red had transformed into a powerful and vibrant symbol for freedom and democracy at the demonstration. To be honest, I was in such fear that I felt extremely uneasy. I had a good reason. I was taken in for questioning in the past for writing about what had happened during the Cheju Massacre and was severely tortured. It was so severe that I even wanted to erase the memory of wearing the red headband. I was suffering from "red" paranoia. I remember the sticky red blood coagulating at the tip of my smashed up finger when I was tortured. After that I even despised looking at red roses.

Now on television, young singers dance wildly, wearing red headbands and even on the program called "Friendship Stage," soldiers rapping and dancing on the stage have red headbands on. Did the meaning and symbolism of the red headband disappear altogether? I feel like I'm living in a different age. Green military uniforms and red headbands stood on opposite poles to each other. The torturers dressed me in a military uniform and beat me severely, calling me "commie" and said I was a disgrace to the military. But the only red they found on my body was the co-agulated blood from my smashed up middle finger. As a middle aged civilian, I was taken in by the authorities and had to crawl on the cement floor like a dog, wearing the military uniform. I realized how powerful and intimidating the military uniform was. I suffered torture because I underestimated the power of the military uniform.

*Little Soldier*

I was never fond of the military uniform. When the war started, it was popular among children because the military khaki was the color of all colors. It was the symbol of power and protection. In those days the soldiers clad in khaki green were called the national defenders.

I also had clothes in military khaki but the dye was so poorly done that the color faded after two or three washings. The military color soon went out of fashion, but I was the only one who had a military winter coat in my classroom. My coat was made out my father's military jacket; it was shabby and worn out, but it truly was khaki green. My father left the jacket when he came to the island with a group of trainees. Mother tried to sell it at first but at the time civilians were forbidden to use military supplies. Even though she tried to sell it dirt cheap, no one would buy it.

She had no choice but to take it for alteration. Fortunately it was enough to make two children's jackets, so she did not have to pay for alteration fees—one was mine and the other was for the son of the seamstress.

Among the things my father left behind were a raincoat and a leather bag. The latter was called a "fanny bag" because it was worn around the waist to store maps and binoculars, but I ended up carrying it on my back. It was much smaller than a regular school backpack but it was altered. Actually it wasn't much of an alteration because only two straps from an old belt were attached to the bag to turn it into a backpack.

This was how I came to acquire the winter jacket and the school backpack. I must have looked like a little solider with the khaki green jacket and the brown backpack. I did not like the way I looked. It was true that the color khaki green was popular, but I felt small in front of those children who wore nice black coats and carried proper school backpacks. I was upset that I was the only one dressed like a little soldier. Some of my classmates teased me and called out, "Hey, private!" Whenever I heard this, I felt insulted as if they were belittling my father. I was afraid I might run into MPs on my way to school. The MPs did not neglect to catch and punish civilians wearing military clothes. Either they made them take off the clothes by force or if the clothes had been altered they marked X with ink on their back or butt. I was afraid of meeting the same fate. My mother told me to stand up for myself by saying that my father was an MP too, but I wasn't sure whether I could actually say it or not.

Luckily the MPs didn't pay attention to me. Perhaps I looked hideous, looking like a little soldier, so when they saw me a smile spread across their scary looking faces.

One time I really got into trouble on my way to school. That day it rained cats and dogs so I had the military raincoat on. Not only was my raincoat confiscated, I had to be on my knees and was reprimanded for over an hour at the MP's office. I told them that my father was an MP but it was useless. Finally I was released but was so overwhelmed with sadness that I couldn't stop crying. I ran to school crying in the rain and was drenched to the skin. I could not enter the classroom because I looked like a drowned rat, so I went back home. I can still remember the feeling of dejection and humiliation as if it just happened.

After that day I became afraid of the MPs and that fear turned into dislike. And my inferiority complex was developed into hatred toward my father, associating him with unpleasant memories. My antagonistic feelings toward my father grew with every single military item I had to use.

*Time*

I am the son of time. I am like a small rock, born from the fountain of time whose existence has been altered and damaged in the strong current. The water flows endlessly over the rocks deeply rooted in the riverbed. I am now well into middle age and my forehead is lined with wrinkles as if time has been eroded and etched. The water flows through once never to return, so when the stream dries up time will stop, like the Pyŏngmunnae which dries up after it flows for a short period of time after the pouring rain. Time is passing by too quickly. Oh, fleeting time! My youth has been filled with the evolution of my life! I know it's futile but I am trying hard to piece together fragments of my childhood memories that have already slipped through my fingers by writing this.

The reason why I felt that time passed by quickly back then was because I grew up too fast. My mother made the khaki overcoat way bigger than my actual size so that I could wear it for several years, but I was only able to wear it for two winters. I wished desperately to grow up and advance to a higher grade. At times I was frustrated because I thought time was passing by slowly. As a child, I always longed for something. I waited for my mother to return from the field. I looked forward to ancestral ceremonies and New Year's so that I could have white rice and a piece of pork meat. I counted the days for school outings and summer vacation. Whenever I waited and waited for those special days, time went by at a snail's pace. However, when the long awaited summer vacation finally arrived, the hot summer days seemed so boring and slow that I could not wait to return to school. My friends and I even bet rice cakes when we played marble games and waited for each other's ancestral ceremonies to arrive.

There were so many things I longed for. Thinking about the times when I ran all over the place to overcome boredom, time did not pass right by me but caught up with me to be by my side so that I could grow up. The time lived is greater than the time to be lived, so I'm reliving my childhood days in my mind while lamenting the fact that time is passing by too quickly.

Remembering a forgotten past cannot be done by the power of reason alone. General events, customs, practices, and institutions can be reproduced with available source materials and witness accounts, but reconstructing personal memories and experiences is not easy. There are more memories that are awakened by the five sensory organs rather than reason. It is common to recall things using the sense of sight, but the sense of smell, sound, taste, and touch can also serve to stir and evoke the forgotten past.

When I read John Steinbeck's short story "Flight," I was able to relate to the main character regardless of the plot. There was a scene where the protagonist hid behind a big granite rock to avoid his pursuer and a bullet flew over and ricocheted, cutting into the granite creating a white streak. When I read this, I got a whiff of an acrid smell of burnt powder that was not described in the story.

What I smelled was none other than a flint stone. In those days, my grandfather lit his pipe using two flint stones and when the stones were struck together, shooting out blue sparks, a smoky smell dispersed quickly about the entire room. I used two broken pieces of earthenware or chinaware to create a will-o'-the-wisp and it had the same smell when struck together emitting sparks. On summer days when fireflies glowed on moonless nights over the stream, my friends and I gathered around the water to make the will-o'-the-wisp. There was a children's cemetery up the stream and on rainy days sparks of phosphorescence flashed in the water so that the true will-o'-the-wisp was illuminated.

*Light and Darkness*

If I recall my hometown in my fourth year of elementary school, it's completely different. Several months into the war, the town went through drastic changes in every aspect. One of the things I remember about those days is small fighter planes practicing firing. The combat planes circled above the downtown area, then aimed at the top of Todu Peak near the beach airport and began firing. It was far from where I lived but I could still hear the machine guns firing. After the military training camp was built, the comings and goings of military trucks were rampant. I collected a variety of things such as dirt marbles, glass marbles, and *ttakchi* cards; I even picked up M-1 carbine casings and machine gun shells.

Town life changed quickly, reorganizing around a war footing. At the beginning of the war, the people were terrified when their sons were drafted and were heartbroken when they went off to the war front but slowly they adapted to the new environment. The refugees from the mainland who were temporarily placed in schools were relocated to different villages; they either rented a room or moved into a shack, and they too began settling in their own way. However, with a sudden increase in population, everyone struggled fiercely to make ends meet. The refugees set up small shops so the streets were overcrowded and the number of street vendors increased dramatically as well. The street vendors selling honey pancakes, doughnuts, and red bean sweets were mainly after children's allowances.

A rice puff vendor came to the village, too. When he first came and popped the rice puffs, the sound resembled the machine gun fire, so the women ran after him and hurled curses. Since they had experienced the explosive machine gun sounds, the islanders disliked the rice popping noise, which was very similar. The rice puff vendor was clever because before he popped the machine, he screamed from the top of his lung to warn them. Strangely people were no longer scared of the popping sound after they heard him scream. I think it is the same strategy nurses use when they slap the butt before giving it a shot. Before the big shock, a small shock is needed to divert the real shock.

One of the major changes in town was the increase in electricity consumption. The main street located on the east side of the pavilion was brightly illuminated even at night. During the time of food shortage, there were people who profited and made a fortune. As more people became wealthy, the number of houses using electricity increased. There were two types of electricity— one was special line and the other regular. For residential use, the regular line was used, meaning electricity was provided once every two days, alternating between two houses, but the blackouts were frequent. Regardless of these frequent blackouts, electricity symbolized civilization and luxury. When my family lived in a rented room, we had electricity but how could we use it when we were poor? A room equipped with electricity cost more, so we ended up moving out to a cheaper one on the west side of Pyŏngmun Stream. My family was forced to leave the civilized neighbourhood. The west side was the dark zone, the poor side. I did not like to hang out in the "poor" section, so I went to the opposite side to play during the daytime.

Military trucks and private trucks increased in great numbers.

Freight trucks were refurbished and used as buses. Most of them were junkers that started when the engine was cranked. I remember how the engine got started. A crank handle that looked like a deformed arm was shoved in the front of the bus and all the weight was placed onto the handle and turned. It was like desperately yanking a stubborn bull's nose ring. After the crank handle was turned fiercely, the engine finally purred and started. Blue smoke belched out from the rear and the smell of fuel accompanied by smoke dispersed in the air. I actually liked the gasoline smell because it was different so I ran after the bus to get a whiff. The strong odor of gasoline represented civilization and was a symbol of power and progress. I can recall the day I got vaccine shots and the smell of rubbing alcohol that saturated the entire classroom. The pungent smell of rubbing alcohol remains in my memory as a wonderful symbol of civilization.

All of a sudden I've just stopped writing and rolled up my sleeves to look at my arm. Those vaccination marks are still visible. I am as delighted as if I have found something that had been lost. Seeing the four vaccination marks is like getting a glimpse of long forgotten memories from my childhood. I vaguely remember the pain when I got those shots but the smell of rubbing alcohol is still vivid. Since the cowpox virus was used as vaccination against smallpox, I feared that I might turn into a cow after I got smallpox. It is still fresh in my memory how unbearably itchy my skin felt when the scabs formed.

*Standard Korean*

The children of refugees infiltrated every aspect of daily living; I saw them everywhere in my neighborhood and in school.

Because of the notorious and cruel counterinsurgency forces from the mainland, I was afraid of everyone, even the children, from the mainland. The children from the mainland were a minority among us locals but we mingled without any problems.

In fact, they were popular because they spoke standard Korean. During a Korean class, my homeroom teacher called on Hyŏngsik all the time to read the textbook out loud. Hyŏngsik, Songi, and Changsu were my first mainland friends from Seoul who lived in my town. Songi and Changsu were brother and sister and I had a crush on Songi. When she spoke in the Seoul dialect, it sounded so soft and coquettish that my heart pounded for no reason. I loved hearing her say "Good morning! How are you?" when we met on our way to school. I had never heard anything more pleasant before. Since I did not know that the Seoul dialect was naturally soft and sweet, I almost had the wrong idea that Songi liked me.

The Cheju dialect was different from the standard Seoul dialect in terms of intonation, pronunciation, and vocabulary. For example, the Cheju people said "ein people" for "eight people," "ding dirt" for "dig dirt," and read "first grade" as "first grain" and "third grade" "third grain." "Unmarried woman" sounded like "inconclusive woman." Well, a marriage is one of the most important affairs so I guess you could say that getting married is like reaching a conclusion. And "becoming ill" sounded like "giving birth to an egg." In the Cheju dialect the word "painful" is used but there is no word for "to become ill." After I learned the word for "to become ill," I tried to use it, but failed miserably. I meant to say "my mom is ill" but when I said it, Songi giggled and said, "What? Your mom gave birth to an egg?" Songi laughed so hard to the point where she couldn't breathe and she literally rolled on the ground.

I was envious of Hyŏngsik and Songi. When they said the following things in their smooth Seoul dialect—the South Gate, East Gate, the Capitol Building, Ch'anggyŏng Zoo, trains at Seoul Station, and trolleys with bell ringing—they all came to life. I was even envious of the freezing cold Seoul weather that froze the Han River. I had never seen an icicle but I sang the nursery rhyme song "Icicle, icicle, crystal icicle" without understanding the meaning. My jaw dropped when they told me that they had crossed the frozen Han River to flee.

When the standard Korean words listed in books simply as letters came to life through Songi and Hyŏngsik, I envied their world so much. It was the world where the smell of gasoline and rubbing alcohol originated and stimulated my olfactory sense. It was the central place of control and domination. I was even envious of the war that was taking place there. To me, the war on the mainland was so remote that it was like a fun action movie.

I played war games day in and day out. I carved a gun out of wood and practiced twelve drill movements; I learned the rules and played imitating surprise attacks and fighting with a sword and bayonet. Whenever I drew pictures, they were always of battle scenes. I drew jet planes, Russian Yak aerial dogfights, naval guns firing at battleships, tanks, and the People's Army and the Republic of Korea Army fighting in close quarters. I also drew the President's face. At the time, his face was on the one hundred won bill. The elders who cursed him as a bad and terrible old geezer had no choice but to accept him as President. The crisp, clean new bill was so precious back then that when the elders complemented children, they often said, "You're good looking just like that new one hundred won bill."

The war had a tremendous affect on young impressionable children. The war determined everything and made people conform. No other war had a bigger influence on the island than the Korean War. To become a part of the central government meant cutting off from the past. Children by nature were good at adapting to a new environment. After I spent some time with the children from the mainland, I soon became familiar with standard Korean. I laughed and made fun of my teachers behind their backs who continued to use the island dialect in class.

*Todu Peak*

The painful memories of the past only dwelled in the somber silence of the adults. For the longest time people could not pass through the village entrance where the cut off heads had been scattered, but after a while everything returned to normal. The road was once again trodden by the villagers. The image of the guerrilla leader hung on the cross in front of Kwandŏk Pavilion gradually disappeared from their memories.

More people and cars passed through the streets continuously. In such busy streets, how can there be any quiet space for spirits to dwell? The fighter planes even scared away all those crows in the sky performing air shows, and they were rarely seen hovering in the air. All those dead bodies and their spirits buried under the runway could not possibly surface because of the loud jet engine noise. There were several large holes where the dead bodies were thrown like salted anchovies, and the rumor was that every night those spirits buried underneath shook the ground. However, the spirits were unable to stir because they were oppressed by the planes. Near the airport, the machine gun fire practice, aiming at Todu Peak, took place every day.

Not only were the spirits buried under the runway discouraged by the firing of the machine guns, but I too suffered a great deal. The horseshoe scar on my head was the root of my trouble again. There was a nice round hill that was caved in at the top due to the gun fire and it was visible from afar. Unfortunately the collapsed part of the hill was compared to my scar. Who else could have possibly thought of such a thing but Lefty? Every time he saw me he spread out his arms like an airplane, flying and circling around me and said, "Aim and fire at Todu Peak! Rat-ta-ta-ta-ta-tat!" I was used to playing dead while playing war games, but I despised it when he aimed at my head and fired.

I found it unpleasant whenever a combat plane flew over my head. Like a hawk looking for food, it would circle overhead.

Then all of a sudden it would start to fire. Unconsciously I would raise my hand to touch the scar because I thought I felt a chill. On days when there was no firing practice, I went to Todu Peak with Lefty and my other friends to collect machine gun shells. The peak was caved in and scarred from the firing. It was not a pleasant sight at all.

My first time going to Todu Peak turned into an unforgettable adventure. I had to walk about two and a half miles to get there and had to pass the ghastly military airport. The airport was located on the main highway right before reaching Todu Peak. There were hardly any people passing by. Mostly the military trucks drove by at an incredible speed, causing dust to rise. My friends and I nervously trotted along the road covered in dust. Along the barbed wire fences, guards were posted, keeping a strict watch, and the combat planes were parked inside the Quonset huts that looked like wrinkly gigantic caterpillars. I knew about the countless bodies buried under the runway but I was more afraid of the American soldiers. How could I not be scared of them when there was a rumor that one of my distant relatives, also a teacher at my school, was picked up by an American driving a jeep and was raped? The American soldiers that I saw walking around downtown every once in a while were based at this airport.

The place where we found shells was close to where the American guards were, so we could not stay very long for fear of getting spotted. We picked up a few shells and made a detour using the beach road, but on our way back we saw something scandalous. There was an isolated house far away from the village; a young woman escorted an American soldier into the house and when our eyes met, she quickly grabbed his shoes and shut the door behind. I was disgusted at the vulgarity, imagining what was happening in that dark room in a broad daylight. Since the man was an American soldier, I was even more appalled, but also scared. However, as if my feet were glued to the ground I could not leave.

I peeked through the hole in the wall, gasping for breath and became agitated. I wanted to do something crazy. Finally, Lefty picked up a rock and said, "This is disgusting! When I throw this rock, we run, okay?"

"What if we get caught?"

"You idiots! They are busy. Besides they are naked. How can they come after us?"

Lefty threw the rock and it hit the door making a loud banging noise, and at that moment everyone ran quickly away. On the horizon of the azure blue ocean, the white clouds blossomed like cotton.

*Uncivilized Night*

After my family moved to the west side of Pyŏngmun Stream, I still hung out on the east side because I did not like the horse manure smell of my town. My school and government and public offices and business sections were all situated on the east side. The Pyŏngmun Stream was on the borderline separating civilized and uncivilized. At night the difference was quite apparent. On the east side of the stream, all the lights were turned on in a flash at dusk and it was a miraculous moment. In summertime, some of the houses had their mosquito nets hung in their bright lit rooms, and the mosquito nets looked absolutely extravagant!

The electric lights on the east side made my town even darker and gloomier, and I associated darkness with my old burnt down house where I used to wait in the dark for my mother to return from the field.

How could I possibly describe the sense of loneliness I felt waiting for my mother in the darkness? It was the longest single hour after the sunset in those days. As the night drew on, I became afraid, as if a nest of snakes were slithering around me, and I felt the tentacles of darkness swallowing and erasing everything around me. It was time for those spirits that had been driven away during daytime to return, whispering to each other shrouded in darkness.

I was afraid of the dark, so I closed all the windows and lit the oil lamp. It soon brightened up the room, but a weak flame could not brighten all four corners of the room. Because of the dim lamp light, the darkness lurking behind those corners looked even darker. I played the shadow game with my sister in an attempt to ease my fear. Our hand shadows created a dog and a cat; the dog shadow I created barked and jumped at the cat. The cat attacked the dog and the dog bit the cat. The cat screamed in pain. For that instant I felt chills running down my spine. The sound of a cat meowing at night reminded me of a crying baby, so I felt uneasy and strange. At the upper part of Pyŏngmun Stream, there were many children's graves, so I was told that at night the sound of babies crying was heard. Some people said it was the sound of cats meowing not babies. In any case, it wasn't pleasant to hear a cat meowing. My sister stopped meowing and called it quits first.

"I don't want to play anymore. You always make me play the cat. I wonder where Mom is?"

"I don't know. I'm sure she's almost home."

"Around the pond?"

"Yeah, maybe."

Perhaps the pond is too close. She needs more time. Maybe she is passing by the Confucian school now. I go out to meet her in my mind, imagining her trudging along with a heavy bundle in the dark. I'm sure my mother is thinking about us as she is walking home. She is unusually late today. Does this mean she's carrying a lot? I can see her taking off the towel wrapped around her head to wipe off sweat. She is plodding along. Now she is at the pond. There is a weeping willow tree that hangs like the tresses of ghosts. Will she be scared of the willow tree? In pitch darkness, narrow-mouthed frogs might be croaking in the water. These frogs are the Confucian school spirits. Many Confucian students were killed during the massacre and the sound of them reading books stopped long ago. So the frogs read out loud. The frogs say, "Confucian says" or "Mencius says," in short "Croak, croak!" Mother safely passes the pond and enters the side street by the stream. She is walking down gasping for breath. Fireflies circle around her. She is getting closer to home. I think I hear her footsteps. The footsteps stop in front of the house. I hold my breath and listen intently. I only hear the buzzing and droning of insects but no sound of the gate opening. I am completely disheartened and tears well up. I hear the insects droning and my stomach is growling. Is she late because she has too much to carry? Or, did she stop by Sungŏn's shoe store next to the Confucian school? Maybe she finished her work late and something happened on her way over Toryŏngmaru. It's the place where the dead bodies were strewn about. The airport runway below is also known as a place where many dead bodies were buried. That's why it is absolutely necessary to carry a torch whenever going over the hill alone at night. No, I'm sure nothing has happened to her.

In my mind, I walk over to the Confucian school again and wait for mother to arrive there.

I have waited for my mother so many times after dark but I don't know why I remember this as one specific event that happened in one particular day. I guess remembering my childhood is like recalling the images of old movies where different scenes are collaged together. And the images do not appear in chronological order but are random.

Although inadequate, I have written my story in chronological order up to this point. And the reason why this has been possible was because of major events that occurred year after year without fail. My past not only includes my personal memory but collective memory as well, meaning history. Historical events have made a significant impact on my psyche and greatly influenced my way of thinking, but no drastic or major events took place for three years until I reached sixth grade. That's why I mistakenly remember the three years from third to sixth grade as very peaceful time. Since there were no big memorable events, narrating chronologically poses a problem and I also find it meaningless to do so.

Thinking back to that time, those three years were like one year, three summers compressed into one summer and several days into one day. Even the things I remember are fragmented and these fragments do not connect to each other. Therefore, it is difficult to narrate in chronological order. It is like all those stars in the sky shining regardless of time and space under one large canopy.

In my writing, certain things, events, ideas, and language comprised of light, sound, and smell are not particular to one day of a particular event. All disparate things ignore time and space and join together to weave one big narrative.

My writing does not reflect every little detail of my thoughts and the events I experienced during my childhood. I do not have a special power or sensibility to remember all those things that happened. I know that I had vague ideas of what was happening back then, but I only understood fully after I became an adult. That's why certain scenes or ideas I have described have been generated after the fact, things I saw and felt when I returned home for visits as an adult. To think about those past memories or images from the present point of view, it is necessary to analyze and reinterpret, because all those things I did not understand back then have become apparent now. And in order to fill the gaps in my memory, imagination was needed; therefore some sections were exaggerated.

The main goal of my writing is to choose and find different fragments of memories nestled in the dark to piece them together to create one complete story.

*Drinks*

I am entering the autumn of my years. Somatic cells are slowing down and even though it's not visible my pulse is gradually weakening, too. My blood is getting thinner. The days when cells multiplied so fast I needed to take naps frequently have passed. I had many dreams then, but those days had been pushed far back to the beginning of time. Cell multiplication slows down after a person fully matures, but every two to three years cells renew themselves completely. Now I'm over that stage as well. Even a small scar does not heal fast, and when it does, it turns into a brownish mark and does not disappear completely. Rib fractures are slow to heal. Last winter, I was attacked by a group of hoodlums and was beaten mercilessly when I fought back in my intoxicated state. I had four fractured ribs and the doctor assured me that they would heal completely, but one of them never did.

Even after the attack, I continued to go home late after drinking. For me, drinking was like an "evil friend" that came to visit once every two days. Now I am too old to keep up with my "evil friend" but I cannot possibly turn a cold shoulder on my old buddy. I find drinking even more enjoyable and drinks never tasted sweeter than now. I do not turn my head when I see a beautiful woman and do not become excited by spectacular and grand plans because they are all outside of my range of interests at this point. I have seen and done those things, plus I have a bad temper so I get irritable and depressed easily. If I don't have drinks to comfort me, how can I possibly survive? When I'm holding a glass in my hand, I'm as happy as a fish in water.

I have entered the degenerative stage of my life. Now I pour drinks to instill hope when my body longs for those bygone days when the cells regenerated fast. One drink warms my blood and gives life to my inactive and shrunken degenerative cells. I act like a child, laughing, and talking nonsense whenever I drink. When alcohol enters my bloodstream, the inactive cells become activated, bringing back my old childhood self again. I like it when I find my old self looking at my friend, drinking and laughing in front of me. It is even better if he is my hometown friend I haven't seen for a long time. With one or two drinks, the wrinkly face of an old pumpkin brightens up as if a light switch has been turned on. Taking advantage of the wonders of alcohol, my friend and I become bold and frank, returning to our old selves again just like the days when we hung out with no clothes on. In our intoxicated state, we go back to being Sea Crab and Sling. We laugh heartily and chatter away.

I smile when I recall bumping into my childhood friend whom I hadn't seen for a very long time. A few years ago, I had to return to the island to take care of some business. I was walking down the main street in downtown Cheju City. I stopped all of a sudden when I saw a junior high school boy. I was so surprised that my feet literally froze to the ground. I almost yelled out, "Aren't you Sling?" and grabbed him by the shoulders to hug him. I had mistaken the boy for my old friend. He looked so much like Sling that I was certain that he was Sling's son. I asked the boy, "Is your Father's name . . . ?" and someone tapped me on the shoulder. I turned around and found a bald-headed, middle-aged man, smiling.

"You're Sea Crab, right?"

"Hey, Sling!"

I could not believe I mistook his son for him when he was standing right next to him. It was funny. I kept looking back and forth at him and his son and laughed. I couldn't stop laughing but at the same I was filled with a sense of despair from the sad realization that we are not young anymore.

He sent his son away immediately and we went out for drinks in broad daylight. In any case, drinks tasted particularly sweet that day. After he had a few drinks, his unfamiliar shriveled up bald old pumpkin head turned red. When his face turned red,

Sling's old self had come alive, casting aside all those years that he had accumulated. His nickname became Sling because he got back at Lefty for having shoved his head in the water by throwing rocks at laundered linens hanging to dry and making holes. Sling was one tough kid.

"I almost called your son Sling," I laughed.

"You silly Sea Crab," he chuckled.

Sea Crab has disappeared into oblivion. He only appears in fragments of my imagination after I have had a few drinks, so I search for him here and there. I'm not the only one who knows about Sea Crab. My hometown friend Sling and others know some things about me that I don't even know about. Every time I return to the island and get together with my old friends, I ask them about Sea Crab. We walk around the beach and wander about the fields where we used to play. It is similar to a father looking for a lost son. Well, it sounds ridiculous to put it like this. When did I give birth to that little boy? That little boy made me who I am today.

### Bones of Mother Earth

The first thing that comes into view when I land at Cheju Airport is a unique landscape. I am so used to the gray skies of Seoul that every time I encounter the natural beauty of my hometown, it's fresh and extraordinary. Because of the higher altitudes and fresh clean air, all the colors look deep, rich, and vivid. The color green looks greener and red redder. Whenever I see red canna flowers or sweet oleanders in full bloom in brilliant harmony with lush shiny verdant leaves, I can't help but be shocked.

The delicate spring scenery, which unfolds after dismal winter days, radiates in brilliance resembling the intense and glorious summer sunshine. The entire beach is covered by black volcanic rocks contrasting the white foam on the water's edge and the azure sea and the blue sky are competing to see which one is

bluer. As the sky boasts of its color, it turns into a chasm of indigo blue. Between the expansive blue sky and the ocean, bright
yellow rapeseed flowers and green barley fields are divided by the
sooty rock walls. Every time I look at that mosaic of different
colors, the colors are so intense and bright that it's painful to look
at. On top of that, my bias toward my hometown intrudes and
makes the colors not only more radiant, but more intense, like
primary colors. Looking at the colors of the landscape, I feel a
strong sense of privilege and a desire to boast about how colors
differ on the island.

I have lived in Seoul for over thirty years, but I am still attached to the island. I'm full of biases when it comes to things
that are found outside the island, and I can't seem to find endearing qualities. No matter where I travel on the mainland, I don't
find places with beautiful landscapes. As the saying goes, "there's
no place like home". When I find hackberry and bead-trees when
I travel I become extremely happy. I do like rivers overflowing
with water and lush green rice paddies, but for some odd reason
they look so plain and uninteresting. Why? It's not because of
dull or pale colors. How should I put it? It feels like all flesh but
no bones. The mainland landscape is flat because it doesn't have
rocks like Cheju Island, and there is no strong wind to stir up and
create an dramatic landscape.

There are rough and rugged rocks everywhere in my hometown—the bones of mother earth. The stark scenery suggests that
the land is sterile. It is a place where the black volcanic rocks by the
beach and the bone white rocks in the dried stream and the bones
of mother earth are ruthlessly exposed to challenge the angry
waves and rain storms, wailing and howling. People have settled
there where the sharp leaf blades of silver grass cut through the
gusts of wind, and they have become tough and arrogant as they
withstand the strong winds. Although the land is not fertile the islanders were not discouraged and continued to live for generations.

The islanders have been tenacious, fighting against the parched and uncultivable land. The hard land is rough so that driving a stake into the soil will reach as far as 30 cm deep, then it will hit rocks. The islanders have lived like densely knitted roots intermingling closely like silver grass on the impoverished land. They are fierce spirits who refuse to succumb to the oppression of the government, and their history is dotted with resistance movements. But their world ended forever when the ravages of the massacre occurred half a century ago. The only thing left after the mass killings was deep resentment and an inconsolable sorrow. There is a strong aura of all those unappeased, angry, and miserable spirits inhabiting the beautiful scenery, but the tourists who experience the luxury of the beautiful landscape pass by happily.

The newlyweds in each other's arms take pictures near the volcanic rock beach of Yongduam. This is the place where I used to play with my friends. What is this ticklish giggling I hear? I get sad looking at women wearing red skirts with green tops contrasting sharply against the black volcanic rocks. Perhaps it's because the black volcanic rocks remind me of that time when the island was burnt to the ground. Volcanic rocks! They represent pride and the stubbornness of the past and the sadness of today. What did nature teach me? I am tough on the one hand, but easily get melancholic on the other, as if I have a split personality. I am unreasonably stubborn so I grunt and moan when I end up getting caught in my own trap. In the past, I couldn't get out of depression without drinking.

I am now near Yongduam. I need to stop the comings and goings of those visitors and drive them out of the volcanic rock beach and bring back all my old friends instead.

*Sŏnbanmul Pond*
After I learned to swim in a small pond near Pyŏngmun Stream, I advanced to Sŏnbanmul Pond. When I entered the fourth grade,

I was able to venture out to Yongyŏn Pond near Yongduam.

I need to explain briefly about Sŏnbanmul since I have just mentioned it. I remember Sŏnbanmul and Yongyŏn as symbols of abundance when everything was scarce in those days. Several villages around Pyŏngmun Stream drew water from Sŏnbanmul and it always had plenty to go around. There is an old saying that even during the severest droughts when fields and pastures are dried up there is plenty of water left. No matter how severe the drought was, Sŏnbanmul and the spring waters around the beach did not dry up. There were two large wells with stone walls and the water gushed forth all the time. The wells were always crowded with women drawing water or washing vegetables, and outside the stone walls there was a place for laundry and the sound of women chattering and laughing never stopped. Occasionally women from a far away village came with loads of laundry and their children; they looked as if they were out on a picnic because they cooked lunch and did laundry and their children played on the beach. But the children did not know how to swim so they held on to a bundle of straw to stay afloat.

A shallow pond where fresh water and seawater met was situated down below the washing place and that was where my friends and I used to swim with a flock of ducks. After playing there for a few years, we saw ourselves as grown-ups and started complaining that, "This place is only good for babies. Women are too noisy. They pee in this water and wash dirty diapers." We complained about the water and then moved to Yongyŏn.

Even after I moved to Yongyŏn, every time I passed by Sŏnbanmul, I was busy looking at where the women were to see what was going on. Believe it or not, there was a time when the noise stopped. It was an interesting sight. When a man dressed in a nice suit with his hair combed in pomade oil passed, the chattering stopped because they were busy looking at him. It was like throwing a rock in a pond full of frogs croaking, then the croaking stopped all of a sudden. They stole glances at him, then the next minute they burst out laughing. The pounding of laundry grew louder and louder and the man in the suit walked away quickly. It was a scene! The women started saying things like, "Whose husband is he? What a life! He's going to Yongyŏn for a walk. He looks slick. He must be from the mainland. Did he fall into a pot of sesame oil or what?" They all giggled.

All the black volcanic rocks and gravel near the washing place were covered with white laundry like wallpaper. It was an unforgettable sight looking at the bright white laundry drying under the scorching sunlight. One time Sling hurled stones and made holes in the laundry, and this led to a fight between Sling's mother and Lefty's mother. They attacked each other with their wet laundry, slapping and whacking. But Lefty's mother was the stronger one since she worked at the blacksmith shop, blowing bellows.

"Bitch, pay me for the blanket cover," Lefty's mother demanded.

"What are you talking about? Kill me and see if you can get a penny out of me!" answered Sling's mother.

*Yongyŏn Pond*

Yongyŏn is situated at the mouth of Han Stream on the west side, not too far from Sŏnbanmul. The Han Stream was a dry stream so the water flowed briefly only after the rain. Similar to Sŏnbanmul in Pyŏngmun Stream, there was a large deep pond where fresh water and sea water met and that pond was called Yongyŏn, meaning Dragon Pond.

Yongyŏn and Yongduam or Dragon Head Rock have always been considered the most scenic spots. The rock walls dropped into the bed of the ocean like folding screens reflected on the surface of the water and in the middle where there were no shadows the water appeared in a deeper and more intense blue color. The solid volcanic texture of the rock walls connected to the white bedrock of dried up Yongyŏn, and below the rock walls the black volcanic rocks extended to the ocean.

My friends and I went from the small pond in Pyŏngmun Stream to Sŏnbanmul then we advanced to Yongyŏn, taking steps that had been prepared for us; we grew out of each pond as if we went through different stages of maturity.

The place where Yongyŏn and the ocean intersected was in the shape of a bottleneck. It was long and narrow and the water was not too deep so the children who were younger than me played there. Even though the water wasn't too deep, the middle part was twice as tall as an average child's height. I first learned to swim breaststroke and I mastered it, then I learned the crawl, the backstroke, then finally diving.

My family moved to Chŏngdŭrŭ when I was in sixth grade and my home was on the other side of Yongyŏn which was very close, so I went there more often. In the summertime, I went to Yongyŏn to bathe after school before going home. My friends and I placed our backpacks on our heads and tied them with our belts and swam across the water.

I liked swimming in those days so I pretty much lived in the water during summer season. I even skipped lunch because I was afraid of getting caught to run errands and do chores if I went home to eat lunch. My mother must have worried a lot for having a son like me. It was not because she wanted me to run errands for her, but she was worried that something might happen to me while playing in the water. After my friend Changsu drowned, my mother strictly forbade me to go to Yongyŏn. She checked my shoes and ears to see if any sand was left. She even licked my hair to see if she could taste salt, but since I was crazy about playing in the water no matter what she did it was useless. She had to give up on the idea of stopping me from going to the beach. After I learned to dive I went deep into the water to win her favor by getting *p'arae* or green laver. The *p'arae* growing where fresh water and seawater intersected was nice and soft, and of an extremely good quality, which made a great side dish. I was completely tanned; after a layer of skin came off like a snake shedding its skin, I was suntanned except for the white part of my eyes.

I crossed the water by swimming below the surface or I held a stone to weigh myself down. At times I went under the water, holding the stone to help me stay down to watch the others swimming on the surface, to experience the silence and stillness of the water. I savored the silence under the water, but it also made me very sad, looking at their arms and legs moving limply like mollusks or shellfish. I could not hear either their cheerful and loud voices or the water splashing underwater. The only thing I could hear was my voice, the drumming noise of my voice. I heard my watch ticking as I held my breath, and it was a sure sign that I was alive. I thought I could even feel the tentacles of death. One's life span shrinks when surrounded by loneliness, fear, and death. My mother's face flashed before me. Am I still breathing? Or did I stop breathing? Their reflected shadows shimmered in the sunlight on the bottom of the water, and I could no longer endure so I went up to the surface. The moment I started breathing, the others' cheerful voices were also brought back to life.

I remember my cute friend Songi from Seoul who giggled a lot and threw white shells in the water; I was like her faithful dog and dived into the water to fetch them for her.

*Family Jewels*

I did not fall behind others on most things, but when it came to diving I was pretty bad.

The volcanic rock wall on the east side of the ocean was used as a diving platform. Depending on the height of the rock wall, there were six designated diving levels. The junior high school levels' seven and eight were situated far from levels one through six, and it was a cliff where the depth of the water could not be determined. Looking at it from level one, which was as tall as I was, the cliff seemed incredibly distant and high.

As long as the different levels of skill existed and were tied to maturity, I could not avoid going through each stage to reach the top simply because I was afraid. I realized unconsciously that life was about overcoming and conquering fears one at a time. My desire to grow and mature by overcoming fears, overcoming myself, and trying to beat boys who were bigger than me enabled me to practice harder. Who was it that was beat up by a junior high school student and said, "Wait till I turn fifteen. You won't see the light of the day! I'm going to crush you!" Was it Sling or Lefty or Chicken Butt? Did we not practice jumping off from places higher than we could manage since we were three years old? No one made us do it. No one watched us. Even when our knees bled from cuts, we jumped off yelling out, "You can break bird's legs but not mine!"

I failed miserably once. I fell from the tree trying to catch a cicada when I was six years old. I fell headlong and crushed my head on a rock. This was not simply a failure but a serious fall. Since this accident, I developed a fear of heights and it took me a long time to get over it.

To learn to dive, I had to practice jumping into the water standing straight up. I was completely naked and held my private parts with my left hand and jumped. I could see how ridiculous I must have looked. I did not hold my private parts because I was embarrassed but because I was afraid of my balls getting hurt. I was afraid of heights so I jumped off in a hurry, so unlike the other kids, I didn't keep my legs straight and together. The moment I hit the water, I felt like I was kicked in the balls, I was in so much pain. That was why I held them with one hand when I dived in.

Even after a lot of practice and after mustering up all my energy and courage, I still did not like my head hitting the water because of my scar. I disliked hanging upside down on monkey bars because I was afraid of falling down on my head. Once Chicken Butt fell from the monkey bars and broke his front tooth, yet he was not afraid of heights and was the first one to conquer level six. I mustered all my courage to get up on the rock wall but then my legs were shaking so much that I had to come down. It was humiliating. My fear and anxiety was so intense that I even dreamt about it. In my dream, I jumped off beautifully but when I looked down it was not water but it was a ground filled with rocks or snakes. When I first learned to dive, I was afraid of my head hitting the water so I fell on my stomach. My stomach hit the water first so it was excruciatingly painful, and my chest and stomach turned red.

I finally overcame my fear of heights, though with some difficulty. I fell behind others but I was able to advance to level six with the rest of my friends when I entered the sixth grade. I think it was around this time that we started feeling embarrassed about swimming naked and wore swim shorts. When we dived into the water, our swim shorts came off and were down by our feet. It was great fun thinking that Yongyŏn wanted to see our private parts so it took off our swim shorts on purpose. At times my swim shorts came off completely so I had to quickly grab them and put them on again before coming out of the water.

*Drought*

In those impoverished days, the millet fields in late summer were affected by drought. The millet fields were parched, so the millet rice I had in those days was as dry and gritty as sand. Is that why I couldn't swallow? When the scorching heat covered the millet that was only two spans tall, the adults sighed frequently looking at the dried up millet leaves. Sparks shot up from the hoes weeding the fields, and the women were busy carrying buckets full of fertilizer to nourish the land.

The heat during the dry season was unbearable. There was no cool breeze even early in the morning. The heralding of glorious mornings with the singing of sparrows was replaced with the irritating droning sound of cicadas. The sun that appeared between the branches of the persimmon tree in the back yard resembled the green leaves set on fire. By midday, the sun had already crawled to the middle of the blue sky pouring down like molten iron. When I left the shaded area, the heat penetrated through my shirt and skin piercing through my bones. I couldn't bear looking at the flowers crouched on the ground such as the moss roses, cannas, marvel of Perus, and cockscombs because of their intense bright colors. Even the chicken's cockscomb became redder. It drank a little bit of water and looked up in the sky and had another sip of water then looked up again. The sky looked ridiculously blue. Similar to the chicken drinking water, my mother looked up at the sky often and sighed deeply. She glared at the sky and cursed, "Crazy sky!"

The drought was inevitable and I could not dream of going to Yongyŏn to swim. The crazy blue sky only had fluffy white clouds floating around, and there was no sign of rain clouds. The volcanic rocks on the beach looked darker because of the burning sun and the ocean was gasping with thirst. Even the water in the ditch dried up so at the lower part of the stream the granites that had been constantly beaten down by the scorching sun faded into a whitish color, resembling huge bones tangled together.

A dried up pool was left with dead white bog moss and another big pool where horses and cattle were taken for water revealed its bottom with not even a drop of water. Countless wet footprints of horses and cattle became hardened and a small pond in a shady area was left with only handful of water filled with dead tadpoles. There were no more frogs leisurely croaking in the water and no more frogs jumping into the water to produce ripples spreading across. Between the crevices of the parched ground disgusting looking tiger salamanders' heads were darting in and out, and earthworms in search of wet ground were dried up dead on the road and lizards on top of heated rocks were panting with thirst. The chickens were frantically searching for water and a wagtail bird was sprawled dead on the ground and a colony of ants was swarming over the corpse. It was a disgusting sight as if the dead bird was still alive squirming.

*Waiting for the Rain*

After the long and loathsome days of scorching heat and drought, the rain finally fell. The burning sun reigning above our heads for days on end changed its color in the western sky, turning into a hazy claret color. Shortly after the sky's color changed, a mass of thick gray clouds started to gather. It was a sign of cumulonimbus clouds signaling the rainstorm. Everyone, exhausted from the drought, expressed delight but at the same time was doubtful whether it was really going to rain.

The black clouds swallowed the red sun and quickly spread to the west side of the sky, rolling onward at incredible speed. The islanders anticipated the rain and wondered whether the rain was really on its way. Suddenly a sense of tranquility descended blanketing the entire atmosphere; it was the calm before the storm. The wind that caused the heat to rise had died down and the serenity before the storm lingered on. Everyone calmly waited holding their breath. Everything on the earth, the mountains and the rivers thirsty for water, quietly anticipated the imminent rain. The wind was faster than the clouds. The black clouds had not quite reached halfway, but the white clouds hanging over Mt. Halla were already chased out by the strong wind.

Finally the wind arrived. From the very beginning the wind was powerful. The landscape trembled and the silence was broken immediately. The storm dust rose from the ground and the red sweet oleanders were shaken by the wind, emitting a strong scent, and a flock of sparrows perched on the persimmon tree landed on the ground like unripe persimmons falling from the tree. The sound of leaves and weeds rustling in the wind echoed widely. I felt dampness from the wind. Mother and my grandparents busily went in and out of the house; they rolled out straw mats and covered the roof, tightening the ropes to prevent things from being blown away in the wind. They also secured piles of barley straw. My friends and I who had lost all our energy from the scorching heat ran here and there excitedly.

Chicken Butt, Sling, and Sea Crab called out to Lefty in front of the blacksmith's shop.

> *Lefty, Lefty*
> *Roll up the straw mat, the rain's coming*
> *Cover the crocks, the rain's coming*

Lefty ran out of the house to hang out with us in the wind.

A strong gust knocked a man off his bicycle. We giggled and laughed even when our pee went flying everywhere and landed on our feet. Dead leaves soared into the air. The dampness in the air felt refreshing and the wind kept smacking our faces. It was great when the dead leaves flew up and got stuck in our faces, and we were happy even when the dust went into our eyes and tears came out. The wind pumped air into our shirts making them blow up like balloons. The back of our shirts were inflated so we became hunchbacks and when the front of our shirts were bloated we looked like we had beer bellies. We staggered and danced and so did passersby. Look at that woman! Her skirt's puffed up so she looks like she's pregnant. She looked hideous from behind; her skirt clung to her body showing the contours of her behind. We giggled.

*Look at that maiden*
*Don't fart*
*Busy powdering*
*Your butt after farting*
*Heat a fire poker*
*Set your butt on fire*

A hen annoyed by the blowing wind showed its red butt as if opening a fan. We chuckled.

"Hey, look at that chicken's butt! Looks just like someone's mouth."

Chicken Butt was upset and drove the chicken away saying that it was humiliating him. We climbed up to the hill to wait for the rain. The wind became stronger. In one corner of the dark western sky, the sunlight streamed through gaps in the clouds like waterfalls. From the pine grove around the Confucian school, the sound of pine trees rustling in the wind resembled the sound of breaking surf. In the pine grove, several crows were frivolously reveling in the wind.

While waiting for the rain, I entertained myself in the wind, too. As if riding the waves in the ocean, I let my body float in the wind. My body felt as light as a feather when my shirt was inflated in the wind. I thought I could float in the air. I leaned forward as much as I could and stretched out my arms in front of me like a frog swimming. I became a fish. The back of my shirt that was pumped up with air was my dorsal fin, and due to the irregular wind dynamics I had to breathe in tandem with the wind. It was difficult to breathe freely against the strong wind, as though my head was completely covered with a scarf. I held my breath and endured. If I opened my mouth unable to endure, the wind went through my mouth, traveling down the windpipe like the time when I drank water playing in the ocean and lost control. The head wind struck my face and the sound of a strong gust kept ringing in my ears. My clothes fluttered in the wind and my mind wandered, so I felt refreshed like in a vacuum state. The leaves and trees all danced for joy.

Finally the rain fell. The miraculous raindrops, sweet and warm drops of rain, fell on the dusty ground and made holes like pock marks. "Hooray! It's raining!" I screamed with joy, jumping up and down. The clouds weren't quite overhead, but the rain came down hard diagonally. I turned around and ran home. I wasn't running away but made a bet with the rain as to who would reach home first. The wind pushed me to run faster and I did.

> *Roll up the straw mat, the rain's coming*
> *Cover the crocks, the rain's coming*

*Monster*

On stormy nights when the wind howled and rattled on, I could not easily fall asleep.

The cold wind penetrated into the room so it was difficult to keep the lamp light on. The holes and openings of the windows were filled up with pieces of rags and all the shutters were closed as well, but the wind somehow crept in and blew out the lamp light. Every time the heavy rain hit the shutters the rice paper covered windows inflated and deflated as if they were alive. The rice paper windows continued to make a neighing noise in the wind. I did not like it when the rain stopped and only the sound of the wind was heard. I liked listening to the rain and wind raging together. When various sounds came to life, I became anxious and disturbed like the rice paper. The house, harassed by the wind, was filled with ominous and strange sounds. It felt as if the enormous hand of a monster held one corner of the house and was shaking it hard.

I stayed close to my mother, lying down right behind her back and thought about the monster. It must be that monster, that tall monster that can easily jump over a house in one leap. It only appears on pitch black nights when there are no stars or moon; since its body is jet black, it's not easily spotted by humans. If a person walks under the monster's legs he or she either dies or falls gravely ill.

That monster has gone crazy, wreaking havoc in the wind. The jet-black body is jumping around and is sitting on the roof like it's riding a horse and shaking the windows and the doorknob, trying to pry them open. My mother and my younger brother and sister are sleeping soundly, and they are completely oblivious to what is going on. My fear does not go away even when I am right behind my mother. The shutters and the kitchen door shake wildly, making creaking noises. What if the doorknob breaks and the monster opens the door? A scary scene is about to happen right before my eyes—the doorknob comes undone and the two shutter doors open and close alternately making a loud noise. Once I got really scared trying to close the door. In the yard, a long stick supporting the laundry line was dancing like a ghost and no matter how hard I pulled it did not budge as if the monster was holding onto the door. I was scared out of my mind.

The monster that was shaking the door relentlessly retreated in silence. In the middle of the courtyard, the monster gathered the dry leaves. Then it grabbed the rotten straw thatch hanging on the eaves and jumped up to the roof. In one leap, the monster went over the roof and crushed the branches of the permission tree. I heard something fall on the tin roof. I wondered what it was. Was the monster throwing rocks? All of a sudden silence fell and the sound of the wind trailed off. I heard the sound of power lines shaking in the wind on the other side of the road. In the midst of an ominous silence, the dry leaves started to rustle in the wind. The wind started to blow again and the monster came back. The whirring sound of the wind was heard. The wind came rushing in and it crushed against the stone wall. It continued to smash against the wall, and the wind went through the holes yelling and screaming sharply. The wind moved upward and suddenly fell headlong in the courtyard. It was crushed and reduced to nothing, then it rose again in a whirlwind. The huge empty crocks in the yard made an unpleasant sound as the wind crashed into them. The windows started to creak again and the tin roof jerked. *Thump!* I heard something fall on the roof. That nasty monster was throwing rocks again. *Thump! Thump!* I was afraid so I tried to wake my mother up, but mother said in a sleepy tone that it was nothing.

"What's the matter? It's the sound of persimmons falling on the ground. Go to sleep. If you go to sleep, the wind will, too. Since it rained, we need to go out to the millet field early in the morning," said my mother.

*Flock of Sparrows in Morning Light*

How did morning appear in my eyes after the violent raging storm? A beautiful image of a flock of sparrows singing in the morning is etched in my memory.

I was slow in waking up in the morning, so I was confused about whether I was still dreaming or awake, unable to connect what happened before I went to bed and the moment I woke up.

I was dreaming about the monster and woke up startled because I heard someone calling out my name. I opened my eyes but couldn't see a thing. Was it still night? I could not see. I could not breathe because of the monster in my dream. I wanted to scream but could not get a word out of my mouth. Was I truly awake? Or was I dreaming? I groped around and looked for my mother but she wasn't in the room. Where did she go? I stretched out my hand to touch the wall as usual every time I woke up from a nightmare. I felt the hard wall. It was hard and real. After that, I was slowly waking up and I was able to see, though not clearly. I felt the pressure lifting gradually. At that moment, I heard my mother urging me to wake up.

"Son, aren't you up yet? Wake up!"

I was not fully awake so my ears were still ringing from the previous night's strong wind. Then I was startled. What was that? The window was wide open and the bright sunlight streamed in through the window. Is it morning already? I quickly put my pants on and ran toward the window situated on the east side. Mother stuck her head out from the kitchen, smiling brightly and said, "The wind is gone and the weather is great. Let's eat soon and go to the millet field."

How I longed for this morning! I puffed out my chest looking at the sunlight shimmering outside the window. The strong wind from the previous night disappeared without a trace. Instead the air was filled with the sound of sparrows singing. Before the sun rose, the sparrows sang continuously, urging the sun to rise.

The surface of the ocean was painted orange and the vast sky was high and tinted a creamy shell color. The sparrows were urging the sun to rise, chirping away noisily, and the creamy colored sky was quickly turning blue. The sun finally came out breaking through the orange color. It was brilliant as if it had washed its face in the ocean. The sparrows chirped even louder and my heart pounded with joy. The newborn sun glowed magnificently and everything on the face of the earth quickly moved toward that light, getting out of darkness one by one revealing true identity. The damp leaves and water puddles in furrows and on the roads also shimmered in the sunlight. The atmosphere cleared up after the rain so Mt. Halla looked closer than ever and the mountain peak shone with luster. The bottom of the small dark creek near my home became bright and illuminated. Sunlight entered my heart and expelled the shadow of gloominess. Where did that thatched roof house come from? I laughed with joy.

"Mom, look! That bead-tree has a straw thatched roof now. It's funny."

The old bead-tree by the stream was covered with straw, like a thatched roof house. The wind was so strong that the straw from the roof flew over and stuck in the tree. I saw houses with collapsed stone walls.

The sparrows flew up. All of a sudden, hundreds of sparrows flew into the morning sunlight. They dove happily, bouncing off the golden light with their white stomachs. The dazzling streaks of light were endlessly drawn horizontally and vertically and the arrows of lights missed each other flying up or falling headlong and shooting upward again. The sparrows scattered and gathered again, then dispersed all over the place suddenly like beans scattering. They dispersed like dots scattered all over the sky then they flew in to unite.

I was afraid of the stormy nights when I was young. The morning arrived in bright sunlight after the wild and furious night retreated. The glorious morning, the proud light of morning arrived after the hardship. I learned the meaning of real happiness from mornings like these. True happiness came after much hardship. A flock of sparrows performed a group dance in delight, the glorious motion of life, in the midst of the splendor of light. I was temperamental and became easily depressed, but one of the reasons I was able to overcome depression was the beautiful memory of the brilliant mornings. Life ultimately means getting encouragement from these mornings and waiting for those mornings to arrive. From the bright morning sunlight, people who are ill or in despair regain the will to fight and the courage to live. I'm certain that at the moment the courageous ones sacrifice their lives for a better tomorrow, the sunlight shines more brilliantly.

*Riding the Waves*

The day after the big storm, the peak of our fun began around noon when we were riding the waves. It was fun picking out edible seaweeds among the piles of weeds swept to the shore by the raging waves the previous night, but the most fun was riding the waves. The ocean has been turned inside out by the roaring storm all night long and the waves continued to roll high even after the wind died down, but by noon it was just right for riding the waves.

When noon came around I darted out of the house like a pony with its reins loosened. Until then I was home running errands for my mother. I ran to the beach straight away. The smell of the ocean tingled my nose, and I could hear the cheerful voices of my friends frolicking in the ocean. I ran barefoot, splashing the water on the road. The soft and sticky sensation of warm dirt underneath my feet felt great. After the sun heated the wet ground, vapor rose, covering the green millet fields in white steam. I dashed to the beach.

My friends, Lefty, Chicken Butt, Sling, Songi and his younger brother Changsu, were already in the water, shouting happily and rolling around in the sparkling ocean. The waves rolled in one after another like a straw mat rolling and washed ashore. I quickly took off my clothes and joined my friends, jumping into the water naked. As they were tossed around by the waves, they were yelling with delight and my voice was soon added to the voices of my friends. My horseshoe-shaped scar head bobbed up and down among my friends' heads. After we were pushed to the shore, we quickly turned around to catch the next wave. The water retreated quickly pulling the sand and pebbles. We held on tight to the rocks inside the water to avoid getting swept away by the strong current. The current mixed in with the sand passed by us, scratching our naked bodies. Like stretching and yawning, our legs were pulled by the current but it felt great. The next wave rolled in soon after, so we got up to ride the wave. We did not dare go near the lip of the surf, though. There was a danger of being dragged into the middle of the ocean. When the wave was high we floated up with it. We were tossed to the side as the wave took a deep plunge the moment our faces touched the white foam of the water. I felt a water spirit inside the ocean. I could feel a strong force grabbing my shoulder and tossing me about. The spirit would grab me by my neck and shove me under the water. Inside the water all my senses became alert. The tingling sensation of tension and excitement ran through my entire body as if the waves were passing through it. I jumped one wave after another even after being tossed around and plunged below the water.

### Water Spirit

What misfortune befell us! Who knew such monstrous disaster was hidden underneath the joy of playing in the ocean! It was the day I followed my mother early in the morning to help her transplant millet seeds and joined my friends at the beach late. How could a treacherous danger lay in wait to shatter our innocent happiness? The day started out great with a flock of sparrows chirping and dancing about. The ground was damp with rain from the previous night, after many days of dry weather, but this day ended in sorrow. Were we too happy? One of us was swept away by the waves and drowned. It was Songi's younger brother Changsu. He disappeared without a trace. The only thing that was left was his clothes. My friends and I could only say, "After we came out of the water really exhausted, we couldn't find Changsu." How could we be so heartless!

Songi and his mother wailed calling out his name at the beach, waving Changsu's clothes. They bitterly called out "Changsu! Changsu!" and we became the guilty ones, sitting together on one side feeling miserable and sad. We waited and watched attentively for the body to float, but there was no sign; I only saw the phantom of a ghastly water spirit grabbing Changsu by the neck, dragging him deep into the ocean. I was scared. I shivered in fear and was overwhelmed by my guilty conscience. Changsu liked me. How could I not know that he was in danger? How could I face Songi from now on? Some sobbed but I could not even do that as if all my five sensory organs were blocked. Instead of tears, chills ran down my entire body and I trembled. I did not even tremble playing in the cold water, but I shivered under the scorching sunlight.

*Flock of Joyful Sparrows*
The shock of Changsu's death must have been great because soon after Songi's family moved to Pusan. Songi did not even say goodbye to me. I found out later and went to her old rented house and sobbed while touching the wall.

I know that the sadness left by the death of Changsu and Songi's move did not last long. Children by nature are not greatly affected by sadness for a very long time; they quickly forget since forgetting is part of a child's nature. Especially for me, after having experienced catastrophe and loneliness in Hambagigul, I detested sadness. My language development was stunted because of that atrocious massacre and I became a stutterer. However, my lachrymal gland overdeveloped, so tears welled up easily. I knew instinctively that sadness was bad for me and that manifested as forgetfulness.

That's why I always wanted to be surrounded by the cheerful laughter of my friends. Being with them made my sadness and frustrations melt away like snow. I often forgot to run errands or forgot where I put things because I was so caught up playing. My mother reprimanded me for being so forgetful and told me that I was a "crow's cousin." Crows were known to be forgetful. I often looked for things when I had them in my hand. But wasn't I closer to a sparrow than a crow?

Those tiny little sparrows, chirping and stomping up and down in staccato, reminded me of my childhood friends and me. Like those sparrows we ran here and there, chatting away not being able to sit still for a long time. We were full of curiosity and energy, our eyes sparkling like those of sparrows that followed mysterious and fun things. We soon forgot even the sadness of losing Changsu.

A flock of sparrows gathered and busily pecked at rapeseeds on a straw mat and a cat appeared out of the blue, stealthily approaching them. The sparrows were not aware of the imminent danger and busily pecked at the seeds, continuing to twitter away. Contrary to the sparrows' staccato movements, the cat's movement was tightly orchestrated and it was ready to attack. As if each movement was connected, it flowed smoothly; then all of a sudden the cat attacked the sparrows like the thrusting of a spear. In an instant, the rest of the sparrows flew up and scattered into the sky like bomb debris. The sparrows were as forgetful as me. Forgetting what had just happened the sparrows returned and perched on the wall, chirping noisily toward the cat holding the bloodied sparrow in its mouth. Perhaps the sparrows were cursing at the cat and at the same time crying over losing one of their friends. *Chirp chirp chirp*! The shock, the sadness, and the anger only lasted for a brief moment. After the cat sauntered along the wall, turning the corner with the game in its mouth, the sparrows happily returned to the straw mat.

In other words, Changsu's death was like that. My memory must have been as small as the size of a bean at the time. Sadness and fear did not last long in my memory.

I witnessed two more deaths in the five year period apart from Changsu's. I can't remember their names but there was one who died a year before Changsu. He was an orphan who lost his parents during the Cheju Massacre and came to live with his relatives. His relatives didn't send him to school, but instead he became their babysitter. Even when he came to play, he carried the baby on his back. All of a sudden he had this growth on his back and stayed away from everyone. Then he became a hunchback and died. As the hump grew bigger and bigger, his body caved in further and further. It was a pitiful sight. He sat crouched, basking in the sun and watched us play from a distance. I felt uncomfortable when he watched, so my friends and I ended up moving to a different place. Witnessing the progression of death in someone of a similar age was unpleasant and disturbing.

*Snake*

There was another boy who died and unlike Changsu his death was quite dramatic. He was a year older which meant he was the same age as Lefty, and he lived in the upper part of town. He was bitten by a snake while he was trying to catch a frog. What was even more strange and surprising was that the snake was found dead next to the boy's dead body. The rumor was that the boy had ripped off the snake that was coiled around his leg and smashed it against the rock. But was that truly possible? Just thinking about it made me cringe. Snakes were like land mines. When you feel something soft under your feet, a mine would go off, similar to a snake biting your ankle and coiling around your leg. The moment I identified a triangular shaped viper's head, the thought that "I'm dead now" would hit me even before the poison. I would lose consciousness and die right there and then.

The boy died a heroic death, putting up a fight until the very end and killing the enemy. It must have been Lefty who interpreted the story like that because he was the only who was not scared of snakes, so it was possible that he concocted that story.

I grew up during the war so I liked playing war games. When my friends and I were out gathering nuts, we did it in a manner in which it resembled battles. Trees with nuts were full of thorns and caterpillars thus they were perfect for the role of enemies. We took off our shirts and spread them under a tree. We yelled and brandished our wooden swords, thrashed branches to shake off the nuts. After a while, the nuts and disgusting looking caterpillars piled on our shirts.

We played battle games, pretending the dense thickets of bushes were enemies. We brandished our swords until the green color of leaves was smeared all over the swords, yelling and slashing grass and flowers mercilessly. When Lefty saw a snake slithering away, he ran after it and grabbed it by its tail. He twirled it under our noses trying to scare us then tossed it into the bushes. He did it just for fun, so he never killed it.

Before the Cheju Massacre, a snake was regarded as the Big Dipper god and the god of fate, so it was something that couldn't be harmed. People believed that killing a snake would bring misfortune and even pointing at it would make that finger rot. The Big Dipper looked like a snake, slithering its way around Polaris in the sky and that's why it was regarded as the Big Dipper god in charge of people's mortality. It also governed food so it was called the god of fate. However, the old belief proved to be wrong. During the Cheju Massacre so many people lost their lives in the fire and many gods were burnt, too. How could there be any faith left? The snake was no longer considered a spiritual being protecting humans, but an unsightly object.

One day, Lefty killed a snake. It was from the same pond where the boy from the upper town had died.

To supplement the protein we lacked in our diet, we often caught frogs in the pond and ate them. It was natural to find snakes where the frogs were. We needed to thrash the weeds around while walking to avoid any snakes. Even I could kill a frog without batting an eye, not realizing how cruel killing was. When I lashed a frog from behind with a whip, it flipped over showing its white stomach and died. It was easy to skin it. I pulled one of its hind legs while pressing down the body with the hill of my foot. That way, the unnecessary parts of the body and guts would be ripped off nicely, only leaving the legs. The frog had turned into a delicious meat showing its white legs. I felt nothing when the frog jerked inside my palm, breathing its last breath.

I killed frogs without a problem but what Lefty did to the snake was utterly deplorable. We played together for many years, but that was the first time I had witnessed a cruel streak in him. Was it because of his brother's death? His muscular brother who had worked as a blacksmith, pounding heavy iron, died during the war. The day his brother's death notice arrived, he wailed, rolling on the ground in front of his house, "My brother died! My brother died!"

Lefty killed the snake that had the nickname Mulp'aegi or Viper because it bit so many people. That day its stomach was swollen as if it had just swallowed something big. Not being able to glide smoothly with its stomach full, it was sluggish. Was it its triangular shaped head and disgusting movement that provoked Lefty to kill it? Or, was it his brother's death? Or, was it the boy's death that generated the impulse? Perhaps he felt hostility toward the ruthless violence the snake had committed by swallowing and ending a life in one gulp and that might have catapulted him, too.

The snake had no strength to resist when Lefty took a firm grasp of its tail. Lefty swung the snake like a whip and smashed it hard against the rock a few times. The snake died with its head crushed and was completely helpless; it was dangling in Lefty's hand. What came next was the cruel part.

"You nasty snake! Spit out what you swallowed!" Lefty yelled out.

Lefty continued to hurl abuse at the snake that was dangling helplessly in his hand. He pressed down by stepping on its tail and held the body between his two hands. Then he began moving his hands upward squeezing it as hard as he could as if he was cleaning out a pig's intestines. Viper's swollen stomach was pushed upward. It wiggled a bit as if it came to life again, opening its mouth, then coughed up a frog with its legs and body intact. There was a saying that if the dead viper smelled dirt, it would be revived, so Lefty crushed its head again with a rock and even peed on it. To make certain that it did not smell dirt he hung the dead snake on thorn bushes. It was such a cruel sight! Later that day I was delighted when I found a piece of fried fish on the dinner table, but when I found a small fish inside the fried fish, I threw up.

After that day, I often dreamt about the snake Lefty had killed. Lefty hung it on the thorn bushes to prevent it from smelling dirt, but I could not stop it from appearing in my dreams. I ran for my life being chased by the snake. And at times I tried hard to get rid of the snake that bit my ankle.

I was not a morning person so during summer vacation when I went out at dawn to attend the west pier breakwater meetings, I ended up sleeping, hiding between the rocks. One time I felt a sharp thing biting my earlobe and woke up startled thinking it was a snake. But what bit me was a sea crab.

Those who have had an experience dreaming about a snake understand how unpleasant it is. No matter how fast you run, you cannot get rid of the snake that is behind your heels. Sometimes in my dream I ran for my life not knowing a snake had coiled around my ankle. And, there was another time when it coiled around my neck and choked me to death. I woke up from my dream and found my hands clenched in fists and soaked in sweat.

*Surrender Game*

I want to believe even nightmares are part of growing pains. The saying "Good medicine tastes bitter" is true in that everything in life cannot be sweet. It is in children's nature to be insensitive to painful and difficult things, but those frightening snake dreams taught me that life is not always good but can be very painful. Did I learn that in order to overcome hardships I have to grin and bear with every ounce of energy I have? Did I ever encounter critical situations in real life like the ones I experienced in my dreams? Did I ever run for dear life in real life?

My dreams reflected significant aspects of my everyday reality. They helped me become aware of my consciousness. In my dreams, I was always chased by a snake but there was a time when I succeeded in getting rid of it. The snake was at my heels but I made a sudden and quick turn at a perpendicular angle, and the snake that was following right behind me died with its body cut in half. I killed the snake coiled around my ankle by pulling it away and smashing it against the rock, the way Lefty had done it.

Playing a surrender game was extremely intense, just like engaging in a battle. Since I was not mature enough, perhaps more spontaneous and free spirited, my instinct to attack came naturally when I was playing the surrendering game. Among us children, it was very important to determine who was strong and who wasn't. I always played the surrender game at breaks and at lunch time at school with my classmates. We wrestled on the floor all the time, so the classroom and the hallway floors' nail heads were nice and shiny. We found a nice grassy area around the two graves near home and wrestled after school, too. Soon the graveyard had very little grass left, and the red dirt was exposed.

The game was between two children, wrestling on the ground, choking the opponent's neck with arms or legs until the opponent called out "I surrender." Kicking and hitting and twisting were against the rules. Every time I played the game, I thought I was fighting a snake coiled around my neck and my body, so I fought really hard with every ounce of my strength.

One time I played the surrender game in my classroom and my opponent bit my chest. The reason why I was able to endure and fight him off was because of the practice I had in my dreams. I was known as a "cry baby" but I had the guts to fight back when I was pushed into a corner. How did I punch him when I was in such pain? I think it was those snake dreams that helped me do it.

When my opponent and I were locked together like two snakes coiled around each other and wrestling on the classroom floor, my head was locked between his arms the moment I let my guard down. I became dizzy and his right arm choking me felt like a snake. I felt suffocated. He demanded, "Say you surrender, shithead!" He choked me even harder, but I held out as long as I could. I escaped from his arm the moment I could no longer breathe. At the same time, I raised my body and threw my left arm around his neck. The situation was reversed. I urged him to surrender, pressing harder. But instead of surrendering, he bit my chest. It was so painful that I felt all of my strength draining out of my body. I let him go, but he wouldn't let go. The other kids watching us yelled out, "Hey! Don't bite! Biting is against the rules!" Still he did not let go. I was in pain but strangely I didn't surrender. The way in which he was biting my chest and squeezing me with his legs wrapped around my lower body was just like Viper. The hostile feeling born out of pain made my hair stand up on end. With all my strength, I struck his chin with my right hand and screamed, "You, nasty Viper!" One blow was enough. He let go of my chest and fell down.

It was a wonderful victory! I think I cried at that time. I'm certain tears rolled down at the moment of my victory. I was always like that. How ridiculous it must have been for a victor to cry but I could not help it. It was uncontrollable since my lachrymal gland was overdeveloped. If you were never a cry baby you wouldn't understand how liberating and satisfyingly sweet it was when tears gushed down after the rampaging violent emotion subsides.

The bite was quite serious, so the wound lasted for a long time. Since I had my shirt on his teeth did not dig deep into my skin, but the teeth mark was distinct. After the bruise disappeared, the teeth mark remained with me for quite a while. How could he have bitten me so hard? He was so cold-blooded! But then I must have been worse because I beat him in the end. How did a fifth grader endure pain and muster up such courage?

After that, whenever I saw him, my heart sank as if I had come face to face with a snake. He walked past by me whenever we met, avoiding eye contact. Later, he became a gang member, whirling and twirling a bicycle chain, but he never tried to pick a fight with me.

### Combat Game

I had the habit of losing myself completely when I was absorbed in playing games with my friends. When I played violent games such as the surrender game, I felt a strange excitement similar to that of madness. And without realizing it, I became violent. My mind would go completely blank and I could not think clearly; I became reckless when I reached a violent state of excitement. It must be a madness that runs in my family.

It was the same when I played a game of hurling stones with kids from the upper town. It was not just a game but a real battle. It happened when I was in fifth grade. There was a major battle on the main street and even the junior high school students from both towns joined in. Adults did not dare interfere in the fight. As the game escalated and became violent, the rule that you could only throw stones below the waist was broken, and it turned into a dangerous battle. The stones whizzed overhead while yells and shouts were exchanged. The dangerous situation drove me into a strange sense of excitement. Without realizing it, I was standing on the frontline throwing stones. By the time I turned around sensing danger, it was already too late. My team was running away and it was at that moment a rock flew and struck my head.

I was hit by a jagged rock. The injury was serious enough to make a dent in my head. I remember picking up dried horse dung, pressing it against the injured area in an attempt to stop the bleeding. I still have a scar on the back of my head; it is a memento from that day.

What comes to mind when thinking about the stone battle is the infiltration firing training I went through as a fresh marine recruit.

I have a bitter taste in my mouth thinking about the three-month training program as a fresh recruit under the scorching sunlight. I was battered until I turned into withered leaves. The training program was so long and tiring that I would not want to take a leak in the direction where the training center was located. What was reasonably endurable was the last stage of the training program, which was the infiltration firing practice. Everyday I went through basic training routines, crawling on the drill ground like a dog beaten with a bat. I felt liberated when I was thrown into a situation much like the actual battle out in the open field. It was like three months of unbearable training was to prepare me for that one day.

The infiltration firing training remained in my memory as something refreshing, like a sudden shower after three months of drought. I crouched when the machine guns were constantly firing overhead and I heard the TNT exploding all around me for the first time. Strangely, in the face of danger, I felt refreshed—as if a sudden shower was falling accompanied by thunderstorms and lightning, and I jumped up and down in excitement.

I was scared at first. I could not move easily because my body was so stiff and tense, and I was under pressure not to fall behind the others. I was on the ground on my stomach and the artillery cover was right above my head. I was afraid that if I lifted my head even a little I would get hit by stray bullets. Since I was struck by a rock once, the back of my head was the vulnerable part of my body. Wasn't it obvious to worry about it?

Fortunately my fear soon dissipated. After I passed the first fence safely, I gained confidence and was seized by a strange sense of excitement. My mind went blank and I was driven by unknown strengths to move forward and forward only. I crawled out from under the fence and jumped over a shelter and was on my stomach again, pretending to shoot. Then I crawled under another fence, and all of a sudden I heard a loud bang from the ditch next to me. Together with an incredibly loud explosive sound, a clump of dirt flew over and hit my face hard that scared me to death. (If this was a real battle, I would have died when I was hit by shrapnel.) I got angry, so I became even more reckless.

However, my action produced an absurd result. I passed all the wired fences set up in an open area and caught up with the other members. When I finally reached the top yelling and running after engaging in hand to hand combat, I realized that the members I caught up with were not my team. They started out before my team. I caught up with them because I was so busy trying to crawl out of those fences as fast as I could that I was out of my mind. In any case, I failed. I should have been punished for breaking away from my unit without permission, but my platoon leader laughed hard and said, "In a real battlefield, I need someone like you. I certainly do. I need someone who can move forward with no fear and to heighten the team's morale."

He meant my action was admirable as a battle expendable, not sure about any other purpose. No matter what my platoon leader said, I was extremely pleased with myself since I broke away from my unit on my own will, though not intentionally. I could not digress even a little from the training routines over the past three months, so this clearly extinguished the oppressive feeling that had been building up.

I became impulsive and reckless whenever I played games with my friends and the episode at the training session could be explained and understood in this context. Since I came from a poor family, I had to help out with errands, chores, and even farming. So I often couldn't hang out with my friends. While helping my mother with grinding, I had this urge to run out of the house when I heard my friends playing outside. So it was possible that when I had the opportunity to hang out with my friends, I was more passionate, pouring all my energy into it. I think my impulsive tendencies were inherent; my over the top sense of passion always produced absurd results.

During my senior year in high school, my craziness acted up again while watching a volleyball final. The moment my school team lost after a close match, I lost my composure and jumped out of my seat, yelling, "Attack those bastards!" There was an outburst at my instigation, so the cheering team all jumped up and attacked the opponent's cheering team and they quickly fled the scene. If they had stayed and fought back, what could have happened, I wonder.

What was the true nature of my blind impulsiveness? There were things I did not know about myself, an unfamiliar self that had nothing to do with courage or foolishness; my impulsive actions came out of nowhere. In medical terms, my action is explained as occurring due to a lack of serotonin secreted from the brain, but I don't believe it. Impulsiveness and violence can be regarded as flaws in the individual, but it can turn into a virtue in a situation when one is pitted against an enemy. That's why I wanted to believe that it is inherent, that it has been transmitted from my ancestors. Believing it otherwise, I find myself to be too pathetic.

I ended up hurting myself several times, exposing myself to danger when I lost all my senses. As the platoon leader had said, I was fit for fighting in battles. I engaged in so many fights because of my flawed personality. Among the countless fights I had, I was caught in four serious ones. I lost four teeth, had four fractured ribs, and my skull was caved in. My impulsive behavior was manifested as self-destruction. When I was going through puberty, I attempted to commit suicide twice.

### Child with a Baby on His Back

My character was full of flaws and what taught me to be patient was labor. I felt the weight of work pressing down on me, prohibiting me from running around here and there.

I started helping my mother in the field when I was in fifth grade. Even before this, I was already in charge of carrying my baby brother on my back. I still remember the refreshing sensation of a cool breeze passing across my back when I put the baby down and handed him over to my mother. Thinking back, even my baby brother was a tremendous burden for me. My brother, ten years younger than me, was born in May of the year of the "the Cheju Massacre."

When my brother was born, my mother—who was very strong in every respect—cried her heart out. Perhaps she was overwhelmed with sadness thinking about father who made a brief visit before the Korean War leading a group of trainees, but since then there was no news of him. No news was good news because news from the frontline was nothing but death notices. Mother cried after my baby brother was born, but she tried hard to think positively. She comforted herself by saying that father was not the type to write letters or that his unit moved around frequently so he could not write.

As for me, I almost forgot about my father because I was busy hanging out with my friends. But even so, whenever I met a mailman, my heart sank. Did he bring a letter from father? I was afraid that the mailman would deliver bad news rather than a letter from him.

The mailman was one of my relatives. He rode a red post office bicycle and went around all over the village to deliver mail. When we met he would say "Hey!" and with a big smile on his face, he waved his hand and passed right by me. I met him several times on the street, but there was no letter from father.

One time the red bicycle that passed by me time and again

finally stopped in front of me. I had my baby brother on my back while I was hanging out with my friends. I was all tensed up thinking that a letter from father had arrived. But what came out of his mouth was completely absurd.

"Whose baby are you carrying on your back?" he asked.

"My baby brother. He's my baby brother."

"Your brother? Your brother, huh . . . strange . . . when did your father come?"

"It's been a while since he came. Since his visit last summer, we haven't received any letters from him."

"Last summer? Of course, I was wondering whose baby it was!" He laughed hard.

My baby brother was my first burden. I couldn't jump around freely with him on my back, so I hung around and watched my friends play. I could only participate verbally and play referee. But I could play marble games with my baby brother on my back because I could use my foot, but not too well though. I rolled the marbles with my foot and only at a crucial moment was I on my stomach and used my fingers to flick the marbles. My brother's head, resting on my back, swung to and fro like a water bucket as he slept. At times I was completely engrossed in playing, paying no attention to him. My brother retaliated by peeing on my back. I often forgot to let him off to pee so my back got drenched.

Actually I didn't mind that much. I guess it didn't smell since it was the baby's. Even a baby's poop was said to be adorable. When my brother cried, I sniffed his diaper thinking that either he peed or pooped. Since he drank nothing but milk, his poop didn't stink and the color of his poop was golden yellow. There is a wildflower named "baby poop." People must have thought the color of baby's poop to be beautiful to name the wildflower after it. I held my brother's soft body and crouched down so that he could take a dump. I encouraged him by saying, "You can do it. Come on!" as if I was taking a dump, straining myself. When

I saw my brother's poop come out, I felt great. I remember my brother crying and kicking when the dog quickly ate his poop.

### Red Bean Worm

When I first started helping out in the field, my grandmother said, "During the busiest farming season, one day of not working means ten days without food later. Just because you are a child doesn't mean you can just idle around. No one does. Everyone works. Adults, children, cattle, ponies, fire poker, grain . . ."

"Even the fire poker?" I asked in amazement.

"Of course, even the fire poker works hard. During the busiest, season cooking rice quickly is important. The fire poker moves busily in the furnace," replied grandmother.

"What about grain?"

"Grain can't be lazy either. People and cattle are working hard so grain needs to grow quickly. It needs to grow strong and tall. That's grain's job. Sometimes no matter how hard we try, we fail. We don't know until the last minute whether we'll have a good or bad harvest. We sigh in relief when rice is cooking inside a pot and is ready to be eaten. Then we can relax."

I always feel happy when I think back on my grandmother's kind words and her warm gaze, encouraging me to work. Of course, one of the most important things for a child was to grow up strong and tall, like grain in the field. For a child, sleeping and playing were two important elements of nourishment, therefore no matter how insignificant or light the work was, it was burdensome. Watching the grain grow tall made the adults happy because it meant a good harvest, but for me I needed to grow more myself so growing something else was not my concern.

During the busiest season, the fire poker busily worked and the adults were so overwhelmed that they were about to hold out their hands to a dog for help, so I could not just hang around doing nothing. When I started helping out in the field, my grandmother always complemented me and said, "My grandson is do-ing a great job. You're better than a dog."

My mother and grandmother helped each other out during busy seasons. My mother worked at my grandmother's field and in return my grandmother worked at my mother's. They usually helped each other out like this, but during lean years we always went to grandmother's for help and freeloaded off of her. My grandmother was a warm-hearted person. Whenever she saw me, she wanted to feed me more. She always smiled warmly and that's why she had a lot of wrinkles around her eyes. I miss her tender smile.

When I helped out with planting, waddling along the field, a day seemed like eternity. My legs kept falling asleep and my back was aching, my fingertips were hurting, but the furrows seemed endless. I got up several times before I could finish one furrow and rubbed my back using a sickle's handle to ease the pain and cursed the sun that seemed to be stuck in the middle of the sky, not moving an inch. After the sun went down, I came home. But I noticed that my right hand that held the sickle was still in a fist. Perhaps what I felt at the moment was a sense of deep despair; hopelessness that I would never be able to get out of that field. What was the point of studying hard when I didn't have a father, and my mother was too poor?

While working in the bean field, I noticed from time to time that a lark flew up all of a sudden as if a small rock was kicked up in the air. The bird flew straight up and stayed in the air in suspension for a long time and chirped happily. The bird looked as if it left this world and had a nest in the open sky. *Chirp. Chirp.* Its singing sounded like it was mocking me, the one who was crouched, crawling and working in the bean field. I was envious of the bird's freedom.

Among the lark's feed, there were different kinds of worms in the field but what it liked the best was a fat worm with a green horn sticking out from its end. It was literally called a "red bean worm" because it ate red bean leaves or other bean leaves. There was a sad story behind the green horn sticking out from the red bean worm's tail. My grandmother told me that the red bean worm was a reincarnation of the oldest daughter of the Jade Emperor. When poor and hungry people came to her begging for something to eat, she gave them rotten food and chased them away. For her sins, she was driven out and fell into a bean field and became a worm. She was thrown out of heaven with only a spoon in her tail. She was clothed in green and led a sad life. She was unable to get out of the field for life. I was afraid that my life would, too, turn out like hers. What kind of food was I going to have with a spoon stuck in my behind?

Every time I helped my mother in the field, I was worried that I was cursed to live a life like the red bean worm. My mother's life was to obey natural cycle of the sun rising and setting, the changing of the four seasons, and tilling the field when the sun was up, crawling between the furrows like a worm. When it rained she stayed home to either mend clothes or keep busy grinding. This kind of life was natural for her, but in school I was taught that it was the life of the uncivilized.

*First Load*

Thinking back on those days when I used to tag along with my mother to work in the field, I remember a young colt that followed her around stamping on the ground. It was on the day we sowed millet. The ground was not fertile so it was important to tamp the soil after the seeds were planted. That was why my grandfather brought the animals to help out. He was the one who plowed the ground. The planting took place when the weeds were all pulled out and were dried out in the sun.

Before planting the seeds, the furrows needed to be leveled. To level the ground, my grandfather placed a heavy rock on a

Japanese holly tree stump and my mother led a horse to drag it. Then my grandfather, following the horse, planted the seeds. My grandmother and I plucked out the left over weeds. What about my sister Yŏngnyŏ? She watched the baby under the cool pine tree shade. I didn't like plucking out pretty pink bindweed flowers even though they were weeds, so I hesitated. I remember my grandfather's foolish way of strewing seeds. I know he did it to plant seeds evenly, but the way in which he hobbled about swinging his arms was ridiculous, as if he was imitating a cripple.

After the seeds were sowed, we had lunch. Then immediately after lunch, the stomping of the ground started again. Grandfather led the horse from the front and from behind my grandmother, mother, and I followed. With every step, dust rose up from the ground and our clothes and hair were covered in filth. The brown horse and our dirt covered hair and clothes blended well together with the color of the ground. It really was boring work—walking back and forth endlessly from the east end of the field to the west end. To alleviate the dullness, grandfather started singing. It was a farmer's song. My grandfather sang in a soft and beautiful voice. He sang slowly, drawing out the melody, then grandmother and mother sang the refrain.

It was such a hard labor for both the adults and the horse alike, stomping on the ground for half a day under the scorching heat in June. It was really unbearable for me. I was so impatient then. Even the water, drawn from the pond, placed under the shade soon turned lukewarm. Our calf could not endure the heat so it kept trying to free itself. I, too, wanted to escape to the cool shade of the pine tree where Yŏngnyŏ was. My grandfather sensed that I was getting crabby and was anxious to flee, so he improvised the song and added lines in an attempt to cheer me up.

> *Hey, look at these colts trying to run away*
> *Whoa! Whoa! These colts are suffering under the June heat*

*But work is your lot*
*One day of suffering will bring days of fun*
*Lazy colts! Work! Work! Work!*

My grandfather sang in a low pitched voice, drawing out like a long sigh, then the voice slowly escalated hitting high notes, reaching the scorching hot sky and floating in the wind. The endless melody was sweet and sad. Sorrows ran through my ancestors' bloodstreams. They were fated to grieve. While listening to the song, I found peace and comfort, and the colt followed quietly with its ears drooped. I became sleepy when the sad yet sweet melody flowed. The colt that was plodding along staggered because it dozed off for a second. I felt my legs getting heavier and heavier. Immediately my grandfather's thunderous voice rumbled, "Hey, you rascals!" I became alert. He sang again.

*You lazy colts*
*Don't doze off. Walk straight.*
*We're almost finished.*
*Stomp harder so we can all rest.*
*Whoa! Whoa! Whoa!*

After two years, the colt turned into a mature horse and became an obedient servant after its mother had been sold at the market.

Even this gentle colt that had transformed into the mature horse did not like it when its first load was saddled. Grandfather loaded slowly, stroking the horse gently, but when the load became heavy it went on a rampage. It kept neighing, violently kicking its hind legs. As a result, the load fell to the ground and the horse ran to the field like it'd gone mad with the saddle on. My grandfather yelled out, "Stop the horse!" Both grandmother and mother who were bundling barley ran after the horse, trying to stop it. The horse could not jump over the high wall so it jumped about wildly inside the field. The loosened reins wiggled like a snake and my grandfather finally caught them. The moment the reins were under his foot, the horse stalled and my grandfather quickly grabbed them.

Grandfather looked extremely angry and said, "Damn you! Just because you don't want to carry the load, you went on a rampage! I'm going to teach you a lesson." My grandfather quickly went around to the back of the horse and put the reins against its hind legs and pulled really hard. Surprisingly the huge horse lost its balance and tilted to one side and finally fell to the ground. It truly was a spectacular sight! It happened so quickly that the horse looked bewildered but got up immediately. The moment it tried to get up and balance its weight, grandfather pulled the reins again and the horse fell once more. This happened a few more times. Grandfather was quick and did not look like he was expending a lot of strength. It was similar to flying a kite, pulling and loosening to make the kite plunge. The horse fell again and again. *Thump! Thud!* It was such a sight! After it went through such an ordeal, the horse became obedient and allowed the goods to be loaded.

I was like that horse when I had my first load on my back. When I trudged along approximately four kilometers with the load, the road seemed rough and endless. The rope was cutting into my shoulders so I became furious and undid the load. Sometimes I endured the pain but the rope loosened and the load came undone. I was just like the horse with its first load.

## Maternal Grandfather

My maternal grandfather was not only good at handling the horses but good at raising them, too. He said he could tell its owner's character simply by looking at the horse. It was a Yuma breed and its body was smooth and was covered in a soft brown coat. Its tail was long and black to match its nice body. A snippet of white hair ran from its forehead to its muzzle. This was such an unusual trimming that I wanted to stroke the horse whenever I was near it.

What fascinated me even more was its voluminous behind that resembled two gourds placed upside down. It was fascinating to watch the horse taking its dump because it looked like shiny green eggs emerged endlessly and its pee came out like a waterfall. I liked that horse a lot, so even though no one asked me to I took the horse by the stream for water and to graze. When the nearby stream was dried up or was reeking, I took the horse to Yongyŏn. During hot summer days, I even dragged the horse into the water to swim with my friends.

My grandfather strictly prohibited anyone from riding the horse because it was only used for transporting goods. He said if the horse was overworked and distressed, it could not maintain an excellent physical frame. If the load was too heavy or was not equally distributed on both sides, the horse's back was sure to get scarred but my grandfather's horse never had any scar.

Not only was my grandfather good at handling and taking care of the horses, he was also good at piling sheaves of straw. He was quick and precise; in a short period of time he made a pile as high as the roof. I was in charge of throwing bundles to my grandfather. He was so quick that I could not keep up with him.

He was a skillful worker but during the winter season, he turned into a poet. He liked to write poems of five or seven Chinese characters in each line. His poetry writing friend was a close relative who lived in the same town. Poets who knew how to appreciate the art needed a delivery boy. I delivered poems my grandfather wrote to my relative and his replies were delivered by his own grandson. I obtained foreign cigarette wrappers for my grandfather and he treasured them and wrote his poems.

## Canteen and Twisted Doughnut

What comes to mind about my school days is a cardboard notebook. It was yellowish and looked as if it was made from simply pressing horses' dung; it was rough and uneven. Wasn't the cardboard notebook a mirror image of myself? I was unable to pay the PTA fee on time so there was no way to buy school supplies. Textbooks were handed down from my cousins and a ruler was cut in half to share with my younger sister. We shared pencils and erasers, cutting them in half, too. When a pencil was about the size of my finger joint, I inserted it into a bamboo tube and used it until the end. (My mom remembered this so when she saw cigarette butts with the white parts showing, she reprimanded me and told me to use a pipe to smoke to the very end.)

I often borrowed crayons from my classmates. My drawings always had lots of empty space that needed to be colored unlike some of my rich classmates' drawings that had every corner filled and heavily colored. Compared to theirs, mine looked pitiful and pathetic. Some even used expensive Japanese brand crayons and the scent of those crayons was sweet and sophisticated.

I was not intimidated just because I was poor. I did well in school and I was even a class president one year. I had no qualms about borrowing my classmates' crayons. Some even bought me candies and doughnuts even though I didn't ask. My parents were poor, but poverty was not mine.

Once I was humiliated in my class because I didn't have the money to buy a new textbook. My math textbook was handed down from my cousin. Since the textbook was old, some parts were different from the new edition, so I was in danger of being humiliated at any time. Some of the math problems were completely different and in some only the numbers had been changed. I got in trouble because of the word "canteen."

"Let's see, whose turn is it to solve the problem? Can someone read problem number four out loud? OK, class president, stand up and read," said my teacher.

"All the fourth graders, two hundred and seventy students, went on a picnic. It was a hot day and everyone was thirsty. Not everyone had a *ppalbyŏng* so per canteen four students shared. What is the total number of canteens?"

Suddenly the teacher struck the desk with a ruler.

"What did I do? Did I make a mistake?" I thought to myself.

"What? *Ppalbyŏng*? What do you mean by that? Huh? Are you making fun of me? Answer me."

The teacher had a red lipstick on and her lips twitched like she was chewing a worm. The other children were curious as to what was to going to happen next and anticipated nervously. There were some who hid behind their books and giggled. I had no idea what was going on. Then all of a sudden a classmate sitting next to me took my textbook and said, "Teacher, teacher! This textbook is old. In this book, the word *ppalbyŏng* is written in the North Korean dialect, not in standard Korean."

Everyone burst out into laughter, but I wasn't embarrassed. I had no reason to because I was already immune to poverty. I scratched the back of my head and made a funny face, smiling at my classmates. When I sat down, my teacher screamed at me again.

"Who do you think you are, giggling like that?"

I still don't understand, even now, why my teacher was so angry. I don't even understand why the word "*ppalbyŏng*" was deleted from the textbook. Isn't it better to use the word *ppalbyŏng*? Why was it prohibited when the word *ppalbyŏng* was not associated with the color red? In any case, the word can only be found in dictionaries but is no longer used. Whenever I think of that word, its disappearance was not gradual and natural, but instead it was obliterated instantly.

The word *ppalyŏng* did not have any association with the color red (though the word *ppal* means red) so it had nothing to do with her red lipstick. Perhaps she was overly sensitive, and she thought I was making fun of her using dialect. Her red lipstick was always the target of our attention. It was natural for her to become sensitive about it since my classmates and I constantly talked about her red lipstick behind her back. And we didn't stop at that. We were so used to seeing teachers with Korean traditional tops and skirts with their bob hair and married teachers dressed in the chignon style. So how could we like her when she looked like a prostitute going to American soldiers in the airfield located across Han Stream? She wore a mini dress that was tight around her waist, permed hair, and red lipstick. On top of that her personality was so bad that she always took her frustrations out on us. We laughed at her, saying that she looked like a cat that just ate a rat.

She was from the mainland and lived in the mansion of the head prosecutor. We had no idea where her hometown was or whether she was the younger sister or the daughter of the head prosecutor. Since she was our homeroom teacher, even if there were things we didn't like about her, we had to grin and bear it. One time several of us went to her home, trying to please her. We bought twisted doughnuts with money we saved from our allowances. Well, I didn't contribute. They all knew I had no money, so they didn't expect me to.

Twisted doughnuts! How great they sounded! In those days what the children liked the most were red bean cakes, honey pancakes, and jawbreakers, but I liked twisted doughnuts the best. I wanted to eat them so badly that every time I passed by a vendor selling twisted doughnuts, I was utterly miserable because I realized there and then what poverty meant.

The twisted doughnut stall was surrounded by children all the time. There were more children watching than those actually buying. Pleasure was not only derived from eating them. Watching how the doughnuts were made was just as fun.

I liked it when a lump of white flour dough was in a huge bowl and was being kneaded. I liked the feel of the soft and white dough, but what was especially fun was the process whereby the shapeless dough turned into twisted doughnuts one after another at an unbelievable speed. He took a small amount of dough then stretched it out into a long string. Then it was twisted at each end in the opposite direction so it wrapped around itself to form the twisted shape. He threw it into a pot of hot oil and when it came out after taking a nice little bath, it turned golden brown. Lastly the tasty fried doughnut was nicely coated in sugar.

We took doughnuts to our homeroom teacher. We wanted to eat together and spend enjoyable time talking with her. The doughnuts were freshly made so they were steaming hot. We carefully carried the bag made out of newspaper thinking that it might break so we placed the bag inside a cap.

The doughnuts that we all liked very much turned into something shabby and powerless at my teacher's place. She did not even bother looking at the doughnuts and refused to even open the bag. She said, "Why don't you eat them?" In that situation, how could we possibly have any conversation? We sat on the floor by the entrance for a short while, and we got up and left. We were unhappy with the situation but those doughnuts tasted great. After we finished eating, we even ate the sugar that was left in the bag and licked the oil soaked bag, too. We came up with a conclusion that our homeroom teacher was a woman who ate rats but didn't appreciate the taste of doughnuts. Her red lips were known as "rat-devouring lips."

She only taught us for a few months. Through her, my classmates and I learned that there were people who were completely different from us. Perhaps what she expressed was hostility toward people who were not ashamed of being poor. I too belonged to a different world. Rather than feeling ashamed, I grew up feeling proud of being poor, as if it was a privilege.

*Classmates*

I remember a classmate who had the nickname Twisted Doughnut.

His parents owned a furniture store, so he often had doughnuts for snacks. But he was selfish and always ate them alone. His personality was all twisted, and that's why his nickname was Twisted Doughnut. Nicknames are difficult to get rid of once people start using them. He must have hated his nickname so much to cause such a commotion. It was the day when he was preparing for a kite fight. One of our classmates passing by him teased him by calling out his nickname when he was spreading glue over the string. He was so upset and angry that he poured glue all over the classmate's head. There was no time to do anything about it and the glue hardened. He was taken to a barbershop and had his hair cut off to get rid of the glue.

There were only a few students in my class who had enough money to buy snacks. Except for Twisted Doughnut, the others were nice and generous about sharing. I often sponged off of my classmates' lunch, but I wasn't embarrassed. I wasn't the only one because there were other poor kids who did the same. Was I a shameless brat acting proud and boasting of my poverty-stricken situation as a privilege of some sort? By thinking this way, I insulted those classmates who happily shared their lunch with me. They did not brag about the fact that they were better off than I was. However, if I had boasted of my poverty in front them, it was the same as inflicting violence upon them. After I graduated from high school, I went to the mainland and entered university with no money. I did not have money to pay for my room and board, so those classmates took turns in letting me stay at their places and shared their meals even though they were hated by their landlords.

Perhaps I wasn't embarrassed about being poor because of my thoughtful and generous friends. If they had not acknowledged me for who I was, I could not have overcome my circumstances of being poor and being raised by my mother alone.

All those classmates who helped me had fathers. They were a civil officer, a banker, a teacher, and a driver. One of them lived in a luxurious house with tiled walls. I thought maybe his pretty glass marbles came from those tiles, too.

I had to stay for afternoon classes when I became a fifth grader. My spending time at school increased so I hung out with my classmates more than my neighborhood friends. As a result Lefty and I gradually drifted apart.

*Candle and MP*

When I was in fifth grade, a letter and a shocking picture from father arrived after a long silence. Surprisingly my father was an MP Lieutenant, and he looked imposing in the picture. I only remembered my father as a sergeant, so it was a pleasant surprise. I was proud of my father. I showed the picture to all my friends because the picture was sure proof of his status.

One time my admirable MP Lieutenant father became the butt of everyone's jokes. It was my homeroom teacher's fault. My teacher always had on a pair of faded army pants and the students did not like him because of his militaristic style of teaching. When he yelled out or gave commands, one side of his mouth became terribly contorted, so his nickname was Warped Mouth. When he said "Attention!" one side of his mouth was twisted and when he said "At ease!" the opposite side. The way in which he opened his mouth widely, it looked as if he could even chew on his earlobes. What a sight! Before he became our homeroom teacher, we only cleaned the classroom with a wet mop but after we had to wax the floor with candlesticks and buff it with empty bottles to make it shine. When he delivered a new order what came out of his contorted mouth was not an "empty bottle" but an "old bottle" which meant MP in Korean. I started to hate him after that.

"Those who will bring candles raise your hand. OK. What about old bottles? Raise your hand. Anyway, you must bring either a candle or an old bottle. OK?"

I became the butt of my classmate's jokes.

"You are lucky! You have an old bottle at home. I only have an empty bottle."

"What?"

"You said your father was an MP. Ha! Ha! Ha!"

"Hey, are you making fun of me?"

I could not get angry because he did not mean any harm. Since I did not have an empty bottle at home, I had to borrow one from him so I was not in a position to get angry.

There were so many things I had to rely on from my classmates. I borrowed books from them. I even went to their homes to borrow reference books to do my homework or study for tests. I borrowed references like *Geography Digest* or *Biology Digest*, encyclopedias, and children's almanacs. I studied much better under the bright fluorescent light at my classmates' homes rather than under the dim oil lamp light at home. Thanks to my classmates I became fond of reading books.

*Blackie*

My classmates and I studied and hung out together. We went to the beach after school and wandered around with our school bags on our backs. We snooped around the main street near Kwandŏk Pavillion to see if we could find anything interesting. We went in and out of the police station where we could not dare go near before. It was around this time policemen were trying to curry favor with children, so they opened "Police School for Children" and handed out T-shirts for free and spent time with us for two or three days. It was a strategy on their part to encourage pacification. I took part in that program and received a free T-shirt that had "Police School for Children" printed on it.

One of the places we often visited was a judo gym in the police station compound. We sat by the door and watched them practice with judo uniforms on. We learned a few moves by watching and used them when we played the surrender game. During the Cheju Massacre the gym was used as a jail. This place was notorious for people dying either of severe torture or cholera. Every day three or four dead bodies were carried out. Since we knew about the place we felt a little uncomfortable. However, we weren't scared because we were already used to the place and knew the gym inside and out. I wonder if the past exists to be forgotten by us children. Five or six years had passed since the "the Cheju Massacre." Those crows, that we pointed fingers at as evil and monstrous, had returned to being ordinary birds. The black police uniform and enamel-brimmed hat that resembled an inauspicious crow and its beak were no longer the objects of fear.

There was another interesting attraction besides the judo gym. By the entrance to the building, there was a shoe repair man who sat pathetically in one corner. He was called Blackie. He was from my village. When the people from Nohyŏngri left their burning homes and were placed in the concentration camp at the beach, he pointed at and picked out villagers among the crowd, sending them to their deaths. He had his trapper hat on and pushed it deep down below his eyebrows and wore a mask to cover his face.

When I heard a rumor that the person who had a deadly finger gun, the one who pointed at and turned his own people in, was fixing shoes at the front gate of the police station, I was scared and nervous about seeing him. There was a group of us who went there and one of them was my cousin. I remember he was so scared that he could not go near him, so he hid behind me. My cousin lost his father, grandmother, and uncle on the same day during the Cheju Massacre.

The shoe repairman was called Kurombo meaning Blackie in

Japanese and his complexion just like his nickname was as dark as charcoal. He resembled a dark angel of the underworld. I could not believe that the notorious and ferocious Blackie had degenerated into a mere shoe repairman. Did he disguise himself as a shoe repairman to spy on people who went in and out of the police station? I was afraid that he would point his finger at me unexpectedly. He worked quietly and steadily at repairing shoes with his head down. Even when he was not working he did not raise his head. He only looked at people's shoes.

That was the fate of an informer. He was thrown out like a pair of old shoes when he was no longer useful. It was like telling him, "Since you worked hard to help us, you can make a living by repairing shoes at the entrance." That was all.

### Tearjerkers

I often went to places nearby the police station such as the post office, bank, and hospital. Watching the pretty young women working in those places was a source of entertainment for me and my friends. But the theater was the most fascinating place of all. There wasn't a place more attractive than the theater. I went in and out of other places for free but I could not get into the theatre without money.

The theatre was used as a place for social gathering. When a movie or a play was scheduled, I would walk over to the theatre without thinking. I snooped around the doughnut stall with the other kids with no money, and I did exactly the same in front of the theatre. I read books I borrowed from my classmates, but there was no way I could see a movie without money in my hand.

My mother had no money but she also did not believe in plays or movies. She did not even like it when I read novels. When I was in fourth grade, I was drawn to the world of fiction, the magical world that dominated and influenced me for the rest of my life. I mostly read western fables and children's stories that were translated into Korean from Japanese. The adventure and action stories like *The Count of Monte Cristo*, *The Adventures of Tom Sawyer*, *The Three Musketeers*, and *The Man in the Iron Mask* were fun to read, but I enjoyed tragic stories like "The Little Match Girl", "The Porter's Son", *The Little Prince*, *Uncle Tom's Cabin*, and "Enoch Arden". I could not read them without crying because of those tragic main characters. My mother hated it when she saw me crying reading books sprawled out on the floor. Since she firmly believed in realism, she didn't think much of fiction. To my mother my tears were cheap and worthless.

"Why are you crying? What's so sad? Your mother died or something? You're crying over nothing. I thought you were smart. I can't believe you're fooled by made-up stories and crying your eyes out. What a fool!"

I was weak and cried even at small things, so it was natural for my mother to worry about me crying over sad stories.

Talk about tragedy, these stories did not even come close to movies or plays. On movie posters, the following tag line often appeared: "You cannot watch this masterpiece without crying." Thinking back on it now, most of the lines from those tearjerkers were exaggerated, unsophisticated, awkward, serious, and tragic, but at the time they sounded wonderful and magical. I had to beg mother to let me go when there was a group school trip to the theatre. I was able to watch two or three times. Watching a movie was not simply watching, it was a powerful and moving experience. The main characters cried all the time but it was so realistic that everyone in the entire theatre cried with the characters. All the children and teachers cried, too. One of the movies I saw was entitled *Prosecutor and Teacher*. After I came home from the theatre, my mother asked me how the movie was. I replied, "It was great! It was so sad that everyone cried."

"Cry, why? You paid all that money to cry? Oh my . . ." said my mother.

"My teacher cried, too."

"Your teacher? That silly man. He should be ashamed of himself, crying over a movie. *Tut, tut!*" she clicked her tongue.

## Paris in England

After the tragic movies, western action movies were introduced. I was deeply engrossed in tearjerker tragedies, so western action movies were refreshing and it was an eye opening experience. I applauded endlessly at protagonists who had the super power and courage to fight their evil enemies. The exaggerated language used in tragic dramas was also found in action movies. Since they were silent films with no subtitles, it was necessary to bring a live movie narrator into the theatre. The narrator spoke in an exaggerated manner. We enjoyed the tearjerkers because they were fun and were real to us. (At the time it was rare to find plays, movies, pop songs, or anti-communism speech contests that were not exaggerated and tearjerkers.) We marveled at the narrator's ability to remember all the characters' lines and recite long lines without any problem. We often imitated the way the narrator spoke. When we ran into him on the street, we were excited and bowed as if we ran into a movie star.

Then we found out that this popular narrator was not as great as we thought, but an idiot instead. I did not see the movie in question, but it was a foreign film. The narrator made a mistake and said, "This is Paris in England." Although the students yelled out that he was wrong, the narrator continued in an unaffected way and said, "Paris was Paris." I heard that everyone burst out laughing. It was so ridiculous that for a while it was popular among us to recite the lines.

"This is Paris in England."

"Rubbish! How can Paris be in England?"

"Don't flies fly in England? *P'ari in Korean is a fly.*"

"Shit! Stop bluffing."

"But Paris was Paris."

*In Front of the Theatre*

I loitered around in front of the theater waiting for luck to fall into my lap. There were always many children who congregated in front of the theatre with no money to buy tickets. I could not give up just because I had no money. I made way for those children who held tickets in their hands, entering proudly. Then I waited patiently. I was more envious of those who entered for free than those who had paid. Some entered for free because they knew the doorman, and some walked arrogantly behind a policeman carrying a carbine gun who was on inspection duty.

By far, the best way of getting into the theatre was with the electrician. The electric problems were frequent at the time so he was treated especially well. Ordinarily he was regarded as a monkey climbing up telephone poles but in the theatre his position was up there equaling the policeman on inspection duty. He always took two or three children with him to the theatre. His commanding presence with a thick leather belt around his waist with various tools reminded me of a cowboy with guns holstered on both sides.

When the bell rang, signaling the starting of a film after the news and previews, I became anxious and tried desperately to find a way to enter, going round and round the building in the dark. There were some old planks that some zealous children shook and shook to loosen the nails. It was possible to crawl inside the theatre holding up one end of a loosened plank, but I needed to brace myself for getting a bloody nose when caught. One time one of the kids stuck his head inside the small opening and got his head kicked when he was caught. When the vigilance became severe, some even tried to enter through the hole in the restroom that was used by the people who cleaned out the excrement. Were they able to enter without dirtying their clothes?

We were quite determined. Nothing could stop us from trying, even the scary doorman who glared fiercely and yelled at us.

Even he knew how persistent we were, so he would allow a few of us to enter first, otherwise we would retaliate and vent our anger at him. We could tear apart the planks on the building walls or kick the boards or shake the emergency door to interrupt the movie and disappear into the darkness. There was nothing the doorman could do after we ran away. So the doorman reluctantly let five or six of us enter halfway through the movie. I was lucky and saw movies two or three times, but the movies I saw were like teasers, one half of a whole, similar to my friend biting a candy in half to share with me.

I was so desperate to see movies that I even thought of stealing money. My mother hid her purse inside a rice jar. One time my hand went inside the jar. I could still recall how desperate I was when I had my hand inside the jar searching for her purse. My heart beat incredibly fast and I heard voices, ringing in my ears. I thought the whole world was yelling at me. "What are you doing now? Why are you searching the rice jar? Just for fun? It feels great when you put your arm in the jar and stir, the way rice touches you, but that's not it, is it? You're looking for something. Unripe persimmons? So, you are looking for unripe persimmons buried in rice, huh? Didn't you eat them last time? Didn't you? Then what are you looking for? Why are you searching the rice jar? Why, why, why?"

I had to take out my hand empty. I had no idea how scary it was to steal my mother's money. When my hand touched the purse, I thought I was touching a burning coal. That's right. I could not betray my poverty-stricken mother.

*Beauty Is . . .*
My mother's sole concern was putting food on the table. Making a living was so immediate that going to the movies was unthinkable. There was no room for hobbies or enjoyment in her impoverished life. She liked singing but she sang not for pleasure in her

leisure time but when she was working. She only knew songs to ease hard labor or lullabies. She couldn't sing a weeding song if she did not have a spade in her hand. To sing a lullaby she had to be next to a baby's crib. If she had any kind of hobby, it was not something that could be separated from work but was integrated within it.

My mother chatted away with the neighbors when she was doing something with her hands. When she knitted, in particular, she chatted endlessly. Since there was no male adult at home, several neighbors came to knit together with my mother on the long winter nights. They talked endlessly, all night long like balls of yarn rolling. Their knitting speed went hand in hand with the speed of their speech. When they were talking about serious things their knitting speed slowed down, but when they were talking fast, their hands moved quickly, too.

Even when a neighbor came over to chat, my mother had a basket full of beans to separate from their pods. It was like a habit for her, working and talking. Threshing beans was usually done during fall harvest so I wondered why there were some that hadn't been threshed in wintertime. When she was in the kitchen cooking rice, she sat by the furnace to watch the fire while separating beans from pods. Not only beans but she also left some millet that needed threshing. At the time I didn't understand why she left a bit of millet when she could have easily threshed everything using a flail.

On sunny days in wintertime, she sat on the millet straw mat in the sunny spot and cut millet ears with a sickle and threshed them by beating them with a club. She never used a flail. In fact, she never had enough millet to use the flail. It was not hard labor but it was enough to keep her busy to get her mind off of other things. For her, free time was something unfamiliar and even fearful. She couldn't relax when she had nothing in her hand. She said, "I know I should be able to relax when I have nothing to do, but if I don't keep myself occupied, I'll be overwhelmed by all sorts of unnecessary thoughts that I'll end up getting sick." I'm using my mother as an example to talk about women in general at the time.

My mother only knew how to live to make ends meet. To her the idea of beauty was insignificant. It existed only when it was in the realm of the practical. Mother did not understand the concept of the aesthetics—beauty that was removed further away from practical everyday life was closer to purity. The only accessory she possessed was a silver hair pin she used when she put her hair in a bun. She put a little bit of camellia oil on her hair when she went out. The accessories were an important part of cultured life. My mother was an old-fashioned person living in the modern era. Calling her old-fashioned might be an overstatement. Perhaps it was more appropriate to call my mother, who worked hard to make a living together with the other victims in the midst of burnt down ruins where only stones were left, a farmer of the New Stone Age.

My mother's idea of beauty was like this. If I said, "That's beautiful!" looking at the red sky in the morning, my mother would exclaim, "Damn! The sky's reddish. It might rain! I was going to go to the field." And she would sigh repeatedly. When I said, "Mom, look! It's so beautiful. It's like all the stars from the sky have fallen," looking at the sparkling fishing boats floating in the ocean. My mother would say flatly, "Stars, what stars? Those are fishing boats." I might be exaggerating here. It was natural for my mother to worry about the bad weather when looking at the sunrise, since she was busy tilling the field. If she sat outside the house on a mat on summer nights leisurely looking at the fishing boat lights, why wouldn't she think they were beautiful? Trying to understand her from the present point of view, one thing comes to mind. Perhaps she reacted negatively to the word "beautiful." In Cheju dialect, there is a word for nice but not beautiful or lovely. I was used to speaking in standard Korean so I must have used the word beautiful rather than nice. Did that get on her nerves?

Even beautiful flowers meant nothing to my mother if they bore no fruit. One night I heard my mother outside the backyard, so I thought she was scolding my sister. When I looked out to see what was going on, she was rebuking pumpkin vines. She pretended to hit the pumpkin flowers with an iron poker.

"What's your job, huh? I asked you for many pumpkins but look at you, you've only produced flowers. You can't possibly forget! You're out of your mind."

My mother said if the pumpkins forgot, she needed to remind them in that manner. It was her way of making sure to get more pumpkins.

Her way of thinking did not change at all even after difficult times had passed and her life became comfortable. When I introduced my girlfriend to her as someone I wanted to marry, her sarcastic comment on her fragile physique was a masterpiece. She said, "Oh my! I don't think she can even carry a water bucket."

*Father*

My mother sighed often after my brother was born. She had a lot of work to do so finding the time to feed him was not easy. She was never free from work. Even when she had beriberi she went to work in the field dragging her swollen feet. She was so tired that she took a nap on the side of the furrow. I could picture even now how she covered her face with a towel, lying on the ground.

"There's no news of my husband since he went off to the battlefield. And how am I going to feed these little ones? No matter how hard I try, things just don't get any better," said my mother.

"What can you do? That's life," replied my aunt.

I heard similar conversations between my mother and my

aunt over and over again when I was young. The only way my aunt comforted my mother was by saying, "That's life."

My mother sighed before she started a conversation. It was like a habit. Even in happy times, she sighed first. She did not easily indulge herself in happiness. She was suspicious of any danger that could be lurking behind happiness. When I brought home an honors award she hid her happiness behind her sigh. Every time she sighed like that I felt helpless.

"If you weren't so smart, I wouldn't need to worry . . ."

At one point my mother thought of sending me to my relative's tailor shop as an apprentice after I finished elementary school.

"Without your father here, how can I possibly send you to school? Even if you study a lot, it doesn't mean you'll be well off. Look at him. His shop is doing well. Learning a skill is the best. You know all those educated people were the first to die during the massacre. Your father graduated from agricultural school . . . It's not good to be ignorant but too much education can bring unhappiness. You need just enough education to be able to write a ritual prayer for your ancestor worship ceremony."

She repeated these words, trying to persuade me to give up on studying. After I began receiving awards she stopped saying about becoming an apprentice at the tailor shop. Her sighs became more frequent, though. She mumbled, "Your father's gone and I have no money . . ."

Strangely there was no news of my father since the last letter and the picture of him in his first lieutenant insignia. My mother, my sister, and I sent several letters to him pleading for him to write back, but every time it turned out to have disappeared into thin air, because there was no reply from him.

Every time I dropped a letter in the postbox, I was seized by fear, fear that I dropped the letter by mistake into a deep abyss; my heart sank. I remember a similar feeling when I had my first baby tooth pulled out. My mother tied a string around my tooth and pulled it out. She held on to the tooth and chanted, "Go away old tooth, bring a new one." After she finished chanting, she threw it on the roof, and at the time, I felt completely at a loss and wanted to cry. I snuck my tongue to feel it and the tip of my tongue constantly went in and out between the teeth. I wasn't sure whether a crow would take the old tooth and return with a new one. Crows were known to be forgetful so I started to worry. What if a crow forgets? The day that I felt a new tooth coming out feeling it with my tongue, I was elated and felt relieved.

Still there was no reply from father.

*Mother's Bosom*

My mother stood at the mouth of a dreadful famine with three children to feed by her side. She was determined to go through the hardship. Her loneliness deepened with my father's long absence. In their ten year marriage, she spent less than ten months with my father. She brought a blanket to share with my father when she got married, but it had remained in the closet for years.

My mother did not completely lose her youth and beauty to poverty and loneliness. Her beauty did not surface ordinarily but was hidden underneath her work clothes. She was tanned, but her beautiful face was hidden under a towel that was wrapped around her head.

At the end of the day, she took off the towel she wore all day long. I remember clearly a streak of whiteness where her hair was parted. It contrasted drastically from her tanned face, so the white line looked unfamiliar and awkward. Not only her face was tanned but her neck, hands, legs, and every part of her body that had been exposed to the sun was dark. Her work clothes were a brownish color, so she was completely brown except where her hair was parted. The whiteness that seemed foreign was her natural color that was hidden underneath. Her tanned faced turned lighter during winter as if dark clouds had been lifted off the moon.

She took off the towel and dusted off her clothes and washed her upper body before breastfeeding my brother. Her inner skin was white. It was an unbelievably milky white. I helped her pour water on her back and her skin was bright white. The softness I felt when I rubbed her back was like a beautiful riddle I could not solve as a child. I saw veins showing through her milky white breasts when she held my brother after she finished washing. She stared at my brother smiling warmly, full of affection, and then she sighed.

The only time I could see my mother smile for a long time was when she was breastfeeding. Watching her breastfeed was such a lovely sight. When she revealed her breasts hidden under her unlined summer top, like two well-ripened large peaches from a basket, my brother immediately stopped crying and greedily sucked on them.

The happiest moment was when my mother returned home after finishing the day's work and smiled happily breastfeeding my adorable brother. My brother kicked his legs while sucking, expressing his happiness. My sister and I touched and played with my brother's plump legs. Was there something more melodious than a child sucking on a mother's breast? *Gulp, gulp*! Listening to my brother was as gratifying as if I was the one drinking my mother's breast milk. My mother's milk was passed down to my brother to fatten him up. I enjoyed touching my brother's plump legs because I was able to experience vicariously my mother's breast milk, which I was weaned off of ten years ago.

One day my mother's milky breast was painted in black ink. After six months, my brother's two front teeth came out. My brother had to be weaned early just like me and my sister. How could a baby from a poor family have the luxury to be breastfed for a long time? My mother was always busy, so breastfeeding was not easy for her. Her ink painted breast was hideous to look at, even to me. My brother whined for days as if someone spoiled his food, trying to suck and spitting out again and again.

After he was weaned and started eating rice, he cried if he was not fed right on time. He was fed white rice after he was weaned. I was jealous. The only time I could have a bowl of rice was on special occasions such as ancestral worship and New Year's. The sweet taste of rice simply melted in my mouth. When feeding him, my mother told me to place a little bit of rice on a spoon, softening it first. But then I would end up swallowing half of it. My brother cried every time I ate his rice.

My brother was exceptionally protective of his own food. He screamed and cried. At times he cried so hard that his faced turned pale as if he was gasping for his last breath. He was just like how I was when I was a baby. My brother cried so hard with his mouth wide open that I could see his uvula. He looked like a baby magpie inside a nest wanting food with his yellowish mouth opened widely covering his entire face. And he cried so loudly, with all his strength, that I thought my eardrums were going to rip to pieces. Listening to his loud cries that came out of his tiny little body, I was reminded of a cicada's loud droning sound that came out of its small frame. What other means were available for a helpless baby who was still soft like a lump of dough to communicate other than crying? No crying meant no food.

*Lullaby*

My brother got cranky at bed time. I used to get angry whenever I put him in the crib, rocking him to sleep. I was not good at singing, so I sang clumsily all out of tune while swinging the crib back and forth to the rhythm of a lullaby. My brother would not fall asleep easily. He continued to whine and whimper. I became impatient and shook the crib recklessly and he fell out; this happened many times. My brother did not like the way I rocked the crib because when my mother did it he soon became quiet.

When he was fussy and whiny for a long time, my mother sang the lullaby in a scolding tone, rocking the crib in a rough manner.

> *Go to sleep, go to sleep*
> *Fall asleep fast, fall asleep fast*
> *I need to prepare dinner, my dear child*
>   *you don't know how busy I am*
> *My dear child, go to sleep, go to sleep*

After the crib had been rocked vigorously like a boat caught in a violent storm, my brother gradually became quiet and my mother's lullaby softened, too. It was a sad lullaby, but it was soft and tender, stroking the sadness gently. I felt comforted by my mother's lullaby, too. The crib swung back and forth softly like a small sailboat gliding quietly along the gentle waves. When my brother was peacefully led to dreamland riding on that boat, I felt like I was on that boat too and was drifting somewhere far away in the ocean toward the origin of existence. I was recalling my own experience as a baby listening to the lullaby that was imbued with sadness.

The crib was mine, and my sister Yŏngnyŏ grew up in the same crib as well. A crib which my older brother—who only lived for five months—used was not passed down to me. The dead baby's crib was not supposed to be handed down so it was left upside down on his grave. I saw small baby graves with cribs on top when I passed by the fields. I heard that on rainy nights, a sad lullaby was heard from the grave.

My father was quite shaken when the first born died. Perhaps his grief was so great that he was reluctant to show any affection toward me. He was afraid to lose another child after pouring out all his love. My mother was worried that her grief and misfortune might reach the baby in the crib. That must be why my mother's lullaby always had a tinge of sadness. The mortality rate was high in those days—small pox, measles and even a cold took children's lives. People had nowhere to turn to except the birth god "Sanshin" or grandmother Sanshin. She was in charge of granting children and protecting newborns. Every child born was her grandchild.

> *Benevolent grandmother, please let my child fall asleep*
> *Let my child have sweet milk and sleep;*
> > *let my child have sweet rice and grow*
> *There's nothing you can't do*
> *This is your grandchild, please take care of him*
> *My dear child is precious like a jade rock under the water*
> *My dear child is soft like a swallow's feather*
> *Let him grow like a cucumber; let him grow like a melon*
> *Go to sleep, go to sleep*

When my mother gave birth to my little brother, I was there. The door of her room was wide open, as was every other door in the house, even the drawers, pot lids, and crockpots. After opening every possible door to invite him in, we waited for the baby, but there was no sign of him. The floor was covered in barley straw and my mother was lying on top of it with her skirt on with no underwear. She resembled an injured animal. She held a rolled up blanket and twisted her body, screaming and writhing in pain. Her contorted face was covered in sweat. Next to her, my grandmother urged her to give another push. My grandmother's voice was shaky and she seemed extremely nervous. I was scared and trembled, watching my mother in such agony. It was an endless moment of stifling tension.

At that precise moment of life or death, the birth god Sanshin was the only thing to rely on. Sanshin granted the fetus; when the baby was filled with father's white blood for three months and ten days and mother's black blood for three months and ten days and waited for nine to ten months, Sanshin added bones using her silvery hands and let the baby out into the world opening the birth door.

The thing that made me realize the secret of birth was not the Sanshin myth, but the smell of blood at the very moment my mother delivered the baby with a loud scream. My mother's dreadful suffering, the newborn baby on the barley straw, and the raw smell of blood were the secrets of my birth as well.

*One Ear*

Sanshin's job was not only delivering babies but watching over them after they were born. She was not visible to people but she sat next to the babies' cribs to ward off diseases. Everyone was her grandchild until fifteen years of age. I almost died of a high fever when I was in fifth grade, but luckily I lived. I barely escaped death because the birth grandmother protected me.

I was running a high fever and was unconscious for four days. I cried because of an unbearable pain in both ears. The only medication I was given was a drop of badger oil inside my ears. The high fever that completely took control over and assaulted my body disappeared miraculously after four days. My ears were infected but the burning fever was gone completely.

The scar left by the fever was found after a few days had passed. I felt different than before but did not know. My mother found out before I did. One day she was angry and yelled at me.

"What are you doing? Pretending not to hear me? You did it to me before."

"Huh, did you say something? I didn't hear a thing," I replied.

"Did you stick a donkey's penis in your ear? You couldn't even hear what I said? I'm talking right into your ear? I said it three times."

"Really? I didn't hear a thing."

"What? Do you . . . ?"

I was lost and did not know what was going on. My mother grabbed me by the ear and said some things into one ear and turned me around to the other side of the ear and said some more things. Then she held me in her arms and wailed.

I completely lost the hearing in my left ear. The high fever damaged the nerve system. It just tells you how high the fever was, and how serious was the danger I had been in. If the fever had lasted longer, I would have lost my life or lost hearing in both of my ears. My grandmother and mother said I was lucky that the birth grandmother helped me at such a crucial moment.

I became deaf in one ear and lost my sense of direction, so it took me a while to get used to the change. A simple analogy would be that one side of my audio system was broken so it turned into mono from stereo. I could not tell where the sound was coming from so when someone yelled out, I had to turn around in a circle to check. I could not hear at all in my left ear so I had to put my hand over my right ear and twisted my neck to face the direction where the sound came from.

Since I could only hear from my right side, I felt like I was overworking that ear to the point where it felt bigger and heavier with all the blood rushing to it. I even had a dream that my right ear grew as big as the palm of my hand. If Lefty was worried about his ear getting stretched out because he often had his ear pulled by his mother and was dragged home while playing outside, I was concerned that my left ear would shrink while my right ear would grow really big. I became overly sensitive about not understanding people correctly. I got into trouble many times because I didn't quite understand what was said so I ended up answering incorrectly or acting completely off the wall.

In school, I marched following the Warped Mouth teacher's command, but I did exactly the opposite of what he said. When he said turn left and march, I turned right and marched; when he said turn right, I turned left and marched, so I kept stepping out of line. I was punished for not following his orders and this experience left a bitter aftertaste.

I was hypersensitive about my hearing loss, so for a while I suffered from incontinence. I peed in my pants without realizing what I was doing, and the crotch area of my pants was stained with urine. My bladder felt full even when it was not, so I felt uncomfortable. I saw pigs getting slaughtered many times so I knew anatomically what my bladder looked like. When intestines were taken out of a pig's stomach, its fresh bladder emerged along side. I felt like my bladder had turned into a pig's bladder my friends and I kicked around for fun. When we kicked the pig's bladder, we sang, "Pee! Poo! You foolish thing!"

Something was wrong with my bladder. What went wrong? I was in a foul mood because I peed here and there without realizing it, especially when I stood up or laughed. So I had no choice but to wear a diaper. It was so pathetic, an eleven year old borrowing a year old younger brother's diapers. I could not even laugh hard because I was afraid I would pee in my pants. It was natural for me to suffer from depression. I lost hearing in one ear and became tone deaf and on top of that I was suffering from incontinence, so I became more depressed.

Later I was able to get by with just one ear because I got used to it. But I think my chronic depression and timidity developed when I lost the hearing in one ear.

*Winter*

That winter I lost my hearing everything was unusually dark and gloomy. A good harvest was expected but it turned out just the opposite; everyone was depressed. My grandmother said you couldn't be certain about rice until it was actually in the pot cooking. The heads of millet, turning golden brown, were listlessly hung like tongues hanging out in the sun. The savory smell of grain maturing attracted insects and a flock of swallows chased away the insects. That peaceful and abundant field lay devastated after a storm swept through the area. What we gathered was barely half of the yield. With only three months worth of food, we had to endure half a year; it was the beginning of famine. A flock of swallows perched on the electric poles creating musical scores, chirping and singing, and after they sang a farewell song, they left for the south all at once. After they left, the dreary winter wind from the north rushed down, bouncing off the power lines.

We had to be frugal with food and so that winter seemed colder than usual because of hunger. The biting cold weather was unbearable for me. My mother and grandparents said, "This weather could even skin a cow," commenting on the sharp cold wind. As winter advanced the violent wind blew as if it was ready to blow away the entire sky. The clouds were moving quickly chased away by the strong wind, and the air was filled with the dismal sounds of power lines bouncing in the wind and the trees and plants swaying. Especially the sound of tidal waves made an ominous pulsating noise.

It rarely snowed heavily in my town, instead just sleet or snow flurries fell. Swept away in strong winds, sleet floated to the surface of the earth like raging currents spewing white foam. I had frostbite, walking on cold, wet, and muddy ground in my worn out shoes. My hands were numb so I couldn't button my shirt. There were days when the weather was moderate, but I was in pain because my frostbitten toes were unbearably itchy. I did not feel it when I was running around, but during class, my toes were so itchy that I rubbed my feet against the foot of my desk. I could not pay attention to what the teacher was saying.

It was that same winter I tried selling newspapers for a month to help out. The biting cold wind at dusk was truly unbearable. To protect myself from the penetrating wind, I put several newspapers underneath my clothes. I rubbed my hands against a warm stone my mother placed in my pocket and sold the papers on the street. I yelled out, "Tomorrow's *Cheju Daily!*" When there was a head wind, I walked right behind a pedestrian on the street. One time I encountered an absurd situation. All of a sudden, the man who was walking in front of me stopped and started talking to me.

"You must be cold. Can I buy you a honey pancake? It's nice and warm."

He spoke in an unfamiliar mainland dialect. The man walked toward me waving a bag of pancakes. He reeked of alcohol. And what was it that came out of his dirty mouth?

"Since you sell newspapers here, you must know your way around, right? Tell me where I can find girls. If you tell me, I'll give you these pancakes."

I was dumbfounded and scared. I had no idea where those girls were but I vaguely knew what kind of place it was.

*Embers*

I was extremely sensitive to cold and what comforted me was not the warmth of fire but love. Love is similar to a heated stone, a charcoal fire in a brazier, a humble yet sincere love, a feeling of relief when my mother wrapped the warm cinder iron in a cloth and soothed the itchy frostbitten toes; it was a cool and refreshing feeling. I wanted to go to the toilet at night but I was afraid that my butt would freeze in the cold so I hesitated. At that moment, I realized the value of the warmth provided by the small brazier.

The brazier was tinged with the color red similar to my dirt marbles that were baked in the kitchen furnace. To feel the heat from tiny embers, three people's hands were gathered around the brazier like a Pao tent used by Mongol nomads. What about my baby brother? He was sleeping on the warmest part of the floor in the room. I often held a reading book in one hand and the other hand over the fire. On those nights, my mother knitted. My sister Yŏngnyŏ learned how to knit from my mother and she knitted, too. My mother had her head down and right in the middle where her hair was parted was white, she had several knitting needles stuck in her hair. I can remember the savory rice cakes that were nicely roasted in the fire that had a bit of a charcoal taste. My mother saved her portion of rice cake brought by a neighbor, and she toasted it in the brazier and gave it to us.

When the night deepened, I crawled under the blanket but it was unbearably cold. My mother saw that my sister and I hesitated to go under the blanket, so she went in first to warm the bedding. My sister and I laid down by my mother's feet and she was holding my baby brother. My mother's feet served as a border line separating my sister and me. When I curled up in the cold bed, my mother pulled my legs, straightening them out, and softly caressed them. "My child, straighten out your legs. If you sleep curled up like this, you'll become poor and unlucky."

Before going to bed, my mother buried the burning charcoal in ashes and covered it well with an iron rod. In the morning, when I dug around I found embers that were still burning, and they were like melted red candies. If the embers were thrown in the kitchen furnace, they turned into a blaze. We had a box of matches but it was precious so we rarely used it, instead we treasured it by the baby's crib.

Using the embers left in the brazier to make the kitchen fire was the method used by our ancestors. The fire that never died out from my ancestors' time had been passed down for generations, the invincible fire. When our family moved, the fire was placed it in an earthenware container and brought with us. It also meant life. Later, when I had my first child, my grandmother passed away; at that time my father hardened the grave by pounding on it with a tree trunk and sang, "Life, life, we are here to pass down the life of fire." He sang the song sadly while pounding on the ground.

It was such a joy to see a small spark turning into a big flame, burning vigorously. For someone who was sensitive to cold, it was a hearty pleasure. The warmth of the kitchen furnace was pleasant and the smell of wood burning was great. I tried to inhale the smell thinking that it had a nutritional value. There is a proverb saying that a beggar gets fattened by fire. Crouching in front of the kitchen furnace, warming myself and smelling the wood burning, I felt like my body was rising like bread, turning golden brown. During wintertime, I volunteered to sit in front of the furnace to watch rice cooking in the pot. After my mother placed cleaned rice in the pot and went out to get water, I sat in front of the fire, absorbed in imagination looking at the dancing flames.

During winter, millet straws or beanstalks were usually used as firewood. The beanstalks were easier to manage than the millet straws when they were thrown in the furnace. The millet straws burnt and spread quickly and overflowed outside the furnace, but the beanstalks burnt evenly and remained contain within. When the fire stuck its tongue out rapidly to devour all the beanstalks, it sort of resembled a horse eating fodder.

I pushed in more beanstalks into the furnace a little at a time. The savory smell of beanstalks burning was really nice. I checked to see if there were any bean pods left. The fire liked the beanstalks just like a horse. I controlled the flames with a poker. The fire swallowed everything I pushed into the furnace. If I fed too much, I hit the stalks with the iron poker to make it eat less. I made sure it swallowed the dampened stalks, too. I had to use the fire poker to entice the fire to swallow the dampened ones. However, if I did not pay close attention it became dangerous like that time I almost got my hand bitten by a horse feeding hay. I saw a bean pod inside the fire, so I quickly took it out with the iron poker. "Hey! You can't have it. I need to eat it myself."

Inside the pod, there were three yellow beans. They were pretty like three siblings, but they were so mischievous. One time I wanted to help my mother thresh beans so I had a flail in my hand and stood before my mother. Oh, boy! I had a hard time because of those aggressive beans! Beans popped everywhere every time my mother threshed with a flail—the beans kept flying, hitting my face. I couldn't even open my eyes because of the dust and I swung the flail the wrong way so I ended up hitting myself. My mother laughed when she saw me and said, "See! You need to move your arms. Don't keep your arms close to your sides as if you have eggs hidden under them." After the threshing was done, I had to gather all the beans and pile them in the middle of the courtyard. I felt good walking over the beans as if they were tickling me but then I slipped and fell on my butt, too. Even after I finished sweeping the floor, some beans were stuck in the cracks and did not want to come out. By the time I picked out each one of them with my hand, the holes left on the floor resembled a pockmarked face. The beans were like mischievous children.

Every time I pushed a bundle of beanstalks inside the furnace I checked to see if there were any bean pods left. I mumbled, "Are those beans shelled or not shelled?" and burst out into laughter. It was funny. If I said it slowly, it was fine, but if I tried to say it really fast it was like a tongue twister. Even if you speak normally, once you start this tongue twister, you say it with a twang and you become a half stutterer. This tongue twister was even in the Korean language textbook because it was difficult to pronounce. During our class, everyone laughed saying it over and over again. I often stammered even in everyday speech. Normally I was fine but when I became upset I stuttered. I had to try not to get upset.

After the fire had been burning for a while, the white foam

started to rise from the pot and my body was so completely wrapped in the warmth that I became lethargic. The bottom of the iron pot was well heated and around the area where it was covered in soot tiny embers glowed. The iron pot bottom looked like a naked butt. Due to the warmth of the furnace, my crotch area felt so wonderfully warm that my scrotum relaxed nicely. The tip of my penis slowly wriggled. I felt ticklish. I knew exactly what the red sparks at the tip of the iron poker resembled. I shoved the red tip of the iron poker into the bottom of the pot. The embers that were stuck on the iron pot bottom fell like sparkling gold dust. Then I stuck the iron pot inside the ashes to kill the embers. I felt so great that I wet my pants a little. I wondered if my bladder had expanded because of the warmth.

I remember clearly that I peed in my pants while sitting in front of the furnace. I think it was the same winter I started suffering from incontinence.

*Lefty*

It was that same winter my family followed my maternal grandfather and moved to the opposite side of Han Stream to Chŏngdŭrŭ Village.

Not long after that my friend Lefty moved, too. Lefty is the first person that comes to mind whenever I remember the old days from my neighborhood. He climbed the tree so well that his other nickname was Monkey. I still remember vividly that he climbed a flagpole to fix a pinwheel during the morning assembly. The way in which he saluted the flag after fixing the pinwheel looked admirable. For five years we lived in the same neighborhood and shared precious moments as I started opening my eyes to the world. He was like an older brother to me since he was a year older and because he was clever and was better than me in every aspect. One thing he did not excel in was studying and later this became a problem. After reaching certain stages of friendship, whether your friend was smart or not entered into the equation and posed a problem. When grades became important, I mostly hung out with my classmates who did well in school and I neglected Lefty. One of the traits of children is their thoughtlessness or cruelty. I needed a rival in studying since I was poor and had nothing else other than school.

How could I not know that Lefty had moved to the countryside? I was beyond inconsiderate. When his brother died, his family sold the blacksmith shop and moved to the country. Before he left, he did not even say goodbye. It was after I had moved to Chŏngdŭrŭ but we were still going to the same school, so if he wanted to, he could have stopped by my classroom. Perhaps his disappointment was so great that he did not want to say goodbye before leaving. It was my fault that our friendship ended like that. Thinking back on it now I feel embarrassed about how we parted without saying goodbye to each other.

Next to the blacksmith shop, there was an empty space covered in weeds, rusted iron scraps, and scrap metals strewn about in the snow. I have this cold winter image in my memory and I wonder if that was the same winter when Lefty and I left Pyŏngmun Stream.

*Chŏngdŭrŭ Village*

My family followed my maternal grandfather and moved to Chŏngdŭrŭ, which was located on the east side of the Han Stream on the flat land by the hillside. The two beautiful scenic spots, Yonyŏn and Yongduam were situated at the bottom of the hill. My aunt and her three children decided to live with my grandparents, so we moved out and rented a room close-by. Since we lived far away from the city, the rent was cheaper. My grandparents' new house had a pretty big backyard, so we built a small place of our own in that yard two years later.

Chŏngdŭrŭ was located between the Han Stream and the

airport. Those people who lost their homes and land for the airport development during the Japanese colonial rule returned after liberation and settled down. There were many who rented rooms like us—those people who decided not to return to their hometown and stayed after the Cheju Massacre, junior and high school student boarders from the country, young women going to a beauty or dressmaking school, young teachers and people working for a company. Every morning there was a long and busy procession of people going to school or work toward the city. Children of my age went to the same school so we were familiar with each other.

I can recall the days I went to school in the biting cold weather, where the rocks and stones crouched underneath the dried up stream, in the middle of winter. Unlike my old hometown in Pyŏngmun Stream where many houses were clustered together among cozy alleyways, Chŏngdŭrŭ was bare, a large open space harassed by strong winds. The road was situated at the top of the steep hill on the other side of Han Stream which led to Purŏri Hill, looking over the ocean. The area was covered with fields so gusts of wind blew all the time. My face was covered in dirt walking down this road in winter and when it snowed it was a blizzard. Even after the snow had stopped falling, the strong wind blew the snowflakes to rise from the ground again creating this blizzard.

Watching the blizzard of the north wind made me think that the snow did not actually fall down from the sky but came from the ocean. The tidal waves attacked the mouth of the river and the sound bouncing off the rock walls of Yongduam reverberated. The calm and quiet water of Yongyŏn undulated violently as if it were flowing backward pushed by the strong wind. The blizzard followed accompanied by the wind, and the snowflakes landed on the trees, the stone walls, and the piles of leaves and stuck like a white dough. Sometimes even before the snowflakes had a chance to land on the ground, the wind blew the snowflakes over to the ditch or into the furrows. When the snow in the barley field furrow or on the road was swept away by the wind, the furrow looked like it was running rhythmically after the wind and the silver grass on the road side swayed back and forth like a pack of weasels dashing with their tails in their mouths. I walked between the furrows following a trail and led my grandfather's horse to Yongyŏn. I wore his hand-knitted hat that covered my entire head except my eyes. The hat was saturated with my grandfather's smell, that musty, stale cigarette smell.

The biting cold wind felt like it had a sharp blade ready to cut off people's ears. To go to school, every single child in Chŏngdŭrŭ, myself included, walked on the ground that was wet and muddy from the melting snow. Our cheeks turned red because of the wind, and we suffered from frostbite all winter long. When the weather finally became warm, our frostbitten toes were so itchy that we rubbed our feet on the desk leg and the rubbing sound reverberated throughout the classroom. I knew when the creaking sound became louder, it was a sure sign that spring has arrived.

Do you know what snail clover is? It is very similar to a four leaf clover. Even now I am happy when I find snail clovers nearby Yongyŏn and Yongduam in winter. The snail clovers are woven together, stuck firmly to the ground, to withstand the strong wind. During a severe shortage of food, the snail clovers served as food for hungry people who were tenacious and full of vitality preparing for the coming winter months. One of the first things people pulled out to eat before other new buds sprouted was snail clovers during a spring famine.

That spring I was in sixth grade, and the shortage of food was serious due to another bad harvest. The barley did not even grow an inch, but my family had already run out of food so my mother boiled snail clovers and we ate them. For two months, until barley was fully grown, both people and animals ate the same food. We ate the barley husks usually fed to pigs and we even ate weeds and wild vegetables that the horses and cows normally ate. We ate mugworts, pigweeds, burr clovers, wild spinach, and more. I ate so many wild vegetables I thought my breath smelled like grass. There is no point going over what it was like to go hungry for days since I already talked about it a lot.

That spring, rallies against the truce were held often, mobilizing students who were suffering from hunger. Even elementary school students participated in the rally. It was led by high school students who had on army uniforms and they swung batons. I was scared because they looked as if they were about to strike anyone. I ran frantically screaming and shouting, "Let's go up to the North and unify!" Everyone yelled out, "No unification, give us death!" Disabled ex-servicemen participated in the rally, too, swinging their crutches. Was not the rally demanding more deaths and sacrifices from the soldiers on the battlefront? Was it not a merciless rally? My father was fighting in the war, too.

One time, a neighbor was so shocked by the rally that she exploded. She was in her twenties and was nervously waiting for her husband to return safely from the war. She was very pretty but she was an illiterate so I had to read and write letters for her. She was not talkative so she reminded me of a beautiful doll. But she went mad when the rally took place demanding the truce to be abandoned. She was as quiet as a mouse but she went crazy. She demolished her own stone walls and screamed, "Murderer! Killing innocent people!" hurling curses and protesting. I also saw a drunken and injured soldier on the ground, with his crutches thrown away, yelling and asking for poison. Those people with money and connections all ended up in the rear and the ones who were dying on the frontline were all those poor people with no money or connections. The word "connection" in Korean means "back," so people imitated the way those soldiers dying screamed "Back!" It was cynical humor which was popular at the time.

I even stole food during the famine. Several huge milk powder cans which had been received as relief goods were placed by the door of the teacher's room. I was frustrated that the milk powder was not distributed quickly enough, so my classmates and I decided to open one. We secretly opened the can and ate it, coughing and choking, but we got caught and were punished. Another time, I went to one of my relatives to run an errand. No one was home so I went into the kitchen and searched for food and found a bowl of cold rice in the cupboard. I was so hungry that I felt no shame. To this day, I am not embarrassed nor do I feel ashamed of what I did.

I wished for the barley to grow fast so that I could eat to my heart's content. Every time I had a dream, it was about food. When it was time for barley to come into ear, the smell of the barley was sweet, glittering in the morning sun, moistened by dew. I remember vividly when the barley turned golden brown and undulated like the golden waves in the wind; the savory smell remained in my memory in close connection with hunger. After the barley was harvested and was hulled in a mortar, a fragrant smell together with warmth hung in the air.

Fortunately the barley harvest was good that year. The barley crop was bountiful and there was an abundance of mackerel but not enough salt to sprinkle on the fish, meaning piles and piles of fish were left rotting away to be used as fertilizer. The stench of leaking rotten mackerels, their fluids dripping endlessly from the carts transporting the mackerel compost, hung heavy in the air. And it was unbearable! I remember the adults saying the foul odor resembled rotting corpses, recalling all those dead bodies during the massacre. They plugged their noses and shuddered violently.

The "season of death" finally came to an end. That summer, the barley harvest was great. What was even greater and more delightful was the news of the truce. The ceasefire was declared and peace came at last. To prove the news was true, the sound of machine guns firing ceased as well. The pier was crowded with refugees returning to the mainland and those boats carrying refugees left the island blowing their whistles loudly. The number of fishing boats and freight ships increased dramatically, and a flock of seagulls that had disappeared without a trace returned to recreate the scenery of the good old harbor days. On the west pier the seagulls flocked around the rotten mackerels like a white sheet spread out. I swam over to a boat floating in the middle of the pier and got one or two mackerels for free.

I anticipated my father's imminent arrival.

*Farting*

During a good barley harvest, farting was abundant, too. What could be more joyful than eating a lot of barley rice to make up for those times I went hungry and then farting away? Barley made me fart a lot. My maternal grandfather slightly lifted one side of his leg when sitting down and farted. Then he laughed out loud and my grandmother, waving her hand, said "Shame on you!" Farting was not something to be ashamed of in those days when food was so scarce, actually it was something to be proud of. We called pretentious people "fart heads."

My friends and I liked to play pranks on each other. When I was about to fart, I didn't waste it but had my butt in front of my friend's face and passed gas. Then I ran for my life. If I aimed it right and farted while swimming, fart bubbles carrying a bad smell floated to the surface and popped under the targeted person's nose. My fart was not powerful at all. It stunk so much that my friends hated me for it, but it did not make a loud popping noise. I wonder if my fart was weak because I was not physically strong. My tough and strong friends farted loudly. I was envious of my friends' rhythmical and cheerful farting sound. Some even controlled their butt muscles to fart twice or more in a row. The so-called "double farting" was so skillfully done that that it almost sounded as if barley grains were shooting out like bullets.

I had white rice only at New Year's or during the ancestral worship ceremony, so I mostly ate barley and millet, which became my staple foods, and a lot of sweet potatoes instead of rice. During fall and winter it was common to have sweet potatoes for dinner. (I ate a lot of sweet potatoes back then that I cannot even stand the smell now.) I passed gas more eating sweet potatoes than barley. My farting was always feeble, but after eating sweet potatoes it was loud and strong. I could even do it consecutively. It was like digging up sweet potatoes with several of them attached in one vine. Sometimes it did not stop after several; depending on my digestion, it continued for a while. I was in trouble because of this when I was in fifth grade. One evening I had sweet potatoes for dinner and went over to a friend's house and experienced multiple farting for the first time.

I often went to my friend's place to study in those days. I did not like being in the same room with my family under the dim oil lamp light, so I used homework as an excuse to go over to my friend's house. I liked his room because it was brightly lit. I liked doing my homework under the bright fluorescent light, but when the light went out all of a sudden we chatted away in the dark and talked about what we read. Due to the unstable electrical power at the time, the lights went out often. My friend shared his room with his cousin but since his cousin attended a night school, he was usually not home. His cousin worked as a clerk at our school during the day.

One time my friend went to the country with his parents, so his cousin was alone. The room opposite to his was rented out to a newlywed couple and her husband was a police officer. That day her husband was on duty, so the wife had a few friends over.

From early evening the lights went out so we started talking. Since I was three or four years younger than my friend's cousin, I ended up listening to him for the most part. In the middle of his story, I farted. I had had sweet potatoes for dinner, and they did not sit well in my stomach. He stopped talking and laughed and laughed. I felt awful. My stomach was full of gas, and I could not stop farting.

Then all of a sudden, he hushed me and whispered into my ears.

"*Shhhhhh*. Quiet and listen."

From the room opposite I heard the women giggling quietly. It was odd and unpleasant laughter. It sounded as if they were tickling each other. Along with the soft giggling noise, we heard them panting. Then all of a sudden they burst out into laughter as if they could no longer hold back. What is that sound? *Slap! Slap!* Are they slapping each other? He whispered again, gasping for breath.

"That sound . . . I think it's the sound of them slapping each other's butts. They must be buck naked. Man, this is driving me nuts!"

At that moment, I farted consecutively. My friend's cousin burst out laughing and the women in the opposite room stopped giggling startled by his sudden explosive laughter. The room opposite became dead quiet and no sound was heard again. It wasn't easy for a pubescent boy to cool down once he became excited, and I continued farting.

Then my friend's cousin began talking about lewd things in a low voice, breathing heavily. I'm sure it was my farting that started the whole thing. In his story, a rumbling sound harmonized incredibly well with my farting sound.

Long, long ago, there was a minister with power and money who advertised far and wide to find a suitable husband for his precious daughter. Suitors stormed in from all over the country and his daughter stayed in her room and peeked at her suitors. The minister interviewed each one of them in the hall. He rejected one suitor after another because there was no one commensurate with his daughter. Among the suitors there was a lazy one but he was not ordinary by any means. He loitered around the courtyard and watched where the daughter's chamber pot was being emptied out. He pulled out his pubic hair and planted it in the area where the chamber pot was emptied. Then something strange happened to the daughter. Every time she relieved herself, it made a strange roaring, rumbling noise. It happened every time. Who in their right mind would like a strange noise coming out of a maiden's private parts? The daughter cried and all the suitors shook their heads and went away when they found out. The arrogant minister was disappointed and discouraged. In the end, he advertised that whoever cured his daughter's illness could have his daughter's hand in marriage. The lazy bum came to the house and pulled out the pubic hair he had planted. The strange noise stopped and he married her.

I think I farted continuously while listening to the story. I was farting in sync with the maiden's roaring and rumbling noise. Even after he finished telling the story, we laughed out loud imitating the sound. We went under the cover fearing that the women in the opposite room would hear us.

That was my first time hearing a lewd story.

For boys, farting was nothing—but it was humiliating for girls. My friends and I could not possibly imagine a pretty girl farting. We engaged in a heated argument about whether girls farted or not. We came to the conclusion that girls didn't fart, but they did when they became old. We were in sixth grade, so we knew to a certain extent the differences between the sexes.

In the storybook we read, there was one about a daughter-in-law who farted.

One time a daughter-in-law carrying her child on her back brought in a dinner tray for her father-in-law and his guest. Then she farted in front of them. She was so embarrassed that she blamed her child. Slapping his butt, she said, "How could you fart in front of a guest?"

And the child said, "Why are you hitting me? You are the one who farted."

Once I was reprimanded by my uncle when I farted while bowing during the ancestral ceremony. "If you knew it was coming, you should've tried to stop it by putting your heel under your butt." So I thought that's how women stopped or didn't fart. Well, I have not exactly checked to confirm whether that's how they do it, so I don't know if my guess is right.

*Rope and Spider Web*

I remember drying myself lying on the bed of stones after I came out of the water during summer. I cupped my right hand around my left armpit and made an up and down motion to create a farting noise and I giggled hard. It was like a whistle ensemble but quite obscene so when the girls saw me doing it, they ran away disgusted.

When I entered the sixth grade, classes were no longer coed. Boys and girls stayed far away from each other, but the girls knew well what kind of games we played and how our minds worked. I even made farting sounds by bending my knee in much the same way as I did with my armpit. When I got bored with it, I pinched the protruding part of skin along the curve of my knee to create a crease that resembled a vulva. I even twisted a wet towel to shape it like a woman's lower part. The girls knew that we did not wear underwear under our swimming trunks, so our testicles hung loose. Until we were in the sixth grade, we always swam naked. Even though we had our underwear on, the girls knew what was underneath. One of my friends had uneven testicles and from afar the girls yelled out, "Someone has uneven balls!" Whenever I heard them tease like that I was afraid that the split in the head of my penis would become the target of their mockery. I did not touch it often but it started to split open. I used to be able to insert barley straw in the tip of my penis and peed but I could no longer do that. The split was so wide that I was too embarrassed. I had my underwear on so I was able to avoid embarrassment, otherwise I would have had another nickname, Split Penis.

We were proud to have passed the stage of swimming naked to the stage of swimming with shorts. I remember a ridiculous scene going to Yŏnyŏn twirling my swim shorts around tied to a towel to show off. Going to the public bath was such a luxury at the time that I only went once a year—the day before New Year's. To let everyone know that I was heading to the public bath, I wrapped some soap in a towel and twirled it around and circled around the pavilion area on purpose.

I felt strange when I wore my swim shorts for the first time. My swimming trunks were made out of a flour burlap sack that was stamped "US Aid." I felt strange when my shorts got wet and clung to my crotch. I felt ticklish inside. My friends and I tried to take each other's swimming shorts off and sometimes I grabbed my friend's elastic waist band area and stretched it out and let it go to hurt him and he did the same to me.

Although the girls' breasts showed no signs of growing when we entered the sixth grade, they were embarrassed to swim with us so either they gave up on swimming or stayed far away from us. Even though they were far away, we could hear them laughing in the vast open sea as if they were very close. When they were near us, we showed no interest but now that they were far away, we noticed them more and paid close attention.

It was fun watching the girls play when the waves broke on the beach spewing white foam because they ran barefoot, yelling and screaming happily. They lifted their skirts up to their calves, and they jumped around in the water as if they were jumping rope. Their playful movements were so enchanting that we watched them lying on our stomachs on a stony beach and did not even realize our backs were getting sunburned. The girls continued to jump up and down screaming with delight, and we were gaping at them. Then we sighed thinking that the white waves were licking their calves.

It was the same for the girls. They pretended they were not interested in us, but they were like spiders waiting for their prey to get caught in their spider webs. The girls utilized strategies that were particular to women. They were endowed with a magnetic appeal, the power of attracting the opposite sex. In particular we could not take our eyes off of them when they were jumping rope. It was fun to watch the cheerful movement of their feet and their short bobbed hair swinging every time they jumped up and down. I felt like I could reach out and touch and feel the rubber band rope wrapped around their calves. As the height of the rope went higher and higher their jumping became swifter and swifter, so that the rope and their bodies became parallel to each other. Finally the rope was above their heads, so they caught the rope standing upside down and snatched it quickly. At that moment their white underwear was shown for a second then disappeared. In other words, the rope was like a spider web because we were caught and couldn't move. The girls were like those spiders waiting for their prey after creating webs. That's why from time to time we let ourselves get caught, then ran away cutting the rope with a sharp blade.

Once I cut their rope and ran away, but I was caught and was humiliated. Sunsim was the one who ran after me. Although she was in the same grade, she was two years older than me. She was the best sprinter at my school and won every year on sports day.

She grabbed me from behind and held me for a while and said, "Are you going to do it again or what?" I felt strange when her soft breast brushed against my back.

*Look, a Bee!*

During science class, we giggled when we read words like "screw" and "nut" and paid close attention to the shape of abalone or sea anemone. We took a great interest in how a cut or injured part healed. To our curious minds a line down the middle of barley was not ordinary. What was real and explicit to us was a horse's behind. Similar to a human, a horse had a nice and round butt. It was fun to look at a mare urinate like a waterfall and its dung come out like laying eggs. Its round and shiny horse dung was like fresh eggs so I thought the mare had two reproductive organs.

When we went to the teachers' room to ask our teacher to inspect the room we just cleaned, we looked up forbidden words in the dictionary. Those were dangerous words that we could not dare mention. We often ran into those words, obscene scribbling, in school toilets or on corner building walls. Those words had a strange power over us and attracted so greatly that it was impossible to reject them. The more dangerous it was the more attractive it became. We secretly had to say the words without our parents knowing because they were forbidden. If the Warped Mouth teacher heard us say those words, we were immediately punished. We had to get into the push up position or assume the "all fours" posture, and he whacked us several times on our bottom and said, "You rascals! You guys are still wet behind the ears!"

We knew what the word was in English. The word "vulva" sounded like "look, a bee" in Korean.

One day in class, Warped Mouth wrote on the blackboard and we copied diligently onto our notebooks. He was glued to the blackboard and continued writing. We couldn't really see everything on the board, so we had to crane our necks left and right.

*Shit! That teacher is always like that. He writes and writes but we can't see what he's writing.* We cursed at him silently and chuckled. We couldn't even chuckle out loud, so we had to do it quietly. Otherwise we would get told off.

At that time a pretty golden colored queen bee flew in and created a commotion. We often had ladybugs fly into the classroom, but it was a bee that caused the problem. The queen bee flew in inviting us to play, but we had to pretend we didn't see it. We really had to be careful what we said when the bee flew in. One time my classmate said, "Hey, look, a bee!" which sounded like "vulva." And the person sitting next to him started giggling, so we all got into trouble. The classroom became absolutely silent and the bee flew all over buzzing loudly. We became afraid of the back of the teacher's head. He had eyes in the back of his head, so he knew what we were doing even though he had his back to us.

We were scared of the teacher, but at the same time we were dying to spit out the word "vulva." We became so giggly that we were ready to burst out into laughter. Everyone in the classroom hid their faces behind their notebooks, constantly rolling their eyes and gasping, as if the queen bee was a dangerous bomber. We sent out signals to each other. *Look, a bee! Vulva! Look, a bee! Vulva!* . . . Finally one of the boys, unable to endure, raised his hand, volunteering to sacrifice himself. "Teacher, I can't concentrate because that bee is making too much noise." The entire classroom shook with laughter. *Too noisy. Shit! Too giddy.* Too giddy to concentrate and study. *Chuckle! Chuckle!*

*Endless Vacation*

Not only insects but even birds flew into the classroom from time to time wanting to play with us. A pretty bird with a light green feathered bird perched on a tangerine tree outside the classroom and sang a song, stealing our attention. A more aggressive sparrow came inside and livened up the boring class.

One time during summer vacation, I went to school and found a sparrow in the classroom desperately trying to find its way out. It kept flying into the window over and over again. I opened the window and let the sparrow out. There were several windows that were not shut completely, so the sparrow had flown in through the opening and could not find its way out. If I had not visited school that day, I would have found the dead bird on the first day of class.

I don't know why I went to school that day. I think I went not just once but several times. There were times when I wanted to go back to school during that long summer vacation. I was seized by the fear that my school would forget about me.

When I took a nap like a lazy dog, flies swarmed around to pick at the gunk in my eyes and various noises disturbed my sleep so I was half asleep and half awake. Then I would wake up startled. I was told that waking up startled from a nap could turn into an illness. There was an old belief that one's soul leaves the body while sleeping and an evil spirit can invade. If one doodles on the face of a child taking a nap, his or her soul cannot recognize the face and leaves him or her forever. For a child, the shock itself was considered to be dangerous so a shaman was called in to exorcise the evil spirit. The evil spirits of the Cheju Massacre were the most dangerous ones. Those children who witnessed the massacre on April 3rd were prone to become ill after waking up startled from their naps.

I woke up startled several times, but luckily I did not get sick. Once I screamed in fright because I woke up but my eyes would not open. I did not realize that mucus had formed around and they were dried up and stuck together. Eye infections were common in those days because there was so much dust in the air. One time I woke up all confused and flustered, saying I was late for school. I grumbled and blamed my mother for not waking me up on time.

When I visited my school during summer vacation, it looked so desolate. There were weeds growing here and there, especially in the courtyard where the students had stopped playing. The newly painted pitch on the wooden fence reeked of a scorching heat wave.

The empty classroom was unfamiliar and strange. From the courtyard dust blew in through the openings of windows and collected inside the classroom. The grayish dust softly covered the floor, desks, chairs, and the teacher's desk. I realized for the first time that the dust which I struggled to clean up during my school days could be beautiful. There were no voices, no expressions, and no gestures of the students in the classroom; things that once shined because the students cleaned and waxed them became dull, covered in dust turning grayish. I heard the soft sound of an organ, though not tuned, coming from the teachers' room. I felt something unreal when I gazed down at my desk and chair covered in dust since they had not been used for a long time. I asserted my existence by writing my name on the dust-covered desk.

My wanting to go back to school and my groundless fear that my school would forget me or summer vacation would never end were all connected to a memory from when I was six years old. In March, 1947, a general strike took place in all provinces. This happened soon after I entered elementary school so I only attended class for two or three days. Then the school was set on fire by the counterinsurgency forces. Even after I moved to town, I often thought of that unfortunate school that ended up with an endless vacation.

In retrospect, those six years of elementary school seemed like one long vacation. I do not have too many school memories, but I do recall clearly working in the field and spending time with my friends. I remember trivial things such as wrestling on the floor with my classmates playing surrender games and those shiny nail heads on the wooden floor because we rubbed them too much. And my classmates who were busy writing, making their cheeks look bloated as if they were sucking on a rock candy and their chewed up pencils. I don't remember anything grand and exciting. I remember standing alone depressed while the rest of the students screamed at a fall sporting event. I ran 100 meters barefoot and came in second and received a notebook as a prize. However, I lost my rubber shoes, so I was really depressed.

I never had proper lessons because this was during the Korean War. Even the classrooms were occupied by refugees. So I roamed around the mountain and the beach under the pretext of having class outside. When I did have lessons they were mostly copying what was written on the blackboard so I was bored. Helping out my mother at home was more important than studying. My teachers did not mind when I was absent from helping out at home. There were holidays for every occasion, such as barley vacation during barley season and millet vacation during millet season. Studying was always the last priority. No one harassed me to study. My future was uncertain and I was miserable because of the bad harvest in the middle of the war. I wasn't even sure whether studying was practical or not. Actually, it was purely by chance that I became interested in studying.

The news of the ceasefire during my second semester of sixth grade blew away my misery. The truce was an opportunity to push back this miserable and tough life as something of the past. Everything moved so fast with such energy and vigor, and it was the same in school. I was busy preparing for the middle school entrance exam. Class lessons became serious and my classmates and I finally understood what it meant to pursue knowledge. Both teachers and students became enthusiastic about teaching and learning. Knowledge was no longer an uncertain entity, but it was a means by which one could succeed in the world.

*Graduation*

My elementary school graduation picture is missing from my old photo album. I did not have my picture taken because I had no money; I regret it and am still bitter about it.

I do not have the graduation picture, but luckily I have two pictures from my sixth grade to show how I looked back then. One of them was taken by a photographer who always hung around the pavilion. The picture was paid for by my two friends who are in the picture. We stood in front of a huge agave in the court-house garden. We looked shabby but we had big bright smiles on our faces. I could not tell what I was wearing on the bottom, but I looked ridiculous wearing a small, outgrown school uniform shirt on top. I must have worn it for about three years. The sleeves came up to my elbow and the black color faded so much that it turned grayish. My cap, sitting on my head like dried up cow dung, looked even more pathetic and ridiculous. I think I wore it for three years or so. When I was in sixth grade, the hat was so small that it was tight fitting but was perfect for playing the cap snatching game. In the picture, I stood with my hand on the giant agave leaf. Like its name, it had leaves as big as a dragon's tongue. I remember scribbling something on the leaf with a thorn from the tree. I think I wrote either "friendship" or "hope."

The other picture was taken by that beautiful but illiterate woman's husband who returned from the war. They lived right next door to my family. To celebrate her husband's safe return they borrowed a camera and took pictures. They took a picture of me to return the favor I did for her. I had written letters for her a few times. I had the school uniform on and the cap but my name tag was torn off. I think this picture was taken immediately after my graduation.

There is something the reader must know. Was my family so poor that they could not even afford a graduation photo? That was not true. We received food rations from the military because of my father when I entered the fifth grade. If we had used the rations, we could have been better off, but my mother exchanged them for cash and saved the money. Not only did she exchange the rations but she also exchanged one head of cabbage at the market for cash. Her determination to build a house within a few years was firm and strong. She did not trust banks, so she relied on *kye*, a traditional way of pooling money together, taking turns in collecting a lump sum, created by relatives.

My father did not return home even after the cease fire. The first letter we received from him immediately after the war ended was completely unexpected, so everyone became excited. After my father left the army, he began a new life as a seafood broker in Inch'ŏn and he was doing extremely well and would send for us to live in the mainland with him. He said I would be the first one to call since I had to be enrolled in middle school.

After I read his letter I was full of hopes, dreaming of going to the mainland. I felt like I was floating on the clouds, but I never heard from him again. I learned later that his business, which he thought was going to succeed, went under after two or three months.

### Juvenile Chick

I am now going to write about my adolescent period when I turned thirteen, about the time I entered middle school. But I am not saying that my puberty began immediately after I started middle school. I was in between stages where my childhood had ended, but something new that could fill the void had not yet appeared. I think I was in a buffer zone during my seventh grade. In many ways seventh grade was an extension of my sixth grade. I was a molecule yet to be separated from nature and could not think of myself as an independent being removed from a group; I was part of an inseparable configuration.

It was not visible and obvious but changes were definitely taking place within my body. By the time July 15th of the lunar calendar came around, even in the middle of summer, the water became cold and crickets started chirping and heralded the beginning of the autumn season. Inside my childish body and mind, a second wave of maturity was taking place and the storm of growth gradually manifested. I was in a period of stasis when deterioration and development simultaneously took place. The child was old. His pure soul and body disappeared, instead his merciless and cruel masculinity started to open its eyes. Neither a chick nor a rooster, in between stages, I was like an ugly juvenile chick. I don't have a picture of myself during this period but I can imagine how I looked. I can imagine how ridiculous I must have looked wearing an oversized school uniform I was hoping to wear for three years. Before my school uniform was too small but this time I looked like a fool with an extremely loose uniform. I was neither a pretty yellow chick nor a hot red rooster; I was a hideous medium-sized juvenile chick of dark color with a half-grown cockscomb and tail.

I was an immature and clumsy seventh grader but I received a scholarship on the first day of school. I was one of three scholarship recipients. My mother realized at that time that knowledge was power. I was lucky to have become interested in studying while others were not. I only had school and studying to rely on since I was from a poor family raised by a single parent. Even after I received a letter informing me that I was a scholarship recipient, I could not believe it until the first day of school ceremony.

Three years of tuition waiver was something beyond my comprehension and I felt extremely fortunate. I thought I was dreaming. I was worried that my school had made a mistake and sent the letter to the wrong person. I was not exactly a lucky person because I never found money, not even a coin, walking down the street, so receiving the scholarship was completely unexpected. The day I entered school, I received the scholarship certificate. I felt great walking home with the certificate in my hand. It was something I felt for the first time in my life, a strange ticklish feeling. Even the streets looked different, and I was under the illusion that everyone was looking at me. I felt awkward and could not shake off the excitement so I ended up stuffing the certificate underneath my sleeve and walked into a bookstore. There I encountered a funny happening. As I was about to leave after looking around the bookstore, a clerk rushed over and grabbed me by the nape of the neck. "You rascal, I caught you. You book thief!" He thought I stole one of the books and shoved it underneath my sleeve.

There were always one or two middle school students who read novels in the store for free and I was one of them. When I got kicked out by one bookstore, I moved to a different one and if I got kicked out from there then I moved to another one. I finished one novel moving from one bookstore to another. There were three bookstores around the pavilion and they did not treat me harshly for reading in the bookstore.

My friends were generous about lending books to me. If one of them bought a new novel, the book circulated until it was torn and tattered. Through reading novels, I slowly understood the meaning of love and the opposite sex. When I encountered words like embracing, kissing, caressing, and exciting, my heart raced. I read Pak Kyeju's *Pure Love* but I completely forgot the plot. The only thing I remember is the first line of the book where a painter tells a nude model, "Take off your clothes."

*Bootleg Squad*

Receiving a three-year tuition waiver scholarship was such a special privilege that even after I started school I could not believe it. I feared that the school would ask me to pay my tuition starting in the second semester.

My mother worried even more than I did. She was always like that. Even when I received awards my mother sighed before expressing happiness, disappointing me immensely. She did not boast of her son in front of others. She believed that if she boasted of her children to others they would envy her and this would in return incur the divine wrath. She was skeptical, so she was in constant fear that something evil would befall me.

She hardly ever visited school to check how I was doing, and the day I received the scholarship award, she was not present at the ceremony. She may have wanted to express her gratitude to the principal, but she did not have the courage to do so. Like most other parents of her age, she regarded all teachers as a different species so she was extremely careful. There was a distinct class difference between those who made a living ploughing the field and those who made a living teaching. She realized that education meant power, since I entered middle school without paying any tuition. My ultimate goal was to become a teacher. That was the only power I could dream of attaining as a child from a poor family.

One day she was supposed to have a meeting with my teacher, which she dreaded and wanted to avoid, but she had no choice. Soon after I entered middle school, there was a home visit where my homeroom teacher made a round of calls at the homes of every single student. Since it was my first experience of having a teacher visit my home, I was extremely nervous. As soon as I got out of class, I ran home to make sure my mother stayed and waited for him. I was afraid that my homeroom teacher might scold my mother, saying "How come you never came to school when your son received the scholarship?" What could I do? What could I possibly do to make him feel welcome? There was no special treat to serve him, so my mother fretted not knowing what to do. She kept rubbing her hands. She contemplated going over to her parents' place to borrow two eggs. She thought of offering hardboiled eggs to my teacher, but it was already too late. My homeroom teacher was already down by the hill. From my window, I saw him walking with another student.

What my mother did was out of the ordinary. Since she wanted to avoid meeting him, perhaps she wanted to believe the person she saw was a bootleg squad, not my homeroom teacher. The bootleg squad usually came from the road my teacher was using. To make money to pay for building the house, my mother made alcohol and sold it illegally from time to time. Therefore, she was overly sensitive about the bootleg squad. Her reaction at seeing my teacher was similar to the time when the bootleg squad appeared. She locked every single door and window, and she even drove me out of the house. Then she disappeared.

I had no choice but to greet my teacher in front of the house and lie. I told him that when I returned home from school, my mother had gone out to the field and no one was home.

*Geyser in the Ocean*

Chŏngdŭrŭ Village was located on the lower reaches of Han Stream. On the way to the beach toward Yongyŏn Pond, there was a small bridge called Hungry Bridge. Although it was called a bridge, it hardly qualified as one. It was built at the lowest part of the stream with no bridge posts. It was nothing but the pouring of cement to build a dyke and a flood gate in the middle. The bridge was only a few feet above the surface of the water, so if the river overflowed, it became completely submerged. Seeing the bridge submerged, people said, "That bridge can't get up because it's hungry. It's lying down on its stomach and it's not moving." The name Hungry Bridge came about when people started joking about it like that. Gently flowing from Hanch'ŏn Bridge was the wide river valley that shrank like a bottleneck and became a rough gorge. The water flowed through this gorge, passing steep slopes and suddenly plunging downward, and it was at Yongyŏn where the pool was created and became famous for its beautiful scenery.

It was rare to see water flowing in Han Stream. Similar to Pyŏngmun Stream, the Han Stream was dry and water flowed for a short period of time only during the monsoon. The water flowed for less than one month in a year. The main player of the Han Stream was not the water but the rocks and stones covering the dried-up riverbed. The bedrock was hardened by lava and rocks clustered together. These rocks were exposed, resembling a wound—under the scorching sunlight they burned in the heat, and in the biting winter cold the rocks froze like bones. This landscape remained in my memory as something beautiful and special. The tough beauty of the earth's bones was exposed, glittering in its whiteness. As much as they were beautiful, those bones signified barrenness.

At the lower reaches of the dried-up stream, there was Yongyŏn. In this pond, there was a geyser that spewed water from the bottom, creating a wide and deep pond. It was so strange that from under the ocean an incredible amount of water surged up. The water vein was beneath the dried up stream. It looked all dried up but underneath it the water had never stopped flowing. When the water reached the ocean, it spurted out breaking through the crust. Even now I often think about the bubbly fresh spring water that gushed out here and there in the ocean, and I feel great, as if my filthy body's being purified.

Yongyŏn, surrounded by rock walls like folding screens on both banks harmonizing with the blue ocean, had breathtaking scenery. During the Chosŏn Dynasty, this place was frequented by *moksa* or county magistrates from the mainland, who enjoyed boating. I remember the name Hong Chongu engraved on the west rock wall. For assassinating Kim Okkyun, his lowly social status was elevated to Cheju county magistrate as a reward: Hong Chongu the assassin. His ambition was so great that he had a stonemason dangling in the air ready to carve out his name. As the name Yongyŏn suggested, a dragon lived in the mysterious blue water. On the east rock wall, old Chinese nettle trees or hackberries were entangled, and there was a temple located in the dark and damp place where services were offered in the name of the dragon. When the drought was severe, they held rituals using *pungmul*, Korean traditional percussion instruments, to entice the rain to wake up the dragon that was sleeping deep underwater. The dragon was thought of as a mystical creature that gathered rain and clouds.

In any case, I used this beautiful place as my base and used to frequent this pond. I was poor but played in the lap of luxury. The children swam in the beautiful water that was shadowed by the reflection of the rock walls. Our loud voices and laughing sounds bounced off the rock walls, creating pleasant echoes. After playing in the water for a while, we came out shivering in cold and the rocks felt so warm. The rocks were enormous and looked rough, but for the children in summertime, they were warm and tender. Due to erosion, the surface of the rocks was smooth without any sharpness, and the rock walls heated nicely from the sun were warm and gentle. During those years, I experienced vicariously the softness and warmth of human touch through those rocks. When I climbed up and down the rocks, I felt the softness on my hands and feet that stuck fast onto the rocks. The salt water was cold since it was mixed in with fresh water. If it weren't for those warm rocks, it would've been difficult for me to swim there. I felt delighted lying down as my shivering body slowly warmed up. A sensual pleasure seeped deep into my skin and my body listlessly spread out on the surface of the rocks like dough. I remember feeling happy lying on my back looking up at the sky. At the top of the rock walls, the tiger lilies blossomed all around like a flower garland, and here and there were small trees on the surface of the rocks with their roots half exposed in the air hanging dangerously like acrobats. It was wonderful. I liked the tiger lilies because they resembled my youngest aunt who had freckles. With her freckles, she looked even more beautiful. The tiger lilies, bearing bright orange flowers with spots, looked like freckles.

Looking up at the rock walls, the two walls look as if they face each other bowing, so the sky appeared very narrow between the two. It looked as if the blue water of Yongyŏn was flowing in the sky—the azure sea gliding in the sky.

I didn't go where the water was deep, the place where the dragon was asleep. I only played in the shallow water with lots of rocks. The deepest water was near the west rock wall and even the adults did not go there. The water was so deep that people said there was no bottom, and it was connected directly to the underworld. According to a legend, there was a tall old woman named Sŏlmundae who sat on the crater Paeknoktam on top of Mt. Halla and put her feet in the ocean to wash clothes. The tallest woman ended up drowning when she went into the water to measure its depth. The water color was unusually blue. It was so blue that it sent shivers down my spine. Like a mysterious magnet, I was pulled to that place. While playing in the shallow water, I was near the abyss without realizing it. I was so afraid that I would get pulled in by the water spirit that I frantically swam to get out of that place.

When I lived near Pyŏngmun Stream, I experienced something similar when I drank water from the well in Mugŭnsŏng Village. The well was extremely deep and roofed over with tin so that it was dark to the point where the surface of the water was not visible. Even during broad daylight looking at the dark water I was able to get a glimpse of death. I am not sure if it's true but there was a rumor that a young woman committed suicide by throwing herself into the well, so I thought of the well as the water of the netherworld. Together with the chilly air that rose from the dark well and the fear of being sucked into it, from the moment the bucket left my hand until it dropped to the bottom of the well, making a clanking noise, I felt so afraid that a minute felt like an eternity. When the bucket dropped to the bottom, I felt as though I was being pulled into the well by the rope in my hand. But what I got was neither darkness nor dark underworld water, but a bucket full of water that, as soon as it was exposed to the sun, turned fresh and real.

From the blue abyss of Yongyŏn, which was thought to have a hole on the bottom connecting to the netherworld, surged fresh and real water—not the water of the otherworld. The fresh water gushed out endlessly and that was why the color of the water was bluer than any other place. It was evident how much fresh water gushed up at low tide. When the water level shrank to half during low tide, the amount of fresh water was more than the seawater, so the water was cold enough to chill the entire pond and the color of the water was even bluer than before. The well that people from Chŏngdŭrŭ used was located on the west side of the pond. That water, which was buried when the tide came in, revealed at low tide the fresh water under the seawater.

Yes, the fresh water under the seawater. This was the best part of Yongyŏn. Even though Han Stream was dried up, revealing its rocky bed, its beauty lie in the fact that underneath those rocks a vein of fresh water was flowing that surfaced when it reached the mouth of Yongyŏn. But sadly the mysterious and beautiful blue water of Yongyŏn became murky due to pollution. In the upper side of Yongyŏn, a town was built so dirty water flowed into the pond. A part of the lower reaches of Han Stream had been covered up, so the beautiful granite clusters that brilliantly shone under the scorching sunlight more or less ended up inside the dark cement tunnel.

So I have internalized this mysteriously blue color of Yongyŏn that no longer exists in real life. It has changed into the symbol of life, lodged deep inside my mind. Whenever I recall the blue water of the abyss where the dragon is sleeping, I feel a surge of great joy piercing through stark reality. The fresh spring water is surging up in the midst of the gray city. The life of the spring water that has not been exhausted, the sweet water within the saltwater, the vein of water that begins from Mt. Halla to erupt when reaching the ocean, the natural water. It is marvelous that the dried-up Han Stream sits on the water vein like blood vessels.

## When the Han Stream Flooded

The Han Stream flowed only when there was a big rain storm on Mt. Halla. My house was located right by the stream so I could hear when it flowed. During the rainy season, I anticipated and wondered when the banks of the stream would break. I had my ear close to the window, which faced the stream, waiting for the flooding to start.

I remember an old pine tree by the Confucian school standing like a hazy shadow undulating in the rain on the other side of the window. Every big crock was overflowing with raindrops from the eaves and the rain kept pounding on the drenched courtyard, creating white bubbles. I also remember those damp matches that would not kindle and a peculiar pleasure I got from scratching my shins like crazy until they bled. I had eczema. The eczema was worse in the rainy season when fungus thrived. I was so sick and tired of the fungus that congealed on my shins that I stayed near the kitchen furnace even during summer to keep my legs dry. Although the atmosphere was heavy with smoke rising from the burning straws, it gently warmed my entire body. And the blue smoke quietly dispersed into the courtyard. My mother roasted beans or barley as a snack. My sister and I crouched in front of the kitchen furnace and shoved dead leaves inside; my mother kept stirring the beans that were popping and cracking in the pot with a wooden spoon. On those days the thunder rolled and lightning struck loudly as if there was a huge iron pot hung in the sky.

There is a folktale I know that is related to roasted beans. In the old days children must have liked eating roasted beans on rainy days, too.

Long, long, long ago there lived a young and wealthy couple. There was no distinction between the living and the dead. One day the husband was called in by the King of Heaven to live in the flower garden of Western Heaven as a gardener. The flower garden of Western Heaven was located where the red evening glow radiated. One could never return once he or she stepped inside of it, so the wife decided to follow him even when she was almost due to give birth. There was only one road and it continued on endlessly in the middle of the field. During the daytime they walked for hours and hours and during the night they slept in the bushes; it was an exhausting journey. It took them several days to reach halfway but the wife who waddled behind plopped down in the middle of the road because her feet gave away. She had blisters all over her feet so she could no longer walk. When they found a village in the middle of nowhere, the wife said, "My dear, I can't walk anymore so why don't you sell me as a slave to a rich family and leave me here."

"My darling, what am I to do?"

"Please name the child before you leave."

"If you bear a son, name him Hallakkung. If a daughter is born, name her Hallattaek"

Thus she became a slave to a rich family but from the first day the landlord demanded her to sleep with him.

"I don't know what the custom is here, but where I come from I can't sleep with another man until I give birth."

She had a baby boy. When the baby was born, the landlord demanded she sleep with him.

"I don't know what the custom is here, but where I come from I can't sleep with you until this baby turns fifteen years old."

She endured difficult times working as a slave. Then Hallak-kung turned fifteen years old. One day when it rained, Hallak-kung asked, "Mother, Mother, roast me some beans."

She put the beans in the pot. Hallakkung hid a spatula and said, "Mother, Mother, the beans are burning. Hurry and stir. If you can't find the spatula, stir with your hand."

She put her hand in the burning pot and began stirring the beans. Then suddenly Hallakkung pushed down her hand and said, "Mother, Mother, why can't you tell me the truth? Tell me where my father is."

"You father is the gardener in the flower garden of Western Heaven."

Hallakkung bid farewell to his mother and set out in search of his father. He successfully escaped from the landlord's dogs that chased after him. He threw a ball of buckwheat dough and ran over two hundred miles and threw another ball and ran ten thousand miles. He went over the mountains and rivers. Finally he arrived at Western Heaven and met his father. After their joyful reunion, he heard from his father that his mother passed away. Her body was cut into four pieces by the cruel landlord using a scythe.

"Hallakkung, on your way here, wasn't there a stream that came up to your knees? That was tears your mother shed when her knees were cut. When you crossed the second stream, didn't the water come up to your waist? That was tears your mother shed when her waist was cut. When you crossed the third stream, didn't the water come up to your neck? That was tears your mother shed when her neck was cut. Go back and avenge your mother's death and bring her to life again."

His father picked a handful of flowers of destruction and re-birth from the garden and gave them to Hallakkung. With both flowers in his hand, Hallakkung returned to the ground. He gave the flower of destruction to the landlord and the flower of rebirth to his mother. The landlord was struck by lightning and died instantly and his mother was revived as if she had woken up from her sleep. She scratched her head and yawned, saying, "I think I overslept because it's spring."

I heard this story from my maternal grandmother when I was young. Many stories I heard were particular to the island and were very different from the mainland stories. During the so-called "childhood period," my mother's control was absolute and it lasted until a few years into elementary school. I believe after I started reading foreign fables and legends written in standard Korean, I slowly forgot about indigenous island stories. I vaguely remember the stories I heard in those days as if they had all been buried in darkness. However, the story of Hallakkung was the only story I could remember with all the details. Perhaps I remember this one because it's a story about a father. I accepted my father's absence as natural and inevitable, so the story of Hallakkung who went on a long journey in search of his father made quite an impression on me. I recall the Hallakkung story on rainy days while eating roasted beans. When my mother roasted the beans, I had the urge to grab her hand and press it down in the burning hot pot.

The savory smell of roasting beans and the warm furnace were the things I remember. Only on rainy days was I able to get old stories out of my mother. I was especially happy because she stayed home all day long. I found rainy days to be peaceful and comforting. My mother mended old clothes and ground grains. The sound of a millstone was similar to thunder, hovering in the middle of the clouds and rain on Mt. Halla. For the Han Stream to overflow, it had to rain a lot on Mt. Halla. On days of torrential rain, the sound of thunder grew louder and louder and the lightning that left Mt. Halla stretched out like tentacles and strode through the meadows. On nights like that, the water from Mt. Halla flowed into the seaside covering the riverbed

The Han Stream overflowed two or three times a year, but it only lasted for ten days. It was rare to see water flowing in the Han Stream, so it was an important event when it flooded. During the scorching summer heat, the rocks revealed the bottom of the riverbed and the dried up stream suffered from thirst. Thus it was a wonderful and magnificent spectacle when the water flooded and flowed freely and lively. I was all ears trying to catch the sound of the water flowing, and the sound of the strong current hurtling down over the rocks, resembling the sound of my mother grinding. The sound of the flowing river, the thunderstorm from the distance, and the grinding sound weaved nicely, creating a harmony as the three most important elements to remember about rainy days.

When the Han Stream flooded, all of us children jumped up and down with joy and ran over to the stream, screaming. It was quite a sight when the stream tumbled down as foamy cascades. But in order to catch the spectacle, it required luck. The cascading happened either late at night or when I was in school. Therefore, even though I lived right by the stream, I only saw it twice.

It took several hours for the water from Mt. Halla to reach the beach. The water flowed down slowly because it had to fill the riverbed on its way. Just because the water flowed slowly, it was not safe to cross the stream. There is an old belief that although he is not visible to human eyes, there is a gray-haired old man at the head of the water who leads the water flow. The first batch of water was muddy and the way it moved slowly wriggling its way through the riverbed was like a giant crawling animal emerging; it was uncanny. A strong smell of dark and damp yet raw arose from the muddy water. The gray-haired old man stood at the head of the water and hit the ground with his cane to divide, splitting the water into many branches. The way in which the water flowed down in several streams resembled crawling snakes. The first batch of water paved its way and then the second batch pounced upon it to make the water overflow. The rocks in the riverbed slowly sank into the muddy current. When Hungry Bridge sank under the water, the stream no longer had any obstacles. It cascaded down quickly with the sound of rocks crashing under the strong current and the water fell headlong toward the gorge in Yongyŏn.

*Horse Cart Swept Away in the Stream*
I mentioned this before but the stream flowed vigorously only for a short period of time. The current was strong and fast, yet short lived; one or two drowning accidents occurred every year. The first few days when the current was strong and rough, I used the bridge located in the upper town, so there was no accident. However, around the time when the water shrank to half its volume, it was dangerous. Some children playing in the water or adults attempting to cross Hungry Bridge were swept away by the current when the water had not quite drained. When the water came up to my knees when crossing the bridge, it was dangerous. It was easy to lose balance and get swept away by the current when the water reached around my thighs.

The first drowning accident I witnessed at Hungry Bridge was the death of a horse. It was the first year I moved to Chŏngdŭrŭ, so I was in sixth grade and it was during summer vacation.

I believe it happened when I was on my way home from school. The water had continued to flow over the bridge, so I did not dare use Hungry Bridge. Only the adults used the bridge, but then all of a sudden, an empty horse cart turned up. The owner of the horse cart was a man who was famous among us as bowlegged because of the dreadful way he walked. One of my classmates was kicked in his face by a horse, so he had a horse shoe scar. Since then his nickname was Horse Shoe. The bowlegged man was my classmate's uncle. He was so severely bowlegged that his entire body seemed all twisted and incapacitated. His legs were curved to the point where his left big toe almost touched his right big toe. When he walked, he waddled, shaking his body from left to right as if he was having a fit. But he was unbelievably fast, and it was fun to watch him lead his horse cart, waddling and swinging the reins. He didn't get mad when we made fun of him. I think he was an idiot. How could he make a stupid mistake?

It might have been after the horse had transported a heavy load because the horse was dripping in sweat. We thought Bowlegged led the horse to the bridge for water. However, after the horse drank water, Bowlegged led the horse to the middle of the bridge where the water was overflowing. Perhaps he reasoned that the water was deep enough for a person to cross with his pants rolled up, so why not the horse with the cart, the horse was stronger and heavier than a person. But the horse cart had a greater surface area to be struck by the current and the horse did not know how to take extra caution in the water. The person who was supposed to hold tight onto the bridle to lead the horse jumped onto the cart so as not to get his feet wet, so you could imagine what the outcome was.

The poor horse went into the water led by Bowlegged, but before it took several steps the accident happened. The horse was swept away by the strong current and one of the wheels came off from the cart. As soon as the man jumped off from the cart, the horse fell over the bridge. The current was so strong that the horse on its side was getting pushed further and further down. The horse sank into the water and only the wheels were visible. The horse died quietly without putting up a fight.

The horse was thrust under the water, drifting and crashing against the rocks. Then it got caught by something and stopped. Surprisingly the horse we thought was dead raised its head high and neighed pitifully. It was dreadful to see the horse with its bleeding head and struggling desperately. I felt so sorry for the horse. It might have been possible for the horse to live if the bridle had been untied. The man jumped like he was insane and wailed. I stamped my feet in frustration, too. There was nothing I could do to help.

The poor horse made its last appearance like that and sank into oblivion, dragging the cart with it. The horse was sucked into a small waterfall at the mouth of a gorge. I screamed and ran to the gorge but by the time I arrived the horse had already fallen headlong underneath the waterfall and sank deep into the swamp. The accident happened and ended in the blink of an eye. It happened so fast that I gazed at the swamp blankly in a state of total shock. I waited hoping that the dead horse would surface but to no avail. Since the horse was tied to the cart, it sank underneath and was buried in the water.

Bowlegged lost his livelihood due to his stupidity, and he whined and cried out loud saying, "O dear, my horse! Oh, my horse!" I didn't feel any sympathy for him. I was rather repulsed. The poor horse died terribly because its owner was an idiot. I often saw horses carrying heavy loads on the street, so I felt sorry because I knew they led a tough life. I thought it was too cruel to leave the horse to rot in the water and not bury it in the ground. The horse could not even free itself from the bridle and to leave it underwater was inhumane even for a mere animal. The swamp would rot together with the horse, reeking in stench. I had often gone there to swim during the scorching hot summer days. I became upset thinking about the swamp rotting away. I cursed at the back of Bowlegged's head when I saw him crying. *What an idiot! Do you think the dead horse would come to life again if you cry like that? Why are you crying when you are the one who killed it?*

I could not leave the place for a while. I stood there staring at the swamp beneath the rock wall. Then all of a sudden the dead horse came up to the surface. The strong current freed the horse from the cart. The horse floated up with its stomach up in the air. Its stomach was bloated with water. It was a pitiful sight, but it was the freedom of death. The horse looked so light after getting rid of the cart, unloading every burden it carried on its shoulder. The dead horse drifted to the lower river floating lightly, even breaking free of its soul. The horse finally reached the sandbank where the water from Yongyŏn and the ocean merged.

### The Girl Who Went to the Dragon King's Palace

I am not certain whether it happened when I was in seventh or eighth grade, but one of my neighbors, a girl, went missing while playing in the water. She must have drowned and died but her body was not found immediately. Her mother was on the verge of a breakdown. Late at night she sat by the water calling out her daughter's name and cried, "Sinok! Sinok!" I believe that was the girl's name. She was not quite ten years old. The young men in the neighborhood searched the water and finally found the body. She was found in the same place where the horse's dead body was found.

When her body was brought to the shore, she was naked but strangely no scars were to be seen. She did not look like a dead person. Her lightly closed eyes looked gentle. She had her knees up in a crouching position, and her small and stiff body was comforting to watch. She was found in this position underneath a rock where there was enough space for her to get in. Her mother, who was on the verge of going mad, was relieved to have found her daughter. She felt comforted when she saw her dead daughter looking peaceful and at ease. I still remember what her mother said in an excited tone of voice. "See, I told you. My daughter's gone to the Dragon King's Palace. She's settled down comfortably in the Dragon King's Palace." If she had not said this, I would've remembered this day as dreadful; the stiff naked body of the girl, something so terrible that I would not want to remember ever again.

After the girl drowned and died, a boy who was the same age as me went around the village crying all day long. People said the boy went crazy because the dead girl's spirit went inside him. So a shaman was called in to perform an exorcism. The boy usually lost when we wrestled together, but after he turned a little funny, he jumped at me crying, wanting to fight. I remember running away from him in fright.

### Naked Woman's Body

It wasn't just the girl. Those who drowned and died in the Han Stream were always found naked. I think I witnessed about five deaths and strangely they were all naked. I believed at the time that the water spirit stripped them of their clothes. I still do believe this to be true. It was natural that clothes came off in the water. The current was so strong in the Han Stream and it had incredible power. But it was not possible to strip a body with strength and force alone. The current had hands and fingers to undo the horse's harness and undress the drowned to have the dead enter the netherworld free from their clothes and their spirits.

I saw the naked body of a drowned woman on the sandbank at the mouth of the river. Several fishermen caught her with their poles when she drifted down. Her pale naked body on a cloudy day was an image of death that still remains with me to this day. For a seventh grader, seeing her body was a peculiar experience. It helped me wake up to sexuality and at the same time to the nature of death. It was my first time seeing a woman's naked body. When my burning desire to see the mysterious part of a woman's body was granted through her dead body, I was completely lost for words. The body was exposed for everyone to see until a straw mat was brought to cover her. She was on her stomach to avoid displaying her private parts. Her prostrate position seemed so natural that she did not look like a dead person. She looked as if she was taking a nap. She must have passed through the gorge before reaching Yongyŏn, but she had no scars or bruises. Her body was clean, even her butt and thighs were plump and firm.

However, a bloodcurdling and ghostly chill emanated from her unscarred body. The color of her body was ghastly pale and icy; it was an aura of death. The fog that rolled upon the sandbank covered her naked body as if devouring it. I ran away in fright when one of the kids kicked the body and the stiffened corpse swayed back and forth.

I become upset even now when the image of her pale body on the cloudy day comes to mind, but there is another image that emerges simultaneously. I think it's my mind's defensive mechanism working instinctively to protect me from inauspicious things. The image of a living naked woman enters my mind as if life is pushing out death, trying to efface the wretched image. I'm not a lucky person. I have never found a coin on the street. But I struck the jackpot and saw a woman taking a bath.

The pool where the girl drowned was below the waterfall, surrounded by boulders and rock walls, so when the water stopped flowing it became a place for us kids to take a bath. It was not as good as Yongyŏn but it was perfect for a quick bath and was near the village. Unlike the cold water of Yongyŏn, it was lukewarm so I could even take a bath in autumn.

I still remember that day vividly since an opportunity to see a young woman's naked body was rare. It happened on one late afternoon in early fall. The pool was nice and warm since it was heated by the sunlight. After the drowning accident, I stopped going there. However, a couple of friends and I went to the pool for the first time in awhile to wash up after we played soccer. And then there she was.

We did not notice her in the beginning because she was behind a big boulder. We got undressed and went inside the water. Then we saw a naked woman sitting against the rock right in front of our own eyes. Her nice and rounded bosom, the secret hidden underneath her clothes which only babies were allowed to see, was plainly revealed. When she saw us, she shrieked and crouched to cover herself. We were as surprised as she was. The only naked woman's body we saw was the dead corpse lying by Yongyŏn. I felt chills run down my spine because I thought she was the ghost of the dead woman. Later my friends told me they had the same thought.

Then all of a sudden she started cursing at us. She said, "You bastards! How dare you come in here! Get out. Get the hell out!" Her screaming and foul words made us realize that the woman covering her chest with her arms in embarrassment was not a ghost. She continued with her tirade, saying, "How dare you come in when I'm taking a bath! You dirty rascals, get the hell out! Hurry! You are still wet behind the ears."

We realized that the woman was a refugee from the mainland who recently moved to a village nearby. She had no idea that the pool was exclusively for boys and men. That's why she was bathing there. In any case, we were the guilty ones for having seen her naked body. We were as embarrassed as she was because we were completely naked, too. I believe my body turned red from embarrassment. But then was it because I was embarrassed or something else? I was embarrassed yet I couldn't suppress my overwhelming curiosity. I could not possibly let this golden opportunity slip through my fingers. So I kept looking her way while crawling out of the pool and being chased out by her screaming and cursing.

*Nude Picture*

The woman's naked body left a deep impression on me. I believe my adolescent period began around this time since the image of this event is vivid in my mind. The fact that I was only a few steps away from the naked woman and that I, too, was naked served as a source of incredible sexual fantasies.

The pool meant something completely different after I saw a woman's naked body. I had not like the lukewarm water before, but strangely, afterwards I had come to like it. I was repulsed by the fishy smell but after the incident it did not bother me all that much. I often went to the pool by myself. I became aware of sensual pleasures while soaking in the lukewarm water. I felt like I was in a daze and the image of a naked woman flashed before my eyes when my naked body was gently immersed in the lukewarm water. The rock bed extended deeply inside the water and the thick moss grew around it. The soft and slippery feeling of the moss tickled my naked body. I rubbed my stomach and groin area against the soft moss, and this was like a calf before its horn grew out, rubbing its itchy private parts.

I had no interest in girls my age when I was thirteen or fourteen years old. I think it was the same for my friends. I didn't think immature young girls were sexually attractive (I'm certain it was the same for the girls). It was natural for the boys who had just begun taking interest in the opposite sex to want to see naked women and to have wet dreams. It did not matter whether they were pretty. I was only interested in discovering the mystery of their body parts hidden underneath their skirts. I found out later why women tuck their skirts between their legs when sitting down. When their inner thighs were revealed by their carelessness, I felt dizzy looking at their white milky skin. I knew it was shameful, but I could not help myself. My eyes gravitated toward that direction. When a woman sat sloppily, my eyes immediately went toward her skirt to catch a glimpse of her milky skin underneath. Until the day I saw a naked woman's body, I was tantalized with bits and pieces of women's bodies, so seeing a fully naked woman was a major event. What did a mature woman's naked body mean for an immature seventh grader?

The answer to the question was in the picture of a nude woman which I saw for the first time. I went to see my Korean language teacher and in his room, I saw a picture of a nude woman that was the size of a business card and was wedged in a picture frame on his desk. Because I had a lot of respect for him, I accepted the nude picture on his desk as something natural and perfectly normal. I came to the realization that nudity was not obscene or immoral but it was something beautiful. I tried hard to emulate my teacher who loved literature, so I kept the image of the naked woman I saw in the pool in my memory without feeling guilty or feeling ashamed. It was like having my own harmless nude picture. I was young so for someone my age a naked woman was beyond my reach, therefore she was not real. She existed only as an idea and fantasy and perhaps that was why it was more beautiful and brilliant.

It's strange. Even after so many years have passed, the image of the naked woman has not faded but remains vivid in my memory. I wonder why? I don't remember what she looked like, but her voluptuous body sitting crouched on the rock remains clear in my memory. During my adolescent period, I often recalled this image in my sexual fantasies. Could this be the reason why I still remember it? The naked body, like the blossoming of a white flower against the background of a gray rock, was even more delicate and soft against rough and hard granite. The reason why I remember it vividly is that it is superimposed with the second naked woman on the cement floor. Unexpectedly I saw a naked woman for the second time in broad daylight six years later.

I need to digress and talk about what happened when I was a freshman in college. I was tutoring a high school student, preparing him for a college entrance examination. So I could not go home during winter vacation. A friend from the island and I rented a small place in Seoul and we lived together. It was a small traditional *hanok*-style house with the courtyard in the shape of "U" turned sideways with the open side on the right. In the past, even a small house had a live-in-maid because the room I was living in was called a "maid's room" next to the kitchen. The husband and wife in question lived on the opposite side of the courtyard.

The couple was in their mid-thirties but had no children. The wife was outgoing and sociable but she was clumsy when it came to housework. She looked as if she was a little girl playing house. In contrast to the wife, the husband was quiet and shy. I heard that he worked for a tobacco company. After he returned home from work, he stayed in the room quietly. My friend and I concluded that they had no children because he was impotent. When the wife started talking to us, smiling for no reason, we wondered if she wanted our sperm. From her facial expression and her manner of speaking, we knew she was flirting with us.

There was only one water tap placed in the middle of the cement courtyard, so to wash rice and to do the dishes, we gathered at the water tap. So we ran into the woman at least a few times a day. She did not care whether her husband was listening or not; she carried on as if she wanted him to hear. She said, "Listen to me, would you? It wasn't even that late, maybe around ten at night. I was coming home after meeting a friend yesterday. I was walking up the alley passing by the briquette shop. The street lights were on so it wasn't even that dark. Then all of a sudden, a man jumped out of this house and grabbed me. He tried to kiss me, you know. He held my waist and pushed me against the wall. It was fine up to that point. Well, he was such a coward! When I slapped him, he got scared and ran away. What a fool! He was an amateur. He had a pretty face, though. I think he was about your age. I was flattered. Do I look that young?"

Something even more ridiculous happened when the landlord was out of the house. Her husband had gone to work. She came to our room, smiling and said coquettishly, "I'm sorry but I really need to take a quick bath. It's too hot right now. Can you stay in your room for five minutes?" Then she shut the door. We were bewildered that we had become prisoners in our own room. We could not let this golden opportunity slip when it was about to happen right under our noses. We could no longer hold off, so we made a hole through the paper door when we heard the water splashing and watched her.

She had nothing on, completely naked. What could be more beautiful than a naked woman's body? The beauty of mysterious wonder! The explosion of brilliant incandescent light reflected on the smooth gray cement courtyard resembled the naked body seen against the gray boulder. Over the years the two images of these naked women fused together as one and remained in my memory as one singular event.

*Sinsŏk*

As I said before, I entered my adolescent period when I was in seventh grade. My childhood period was over but new things had not quite filled the void. I was curious about the opposite sex but had not reached the stage where my curiosity was manifested as an obsession. I was standing on the threshold of my adolescence, looking inside full of curiosity and desiring to see many mature and naked women. Perhaps this meant I wanted to mature quickly to act on my desires. I envied those high school boys in my neighborhood who had muscular bodies from doing sports, and I realized for the first time that men's bodies can be beautiful, too. For a medium-sized chick with a yellowish cockscomb, the beauty of a fully-grown bright red cockscomb was an object of envy.

Among the neighborhood guys, there was a soccer player with the nickname Water Spirit because he was good at harpooning fish, but Sinsŏk had the best body. He lived two houses down from where I lived. He was very good on the parallel bars. He set up the parallel bars in front of the house and worked out everyday. When he took off his shirt, his trapezoid torso and his toned muscles bulged out and he looked great. His arms were naturally held wide because he had muscles. Those muscles were called "*kappakin*" in Japanese. Although this is the Japanese word, I'm happy that I can remember it as if I found a lost object. I put my pen down for a minute to look at an anatomical chart. The word "kappakin" means the latissimus dorsi muscle. When he flexed all of a sudden without his shirt on, both latissimus dorsi tightened up as if the wings of a bat were extended, and his arms raised automatically. I learned more words like biceps and triceps because of Sinsŏk.

I was not only attracted to his muscular physique. I was more captivated by the way in which he set up his goal and struggled to attain it day and night. He swung around on the parallel bars like a bird, but he was also very diligent about studying. He shut himself in his room to study and came out for a brief moment to take a break and work out on the parallel bars. For him, exercise was a kind of breather he needed between long and boring studies, serving as a diversion.

He was a graduating senior but surprisingly his dream was not to become an elementary school teacher. As soon as he finished school, he planned to go to the mainland to take the college entrance examination. He was not financially well off; he was poor like me, so how could he go to a college? He lost his father during the Cheju Massacre and lived with his mother in a rented room. His village was completely burnt down, only two and a half miles away from his present home. However, his mother did not have enough money to build a house when the reconstruction was underway so he couldn't go back to his old village. Even so, his decision to enter university did not change. He said he did not need money, as long as he passed the exam and was admitted to a prestigious university. If he was accepted to one of the top universities, he could afford it by working part-time as a private tutor.

His grand plan to change his current situation made a deep impact on me. What a delightful revelation! It was possible to change your lot if you put your mind to it. For me who was poor, Seoul was like an imaginary and remote place that was unreachable. However, it was that very place which existed as real in Sinsŏk's future plan, not as an imaginary space. Seoul was not a mere picture on the wall; for Sinsŏk it was his goal, a straight line he needed to walk on without getting distracted. His dream now became my dream.

Sinsŏk became the first person I worshipped as my first hero. Like most heroes, he did not pay any attention to me. He didn't even take notice of me and only my one-sided hero worshipping existed between us. He was a senior in high school and I was a seventh grader, so he took no interest in me and had no time because he was busy studying for the examination. He smiled when I bowed to him and that was enough to make me feel great. I lingered outside his home trying to get a taste of what it was like to study day and night. I went to his place in the middle of the night and was deeply impressed when I saw a light coming out of his room.

Without realizing it, I started imitating him. I began working out on the parallel bars he had set up in front of his house. One time I tried to take large steps to walk like him and pulled my groin. Sinsŏk was not the only one with big strides; all the others his age were the same. I don't know why I rushed to school every morning when I wasn't even late. It was a habit of mine at the time. Recalling those passersby who walked hastily down the street reminded me of those characters in silent films walking in a hurry as if they were being pursued.

It was a time when people relied on walking on foot because they had no other mode of transportation; walking twenty-five miles was common as if it was an everyday occurrence. In a traditional agricultural-based society, walking fast was also an important part of daily life. Most of the students were sons and daughters of farmers. Didn't we, the sons and daughters of farmers, rush to school every morning in groups like the strong wind to attain a better and higher status than our own parents? I ran in order to catch up to Sinsŏk and others his age. And as I was running, I thought of the hero Yi Chaesu who lived at the turn of the century. Before Yi Chaesu became the insurrection leader, he was a slave and worked as an errand boy at the local government office. He was known for being quick to action. Fifty years ago in 1901, he met his tragic death when he rose as the leader of *minjung*, the people, from his lowly status as a servant. Yi Chaesu was the only hero I could openly praise when I could not do the same for Yi Tŏkku, commander of the armament unit during the Cheju Massacre.

I can recall even now when the students from Chŏngdŭrŭ trotted like a herd of horses through the narrow alley to go to school in the morning. The high school students walked in big strides and the junior high school students followed taking short and quick steps. I was always behind Sinsŏk. I remember his unusually huge behind and the English vocabulary notebook in his back pocket.

*Pleurisy*

I went too far in wanting to be like Sinsŏk. For a junior high school boy with narrow shoulders, the parallel bars were too difficult, so I became ill. I had pleurisy. I think my breast bone was badly strained and got infected. Luckily it was not chronic, so hot and cold massage was sufficient but I was bedridden for a month.

I had a slight fever the whole time I had pleurisy. I was miserable. I remember my mother feeding me rice mixed in with a spoonful of sesame oil. It was savory and delicious! I was not distressed by the lingering fever, rather I was enveloped in an atmosphere of peculiar sadness. I have never been sick for that long, so I can remember it clearly. It must have been traumatic for me.

I was sinking deep into an abyss of powerlessness and depression. Even during the daytime, I was in a daze, half-asleep and half-awake. Yet, I was sensitive to my mother's presence, so I was wide awake when I heard dishes clanking in the kitchen. The sound of dishes clanking, the sound of chopping on the cutting board, and the sound of water splashing when my mother came back from the well and poured it into the jar penetrated deeply into my mind when I was in my semiconscious state. While I was sick, I became awfully frail and my sole focus was on my mother. I had an invisible string attached to her back and held onto it all day long. I followed her every move, going in and out of the house, and how I waited eagerly for her to come see me. I waited for the moment for her to open the door to check up on me. I only had my mother to depend on. In the past, I waited for my mother's return many times when she came home late, but I had never realized the importance of her presence until then.

I felt my mother's strong presence in my life. I have the habit of drifting away in the middle of a conversation and I think this started around this time. I had never stayed away from school or my friends for a long time. During the daytime, I was alone in the room separated from my family. I had to endure the silence alone. Gradually I became familiar with silence and began to see myself clearly in that silent environment. The room was filled with only my existence. While I hung out with my friends, I tried to be one with them, not stand out in any way. That was the way I had existed until then. Then I became aware of myself and my own existence. I, who was independent from my friends and my mother, questioned for the first time who I was. I became aware of the void and it weighed down on me heavily in helpless dejection. I confronted myself in the depths of this languid and despairing powerlessness; in other words, I looked inside myself.

When I woke up after being in a state of half-sleep, the wallpaper design on the ceiling resembled snakes writhing. I remember lying on my side facing the paper-covered window and gazing absentmindedly at the bright paper that was in touch with the outside world. The window paper had many tiny strands or fibers, but to me even those took on the various shapes of animals and people. What caught my attention was a profile of a boy with long eyelashes. It resembled a sad-looking boy character who appeared often in the illustrations of serials in young boys' journals such as, *Boy's World* and *Academy*. A boy with long eyelashes was like a girl. Gazing blankly at the profile of the sad boy reflected on the window paper, I felt as if the boy possessed making me sad and ill. I wept staring at the boy overwhelmed by an unknown sadness. I could not move at all because I felt heavy with the boy inside me. I was in despair because of my powerlessness, yet there was something sweet about sadness. I tasted sweetness when slipping into the deep abyss without struggling. I must have liked the boy who possessed me while I was ill, but the boy was none other than myself. I was told numerous times how I looked like a girl because of my big eyes and long eyelashes. I cried often like a girl, too.

*Writing*

Even before I became ill, I was prone to bouts of melancholy, but I became even more sensitive. After I recovered fully, the boy with the long eyelashes and sadness lodged deeply inside me. I clearly saw myself as different from others and broke away from the group. I no longer walked after my seniors struggling to catch up with them. I walked alone and stayed away from the morning procession to school.

There was someone else who influenced me as much as Sinsŏk. He was two years older than me and his name was Yŏngdae. Later he became an assemblyman during the Fourth Republic and was like a Triton among the minnows. He was from the same clan and from the same hometown, so we were close from elementary school. He lost his parents during the Cheju Massacre and came to live in the same village where I lived. Yŏngdae lived with his older sister in a rented room. Even in his impoverished situation, he excelled in his studies and there was no one who could surpass him.

He was good at giving speeches, so every time he entered a contest he was placed either first or second. He even composed his own speech when he was in seventh grade. But one of his flaws was that he was short. Once at a speech contest he compared his height to Britain's Prime Minister David Lloyd George and surprised us all. I learned about David Lloyd George at that time and the story about his height made a deep impression on me. "David Lloyd George was short like me. He was running to be an assemblyman and gave his speech for the first time. When he got up and stood in front of the podium, he was so short that only his head was visible. People burst out into laughter, but guess what he said? He said one does not measure a man's height from his head to toe, but from the chin up. He said only the size of the head was important and he received a standing ovation."

Yŏngdae, too, received a standing ovation. Lloyd George was his dream. He had already chosen a symbolic figure and was climbing up step by step toward his goal through appropriate training. The road had been decided, and he simply needed to walk toward it. No one had any doubts about his success. He was an orphan who survived the Cheju Massacre. How could anyone not give him a big round of applause, watching him running energetically toward his goal with his strong will to survive? He was my role model in every respect. The reason why I did reasonably well in school was because I had an excellent competitor like Yŏngdae.

After I had pleurisy, I became a completely different person. My long forgotten depression, suffered when I was five or six years old, surfaced again. It was that dark and dreary hopelessness of my old home in Hambagigul. The experience I had at Hambagigul was so severe that even after I moved to town, I suffered from the aftermath of the Cheju Massacre for a long time. I stuttered and cried for no apparent reason after the fearful and painful event had long passed. I did not cry because I was sad, and it was utterly embarrassing to shed meaningless tears. I stammered like I had a mouthful of unhulled rice. I felt heavy-hearted. To overcome my stuttering, I entered a speech contest when I was in sixth grade and a stand-up comedy contest in seventh grade. For a while my efforts were rewarded and I noticed some improvement in my speech. However, my depression, which I tried so hard to overcome, returned when I had pleurisy and took control of my mind. I became weak from illness and my adolescent period coincided at this same time.

I started puberty when I was in seventh grade and from this time on my inner landscape changed completely. I wanted to be left alone and cried for no particular reason. I broke away from my friends and walked alone feeling dejected. I walked with my head down, looking at the shadow created on the ground. I did not even like the sunlight, so I walked in the shade on the edge of the street. Similar to when I was sick, this sense of dejection had a strange sweetness to it. Those who experienced the sweetness of solitude during puberty would understand. In fact, I relished in the sadness and wore a gloomy look on my face on purpose. Therefore, this melancholic depression was in part intentional and staged.

I was accustomed to silence because of my prolonged illness. A quiet boy with a gloomy face. I decided not to get attached to something that did not belong to me, such as speaking eloquently. I was deaf in one ear and a stutterer, so silence suited me better than talking. Therefore, I realized that what I needed to choose was writing, not speaking.

My Korean teacher became the object of my worship, my new

idol. He was young and single, and he was aspiring to become a writer. His genuine passion for literature was passed down to me. I remember the way in which he recited a poem in his clear voice and his radiant expression, while toying with a chalk in his hand. I'll never forget him saying that at times a noise can emphasize silence. I was impressed when he said that deep into the night when everything was asleep, the sound of leaves falling down could highlight the silent night even more. I was deeply moved by his words. What a revelation! What he said sounded poetic, something I had never heard of, and there I found the secret of literature.

It was around this time I started imitating the writing of the high school students who were published in a journal called *Academy* and I created my own story for the first time. It was during my second semester in seventh grade and fortunately my writing won the junior high school competition. Then my Korean teacher took notice of me, granting me special privileges to enter his room and let me borrow his books.

My very first, the so-called fiction, was entitled "Mother and Mother."

*"Mother and Mother"*
In "Mother and Mother," the second mother referred to my father's new wife. I just explained that my depression had generated as an aftermath of pleurisy, but a contributing factor was my father, who abandoned the family. "Little Mother" in Korean meant a stepmother and I thought it was utterly wrong to have two mothers. It was like my father who went to work at the garden in Western Heaven only to be charmed by a witch and never return home.

My father's secret came to light in the summer of my seventh grade. It was after we received a letter from him saying how he worked as a seafood broker in Inch'ŏn, then we never heard back from him again. My uncle went to Seoul on a business trip and came back with the news that my father had taken a new wife and settled down in Inch'ŏn. My father told me that after I finished elementary school, he would enroll me in a junior high school in Inch'ŏn. How could he do this to me? My uncle could not pass on the news to us, so he asked someone, a mediator, to break it to us gently. The woman my father was living with was someone he met recently; he had lived with her since he was discharged from the military. My uncle did not say it directly in so many words, but he wanted to suggest that since my father had been living with the woman for a long time, we had no choice but to accept it as a fact. For a while my mother disliked my uncle.

Since I had no idea what went on with my father for almost a year, I was very disappointed. When Sŭngŏn's father had an affair, I regarded it as something remote. Once I passed through the market, I saw Sŭngŏn's mother dragging a woman by her hair. I found out later that was the woman Sŭngŏn's father was having an affair with. The woman, surprisingly young and pretty, pleaded with Sŭngŏn's mother and said, "Please! Please!" Sŭngŏn's father had a limp because he had polio, but he made a lot of money in poultry farming. Sŭngŏn was in a precarious position. He was caught between his father's new woman he was living with and his mother who was bedridden. His mother tied a thin cloth around her head to show she was ill. I felt so sorry for Sŭngŏn. He was chased out of the house at his mother's urging to bring his father back home, but he had no courage. So he hung around the street, pacing up and down not knowing what to do. One time he pleaded with me to go with him to find his father. When we arrived at his father's mistress's house, the woman came out and Sŭngŏn said hello and bowed, calling her "Little Mother." She was just old enough to be his older sister, so I was shocked when he addressed her as "mother." How could he when his own mother was suffering because of her?

I was in the same situation as Sŭngŏn. Now that my father had a new woman, what was Hallakkung supposed to do? I could not even fathom calling her "Little Mother" because it was a word forbidden in my vocabulary. She was nothing to me, other than my father's woman. I had no idea that the image of my father I had longed for for such a long time would be ruined like this. I was disgusted at Sŭngŏn's father, so I sneered at him inwardly when I ran into him in the street. I made fun of his uneven way of walking, saying "teeter totter" in the rhythm of him hobbling along.

My mother tied a thin cloth around her head, and I had to endure her harassment just like Sŭngŏn had. I could understand how shocked and miserable my mother was through her crazy behavior. My mother's gentle face was twisted and warped with hatred, and I had never seen her like that.

I wondered how bitter she was at my father's betrayal. She was a proud woman. She said she could not possibly walk around with her head held high because of the humiliation. She said she just wanted to die. I think disgrace was more painful than despair. To put it crudely, a letter informing of his death during battle would have been less painful for her. Mother was so afraid that the other people might find out, and she seemed to fear that the most. She could not vent her frustrations out on her neighbors fearing that they might find out. So she could not even cry out loud, and she shut herself in her room and shuddered in shame.

"What am I going to do? How can I go on living with this shame? I'll die. My heart, head, and organs will all burn. You bastard, deserting your wife and living with another woman! Drown in the middle of the ocean and die."

Since the object of her hatred was far away, outside the island, I, the oldest son, had to take his place and become the target of her tirade. I was told that I came to look more and more like my father, so perhaps my mother saw my father in me. Therefore, she vented her hatred of my father on me.

"Talk to me. Tell me the truth. Aren't you happy that your father's taken another woman? You'd like that bitch, too, wouldn't you? You must be excited that you have 'Little Mother.' What? You don't like it? You are lying. You are waiting for your father to return, aren't you? When you hear from your father, you'll leave your poor mother alone and leave for the mainland, right? Am I not right? Am I wrong? You're lying. I won't stop you from leaving, so go. Leave your poor mother. Run to your father. Go live with that bitch. Eat the food she cooks for you and wear the clothes she buys for you. Call her mother and live happily ever after. Don't pretend you're crying. Tell me the truth. No? It's not true. What isn't true? What have I done to deserve this?"

My mother often went off saying all those things to me, linking me to my father. Every time she did that, I was upset and wanted to cry, too. She would then find a fault about my crying and say, "Why are you crying? Did your mother die? I'm not dead yet. Why are you crying when I'm still alive and kicking? Is it because I'm cursing you out? Or, is it because I'm calling her names? I'm going to die. When I die, you can live happily ever after and call her mother. I can't live like this. I need to get away or die. I'm going to leave all three of you and run away. I really can't live like this. I can't. Go to your grandparents and bring them and your uncle. I'm going to leave you guys with them and run away."

It was more unbearable listening to her piercing voice than being beaten by her. How could I endure her endless tirades without crying? I answered her back at times, but I stuttered when I was agitated. I became even more angry and frustrated because of my stuttering.

I don't know how to explain the tension between my mother and me. When she started venting, she was a completely different person and I became afraid of her. She knew it was not right to vent to her young son but she could not help herself. She could not suppress the anger that was burning her alive. She had no one else to vent to other than me. My mother was in pain, so I had to endure it at all costs. I was afraid that she would leave us in help-less despair. However, when she started venting, I could not help but become enraged, too.

The word "father" became a dangerous word that could not be mentioned around her. She became so sensitive that her nerves exploded even at the slightest provocation. For example, when I asked her for money to buy school supplies, she made sarcas-tic remarks such as "Why don't you ask your father or your new mother?" Then she gave me the money. Sometimes I could no longer endure her sarcasm, so I exploded and talked back at her. Once I was in such a rage that I lost my head completely. I felt numb in my brain and stuttered severely. I yelled and screamed, "I'm going to die. I'm going to die first," ripping the T-shirt I had on to shreds and scaring my mother. Whenever I had a fight with her or something sad happened, I ran to the beach near Yongduam and cried my heart out, crouching between the rocks. I let my cries be washed away by the waves, so that no one could hear, and I felt better after that.

My mother and I hurt each other like this, but we bonded tighter as mother and son by sharing painful memories. I wrote to my father in Inch'ŏn often at my mother's urging. I wrote to him saying "Drop everything and return home at once." I added that mother was crying everyday saying she'd run away, so if fa-ther did not return she would truly leave the house. The letter was melodramatic, full of lies and exaggerations, but it was a device to move him so those lies and exaggerations were true to me. I cried often so I had no problem dropping a couple of tears on the letter to make the ink run.

Not all my letters to him were melodramatic, full of tears pleading for his return. I subtly threatened him, too. Is it not true that all fathers feared their first sons? I needed to show to him that I was not to be taken lightly. I exaggerated about how smart I was. It was true that I received a scholarship, but I boasted it as if it was a sure ticket to become successful. I even concocted a story where I painted myself as a hero to impress him. In other words, I wrote a fiction not a letter. I realized at that time that fiction that was created like a real story was more believable than a true story. I knew lying was the best way to move him.

I wrote "Mother and Mother" based on the situation at home. However, this story was not entirely a confession based on my experience. I was embarrassed by the fact that my father had another woman, so I concealed it in the story. The story was based on my experience, but it was fictional. The protagonist of the story was neither Sŭngŏn nor I, but an amalgamation of the two, producing a completely different character. I named the character Chun with long eyelashes and sad eyes.

Who knew something I did not understand fully would determine my future career? It was the beginning of a long battle with no hope of winning. Writing was a battle that I could never win. I have no regrets, but my long painful life as a writer began with this piece of writing, "Mother and Mother." If my father had not abandoned the family, this writing would not have existed. Thinking this way, my heartless father was a key person who led me down this road. To be exact, my fiction writing began as letter writing to my father, which lasted for nearly seven years.

### Mountain Returned

The year after the truce was declared the confinement decree was rescinded and people were allowed to enter and cut wood on Mt. Halla, and I was in seventh grade. Mt. Halla had been bound like a criminal, but after seven years it was freed from the bondage and returned to the people. When the confinement order was in effect, no one was allowed to enter Mt. Halla or set foot in the expansive prairie. After the repeal, horses and cows grazing in the mountain meadows and the procession of people going to and fro cutting fire wood and carrying wood in their backs were seen on the road.

Thinking back, there were many newlyweds that year. There were hardly any wedding ceremonies for seven years, but it became popular after the young men returned safely after the war ended. My cousin was one of them. I remember how happy he was marrying a beautiful woman he met in the mainland. He had a tailcoat on and his shoes were shined so well that a fly would slide right off them. He looked absolutely great. His bright smile glowed and his entire body radiated brilliantly.

My two aunts got remarried that year, too. Their husbands were refugees from the mainland. I could guess what the situation was like at the time through my two aunts' weddings. After seven years since the Cheju Massacre, widows were permitted to remarry because so many island men had died, and they were grateful even though their marriage partners were from the mainland.

In any case, the season of death ended. Life penetrated through death, and the grand project of creating new life was under way. From the heap of ashes, a spark of new life blossomed to cover the burnt ground with verdant grass.

In regard to this, I recall an image. I witnessed something bizarre when I went to my paternal grandparents to attend the ancestral ceremony. They lived in a shack, still confined within stone walls. A lot of people gathered in the next shack, so I thought they were having their ancestral ceremony, too. It turned out that the people gathered in the next shack because someone was giving birth. Some of the women were standing outside the hut to encourage her and they looked gravely serious. I don't know why they did that. She wasn't giving birth to a prince. I guessed their losses during the Cheju Massacre had been severe because childbirth was the most urgent priority.

The lifting of the ban created a euphoric feeling and this wave of euphoria was reflected in the reconstruction project of my hometown at the time. It was the same year that the relocation camp under the name of "settlement construction" was abolished. The settlement construction was a euphemism for concentration camp. The counterinsurgency forces burnt down the villages and many lives were sacrificed; those who escaped death were placed inside the stone walls and kept under surveillance. This place was called the settlement construction. The true meaning of reconstruction began after the settlement construction was abolished. The people from Nohyŏngri returned to their burnt-down homes and took the stones used to set up the concentration camp walls to build their new homes. They went to Mt. Halla to look for lumber since the confinement decree was rescinded. Many people who took shelter behind the stone walls returned to their own villages. It was around this time the name Cheju Town was changed to Cheju City.

My family did not return to our old home. We could not think of moving back to our old home because we had settled into town life. So my mother decided to build our home in my grandfather's backyard. Her plan materialized sooner than she had anticipated. My aunt's new husband was a carpenter, so he was a great help. Carpenters were popular and in great demand because everyone was building or rebuilding a house. My mother bought lumber for columns and crossbeams with the money she had saved, and she went to Mt. Halla to cut wood for rafters. She also went to Mt. Halla to gather firewood because the barley and millet straws were not enough.

When people started going to Mt. Halla to gather firewood, the paths in the field that had disappeared from sight, covered in weeds, reappeared here and there, connecting the seaside road to Mt. Halla. On Sundays when there was no school, I followed my mother to gather firewood. Since entrance to Mt. Halla had been prohibited for a long period of time, there were plenty of dead branches. It took an entire day to gather wood, and it was my first time walking such a long distance.

When I recall that path that begins at the bridge over Hanch'ŏn, the first thing I remember is an open manure tub located not too far from the entrance of the path. On windy days in wintertime, children were engaged in kite battles in the field near the stream. One time a boy, busy looking up at the sky following his kite with its broken string, fell into the manure tub and almost died. The manure tub was filled with thick, black excrement and the stench was so bad that whenever I was near the place, I held my breath and passed by quickly. Walking along the path, at the end of the rice paddies there were two small mountains called Minorŭm and Namjosunorŭm. The vast grassland areas that people were prohibited to enter started from these two small mountains.

I feared Mt. Halla which seemed remote and marginal because I was not able to enter. After I started going to Mt. Halla to pick firewood, I changed my mind. My narrow vision, which had been limited to the seashore, expanded infinitely when I was at the foot of Mt. Halla. The vast space created by the expansive plain, the ocean, and the sky was a wonderful and marvelous world to me. But it was also a closed space, a world situated in the margins. The horizon that seemed close enough to touch my forehead when looking from the seashore was far away, creating a beautiful semicircle curved line from the foot of Mt. Halla. I could not find, not even the tip of the mainland, anywhere in that extensive sea touching the island. Then I realized that the island was surrounded and confined within the water. I must have thought someday I needed to penetrate through the horizon to escape from the island.

*Waiting for Mother*

When my mother went out to get firewood on weekdays, I carried a strap to bundle up the load to meet her as soon as I returned home from school. I walked two and a half miles to meet my mother and carried half of the firewood. My mother carried a lot knowing that I would come out to meet her halfway, so I had to go and meet her no matter what. It was such a joy meeting her on the way, though. My mother's head was pressed down by the heavy load and she plodded on, looking extremely exhausted. I ran calling out "Mother" trying to unload her burden as soon as I saw her. My mother lifted her head at my calling and smiled brightly. A warm feeling engulfed us, something that we could not feel when we were at home.

The joy of seeing her was sometimes ruined because of my mother's stubbornness. My mother would not unload firewood unless she needed to rest, so I was upset.

"Mother, unload quickly."

"I just rested. I can go a little more."

"What's the point of me coming out to meet you then?"

"Don't get upset. Look behind me. I have wild berries for you. Eat those berries and follow me."

"I didn't come out to eat. I came out to get firewood. Hurry and unload."

Once I went out to meet her but I missed her. It happened when I was in eighth grade. Since there was only one road, we could not possibly miss each other. However, on that particular day many people came down carrying hay stacks. It was the season for gathering hay for cows and horses to get ready for winter. Everyone carried a huge stack since hay was light and dry. I saw a horse carrying a stack as big as a house. People, cows, and horses all carried huge stacks. The lifting of the ban signified going back to the old lifestyle. Fall harvests were always bad, so gathering firewood and hay to prepare for the coming winter season made up for the bad fall harvest.

In late autumn, everything in the mountain came down to the village to spend winter. People who were working on the plain, cows and horses grazing, grains in the field, hay, firewood, in other words every single part of nature came down to the village in a long procession in late autumn.

That day I walked pass the long procession of people carrying huge hay stacks and looked for my mother among the crowd. The procession continued for a long time, but my mother was nowhere to be found. My friends who came out with me all met their family members and left, and there were no more people with stacks so I was left all alone. After the sound of people, cows, horses and carriages with loads became distant, a gloomy silence surged upon me. I was baffled at the sudden change of situation. I became afraid of the dreary silence. The shadow of the mountain became bigger and the sound of insects grew louder and louder as the silence deepened. In that absolute silence, I felt alienated. *Did something happen to mother? She never fell behind like this before even if her load was heavy. Did she get hurt? No, that can't be. We must have missed each other.*

I had to stop when I reached Minorŭm, where the rice paddies ended and the grassy land began. The sun was disappearing below the horizon. I stood between the two mountains and gazed at the path extended right in the middle of the prairie. The color of the sunset deepened and the prairie was covered in a gold color. The grass undulated in the wind like a living organism and it seemed unreal. I did not feel comfortable walking around the prairie alone even during the day because so many lives were taken away during the Cheju Massacre. Rusted shell casings, rubber shoes, bones that had been buried continued to turn up.

The shadows of the two mountains gradually grew larger, becoming darker than the prairie area. My mother did not appear with a load of firewood and as the night drew near the two small mountains froze like a fossil, leaving only the dark outlines. I, standing alone on that path felt as if I, too, had changed into that fossil. I wrote a poem entitled "Fossil" based on this experience; it was my first poem. I do not remember the lines exactly, but I still remember vividly how I felt at the time.

*Home*

My home was built within the walls of my maternal grandparents' yard in spring of the year I entered the eighth grade. One of the reasons why the house didn't get completed as planned was because my uncle was always busy. He only worked on our house between building other houses. Among the construction materials my mother bought, there were some old and new; some of them were relief materials and were as good as new but the pillars and cross beams were not new. The old ones were collected from the houses that were burnt down during the massacre. The pillars and beams were worn away by the wind and the rain and had burnt marks here and there. The stained parts were all shaved off with a plane saw and became as good as new.

On the day the framework of the house was completed, I bowed to the guardian spirit of the house in place of my father as my grandfather had instructed me. I felt so proud when I saw the ridge beam standing high up with a ceremonial letter written by my grandfather flapping in the air. My long dream of having "my home" finally came true and I was to become the head of the household.

After the framework was completed, the work progressed fairly quickly. Especially when the mud was being plastered, everyone was extremely busy. The neighbors helped us getting water and soil. I think it took about four days to use up a pile of soil in the middle of the courtyard. During those four days, everyone moved about busily. Even I had to work hard. I think it was during my spring break. I was mainly in charge of mixing water with soil. I poured water in the middle of the soil to create a pond and rolled up my pants and mixed with my feet, walking all over. It was simple and easy, but I hated the cold feeling I felt around my feet. It was early spring so it was still a little chilly. But I endured it. I was to become the future head of the household in place of my father.

I did well until one day when the temperature dropped drastically, and I made a complete fool out of myself. I should've stopped when I could no longer endure the cold soil mix, but I continued on. Then I burst into tears. When my grandfather saw me crying, he laughed and said, "Hahaha! Look at him, he has a foul temper!"

At last a small house I called "my home" sprung forth, reeking with a fresh smell of soil. There was not enough money to build a porch, so it was decided to add it later. Everyone in my family was excited about having our own home even though we had to rent out one of the two rooms. It was a drastic change going from renting a room to renting out.

The room was rented out to two women who were several years older than me. They came from the country to attend a dressmaking school. Even though we lived under the same roof, there was not much interaction between us. I did not get along well with people. How could I pretend not to notice when the women were in such close proximity? I simply hid it well, pretending not to care. Because I was always quiet, they thought I was a difficult person to approach, so they did not approach me unless they absolutely had to. When they did ask me something, surprisingly they used formal speech. I felt weird hearing formal speech from the women who were several years older than me. At night I heard them laughing loudly and I felt distracted. From time to time, some boys from the technical high school, not very studious looking, followed them and hung outside the house, whistling.

The story of these women was cut short because my father returned. My father and I ended up using that room.

*Father Returned*

At last my father returned. His return meant that his life in the
mainland had failed. If his business had not failed, making him
penniless, would he have returned home? He acted indifferently
toward us as if he had returned unwillingly at the urge of my
mother's and my letters begging him to return.

My father returned around four months after the house was
completed, and it was during evening in summertime. We were
having dinner in the courtyard with my grandparents and my father walked in without any warning. I was in a state of confusion
rather than feeling happy to see him. I sent him letters begging
him to return but seeing father like this, I felt uncomfortable—as
if I was meeting a complete stranger. We were estranged from
each other after seven years of separation. For a fourteen year old
boy, seven years seemed like an eternity and my father's absence
was deeply ingrained in my heart and could not be erased forever.
Seeing my friends reprimanded by their fathers, I was relieved
that my father was not around. I wrote to my father because my
mother urged me to do so, but it meant nothing to me as if I had
written it to an imaginary person. So I thought my father's return
was impossible. My father existed as an idea not as a real person.
He broke the long silence and appeared in front of me as someone real. I had lived not knowing what it meant to have a father
around and from then on I experienced it to the full extent.

Not only was my father a stranger but the epitome of total
failure. At first, his leather luggage seemed so luxurious that I
doubted that he was broke. The smell of the leather bag was so
good that I still remember it. However, everything inside the
luggage was pathetic and pitiful. Later there was no sign of the
leather luggage in the house; I think he pawned it or sold it. He
only had one suit; the jacket was black and looked decent, but the
trousers were faded serge blue army pants. My Warped Mouth
teacher I disliked so much dressed like my father. They were not

only similar in what they wore but they carried themselves and talked like soldiers, too. I became depressed.

My seven years of grace was over and my living with my father began. I was fourteen years old and was full of discontent. My childhood had passed but my new self had not quite formed to fill the void, so I was in pain and unhappy. Therefore, my father's sudden appearance made me hostile. I was beginning to see who I was. To strongly feel oneself completely as distinguished from another meant that the other me that was relative was overwhelmingly magnified; for me, that other me was none other than my father.

At first I tried very hard to accept and get used to the new environment, meaning my father. I had to be in the same room with him and sleep under the same blanket, so regardless of whether I liked it or not, I had to get used to it. I volunteered to massage my father's feet at that time, which became habitual and lasted until he died; it was tedious and tiresome. I slept by his feet, so I had to get used to smelling my father's feet. Luckily my father always washed his feet before going to bed, so they did not stink. Perhaps it is correct to say that he washed his feet to make me massage them. When I was in third grade, I was taught how to massage by a blind refugee boy and I certainly made good use of it. My father was difficult to please, but he certainly approved of my massaging skills. He said he fell asleep easily when I massaged his feet.

My father had nightmares often. I hated so much when he shouted in his sleep,. How many nights had I endured him shouting? His nightmares were symptoms of postwar trauma. There was no one who could comfort him and heal the scars that were deeply lodged in his heart. If war was cruel in trampling upon peace, peace was cruel in forgetting the memories of war and wounds too quickly. Even my mother did not want to know about his wounds. It was best to forget the painful memories as soon as possible. If he hung onto those painful memories for too long, he would only become a social outcast. For my father, the war that had ended in real life continued to take place in his consciousness. Everyone was intimidated by his army-style speech and demeanor. Hearing him scream in the middle of the night, I was extremely disturbed and felt uneasy, as if divine wrath had struck me.

One time I happened to massage his feet and he slept well. Since then I had to do it every night even though I did not want to. What started as something I volunteered to do ended up as a yoke of bondage. I felt good about helping him, though.

My father always had his socks on, so his feet were pale. I was used to seeing tanned farmers' feet, so it was strange seeing a pair of such white feet. His feet felt cool and damp even during the summertime, so I felt like I was touching mushrooms in the shade. His feet endured several years of war, tired and weary wandering around the battleground. They were frighteningly cold during the summertime, too. Thinking back now, my father was trying to warm his feet by borrowing his son's hands in place of my inattentive mother. What I touched and stroked with my hands was my father's sadness. Sadness that no one could console, not even my mother, whom he had not seen for a long while. After he returned, they slept separately from the first day. His sadness of sharing the blanket with me rather than with mother also included the pain of saying farewell to his woman in Inch'on. However, I couldn't understand or try to understand what went on inside my father's mind, or my mother's for that matter. My father was nothing but an object of fear. I could not stop massaging my father's feet because I was afraid of him.

My father's first job was a clerk, working at the county office. It was temporary but he was told he'd get a permanent position within several months. He should've been grateful since unemployment during the postwar period was severe. I was proud of seeing my father going to work in his newly made suit. My entire family wanted so much to have a father who earned money. At the time the majority of the islanders were engaged in farming; we were still living in the agricultural age. So a person working in an office and getting a salary was treated like nobility, and civil servant jobs were especially popular. Going against our expectation, my father quit working after a month. He did not quit because he found a better job, but he simply did it because it did not suit him. I was disappointed in my father for leaving such a good job. All he had to do was do his work and every month he would receive his salary. Of course, my father had his own plans. I'm certain he was confident about his future like any other thirty five year old man. After he quit his job, he started raising pigs.

*The Sow Ate Her Young Piglets*

I mentioned earlier that it was a custom in Cheju Island to raise pigs in the outhouse of each house. After our house was built, we raised a pig, too. Since we could raise a pig with our own waste, it was a joy going to the outhouse. We bought a baby pig and it was so adorable. I remember coming home to use the outhouse when I was at my friend's so that I didn't waste my dump. It was common to have a pig when you had your own home. My father also had another pig he raised, borrowing our neighbor's outhouse. The neighbor who let us use his outhouse was the trucker named Mr. Kim. He came to the island as a refugee from the North during the war, so he had never raised a pig.

My father bought a pig and raised it in Mr. Kim's outhouse, but it was my sister and I who had to take care of it. My mother was busy with farming, working in the field, and my father was always out. I had no idea what he was doing outside, but he did odd jobs here and there. He worked as a broker for cows and went to the country; he even helped out with thatching roofs. At the time, even the houses downtown were thatched roof houses.

Those people who weren't engaged in farming had to call in people for help. I went to my teacher's house to borrow a book and was surprised to find my father thatching roof. I found out that day that my father did odd jobs. When he saw me he didn't say a word, but he just winked at me and smiled awkwardly. He did not ask why I was there, and I did not say it was my Korean language teacher's house.

My father said he was working odd jobs to save enough money to start his own business. He seemed like he was working hard, but didn't have much money saved. He busied himself for nothing. My mother spoke ill of him saying that his diligence was like a "straw basket," meaning that all his efforts escaped through the holes. If he were simply a lazy person, I would have accepted it and felt better. I think he was cursed.

Because of my father's "futile diligence" my sister and I became busy raising the pigs. Twice a day we had to take turns in feeding the pigs. My father said the pigs needed solid fodder, so he made us go outside and gather seaweed from the seashore and outer leaves of Chinese cabbages from the cabbage field. I did not know what the word "solid fodder" meant but did not bother to ask. I didn't even want to ask. I shut my father out completely. Why do I need to know that fancy word raising a few lousy pigs? Is he trying to brag that he graduated from the agricultural school? Shouldn't he be embarrassed about raising pigs, an agricultural school graduate and former MP Lieutenant? I couldn't open myself up to my father because of these reasons. Whenever I think of my father's failure, the word "solid fodder" comes to mind as if it's the symbol of his defeat.

His attempt to raise pigs ended in failure. One year worth of hard work, a baby pig that grew big enough to be a mother pig, went down the drain over night.

I believe it rained on the day that mother pig gave birth. It was during the monsoon season, so it rained for days and the outhouse flooded. My father had that worried look on his face, fretting about water getting into the pig's shed. He placed stacks of dried barley straw, but he could not stop worrying about the pig. He anxiously waited for the pig to give birth, and when he saw a baby pig squirming inside the shed, he thought his worries were over. He went to the kitchen to make fodder for the mother pig so that she could provide milk for her young. Usually a pig gives birth to five or six baby pigs. He could not ascertain how many were born since it was dark, but he didn't doubt for one second that five or six would be suckling.

However, the outcome was an utter fiasco. It was something that rarely happened, a mother pig eating her young; but it happened to us. The baby pig that my father saw was the last one left, but after a day it was nowhere to be seen; it was the last one to be eaten by the mother pig. There is a saying that a mother pig eats her young when the area is tampered with. No one was supposed to peek inside the shed when it was time to give birth or make any noise. We knew this so well that no one in my family would go against the rules, so there was no reason for this to happen. How could something like this happen? How can this be explained scientifically? Did the mother pig decide to consume its own young because they were born too weak or the environment in which they were born into was so poor and inadequate that they had no chance? Later when we looked at the shed, there was a puddle of water despite the fact that there were stacks of straw on the ground.

Everyone in my family was unhappy that something inauspicious happened. I was disgusted when I read the section where the Three Witches from *Macbeth* made a potion by throwing in various creatures in a cauldron and adding blood from a female pig that ate her own young. *Macbeth* was my middle school graduation play in which I had a part.

My father was so disappointed that all his hard work, more

than a year's worth, went down the drain. However, he never thought about how disappointed we would be. He sold the despicable mother pig at a market and spent it all on gambling, ignoring my mother's plea to leave half of the money.

The image of my father was that of a failure and was deeply etched in my mind. My father failed one thing after another. I don't think he was unlucky, but he was cursed.

### Books

I hated my father. I needed an object of hatred at the time, too. I was standing on the threshold of maturity, physically and psychologically. My new self was struggling to come out. In order for the strong-willed self to be created, completely distinct from the other, a collision with my other, meaning my father, was inevitable. I realized my "self." No, not only did I recognize my "self" but this presence of my "self" pressed down, weighing heavily on me. As I recognized my "self," everything around me seemed unfamiliar. Not only my father but my mother was objectified and seemed very far away. I was only thinking of myself. I was the truth and the most important thing. The only thing that was real around me was my "self" and everything else was false or unreal. I was under the impression that nothing would happen in my absence. I'm sure all of you have experienced this at that age. Similar to those puppets on a stage, they only move and talk when I'm watching them, but once they are out of my sight, they stop moving. In other words, I was under the illusion that without me nothing would happen and nothing would matter.

My delusion was so fragile that every time I confronted the finitude of my existence, a painful awakening, it completely shattered to pieces. I still remember this sharp pain that trampled upon the fragile heart of a ninth grader. That was why I was often depressed like an abandoned child. No one had abandoned me. In fact, I was the one who stayed away from them.

Whenever I felt depressed, I stood alone at the beach and gazed blankly at the waves or the clouds in the sky. For the first time in my life, I skipped school. I hid my school bag between rocks and wandered around the beach all day long. I was upset thinking that all my classes went well even when I wasn't there. It meant that I didn't need to be present for things to happen and that even after I died, everything would continue as usual. I think it was around this time, my third year in middle school, I entered a writing contest and the title of my entry was "Me." I won the first prize. I forgot all the details, but I remember writing about the endless darkness and fear before birth and after death.

I believe my gloomy inner self was aggravated by reading. I read everything that I could get my hands on. I was over the stage of reading young adult books or popular fiction. I was absorbed in reading the so-called "pure literature." Luckily my teacher Mr. Kim's library was always open to everyone in school. I borrowed the collected works of Yi Sang, Kim Yujŏng, Hwang Sunwŏn, Kim Tongni, An Sugil, and O Yŏngsu and a monthly literary journal, *Modern Literature*.

There were parts I could not understand when reading some of these books, but somehow they deeply touched my heart. In Hwang Sunwŏn's *To Live with the Stars* I was startled to encounter a passage about a blood stain in the female character's underwear. No one had taught me nor was there a detailed explanation, but I knew instinctively that the blood stain meant her first period. I particularly liked Yi Sang and the word "hemoptysis" that appeared in his writing was quite shocking even though it meant coughing up blood.

Reading suited my melancholic mood well. In place of speaking, I filled the silence around me with reading. After I finished reading, I felt content as if I had met a good conversation partner and had a great discussion. Books taught me about sadness that had no particular cause—in other words, loneliness. I often wept even though I wasn't sad because I felt a sense of emptiness. Tears of that sort were even sweeter. My future didn't seem bright. I thought that my depression would surely block my happiness. An impoverished writer . . . I think that's how I saw myself in the future. I just wanted to write something, not necessarily literary works.

I particularly liked Yi Sang and Kim Yujŏng who died young, so I felt closer to them than my own blood kin. I was even envious of their tuberculosis. They both died young having contracted tuberculosis, but even their illness seemed like a laurel wreath. I was dying to contract the same disease—spitting up blood into a white handkerchief, a beautiful flower.

*Untimely Death*

In real life, it was different. The tuberculosis that existed in my imagination as an abstract thing materialized as something real. My idol Sinsŏk contracted tuberculosis and became ill. I was in ninth grade at the time. After he graduated from high school, he found a job at a local elementary school. He had decided to work for just one year to save money for his tuition to go to college in the mainland. He had high hopes of entering university to continue his studies. Who knew a seed of death was growing inside his muscular body? At the time, tuberculosis was incurable.

He passed away that summer. He returned to the countryside and died there. I found out when his mother came to collect his things in his boarding room. Since her son died, it was useless to keep the room. She packed everything and cleaned out the room. I saw her before she left when I went to the beach situated below Yongduam. She had her feet in the water, gazing out blankly.

That particular pool was only for men so normally women did not use it. It was during the daytime, so there were no bathers. Usually people came either early in the morning or in the evening after work. Children frequented this place to wash after they played in the ocean. Young men liked to soak in the cold water rather than swim in the ocean. The cold water was good for cooling down their burning sexual desires. They bathed naked, but when they saw young women passing through the beach over on the cliff side, they held their penises that shrunk in the cold water and caressed them. They shouted like horses neighing when they were in heat. I didn't think it was obscene at all because it was something I often witnessed. Rather I thought it was quite playful and mischievous.

Sinsŏk was one of those mischievous ones. When he took off his clothes, his muscular body looked strong and wonderful. But then inside his healthy body, like a worm in a fruit the deadly disease was hiding. I was no longer able to see his beautiful body in the water, but his mother visited the place to find traces of her dead son.

I said hello and quickly turned around to leave, but she stopped me.

"Come over here. Don't try to run away. I'm just an old lady so no one will think ill of me for coming to this place only for men and staying for a while, right? I came because this is where my son used to come."

She had her feet in the water and I approached her with a heavy heart as if I were about to be reprimanded. I had yet to express my word of condolences, so I was afraid to face her.

"Good thing that I ran into you. I have something to tell you."

She looked as if she had something important to say. *I wonder what it is. I'm just a kid. I don't know what to say to comfort her. What's so important that she needs to tell me? What if she starts to vent or grumble about how miserable she is?*

"Would you like to have my son's desk and chair? I want you to have them."

My ears pricked up. Since I didn't have a desk, I used the folding table we used for meals, but it always reeked of a dishcloth. So I could not believe that she wanted to give me a real desk and a chair.

"Say something. You don't want them?"

"No, no! It's not that. I just don't know how to thank you. Thank you very much."

"Then come over in the evening and pick them up. He bought the raw material from the wood shop and made the desk and the chair himself. They are strong and sturdy. He did a good job."

I knew he was good at making things, so I did not lose my opportunity and added, "I know. I saw the desk before. It sure is well made. What about the parallel bars? They were well made, too." I said these things without giving much thought, but surprisingly she became animated and her eyes sparkled.

"You know my son very well. He was good on the parallel bars."

"I know. He was good at everything. He was like a Jack of all trades. People who did well in school were poor athletes, but Sinsŏk was good at both, studying and sports. He was very popular."

"He was such a good son, too. He was really good to me."

"Sinsŏk took cold baths here naked even during winter in heavy blizzard. His body turned red and a hazy white steam rose. We shivered in cold just looking at him, but he did not even bat an eyelid. He stood firmly and yelled out, 'Attention! At ease!' looking over the ocean. He looked great! He was captain material."

"Yes, yes. You know him so well."

Tears welled up in her eyes—not tears of sadness but happiness. I was glad that I expressed my words of condolence to her.

I remember one winter day when he took a cold bath in the pond. His strong and muscular body turned red from scrubbing too hard with a towel and steam arose from his body. He stood firmly and screamed loudly toward the ocean. His voice spread far out into the ocean, making the ocean look grander and the rolling waves kneel before him obeying his command. A pack of wild horses running with flying manes in the waves galloped fiercely but there was no white horse that came forth to claim him as its owner. He died at the peak of his beauty and strength. The image of Sinsŏk I have is conflated with a legendary character and has made a deep impact in my memory.

*White Horse in the Waves*
The beach near Yongduam, often called Yongmŏri meaning "Dragon Head," has two legends, one is that of a dragon and the other a horse. Malmŏri or Horse Head is located on the west of Yongmŏri. The legend was that for a long time a dragon wanted to ascend to Heaven and the moment it was about to rise out of the water, it froze, thus the name Yongmŏri. A white horse searched for a hero in the ocean but could not find him, and it died so the place was named Malmŏri. Both myths bemoaned a sad demise.

Once upon a time there was a boy with incredible strength and he lived with his mother by the harbor located on the west side of Yongmŏri. When the boy turned fifteen years old, he ate about five bushels of rice and one whole pig. Thus, his strength was comparable to the amount of food he consumed. It was difficult to feed him since his mother was poor. His mother could not watch him die of starvation, so she went to the local government to ask them to take her son as a slave. She asked to make her son do the work of ten people and feed him the equivalent of ten people's. The governor plotted to kill the boy instead of trying to help him. He did not want him to stay alive for he was afraid that he might become a traitor later. The problem was how to tie him with a rope. Over twenty constables were sent out to capture him, but they did not dare put a rope around him seeing his tall stature. Surprisingly he was submissive and said, "Dying of starvation is the same as being killed, either way dying is dying. Let me eat to my heart's content before I die. If you provide five bushels of rice and one cow for me to eat, I will turn myself in." Five bushels of rice were cooked and one cow was slaughtered. After he finished eating, he became drowsy and fell asleep. The constables bound him and attached heavy rocks on his legs and arms and dumped him in the ocean near Yongduam. The giant did not sink easily. He was floating on his back in the water for three days and yelled out, "Mother, mother! Should I die or live?" His mother could not say to live, so she kept quiet and wailed, watching him by the seashore with other villagers. Since the local government official was plotting to kill him, he would die sooner or later. Even if he were to live how was he going to feed himself? Then after three days he said, "Mother, please live long. This unfilial son will leave you now," and sank into the water. A white horse sprung out of the water all of a sudden. It reared up and shook its head and neighed three times. Then it disappeared into the water. The white horse was meant for the giant. He called out to its master, but there was no reply so the horse went back into the water. If the giant had lived for a few more minutes, he could have become a general commanding the world riding on that horse. The name Malmŏri came about because the horse raised its head above the water and then disappeared.

The reason why I draw parallels between Sinsŏk's death and this legend is because I came to understand the real meaning of this myth. There were various legends about giants from all over the island. The giants who were killed because they posed a threat to the government as possible rebels represent all the islanders who were discriminated against. They signify the sad demise of those people who fought hard trying to overcome their difficult situation. The countless young people who died during the Cheju Massacre were those giants. Those young men who wished to fly high up in the sky felt the weight of the enormous rocks that hung around the giant's arms and legs.

### The Sorrows of Young Werther

This was how I inherited Sinsŏk's desk, but it did not mean that his dream was handed down to me as well. My dream was heading toward a completely different direction. I was interested in literature, therefore I no longer liked muscular men; Sinsŏk was the last. Words like muscular physique, magnanimous, a man of noble spirit were detestable to me. I thought femininity was the key to literature; rather than masculine energy and vigor, the effeminate qualities were important elements in literature. Pale and sickly looking was more important than looking healthy. Here I am not referring to physical sickness. I liked Yi Sang and even the tuberculosis he contracted seemed wonderful, but I could not imagine myself suffering from tuberculosis. After I brought Sinsŏk's desk and chair, I cleaned them several times with soapy water for I was afraid that tubercular germs might remain. When I said illness, I meant mental not physical. I wished to have the symptoms of mental illness described in Yi Sang's works because I thought I needed to become ill to write. For me, the name Yi Sang signified idiosyncrasies, psychological abnormality.

Unknown desire, sadness, and conflicts were stirring deep in my heart. These feelings were in the process of formation, so they were not quite in solid form. They were mere concepts or notions yet to be manifested in concrete forms, but they stirred my heart like the prelude before a storm.

I began to wear a sad face like a mask. I pretended to be depressed or melancholic before I entered puberty. I was often depressed before, so it was not difficult to walk around putting on a sad face. At the time I thought I was being true to myself because that's how I felt and I didn't think I was imitating, but I was wrong.

Every time I encountered young protagonists with scarred souls in the works of Yi Sang or Kurata Hyakuzō's *The Beginning of Love and Awareness*, I was eager to imitate them. For someone who wanted to imitate characters undergoing pain, I slept way too much. How can a sleepyhead like me contemplate life? It was impossible. The characters I knew from the novels I read spent all night long contemplating, and how I envied their sleepless nights. I never succeeded in staying up all night. I was absorbed in reading and I cried, but when it was nearing midnight I could not keep my eyes open and dozed off. I tried to think of Sinsŏk's sad fate, Sinsŏk who died young before realizing his dream, but even that could not keep sleep at bay.

I attempted a few drastic measures to overcome the midnight wall. I turned off the oil lamp and lit a candle and placed it on my desk around eleven at night. I swore to stay awake until the candle went out. I even had a kitchen knife next to me. I wanted the god of sleep to run away seeing the knife. I thought I could stay up by creating this kind of environment. I said to myself that I was an idiot if I could not stay up until one whole stick of candle finished burning. I tensed up and read *The Sorrows of Young Werther*, following Werther's every movement. I arrived at the sad part and closed the book in sorrow, staring at the candle light. The candle was shedding sad tears. Watching the candle, tears welled up in my eyes, too. I quickly took out a mirror and looked at my face. My face illuminated by the candlelight made me look beautiful as if I was not myself. It was a beautifully choreographed expression of sorrow; what I found in the mirror was Werther crying in pain.

I could not stay awake with fake tears or fake suffering no matter how many times I said, "Ah, I'm sad! I'm in pain." By midnight I could not ward off sleep and ended up dozing off at my desk with tears in my eyes.

### Joy of Suffering

I tried not to talk too much because a person suffering couldn't be talkative. I was practicing to be silent. I did not do this to imitate suffering or feign loneliness. At the time I was going through the voice change and it was so severe that my voice sounded hoarse. Every time I tried to talk I sounded like a rooster with a bone stuck in its throat. I was embarrassed because among my friends I was the only one with the problem. I was afraid that my vocal cords would stay that way forever. I avoided talking because I was embarrassed about my voice.

It was not difficult to keep my mouth shut for half a day if I had things to read. I was conversing with the characters in the story in my mind so the true meaning of silence did not apply. I borrowed any books I could get my hands on, difficult or easy. Philosophical books were difficult to understand but they made strong impressions on me. I read Camus, Schopenhauer, and Kierkegaard. I read them fast, not fully understanding, as if a dog was licking wild grapes, but I certainly understood their pessimistic views. One of the philosophical books that I read and understood fully was written by the Japanese philosopher, Kurata Hyakuzō, entitled *The Beginning of Love and Awareness*. It was written in a sentimental tone, but it was heavily laden with pessimism. The writer perfected the dramatic effect of pessimism by committing suicide by jumping off a waterfall. The negative understanding or awareness began to sprout in the heart of an adolescent boy, the realization that the world was neither good nor perfect nor beautiful.

I could endure the classroom noise during breaks if I had a book or a magazine to read. This realm I created for myself, remaining silent while everyone else was talking and making noise completely absorbed into a different world, was exquisite and precious. I was like a frog in a pond shutting out noise while the other frogs were croaking wildly. When I had my ears covered with my hands, the noise the kids made sounded like bees buzzing. My friends around me were the embodiment of "noise," meaning illusions, and the only thing that was true and factual was me.

I preferred to be in dark places and kept my head down when walking down the street. Everything I saw seemed to be a depressing gray color. I don't know when it started but I began to see the world as a place full of detestable things. I told myself over and over again that I'm walking with my head down because I did not want to see those ugly things. I did not even want to hang out with my friends, so I kept my distance from them. I did not want to see them acting like idiots and I hated those book smart ones because they were studious and diligent. I despised my teachers. I was disappointed with my father, so I felt hostile toward teachers who weren't capable but attempted to exercise their power by disciplining students and hitting them. I kept silent suppressing my desire to raise my hand to answer the questions my teacher posed which no one else in the classroom knew but I knew. I took great pleasure in this.

Like I said before, my thoughts and actions were in fact abstract ideas of joy, although I did not realize it. I wasn't confronting reality. I consciously created my depression or I silently withdrew and then became depressed. After experiencing this kind of pleasure, the world was no longer gray but more beautiful than ever before. The joy I felt was greater when I returned to my friends after I kept silent for a long time. This feeling of accomplishment swept over me when I finally spoke again with my friends after successfully enduring not talking to them. The longer I held off speaking the greater the pleasure I felt when I went back to my friends, laughing and talking.

Thinking back to the time when I was standing on the threshold of puberty, I was not myself in terms of my psychological frame of mind. I felt alienated from myself. Although I am the same person as before, I was completely different then. My genuine passion had died and changed into something disgraceful and unsightly, so how could I be the same person as before? (My uncontrollable drinking habit!) My old self is closer to today's middle school students who are crazy about rock music and hip hop dancing rather than my present self.

## Female Students

I ran into female students on my way to school because the middle school I attended was located near the girls' middle school. It was around this time I started to feel attraction toward girls who had previously only existed for me as the "dark blue colored skirts" of their school uniforms. I began to notice the girl's physical attributes, like their chests sticking out. I was more interested in the high school students who were physically more mature than the middle school students.

I explained already how I had my head down trying not to see things I did not want to see when walking down the street. I wanted to avoid seeing those girls for other reasons. When I said I did not want to see the girls what I meant was I was trying hard to resist their attraction. I could not help but look when the girls appeared. I was disappointed in myself, so I had my head down so as not to see at all.

Even if I had my head down, I could see everything. I looked as if I carried all the troubles in the world and dragged my feet looking miserable. My eyes were lowered, but I slyly stole a look at the girls' legs. I felt dizzy when they passed by me with their skirts flapping, their joyful strides revealing the contours of what was beneath and their plump thighs, and I sighed unconsciously. Finding a resemblance to Werther in my sad appearance, I wanted to hear the girls to say, "Look at him! He looks so sad!"

Unfortunately the person who found me first was my mother. Well, it's more accurate to say I was discovered, not found. I ran into my mother in front of Sŭngŏn's shoe store after school. I had tucked my school bag under my armpit, had my hands in my pockets, and had my hat all the way down to my eyebrows, I walked sluggishly with no strength dragging my feet with my head down. When my mother saw me looking pathetic, she was surprised. I had a bad feeling, so I raised my head. There was my mother only a few steps away from me, glaring. I was embarrassed so I took my hands out of my pockets, fixed my hat, and pretended I never dragged my feet. I smiled sheepishly and puffed out my chest. She was holding a pair of white rubber shoes she just bought.

"Mother, did you buy new shoes?"

Mother was really angry.

"What, shoes? Are you taking me for a fool? You looked so sad, as though you had just been crying at my funeral."

"Sad? I was not."

"I saw you coming from over there. Why are you walking like that? You had your head down like your mother died. Are you in trouble?"

"No, nothing like that. I'm not in trouble."

"Then why are you walking gloomily with your head down? Are you trying to find barley ears like your grandmother?"

"No, it's not that. I did it for fun."

"For fun? Don't lie. Tell me the truth. What's troubling you?"

"Nothing."

"Anyway, don't walk like that from now on. You need to walk in the middle of the street ... don't wear your hat like that. You look sneaky and devious."

Although I was reprimanded, I continued to walk like that. The girls showed interest in me, even though insincere and superficial, when I walked around with all the troubles in the world on my shoulder with my head drooped down. They giggled softly. When they passed right by me, my heart pounded so loudly that even though I had my head down I could feel they were staring at me.

Once I made a fatal mistake. There were two female students who walked toward me and as soon as we passed by each other, they burst out into laughter. It was clear that they were laughing at me. So, I raised my head to see what was going on. When I checked, a button came off from my pants so my fly was open.

I was embarrassed but listening to the girls laugh always made me feel great. I could never understand what the girls were saying because they were always at a distance so all I could hear was them laughing. Until fourth grade the girls and boys studied together, but now those girls who were once my classmates seemed like total strangers. Their laughter was magical like I was under their mysterious spell and it was irresistible. Every time I heard them laugh I was frustrated that there was a distance between us and that I could not get close to them. Their laughter was ringing in my ears day and night. The girls existed as phantoms, laughing from a far off place where I could not reach them. I wondered if there was a way to get close to them.

### Women's Public Bath

The charming laughter of bathing women coming from Yongyŏn was incredibly stimulating. Young men passing by the place were ill at ease and became nervous when they heard women's voices coming from the pond. Even to me the sound of their laughter was extraordinary. I felt uneasy hearing them splashing water and laughing and giggling. Like one of my classmates, I was compelled to jump into the water with a towel wrapped around my head. I laugh even now thinking about my classmate who had a towel wrapped around his shaven head and a cloth around his waist like an apron, carrying a water jug.

He was from the country and lived in a rented room near the

bridge. (I remember eating cheese for the first time at his place). What he disliked the most about living alone was drawing water from the well called Sŏnbanmul. He did not have enough money to buy a bucket so he used the landlady's water jug which only women carried in Cheju Island. He was made fun of for carrying a woman's water jug, so he went to the well only at night when no one could see him. That was why he dressed like a woman with the towel on his head covering his bald head and had the wrapping cloth around his waist like an apron.

One time there were many women taking a bath at night because hot weather had continued for several days. The well for drawing drinking water and the bathing pool were next to each other so he was afraid to go in. But he could not go home without water so he risked being found out and went in. Fortunately the women were busy talking to themselves in the dark, so they did not notice him. The first few days he was busy trying to get out as soon as he got the water, but after several days he had time to look around and relax.

"It was great watching them, more than ten naked women taking a bath. They didn't even have their underwear on. They were completely naked!"

"Completely naked? Really?"

"Really. They had nothing on. Their white butts were round and plump."

"Don't lie! How can you see when it's so dark?"

"No, you can see them. I saw. Don't tell the others, okay? If this gets out, I'll be in trouble. I couldn't see well because it was dark, so I got undressed and went into the water myself."

"What? You're lying. You're such a chicken. You couldn't have."

"I'm telling you the truth. I went in naked with a towel around my head. I took off my underpants, too."

"What? You took off your underpants?"

"Everyone was naked so if I had the underpants on, they would get suspicious, right?"

"Shit! Then what? Hurry, tell us."

"I pretended I was taking a bath, but I watched them. It was such a sight. They were squeezing their breasts and oh my god!"

"Shit head! You are making things up."

After this, in my sexual fantasies I often saw myself naked with only a towel wrapped around my head, jumping in between the women in the pool. A similar image came to mind when I went to the public bath once a year.

In a public bath, a partition was the only thing that separated the women's and men's sections. The partition was a slightly taller than average male height, so I could hear the women talking on the other side. The men were always so quiet because they were either intimidated by the aggressive sound of naked women that travelled with the water vapor or busy trying to appreciate the sensual meaning of women. The thick water steam rising from both the men's and women's baths was blended to create a dreamy atmosphere and the sound of laughing, talking, and water splashing travelled to the men's side. And through the side door where the wall ended, the dirty and soapy water flowed into the drain gutter to the men's section.

Not only did the dirty and soapy water flow into the men's side. One time a naked woman ran inside screaming when a gold ring drifted into the men's section. She flung open the door and screamed, "Oh no! My ring!"

After this incident, I imagined a naked woman flinging the door open and rushing in whenever I looked in the direction of the door. There was the cold water tub for both men and women on the side of the wall where the partition was. The women pouring water over their bodies were close enough that if I stretched my hand out I could reach them. Watching their bare arms pouring water drove me mad.

## Pubic Hair

I noticed changes in my body. Around the time I had facial hair, I found something similar growing around my pubic area, too. I was more concerned about my pubic hair than a mustache. When I found fine soft hair growing yellowish then turning black, I was so surprised that I shaved it off using my father's razor. I did it without thinking too much but after that it came out darker and thicker than before, so I was utterly dismayed. I heard afterwards that if you shave hair it would grow thicker, darker and faster.

I don't know why I shaved it off when it was normal to have pubic hair. It was a sign of manhood. I felt uneasy about pubic hair because I was not prepared at all. Perhaps subconsciously I was thinking "What's the point of having pubic hair when I haven't even matured at all? I can't reach out and touch them because they are hidden beneath their skirts and the only thing that is real is the sound of them laughing."

The growing of pubic hair marked the second phase of puberty and all those male fantasies began to take concrete form inside me. I felt unfamiliar desires squirming inside me and became afraid of myself and felt extremely uneasy. I thought the seed of sin was growing and disgusting bodily desires were blossoming. Perhaps I shaved my pubic hair because I was afraid. I wanted to stop growing and remain a child forever.

I wanted to see the same change occurring in a woman's body, too. I wanted to see a woman's mound covered in pubic hair. That was my most immediate wish and hope at the time. I revealed my wish to my friends without any reservations. My friends had the same thoughts, so I found comfort in talking about it. I think sex was our utmost concern when we were in ninth grade because no matter how many times we erased lascivious graffiti on school toilet walls, they were back on the walls again and again. We were envious of those pigs raised in the outhouses. So we sang a song, "A maiden sat on a toilet and relieved herself. A pig that came to catch her dung looked up and, 'Look, it's making a thunderous noise. Wow, it even has hair and is spewing water. Ha ha ha!'"

*Burnt Skin's Crush*

Mixing human and pig excrements with straw became an important fertilizer for barley farming. When the barley tilling season neared, fertilizer piled up outside everyone's house. I never thought of that straw covered in feces as dirty. In fact, I thought it was the symbol of fertility. The adults had no qualms about handling the straw with their bare hands. They couldn't possibly have thought of it as dirty when it served as nutrients to grow barley.

Feces that was once regarded as an important fertilizer became filthy, so western style toilets became popular to make the waste disappear by flushing it clean. I could not help thinking what a waste of resources that was. I remember there was an order to cover the feces straw piles with barley straw when the former President Syngman Rhee visited the island and was touring around Yongduam. The piles were covered to be disguised as hay stacks. This happened when I was in ninth grade.

When my friend Burnt Skin whined and begged his mother trying to get out of cleaning the outhouse it was not because he thought it was dirty. His nickname was Burnt Skin because his arm was burnt in scalding water. He had to take over the outhouse cleaning work after his older brother went to Japan as a stowaway. He did not want to do it because it was the house of a girl he had a crush on.

His mother wanted to have more fertilizer, so she had the neighbor's excrement as well. The house next door was renting the entire house because the owner from the mainland had his own business, so the family had no use for fertilizer. My father borrowed our neighbor's outhouse to raise the pig and Burnt Skin's mother had been placing straw in the neighbor's outhouse for a year to prepare fertilizer.

The girl he had a crush on was Yŏngi. He only knew her name and never talked to her. She was pretty and was also a ninth grader like us. Since he had a crush on her, going there to clean the outhouse was not easy. He asked his mother to hire someone to do it, arguing he couldn't do it because there was a girl in the house. But his mother didn't budge at all.

In the end, Burnt Skin had no choice but to do it. I caught him cleaning the girl's outhouse. He wore his hat low over his eyebrows, but he could not fool me. When he saw me, he looked miserable. I giggled and teased him.

"Hey, Burnt Skin! What are you doing over there?"

"Shit! Can't you tell?"

"Did Yŏngi ask you to clean her outhouse?"

"Shit! Don't make fun of me! I'm ready to explode."

"Why are you taking it out on me? Your girlfriend's shit is there so you should be happy."

"You asshole! Stop it, okay?

I think it was after this incident that I ran into Yŏngi in the alleyway. I must have walked with my head down pretending I was depressed. I saw a large bill on the ground. It was flying toward me. I saw not one but two bills. I thought I struck a gold pot. My mother often reprimanded me for walking with my head down, saying I was looking for barley ears. I had never found a coin on the ground until then. Two large bills! I ran frantically trying to catch the bills.

After I caught the money I realized there was someone near me. It was Yŏngi who was all out of breath and stood in front of me. She ran trying to catch the money. When I heard her gasping for breath, my face turned red. I had never stood so close to a girl before. Surprisingly Yŏngi's face was red, too. When I handed her the money, she was a little hesitant and seemed embarrassed. After she received it, she turned back and left quickly. It happened so quickly but I could not believe that Yŏngi turned red because she was embarrassed. I experienced for the first time, so I wondered if she had a crush on me. Burnt Skin continued to have a crush on her, and nothing happened between Yŏngi and me.

*Sea Anemone*

I was very much isolated from women (all of my friends were the same) to the point where I could not even strike up a conversation with my neighbor Yŏngi. So my interest in women was manifested in a bizarre and perverted way. Even female pigs and horses that were in heat did not seem ordinary to me; the female pigs' swollen genitals and the horses' genitals quivering after urination were enough to stimulate my sexual fantasies.

However, they were not the mysterious women's mounds beautifully covered with hair. I was eager to see so my friends and I played with sea anemones found on the shore. The sea anemones with numerous feelers were dense and resembled women's private parts covered in pubic hair, so my friends and I had an impulse to stick our hands inside. Like a pretty bloomed flower in the water, if you stuck a finger inside the opening it would bite. Even though you take out your finger immediately, you suffer painful stings from sea anemones, because of the poison that was discharged from the feelers.

One of my friends said, "You know that el cheapo? That guy who goes to business school. He made a bet with his friend. Do you know what kind of bet it was? Putting your penis inside a sea anemone. I'm not lying. I saw it with my own eyes at Yongduam. His friend promised to buy him a bowl of noodles if he did it. You know he's gullible. He thought it would be a piece of cake so he fondled it to make it hard and inserted. As soon as he put his penis inside, he screamed and fell on his back. He was stung by the sea anemone poison. His penis was swollen and it was bigger than an eggplant. Ha ha ha! I'm sure it was painful."

Then there was someone who got extremely lucky. It was

Kwangi from a drinking tavern. On days when there were many customers, the room where his school uniform was hung had to be used. From time to time he smelled of cigarette. One time he got lucky and saw a woman's private parts. He did not even see secretly. The woman offered to show it to him. She worked at the drinking house. She showed it to him right up close. We went crazy listening to him.

My classmates and I were practicing our graduation play *Macbeth* during winter vacation. It was before the director arrived, and all of a sudden Kwangi who had the part of King Duncan came in with a broom like an insane person.

"Shit! Listen carefully. It's an interesting story. It happened last night. You know that woman from Mokp'o. It's only been fifteen days since she came. She's pretty. I was in the room alone last night, and she opened the door and came in, saying she was in pain. She was drunk and was relieving herself in the corner somewhere in the courtyard and her butt got pricked by a thorn or something. Then she had her butt right in front of my face. It was such a sight. Idiots! Do you know what I'm saying? That woman had her butt in my face, you idiots! Do you know what she said? She asked me to take a look, whether a glass or thorn was stuck and if so, take it out. So, I looked. A cactus thorn was stuck so she bled a little but it was nothing serious. Anyway, I got a good look at it. That thing was black and scary looking."

After he finished with his story, he said, "Oh shit! I'm getting horny!" and stuck his broom stick between his crotch and started poking the desk as if he was doing it. He was usually quiet but the reason why he acted so crazy was because he was in such a shock from the night before. Since he was two years older than me, his sexual drive was even more intense.

Since it happened during one of our play practices, I remember it vividly, moreso than any of the scenes from the play. Kwangi's performance as King Duncan in *Macbeth* was memorable, but in no scene was his performance as great as the performance he gave us that day.

## Lily of Purity

We maliciously associated sex with feces, urine, pigs, and sea anemones and made it vulgar, but as soon as we saw female students in school uniforms we became quiet. We could not possibly defile with our vulgarity the brilliant white of their uniform collars, which symbolized purity.

Like most of my friends, the opposite sex was not one particular person but existed in multiplicity. The girls existed as the fluttering skirts, the brilliant white collars of their uniforms, and the sound of laughter. There was not even one face that came close enough for me to recognize. I wanted to know what made them giggle like that and was curious what they were talking about, but they were always so distant from me that I could only hear their laughter. I tried to get close to them so I started going to a Catholic church with a friend who was an alter boy under a foreign pastor. One of the two girls' middle schools was a mission school ran by a Catholic church so if I stopped by there after school, I could see many girls like beautiful flowers in bloom here and there under camphor trees. If only I could hear what they were saying and what they were laughing about.

I had a sure way of getting close to the girls and that was to befriend someone who had an older sister and frequent his house. If I visited his house often, I would get a chance to see his sister's friends up close who came to visit her. And if I got lucky, I could become one of her friends' adopted brother. This was why boys with older sisters were popular then. Even so, I could not become friends with someone I did not like.

One of the reasons why the girls kept to themselves and did not come out of their group was because they had fears about the opposite sex. Dating was not permitted at the time, so the girls were extra cautious. If people found out that you were dating, even it was her first time she would be labeled as Miss Promiscuous or Dating Coach or flappers and would be shunned and treated unfairly. Even though one could endure all those abuses, there were no efficient birth control methods so the girls could not escape from the fear of becoming pregnant. It was true that "platonic love" was popular at the time. To avoid being found out, dating had to be done discretely and writing love letters was the means of communication. "Platonic love" was popular but in reality one-sided love outnumbered mutual love relationships.

In this kind of situation where dating was not condoned, calling on someone as so and so's sister or so and so's brother, adopted sister and adopted brother was popular. Boys who had pretty faces like girls were popular. A boy with an adopted sister could be spotted right away because he would have a white handkerchief. This handkerchief was made from the white gauze used in a hospital and the edges would be sewn nicely with embroidery thread. For someone uncivilized like me, I used my thumb and index fingers to blow my nose, a white handkerchief was something I coveted. The reason why they bought the gauze from the pharmacy and made handkerchief was because the color white symbolized purity.

The gauze was used elsewhere more importantly before bras became common and popular. I heard that high school students wrapped their chests with the gauze to make sure their breasts didn't jut out. How did they come up with the idea to wrap their chests with the gauze? Perhaps it was suggested by the sisters at their school. Since it was a missionary school, education on purity was emphasized. Their growing breasts were their source of fear. Were they afraid that their purity would be tainted, so they wrapped them tight with the antibacterial gauze? Well, I could be completely off on this.

The collar of their school uniform was white, signifying purity. Starched and pressed crisp with an iron as if when chewed it would make a crunchy sound like a rice cracker. This too was a symbol of purity. The collar looked like two large lily petals. The Catholic sisters were wearing white hats that looked like lily flowers in full bloom, and the girls' school uniform collars resembled the pure lily flower petals, too.

It was a different kind of vigorous beauty from a girls' notion of purity and the Catholic sisters' idea of chastity. If they had abided by the strict rules of purity as they were taught, how could they possibly lure pretty-faced middle school boys as their objects of love?

The white collar of the girls' school uniforms cast a powerful magic spell, making the boys' hearts throb. At home they wore old and worn out clothes like their mothers and worked on all different kinds of house chores. They even carried buckets filled with foul smelling excrement and poured them on the garlic field. I don't know why, but those girls who covered their faces with towels, carrying the fertilizer buckets and walking hastily became graceful and beautiful when they had on their white school uniforms. They might have wrapped their chests with the gauze not because they were fearful of sinning but for the pure beauty of it. For boys it was such a pleasure imagining their white breasts wrapped with the antibacterial white gauze.

That's right. We imagined how their breasts pressed underneath the gauze would feel by touching soft tennis balls. During those days tennis was a hobby for upper class people, so tennis was popular and the tennis balls were made with good quality rubber. I remember a boy who let me touch a tennis ball for the first time. His father was a customs inspector with two gold stripes around his jacket cuff who was a good tennis player. The tennis ball was soft like a living organism. When the boy compared the feel with a girl's breasts, I was completely taken aback. I felt the softness inside the palm of my hand. Even if he had not explained it to me, I might have related this feeling instinctively because I had not completely forgotten the feeling of my mother's breast when I was being breastfed. When I made marbles out of dirt, the feeling I got from the dirt marbles and flour dough reminded me of the forgotten memories of my mother's breasts. The tennis ball was much more sensual. There was a small hole that was projected where air could be filled with an injection and it felt like a nipple. The secret underneath the white gauze could be touched only if one was lucky enough to be an adopted brother of so and so's sister.

*My Love Anima*

Since I hadn't had any relationships with women, every single one of them who appeared in my dreams was a stranger. I had my first wet dream during my ninth grade winter vacation, so it was around the same time an unknown woman started to appear in my dreams. This enchanting naked woman came out in my dream and wrapped my body with hers. She felt soft like mud, but I had never seen her in real life. In a way, it was this woman in my dream who taught me the pleasure of sensuality for the first time. She embraced me with her naked body and I was burning and became exhausted in the end. Who was this woman? I forgot her face as soon as I woke up. Every time I had a wet dream, she appeared.

I still don't know who she was; it's like a riddle that cannot be solved. The image was too vivid and real to be thought of as a mere fantasy or fabrication generated from my sexual desires. Her image was lucid yet as soon as I woke up, she was quickly forgotten. Was this woman real? Was she someone in a picture my classmate showed to me? Or, was she a woman from my past life? Since I read a little of Karl Jung's introduction to psychology, I wanted to believe it was my other self, my alter ego. Jung had designated anima as female characteristics existing inside a male.

In my case, the female tendency was so excessive that it bled out and manifested externally. I was sentimental, extremely fickle, and sensitive. I was embarrassed about crying over little things like a girl and was easily hurt over insignificant things. But I was no longer embarrassed but wished to be more feminine. I thought I could not get close to girls without being feminine. I felt as if I had become a girl when I imitated the way they walked, trying to understand them better. I tried to imitate their facial expressions so I looked in the mirror and practiced. I felt strange as if I had really turned into a girl. At this time I was caught by my grandmother walking down the street and was reprimanded.

My inclination toward the feminine intensified when that unknown woman appeared in my dreams. I was completely cut off from any kind of communication with girls so I was in love with the woman in my dream. She was my other self, my alter ego, and I was in love with myself. I became more like a girl when I saw my reflection in the mirror. It was around this time I had a double eyelid on one eye. I wished for my other eye to be the same.

I placed the desk and chair I got from Sinsŏk in one corner of the room and did my homework and read novels. Deep in the night when silence finally dominated the house, I attempted a transformation. I turned down the wick of the oil lamp low (if I had a small used candle, I lighted that instead) and covered my head with a bandana like cloth and looked into the mirror. I found a pretty girl in the mirror. The girl in the mirror looked at me and smiled, and suddenly she glared at me with a distorted face. Then her expression changed again and I noticed her grief-stricken face. I was really good at crying, almost a pro, so tears soon welled up wetting my long eyelashes. I truly loved the girl, looking sad in the mirror.

When Narcissus gazed at his reflection in a pool, he wanted to see not the image of himself but someone who looked just like him, his doppelganger, in other words, an image of his dead twin sister. I, too, was attracted to my other self, my anima. Unlike self destructive Narcissus and his hopeless passion, my love for myself was temporary and only lasted during the transitional period. When I was forced to defer to acting like an adult and sex was considered taboo, my desire to find the opposite sex could not be fulfilled and I had to look internally. As I mentioned previously, my love for my "self" was sexual so by loving the feminine side of myself, I was trying to destroy my desire for the opposite sex in real life.

### *The Need to Blow My Nose*

I learned to masturbate around this time and this too was a form of narcissism. For example, on Sundays, I took my grandfather's horse to the west side of the beach for grazing and there I read books. I didn't mind taking care of the horse when I had my book and the blue sky and the azure sea spread out before me. When I became bored with reading, I got on the horse and played. I had taken care of her since she was a colt so I was particularly attached. The horse had a nice body and had really nice brownish coat, so when it was by my side I wanted to stroke it.

One day my attachment to the horse went over the top. I don't know how it happened. I wonder if watching it pee made me feel a bit strange. After the horse peed like a waterfall, its genitals seen through its brawny and supple behind resembled the soft part of abalone swaying to and fro gathering slowly. I didn't feel anything before but on that particular day I became aroused.

My heart started beating fast and I felt dizzy. When the horse's genitals shrunk completely it seemed satisfied and swung its tail back and forth. She was so busy trying to get rid of all those flies that swarmed to her body that muscle spasms in her thighs travelled to her well-rounded and supple behind, supported by her nice and lean legs. I looked to see if anyone was around and walked over to the horse's stomach. I was aroused so I couldn't walk properly. Not knowing what was going through me physically, the horse continued grazing. I started stroking its back, glittering in the sunlight, then I grasped its mane and got on its back. The horse did not mind what I was doing and continued grazing. She kept eating and eating. I thought if my fingers got caught between those teeth they would be crushed. I could not believe that an animal with such strength was docile and obedient. Regardless of what I wanted to do, the horse would not go crazy, I thought. I squeezed softly its full stomach with my legs. When my crotch touched the horse's backbone, I felt stimulated. I embraced the horse's neck with my arms and buried one side of my cheek into its mane and I was on my stomach. As soon as my groin area touched the horse's back, I started rubbing left and right and back and forth. I was worried that the horse might figure out what I was doing but when the tingly sensation spread all over my body, I became fuzzy.

Then I realized I was sliding toward the horse's behind and stopped myself in surprise. No, this is going too far! It's dangerous. What if the horse gets angry and throws me off its back? I continued to rub my crotch imagining myself stuck fast to its behind. Suddenly I felt the urge to relieve myself in my hazy consciousness. I got off the horse and walked over to the bushes. Because it got hard, I couldn't walk so I waddled. I stood in front of the bushes and unbuttoned my pants and took it out. It was incredibly hard. I concentrated and tried to think I was peeing. *It's coming out. It's coming out.*

What came out was not urine, but something white and of a porridge-like consistency. I don't remember whether that was my first time masturbating. Even if that was not my first, I must have begun masturbating then.

I started masturbating and I could not free myself from the bondage. I was attached to this act, almost like an illness. I think I did it at least two times a week. What followed after the act was nothing but deep despair, regret, and guilt. Because of sudden calorie consumption, I was weak to the point where my eyes sunk in deeply. When my strength drained, I felt as if I was falling into an abyss of despair and even felt death approaching. It was the taste of hell. I feared that I might go to hell because of my sin. I felt guilty. I didn't even go to church, so I don't know why I felt that way. Did I read this in a book? Or, did I learn this from an alter boy? The Holy Spirit dwelled in each person's body, therefore masturbating was defiling the holy spirit.

Before, I only had a double eyelid on one side but it was around this time I had one on both eyes. After I finished masturbating, I looked emaciated and my eyes were sunken. I think this is how I got my double eyelids. I looked at myself in the mirror and found a perfect girl's face.

Even during class, my mind was fuzzy and I could not concentrate. Every single class was boring. My dandruff fell on my open book and what stood between me and the book was nothing but cloudy fogginess. In this state of fuzziness, I squeezed pimples or stuck my hand inside my pants to fondle.

One day, a miracle happened during a boring class. A miraculous salvation! An unmarried science teacher freed me from my guilty consciousness in a clear and succinct manner. He was explaining about horse power and all of a sudden the talk about masturbation came out of his mouth. I was so surprised.

"How do you say *maryŏk* in English? Mal is horse and ryŏk is power. Yes, strength is power. That's why maryŏk is horse power; HP for short. HP, understand? I will tell you something even more important. HP stands for horse power but it also stands for something else. Do you know? I know you guys do HP. HP stands for 'Hand Play.' Don't pretend you don't! Are you afraid that I'm going to punish you? It's okay. Those of you who doze off in class are tired from doing too much. Isn't that true?" Everyone laughed.

"Listen carefully. This is very important. I'm sure some of you are worried sick because of your HP. Some may feel guilty, entertaining the thought of committing suicide. But it's not a sin. Why worry when you haven't committed a sin? You need to blow your nose when it's stuffed up, right? It's the same concept. So it's nothing to feel guilty about. I'm telling you this because I think you guys might worry too much. Young boys who stress too much could easily fall ill. What you do need to remember is that even though you do HP, don't do it too often. If you do it too often you become weak and won't grow, okay? Remember! One HP equals 6 pints of blood. Yes, 6 pints of blood! If you are alone you tend to touch your thing so try to spend more time with your friends and play sports or sing a song. It's good to take a cold bath in the pool near Yongduam, okay?"

What a great explanation! HP was like blowing your nose and one HP equals 6 pints of blood. It was a lucid and wise explanation.

*Macbeth*
The reason why I went through a tougher adolescent period compared to others was, of course, my bad temperament. I was completely ignorant about the psychology of the opposite sex. My friends or classmates who had older sisters and went to church did not have a tough time like I did. I was so envious of them; they easily carried on conversations with girls without any reservations. To me, the girls were like a mirage that was beyond my reach.

The saying "Where there's a will, there's a way" meant I finally saw the light at the end of the tunnel. The opportunity came during the middle school graduation play. It wasn't a simple school event. This was the second year the play was put on. The school rented a theatre downtown and staged the play over two days. The fact that the middle school was able to put together a big event regardless of financial losses, meant that the school was progressive since the economy was unstable at the time. The school administrators and teachers were ambitious. If not, how could they make us, middle school students, not fully matured, do a Shakespeare play? The class before us played *Hamlet* and we were stuck with *Macbeth*. I heard good reviews about *Hamlet* played by my seniors, so my class was pressured to do even better.

The director was one of the teachers from the girls' Catholic school who taught mathematics. I could not understand how an unmarried male teacher could teach female high school students. At the same time I was jealous of him because I thought his body was an embodiment of all those female students' gaze and their laugher. He made quite an impression wearing a black beret. I remember him saying that, "To wear a beret with style, you need to wear it slanted." He proved how popular he was with his female students with his beret and his gaudy and exaggerated gestures when instructing us what to do. He often encouraged us to do well, saying, "You need to do well. My students will be coming to watch this. You can't be humiliated. You need to do well. OK?"

In order to attract the girls' attention it was important what character I played. If I couldn't play Macbeth I needed to play a supporting role, but unfortunately I ended up playing a minor role, Ross the nobleman. Those who played Macbeth, Lady Macbeth, Duncan, Macduff, and Banquo were all a year or two older than me. Even a one year age difference made a drastic difference in physical appearance, so the important roles like king and general all went to older upperclassmen. All the major characters except Macduff get murdered, but I had such a minor role that I was not even worthy of death in this blood-soaked play. I didn't volunteer to play one of the three witches because I thought they were unimportant, but my role ended up being nothing compared to the three witches. I didn't die until the end but appeared sporadically throughout the play. I served as a set off for other characters, and I didn't even have proper lines.

My lines were like, "Gentlemen, rise! His Highness is not well." Or, "Lady Macbeth, please calm down." My lines were short and insignificant. One time I added a few lines that were not in the script, and the director reprimanded me. Since I didn't have many lines to practice, I spent time memorizing other people's lines. I particularly liked the Macbeth and Three Witches' lines. Macbeth had tragic lines and the Three Witches sporting with Macbeth were dismal and dreary. I still can recite some of the lines. It was a soliloquy after Macbeth murdered King Duncan, he was wrapped in fear:

> *Still it cried "Sleep no more!" to all the house:*
> *"Glamis hath murdered sleep, and therefore Cawdor*
> *Shall sleep no more: Macbeth shall sleep no more."*

What great rhetoric! I learned later in college that this passage was so famous that British people liked to recite it. I was as happy as if I had found something after losing it.

As the day of the performance drew near, everyone was busy getting their costumes ready. The school only provided armor made out of corrugated cardboard and the rest was up to the actors and actresses. Although I had a minor role, I too had to think about what to wear. It was my first time standing in front of all those female students, so I could not possibly go out there looking shabby. I had to find a velvet skirt I could use as a cape, a beret, and a pair of women's stockings.

At that time a velvet skirt was a luxury item that only educated women wore. The only person in my family who owned a velvet skirt was my cousin's wife. I knew that she only wore the skirt on special occasions, treasuring it, so I didn't have the courage to ask her to let me borrow it. I was playing a minor role so I hesitated to ask. But when I finally did, she gladly lent the skirt to me. I was so grateful for her generosity that I felt a lump in my throat. I was lucky and was able to obtain a beret and a pair of stockings. I would've been grateful for a simple knitted hat, but my oldest cousin had a friend who owned a hat shop so she borrowed a beret from her. It was brand new, and the hat had to be returned to be displayed at the store after the play was over, so I had to be very careful. It was a great green hat. Among the actors and actresses, I believe the beret I wore was the most expensive item. When I had to stick a pheasant feather into the hat, I was worried that I might make a hole. Thinking back, the green beret was like a bird that landed on my head briefly and flew away. I borrowed a pair of old stockings my cousin's wife wore. I wore my shorts over the stockings.

Among the costumes, the shorts were the last to arrive. Shortly before the opening, the director brought a bag of something and threw it on the floor in front of us and said, "Pick one and wear it." What was in the bag? Surprisingly they were bloomers, girls' gym shorts. The director brought his own students' bloomers that they wore during their physical education classes. There was a string that you can pull above your knees and the shorts gathered at the bottom in the shape of a bell. We were told that during the Shakespearean period the trousers looked like bloomers.

Everyone went wild at the prospect of wearing the girls' gym shorts. I wondered what kind of girl owned the shorts I had. There was a tag inside the shorts but it only had the classroom number with no name, so it was difficult to decipher whether it belonged to a middle school or high school student. We were fantasizing and pulled the rubber and twisted our bodies laughing. The gym shorts, when crunched up, were small enough to fit in one hand. In any case, we needed to do well. The owners of the gym shorts and the city's two girls' schools were coming to watch. We weren't interested in the immature middle school students but the older high school students.

Finally the day of the performance arrived. I looked pretty good as Ross the nobleman. With the black cape that was trimmed with a strip of sparkling silver paper, the green beret with a pheasant feather, I was particularly surprised at my powdered face. I looked pretty. After my entire face was covered with power, my cheeks turned pinkish with a dab of blush, and I even had lipstick on. If it weren't for the mustache, I would have looked just like a girl. I erased the thick mustache the director had drawn on and instead I drew a thin one. When the director saw me with the thin mustache, instead of reprimanding me, he said "Oh, you look like a girl." When I heard him say this, I was so happy. This was what I wanted to hear.

I was nicely transformed in appearance, but when the curtain went up I was so nervous that I became scared. The only thing that I didn't borrow from others was my shoes, but something I wanted to hide was precisely my shoes. The white sneakers were washed so they looked clean but both soles had holes in them. I was certain that the audience would not pay attention to the holes, but before I stood on the stage I started to worry. I never asked my mother to buy me a new pair unless she bought them of her own accord. Not only shoes but other things, too; I never asked my mother for anything, so I could not ask her just for the play. I was not even playing one of the main characters, so my mother did not even come to watch. She said, "The person who knows the taste of tail soup knows how good it is. I've never seen a play so how could I enjoy it?" The holes in my shoes were not the only things that worried me. The stage props were recently painted so they were still wet and sticky. If the paint was to smear on the velvet skirt or the beret, I was in big trouble.

When I stood on the stage for the first time, I was cautious as if I were walking on thin ice. Regardless of my worries, the play moved along smoothly. While I was practicing for nearly three weeks during the winter break, I had no idea how it would turn out but once it started, the play moved along as if it had its own life. The costumes, the lights, and the stage props all worked well and between the scenes the brass band played to make the performance livelier. The high school band was situated at the bottom of the stage. The band was quite famous. Every year they were invited to play at festivals in the city of Chinju on the mainland.

As the play moved along, everyone's acting became smooth and natural. My worries dissipated and I went with the flow. The actors with minor roles ran here and there and I was one of them. Everyone acted well, but Macbeth's acting was superb. Macbeth was led to destruction due to the Three Witches' prophesy. As foretold, Macbeth murdered the king and seized the throne but what he discovered was not glory but destruction. The band urged the destruction and with the roaring sound of the cymbals Macbeth was supposed to stab Macduff to death. Ansik who played Macbeth was excellent.

As I scanned the audience I was able to make out the caps of some male students and the bobbed hair of female students. I heard sighs and lamentations of "Oh no!" and "Oh my gosh!" coming intermittently from the audience. It was natural to have such reactions because this tragedy was made up of murder, intrigue, madness, and destruction.

In this intense moment, a reaction that was completely different changed the atmosphere. From time to time a girls' giggling sound was heard; this play had no room for laughter, though. So it meant someone was making blunders. I was gripped with fear that I was the culprit, the source of their laughter. Either my acting was terrible or they had discovered the holes in my shoes. After the curtain came down, the director said we did well and did not mention anything about the girls' giggling.

The truth of the matter was revealed after the second day which was the last day of the performance. While the play was going on, the director asked me to do something absurd. "Hey, you look like a girl! OK. I'll create another scene for you, so enjoy!" A scene that was not in the original play was added. I was merely an insignificant character appearing here and there, but I was to stand on the stage alone. I lucked out! I was to appear in a battle scene, and I was to call out Fleance's name and walk over to the other side of the stage. Fleance was the son of Banquo who was murdered by Macbeth.

It was a minor scene, but I had a difficult time acting this out. With the lively music, several actors engaged in sword fights, and they disappeared to the other side of the stage. When the music stopped and the stage became quiet, I entered the empty stage. I had the sword in my hand and lowered myself taking extra caution, stepping onto center stage. Then the sound of drumming was heard, and a spotlight shined on me. I was so nervous that I felt dizzy. Walking on the stage felt like I was walking on thin ice. I took each step hesitantly while the intense light was shining on me. Then I heard the girls' giggling. It was the same giggling sound as the previous night. I felt suffocated. What was I doing wrong? Did they see the holes in my shoes? I dragged my feet so that the soles of my shoes could not be seen. "Fleance!" I looked left and right and pretended to brandish my sword. "Fleance!" The sound of laughter became louder. Walking toward the other side of the stage seemed to take longer than entering Nirvana. I finally reached the other side of the stage and was about to call out Fleance's name for the last time, but I was so nervous that my voice cracked. I sounded like a chicken with a bone stuck in its throat. Everyone burst out into laughter.

I ran to the back of the stage and my entire body shook in embarrassment. However, my mistake did not stop there. I got some paint on my cape. It was very small only the size of a coin, but the problem was it would not come off easily. I tried to scrape the paint off with my fingernail. I felt miserable so I left the theatre. I took off my velvet skirt and beret and wrapped them up. The play had not ended, but I was done with my part so I didn't need to be there. I ran through the dark after passing the theatre lit up brightly with international flags flying. I went to the beach near Yongduam. I cried my heart out, crouching between the rocks and gazing at the dark ocean.

I was so humiliated I wanted to kill myself. But when I went to school the next day the situation was quite the opposite. Well, the situation was the same but I had interpreted it the opposite way. The laughter from the audience was not to ridicule my mistake, but it was their way of expressing interest and goodwill. I heard that the reason why they giggled was because I looked pretty like a girl with the makeup on. I knew then why the director made an extra scene for me on the second day of the performance. "You look like a girl. OK. I'll create another scene for you. Enjoy." To be honest, I worked hard to look "pretty" rather than spending time playing the nobleman character Ross. I wanted to hear that I looked like a girl. I tried hard to bring out the feminine side. To get closer to the opposite sex, I thought I had to look like them, in other words to become a "pretty boy."

*Pretty Boy*

I had several offers from the female students who wanted to adopt me as their brother. I was called here and there until one high school student made a successful bid. One of the girls tried to impress me with her singing about loving someone who was out of her league, but I was utterly disappointed. I don't know whether she was ignorant or an idiot, but in the middle of our conversation she left the room to relieve herself in the chamber pot right outside the room; I was flabbergasted. Thinking back on it now, it was funny.

The student who became my adopted sister was three years older than me. In a way, she was my first "woman." I was not the active one seeking this relationship and did not choose but was chosen. I was in bondage for two years and thinking back, those were sweet memories but at the same time pathetic. Love is something that one chooses; one does not want to be chosen. It was understandable for a short period, but two years was too long. She graduated from high school but was not admitted to a university, so she spent another year preparing for the college entrance exam. Then she entered a university in the mainland and left the island. If she had stayed longer, my senior year would have turned out to be disastrous. I might have given up going to college. I could not escape that pretty boy image from the play *Macbeth*.

There were others who had an even more difficult time escaping the aftereffects of the play. I could still hear the laughter of the Three Witches. Some of them became female students' slaves and ruined their senior year in high school. After graduation they were good for nothing. Kwangi who played King Duncan and Munsu, one of the Three Witches died early wasting their time drinking.

For those immature boys, the sweet and sensual pleasure of kissing they experienced served as a poison. When I was young, I heard a story about how a boy on his way to school met a pretty girl and kissed, playing the marble game. Once you kiss you become a slave to inertia. Kissing was so bewitching that you could lose your mind completely. It was difficult to swallow the marble to end the pleasure. In the story, the boy mustered up the courage and swallowed the marble. Then the pretty girl turned into a fox with nine tails and ran away.

I have a lot to say as a "pretty boy" who was dominated by one woman for two years. But then talking about this only means digressing. In this story, I have tried to ruminate on how an individual was born and grew. So I should end it around ninth grade when I lost my childhood innocence.

Since the play was a graduation performance, my childhood

ended with the play, too. As the demarcation point, my life before and after had changed dramatically. Entering high school meant losing innocence and being initiated into the dishonesty of worldly affairs. During my high school years, I was a powerless slave dominated by a woman on the one hand and I fought against my father who was the object of my hatred on the other. I was experiencing the split self.

*Returning Home*

Lately I have been thinking a lot about my hometown and unlike before I dream frequently about it, too. My visits to Cheju Island have increased along with my dreams about it. There is a saying that as one grows older he or she tends to regress. That might explain my frequent visits back home. I believe these changes took place after my father passed away. Before, death stood between my father and I, but now that my father is gone, there is no buffer zone; I am directly linked to death. I am to return to my hometown some day and lay beside my father. I have been seriously thinking about returning to Cheju Island lately.

Once I got on the plane on a whim when I felt the late autumn warm sunlight on my arms. When the late autumn sunlight filled the veranda of my home in Seoul, I thought of a large straw mat spread out in the courtyard, drying yellow millet in my hometown. I thought it was such a pity wasting the precious sunlight, so I went to the market and bought shiitake mushrooms and wild vegetables and dried them. Only then did I feel relaxed. That's why I find every opportunity other than New Year or Ch'usŏk, Full Moon Harvest to get on the plane and head home. I go there to meet the boy with a pure and innocent soul who opened his ears and eyes wide with curiosity surrounded by nature, the cradle of his childhood.

I have changed but so has my hometown. The old buildings have either been demolished or left in ruins and what's left are dominated by the madness and superficiality of pleasure-seeking consumer culture. From the airport, the landscape seem to be a mere extension of Seoul. This city landscape has even extended to my village so that my vain efforts to find traces of the old and my past childhood fill my heart with heaviness. The places remain the same, but something fundamental and truthful about my past has been buried underneath the concrete and asphalt of those places. I shudder at the cruel and heartless sights that reject my glare. The beaches and the streams have been plastered with concrete and have transformed into something ugly. My old home in Chŏngdŭrŭ has disappeared, too. The only thing left is the ocean. I rush to island to feel the cool ocean breeze caressing my face.

I pass by my old home in Chŏngdŭrŭ on my way to the beach near Yongduam. Everything has changed completely and the traces of old things are nowhere to be found. I feel strange as if I have come to a different neighborhood because all the houses have been rebuilt with bricks and cement. It is like being in the outskirts of Seoul.

My old house has changed into this red brick multi-complex housing building. It was built three or four years ago. Where is that small and cozy house? I am in deep thought and tell myself that the old house has not been demolished in order to build this multi-complex housing but has been buried underneath after it has been worn out due to the weather and old age. I feel better thinking this way.

My old house was built with the help of my grandfather when I was in the eighth grade, and it was taken over by the creditor along with the land when my father's business failed. It happened when I was a senior in high school. I did not want to be reminded of the painful memories of losing the house, so I had avoided passing by. But now it has completely disappeared from the earth. I am reminded of the painful memories of how I shouted out loud in anger, "Neighbors, come over to our house! My mother and father are fighting. Come over and watch." It gives me the shivers that I shouted this out loud. I said mother and father but I meant my father. After his business failed, he started gambling which made my mother even more miserable. He found the money box hidden under the floor and rushed out to gamble. The image of my mother running after him is still vivid in my mind.

My father failed in his business. Actually, it is more accurate to say he was a sacrificial lamb of deceit from the very beginning. I was disappointed in my father not because he failed but because he was gullible.

The next door neighbor Mr. Kim, the truck driver, was the mastermind of deceit. It was the same driver whose outhouse my father borrowed to raise a pig. He was the truck driver from the North. His business proposition was a second hand tire shop. Mr. Kim enticed my father by saying that he was a tire technician. I think my father thought that it was as easy as mending rubber shoes.

With a huge drum, a smelting furnace was made to melt old rubber shoes and make tires together pouring the liquid and old tires in a molding frame. It looked believable even to my eyes. However, the tires made of mixing the two were a complete failure. When the reproduced tires were tested on a truck they did not even make five hundred meters and just tattered and went flat. Mr. Kim said since it was his first try it could happen and my father believed him. My father found out that he'd been scammed after Mr. Kim left to the mainland to obtain supplies for the business and never came back. Overnight my family became homeless and landless.

We were thrown out of the house toward the end of my senior year. It was around the time of the college entrance examination, so I was getting ready to go to the mainland with my friends. I had decided to go to college, so I had saved up some money. My father used my money to gamble. At that time, my disappointment was so great that it was beyond description. I was in despair and my anger made me lose any sense of propriety that I ended up committing an unfilial act. When all of my friends left for the island to take the entrance examination, I couldn't go and had to give up on the idea of going to the mainland. To make my father feel bad about what had happened I decided to starve myself. We were going to be thrown out of the house in four days. On the moving day even when the last item was taken out of the house, I grabbed my stomach enduring hunger and rolled on the floor. I did not stop until my father apologized to me. I could not believe I had made my father give in. It was beyond unfilial; it was a merciless cruelty. I did something terrible, something I should have never done. Thinking back on this, I feel something heavy pressing my chest. I left the town in a hurry.

At the end of the residential area, an unexpected landscape came into view. I could not believe my eyes that the old landscape had remained. There is a narrow path between the two fields and the horizon on the other side of the sky seems to be floating in the air. This is the path I used to run around barefoot to jump into the cold water of Yongyŏn on hot summer days. Halfway along the path, there is a steep slope before reaching the beach so Yongyŏn is not visible yet. The main road leading to the beach is located on the other side of the fields twenty meters to the west. On that asphalt road, cars pass by with loads of tourists. It is almost a miracle that this small old path still exists right next to the road with so many cars. In the old days, this narrow path had been used by everyone going swimming or to water horses and cows, and the village women frequented this path to draw water from the well. The path has since been covered with overgrown weeds because there are no longer passersby.

I enter the path and my heart starts pounding. At this very moment I recall the old days standing on this path. This is the path on which I used to run to the beach whether happy or sad. The smell of strong green grass wafts through the air and the loud singing of grasshoppers is ringing in my ears. When I go near, the grasshoppers stop singing as if they are scared. A momentary silence. In this silence, I can hear the grasshoppers asking who I am and I answer "I'm Sea Crab." The various wildflowers growing along the path look familiar. The different kinds of flowers and plants, such as wild chrysanthemums, spiderworts, clovers, honeysuckles, have been grazed by my maternal grandfather's horses. The sound of horses eating still rings in my ears. The honeysuckles gently brush my arm as if to greet me. The wildflowers and plants are densely grown, not caring about people or horses.

I get off the path and go down to Yongyŏn. This place has changed so much that I can't recognize it. The way in which it has changed is atrocious. The harbor, where the low thatched roof houses congregated together, has changed into a cluster of sashimi places in the last one or two years. The beach across Yongyŏn has been reclaimed and now only huge concrete trivets that had been used to build the breakwater are strewn all over the place.

Even the Yongyŏn water is not the same. Where are all the children? I am disappointed to find only three children playing in the water. It's because dirty water from the houses flows into the pond. The water is murkier than a year ago. The rock that has been used as a diving board has turned into a useless thing buried under a pile of small rocks washed up by the waves. The three children are taking turns, diving from a wooden boat that is tied up and they play in the water. But I feel as though this has been orchestrated to ease my distress. The water is not how it was before, but it is saying it's still okay. I think the water is fine since there are three children in it. It has not dried up. As long as the water does not dry up there is hope. I often think about this clear water, as I lead a murky city life in Seoul.

I pass the sashimi restaurants and head toward Yongduam.

There is an oncoming crowd of tourists. I quickly take the side road to avoid them since I am not a tourist. I leave the path and head directly toward the beach. This path I'm on now is not used by many people since the slope is very steep. There is a huge volcanic rock mass underneath and the ocean water flows on both sides of the volcanic rocks and runs deep to create a cape. It is low tide so the bottom of the rock that has been submerged in the water glows like solid amethyst. When I was young, this cape was my playground as much as Yongduam.

I get on the rock that looks like a giant dinosaur. The surface is so uneven with many sharp edges that I can't walk easily with my shoes on. The unevenness is created by the hardened lava. I have this image of lava boiling over like a pot of red bean porridge. The name "*hyunmuam*," meaning basalt, is great to hear. It is the same as my last name, Hyun. I take off my shoes and socks and place them on the lava boulder. When I was young I walked barefoot all the time. On this dark black lava boulder, my white feet look immensely foreign. My feet are so white that they even look ghastly. My toes, always inside my socks and shoes, start to wiggle when they are exposed to the bright sunlight. When the soles of my feet absorb the heat from the hot surface of the boulder, I feel a stinging sensation.

I leave my shoes and socks on the boulder and walk down. When I was young, I ran up and down with no problem but now I sweat profusely and I have to crawl down. My body feels heavy! But my feet and toes still remember the old days. My toes are slowly recovering, remembering the good old days. I feel strange looking at my toes. My usual scrunched up toes are wiggling, trying to get used to the uneven lava boulder. I'm amazed at how long my toes are. All my toes stick fast to the boulder like an octopus. My toes move as if they are independent organisms, not part of my body.

At last I come to the edge of the rock. The waves are breaking on both sides as if a boat is gliding across the water. I can now see a part of the city that had been hidden behind the shade, glittering brilliantly in the afternoon sunlight. I can also see the long embankment on the western pier.

I climb up the rock near the water. This is where I used to enjoy fishing. Using this boulder as my base, I fished using a spear. The flat rock has not changed. I am happy to find crawling baby crabs, mussels, and shellfish crammed in the rock crevices. I'm so familiar with these creatures. I feel as if this boulder has been waiting for me. Does it recognize me at all? This rock that has not aged at all might not recognize who I am because I have aged. The rock is eternal and I am ephemeral.

I take a deep breath, looking at the vast open space. My white feet scream out, enjoying their freedom. The wind blows my hair in the vast space where the deep azure sea as fresh as mackerel, the white clouds blossoming in the horizon, and the sky above the horizon coexist. It is not the ordinary wind but a gentle breeze blowing ozone and iodine. I feel as if my spirit has been lifted and is blowing in the gentle breeze as well. My body feels very light melting into the indigo ocean. I can see myself swimming in the water naked.

Holding a spear in my hand, I dived into the water. There I found a school of beautiful fish—sea bream, leather fish, and rock fish—swimming between the fronds. Once I was in the water time passed by so quickly. When I became tired from swimming, I let myself float and rested for a while. At that time I think I had fish scales and gills.

My body and soul were one, but after I graduated from middle school, I became a completely different person. I came here and cried my heart out when I was shocked at hearing the girls' laughing during the graduation play. I returned to this boulder during my high school year but not to fish. I came here to scream with joy or cry when upset. When I was happy, this boulder served as a boat cutting across the ocean and in despair the horizon seemed like a cage incarcerating me.

I remember jumping into the water to kill myself, but I failed. Even after my father gave in when I went on a hunger strike, I still was not satisfied and went up to Mt. Halla in winter. I didn't have a tent and spent a night on the mountain with a bonfire lit. One time I sold all the books I was using to prepare for the college entrance examination at a used bookstore and wasted all that money drinking. When I was drunk, I jumped into the ocean. This was the boulder where I jumped in. I was so drunk that I thought perhaps I would die of a heart attack or from exhaustion. But it did not happen. While I was swimming in the cold water, I had this unknown strength that kept me going. The cold waves woke me up so how could I swim toward death?

Everyone has to go through puberty, but I think my adolescent life was more complicated than other people's. It was the conflict between soul and body. My soul and body each desired something different; what my soul wanted was something my body could not provide or vice versa. Thinking about the innocent boy struggling in the midst of discontent, I sigh deeply.

The conflict between body and soul meant I broke away from the world of nature that I was once a part of. I equated nature with barbarity, ignorance, and boundaries, It was something I needed to overcome. My future was uncertain because I was poor. Moving from the margins to the center for a poor boy like myself was a dream beyond reach. Going through high school was difficult enough so how could I possibly cross the ocean to go study at a university? I was nurtured by the ocean but this very thing that nurtured me was going to hold me back when I was ready to fly. It was a painful realization. I was trapped by the horizon on the ocean.

I rejected nature's womb and confronted my father face to face after struggling with the violent rages inside me. I thought of my father as an obstacle blocking my path, for I was blinded by my ambition. I went on a hunger strike for four days. How could I have fought my father? I was heartless. This was unforgiveable for my father and because of this he and I remained awkward until he passed away. After I entered university I got down on my knees asking for his forgiveness but there was no point crying over spilled milk. I wrote him a letter, too, but it was useless. Thinking about the boy who knew only himself and did not listen to other people makes me sad.

If it weren't for literature I wouldn't have become so cynical. I'm certain literature had a bad influence on me to a certain extent. Even if I were born cruel and wicked and if it weren't for literature I would not have behaved in such a ruthless manner. When I started worshipping literature, I considered Yi Sang or Camus closer to me than my own blood related family members. I regarded their teachings such as eccentricity, rebellion, and unfaithfulness to be the golden rules. I thought that growing up was all about rebelling and going against the norm. Even though there are many variables involved in the equation of growing up, there is one constant. That is the beginning of creation, a hard seed that was made by the soil of Cheju Island and this fundamental foundation could not be changed.

I left my hometown to attend university and since then I have been living in Seoul. My dream came true. But what does it mean? What is this literature that I regarded as my calling? Since my father died I am looking more and more like the picture of him hanging in my room. Father's death eliminated all those uncomfortable memories that existed between us, moving right in to take over his place. I am now directly connected to death. There is no buffer zone between myself and death anymore since he passed away. The fact that I look more and more like my late father means that it will soon be my turn.

Death will eventually take me back to nature. That's the reason why I'm practicing going back home. I'm practicing in order to return to nature. My days in Seoul seem useless, the days I have wasted. Standing in front of the ocean, I cannot help but acknowledge my failures. The ocean has made me realize that this place I left is not at the periphery but is at the center of the world. I am transient but the ocean is eternal. I am on my way back to the womb, where I will once again be closer to eternity.

HYUN KI YOUNG was born on Cheju Island in 1941 and graduated from Seoul National University. He has served as the Managing Director of the National Literary Writers' Association and as the President of the Korean Arts and Culture Foundation (2003). Hyun was also the director of the Committee for the Investigation of the April 3rd Cheju Uprising, as well as the President of the Cheju Institute for the Investigation of Social Problems.

JENNIFER M. LEE teaches English in the Department of English Language and Literature at Konkuk University Glocal Campus. Her translations include Yi Ch'ongjun's short story "The Wounded," and his classic novel *Your Paradise*.

## The Library of Korean Literature

The Library of Korean Literature, published by Dalkey Archive Press in collaboration with the Literature Translation Institute of Korea, presents modern classics of Korean literature in translation, featuring the best Korean authors from the late modern period through to the present day. The Library aims to introduce the intellectual and aesthetic diversity of contemporary Korean writing to English-language readers. The Library of Korean Literature is unprecedented in its scope, with Dalkey Archive Press publishing 25 Korean novels and short story collections in a single year.

The series is published in cooperation with the Literature Translation Institute of Korea, a center that promotes the cultural translation and worldwide dissemination of Korean language and culture.

MICHAL AJVAZ, *The Golden Age.*
*The Other City.*
PIERRE ALBERT-BIROT, *Grabinoulor.*
YUZ ALESHKOVSKY, *Kangaroo.*
FELIPE ALFAU, *Chromos.*
*Locos.*
IVAN ÂNGELO, *The Celebration.*
*The Tower of Glass.*
ANTÓNIO LOBO ANTUNES, *Knowledge of Hell.*
*The Splendor of Portugal.*
ALAIN ARIAS-MISSON, *Theatre of Incest.*
JOHN ASHBERY AND JAMES SCHUYLER, *A Nest of Ninnies.*
ROBERT ASHLEY, *Perfect Lives.*
GABRIELA AVIGUR-ROTEM, *Heatwave and Crazy Birds.*
DJUNA BARNES, *Ladies Almanack.*
*Ryder.*
JOHN BARTH, *LETTERS.*
*Sabbatical.*
DONALD BARTHELME, *The King.*
*Paradise.*
SVETISLAV BASARA, *Chinese Letter.*
MIQUEL BAUÇÀ, *The Siege in the Room.*
RENÉ BELLETTO, *Dying.*
MAREK BIEŃCZYK, *Transparency.*
ANDREI BITOV, *Pushkin House.*
ANDREJ BLATNIK, *You Do Understand.*
LOUIS PAUL BOON, *Chapel Road.*
*My Little War.*
*Summer in Termuren.*
ROGER BOYLAN, *Killoyle.*
IGNÁCIO DE LOYOLA BRANDÃO, *Anonymous Celebrity.*
*Zero.*
BONNIE BREMSER, *Troia: Mexican Memoirs.*
CHRISTINE BROOKE-ROSE, *Amalgamemnon.*
BRIGID BROPHY, *In Transit.*
GERALD L. BRUNS, *Modern Poetry and the Idea of Language.*
GABRIELLE BURTON, *Heartbreak Hotel.*
MICHEL BUTOR, *Degrees.*
*Mobile.*
G. CABRERA INFANTE, *Infante's Inferno.*
*Three Trapped Tigers.*
JULIETA CAMPOS, *The Fear of Losing Eurydice.*
ANNE CARSON, *Eros the Bittersweet.*
ORLY CASTEL-BLOOM, *Dolly City.*
LOUIS-FERDINAND CÉLINE, *Castle to Castle.*
*Conversations with Professor Y.*
*London Bridge.*
*Normance.*
*North.*
*Rigadoon.*
MARIE CHAIX, *The Laurels of Lake Constance.*
HUGO CHARTERIS, *The Tide Is Right.*
ERIC CHEVILLARD, *Demolishing Nisard.*

MARC CHOLODENKO, *Mordechai Schamz.*
JOSHUA COHEN, *Witz.*
EMILY HOLMES COLEMAN, *The Shutter of Snow.*
ROBERT COOVER, *A Night at the Movies.*
STANLEY CRAWFORD, *Log of the S.S. The Mrs Unguentine.*
*Some Instructions to My Wife.*
RENÉ CREVEL, *Putting My Foot in It.*
RALPH CUSACK, *Cadenza.*
NICHOLAS DELBANCO, *The Count of Concord.*
*Sherbrookes.*
NIGEL DENNIS, *Cards of Identity.*
PETER DIMOCK, *A Short Rhetoric for Leaving the Family.*
ARIEL DORFMAN, *Konfidenz.*
COLEMAN DOWELL, *Island People.*
*Too Much Flesh and Jabez.*
ARKADII DRAGOMOSHCHENKO, *Dust.*
RIKKI DUCORNET, *The Complete Butcher's Tales.*
*The Fountains of Neptune.*
*The Jade Cabinet.*
*Phosphor in Dreamland.*
WILLIAM EASTLAKE, *The Bamboo Bed.*
*Castle Keep.*
*Lyric of the Circle Heart.*
JEAN ECHENOZ, *Chopin's Move.*
STANLEY ELKIN, *A Bad Man.*
*Criers and Kibitzers, Kibitzers and Criers.*
*The Dick Gibson Show.*
*The Franchiser.*
*The Living End.*
*Mrs. Ted Bliss.*
FRANÇOIS EMMANUEL, *Invitation to a Voyage.*
SALVADOR ESPRIU, *Ariadne in the Grotesque Labyrinth.*
LESLIE A. FIEDLER, *Love and Death in the American Novel.*
JUAN FILLOY, *Op Oloop.*
ANDY FITCH, *Pop Poetics.*
GUSTAVE FLAUBERT, *Bouvard and Pécuchet.*
KASS FLEISHER, *Talking out of School.*
FORD MADOX FORD, *The March of Literature.*
JON FOSSE, *Aliss at the Fire.*
*Melancholy.*
MAX FRISCH, *I'm Not Stiller.*
*Man in the Holocene.*
CARLOS FUENTES, *Christopher Unborn.*
*Distant Relations.*
*Terra Nostra.*
*Where the Air Is Clear.*
TAKEHIKO FUKUNAGA, *Flowers of Grass.*
WILLIAM GADDIS, *J R.*
*The Recognitions.*

JANICE GALLOWAY, *Foreign Parts*.
*The Trick Is to Keep Breathing*.
WILLIAM H. GASS, *Cartesian Sonata and Other Novellas*.
*Finding a Form*.
*A Temple of Texts*.
*The Tunnel*.
*Willie Masters' Lonesome Wife*.
GÉRARD GAVARRY, *Hoppla! 1 2 3*.
ETIENNE GILSON,
*The Arts of the Beautiful*.
*Forms and Substances in the Arts*.
C. S. GISCOMBE, *Giscome Road*.
*Here*.
DOUGLAS GLOVER, *Bad News of the Heart*.
WITOLD GOMBROWICZ,
*A Kind of Testament*.
PAULO EMÍLIO SALES GOMES, *P's Three Women*.
GEORGI GOSPODINOV, *Natural Novel*.
JUAN GOYTISOLO, *Count Julian*.
*Juan the Landless*.
*Makbara*.
*Marks of Identity*.
HENRY GREEN, *Back*.
*Blindness*.
*Concluding*.
*Doting*.
*Nothing*.
JACK GREEN, *Fire the Bastards!*
JIŘÍ GRUŠA, *The Questionnaire*.
MELA HARTWIG, *Am I a Redundant Human Being?*
JOHN HAWKES, *The Passion Artist*.
*Whistlejacket*.
ELIZABETH HEIGHWAY, ED., *Contemporary Georgian Fiction*.
ALEKSANDAR HEMON, ED.,
*Best European Fiction*.
AIDAN HIGGINS, *Balcony of Europe*.
*Blind Man's Bluff*
*Bornholm Night-Ferry*.
*Flotsam and Jetsam*.
*Langrishe, Go Down*.
*Scenes from a Receding Past*.
KEIZO HINO, *Isle of Dreams*.
KAZUSHI HOSAKA, *Plainsong*.
ALDOUS HUXLEY, *Antic Hay*.
*Crome Yellow*.
*Point Counter Point*.
*Those Barren Leaves*.
*Time Must Have a Stop*.
NAOYUKI II, *The Shadow of a Blue Cat*.
GERT JONKE, *The Distant Sound*.
*Geometric Regional Novel*.
*Homage to Czerny*.
*The System of Vienna*.
JACQUES JOUET, *Mountain R.*
*Savage*.
*Upstaged*.

MIEKO KANAI, *The Word Book*.
YORAM KANIUK, *Life on Sandpaper*.
HUGH KENNER, *Flaubert*.
*Joyce and Beckett: The Stoic Comedians*.
*Joyce's Voices*.
DANILO KIŠ, *The Attic*.
*Garden, Ashes*.
*The Lute and the Scars*
*Psalm 44*.
*A Tomb for Boris Davidovich*.
ANITA KONKKA, *A Fool's Paradise*.
GEORGE KONRÁD, *The City Builder*.
TADEUSZ KONWICKI, *A Minor Apocalypse*.
*The Polish Complex*.
MENIS KOUMANDAREAS, *Koula*.
ELAINE KRAF, *The Princess of 72nd Street*.
JIM KRUSOE, *Iceland*.
AYŞE KULIN, *Farewell: A Mansion in Occupied Istanbul*.
EMILIO LASCANO TEGUI, *On Elegance While Sleeping*.
ERIC LAURRENT, *Do Not Touch*.
VIOLETTE LEDUC, *La Bâtarde*.
EDOUARD LEVÉ, *Autoportrait*.
*Suicide*.
MARIO LEVI, *Istanbul Was a Fairy Tale*.
DEBORAH LEVY, *Billy and Girl*.
JOSÉ LEZAMA LIMA, *Paradiso*.
ROSA LIKSOM, *Dark Paradise*.
OSMAN LINS, *Avalovara*.
*The Queen of the Prisons of Greece*.
ALF MAC LOCHLAINN,
*The Corpus in the Library*.
*Out of Focus*.
RON LOEWINSOHN, *Magnetic Field(s)*.
MINA LOY, *Stories and Essays of Mina Loy*.
D. KEITH MANO, *Take Five*.
MICHELINE AHARONIAN MARCOM,
*The Mirror in the Well*.
BEN MARCUS,
*The Age of Wire and String*.
WALLACE MARKFIELD,
*Teitlebaum's Window*.
*To an Early Grave*.
DAVID MARKSON, *Reader's Block*.
*Wittgenstein's Mistress*.
CAROLE MASO, *AVA*.
LADISLAV MATEJKA AND KRYSTYNA POMORSKA, EDS.,
*Readings in Russian Poetics: Formalist and Structuralist Views*.
HARRY MATHEWS, *Cigarettes*.
*The Conversions*.
*The Human Country: New and Collected Stories*.
*The Journalist*.
*My Life in CIA*.
*Singular Pleasures*.
*The Sinking of the Odradek Stadium*.
*Tlooth*.

JOSEPH MCELROY,
Night Soul and Other Stories.
ABDELWAHAB MEDDEB, Talismano.
GERHARD MEIER, Isle of the Dead.
HERMAN MELVILLE, The Confidence-Man.
AMANDA MICHALOPOULOU, I'd Like.
STEVEN MILLHAUSER, The Barnum Museum.
In the Penny Arcade.
RALPH J. MILLS, JR., Essays on Poetry.
MOMUS, The Book of Jokes.
CHRISTINE MONTALBETTI, The Origin of Man.
Western.
OLIVE MOORE, Spleen.
NICHOLAS MOSLEY, Accident.
Assassins.
Catastrophe Practice.
Experience and Religion.
A Garden of Trees.
Hopeful Monsters.
Imago Bird.
Impossible Object.
Inventing God.
Judith.
Look at the Dark.
Natalie Natalia.
Serpent.
Time at War.
WARREN MOTTE,
Fables of the Novel: French Fiction
since 1990.
Fiction Now: The French Novel in
the 21st Century.
Oulipo: A Primer of Potential
Literature.
GERALD MURNANE, Barley Patch.
Inland.
YVES NAVARRE, Our Share of Time.
Sweet Tooth.
DOROTHY NELSON, In Night's City.
Tar and Feathers.
ESHKOL NEVO, Homesick.
WILFRIDO D. NOLLEDO, But for the Lovers.
FLANN O'BRIEN, At Swim-Two-Birds.
The Best of Myles.
The Dalkey Archive.
The Hard Life.
The Poor Mouth.
The Third Policeman.
CLAUDE OLLIER, The Mise-en-Scène.
Wert and the Life Without End.
GIOVANNI ORELLI, Walaschek's Dream.
PATRIK OUŘEDNÍK, Europeana.
The Opportune Moment, 1855.
BORIS PAHOR, Necropolis.
FERNANDO DEL PASO, News from the
Empire.
Palinuro of Mexico.
ROBERT PINGET, The Inquisitory.
Mahu or The Material.
Trio.
MANUEL PUIG, Betrayed by Rita Hayworth.

The Buenos Aires Affair.
Heartbreak Tango.
RAYMOND QUENEAU, The Last Days.
Odile.
Pierrot Mon Ami.
Saint Glinglin.
ANN QUIN, Berg.
Passages.
Three.
Tripticks.
ISHMAEL REED, The Free-Lance Pallbearers.
The Last Days of Louisiana Red.
Ishmael Reed: The Plays.
Juice!
Reckless Eyeballing.
The Terrible Threes.
The Terrible Twos.
Yellow Back Radio Broke-Down.
JASIA REICHARDT, 15 Journeys Warsaw
to London.
NOËLLE REVAZ, With the Animals.
JOÃO UBALDO RIBEIRO, House of the
Fortunate Buddhas.
JEAN RICARDOU, Place Names.
RAINER MARIA RILKE, The Notebooks of
Malte Laurids Brigge.
JULIÁN RÍOS, The House of Ulysses.
Larva: A Midsummer Night's Babel.
Poundemonium.
Procession of Shadows.
AUGUSTO ROA BASTOS, I the Supreme.
DANIËL ROBBERECHTS, Arriving in Avignon.
JEAN ROLIN, The Explosion of the
Radiator Hose.
OLIVIER ROLIN, Hotel Crystal.
ALIX CLEO ROUBAUD, Alix's Journal.
JACQUES ROUBAUD, The Form of a
City Changes Faster, Alas, Than
the Human Heart.
The Great Fire of London.
Hortense in Exile.
Hortense Is Abducted.
The Loop.
Mathematics:
The Plurality of Worlds of Lewis.
The Princess Hoppy.
Some Thing Black.
RAYMOND ROUSSEL, Impressions of Africa.
VEDRANA RUDAN, Night.
STIG SÆTERBAKKEN, Siamese.
Self Control.
LYDIE SALVAYRE, The Company of Ghosts.
The Lecture.
The Power of Flies.
LUIS RAFAEL SÁNCHEZ,
Macho Camacho's Beat.
SEVERO SARDUY, Cobra & Maitreya.
NATHALIE SARRAUTE,
Do You Hear Them?
Martereau.
The Planetarium.

ARNO SCHMIDT, *Collected Novellas.*
  *Collected Stories.*
  *Nobodaddy's Children.*
  *Two Novels.*
ASAF SCHURR, *Motti.*
GAIL SCOTT, *My Paris.*
DAMION SEARLS, *What We Were Doing*
  *and Where We Were Going.*
JUNE AKERS SEESE,
  *Is This What Other Women Feel Too?*
  *What Waiting Really Means.*
BERNARD SHARE, *Inish.*
  *Transit.*
VIKTOR SHKLOVSKY, *Bowstring.*
  *Knight's Move.*
  *A Sentimental Journey:*
    *Memoirs 1917–1922.*
  *Energy of Delusion: A Book on Plot.*
  *Literature and Cinematography.*
  *Theory of Prose.*
  *Third Factory.*
  *Zoo, or Letters Not about Love.*
PIERRE SINIAC, *The Collaborators.*
KJERSTI A. SKOMSVOLD, *The Faster I Walk,*
  *the Smaller I Am.*
JOSEF ŠKVORECKÝ, *The Engineer of*
  *Human Souls.*
GILBERT SORRENTINO,
  *Aberration of Starlight.*
  *Blue Pastoral.*
  *Crystal Vision.*
  *Imaginative Qualities of Actual*
    *Things.*
  *Mulligan Stew.*
  *Pack of Lies.*
  *Red the Fiend.*
  *The Sky Changes.*
  *Something Said.*
  *Splendide-Hôtel.*
  *Steelwork.*
  *Under the Shadow.*
W. M. SPACKMAN, *The Complete Fiction.*
ANDRZEJ STASIUK, *Dukla.*
  *Fado.*
GERTRUDE STEIN, *The Making of Americans.*
  *A Novel of Thank You.*
LARS SVENDSEN, *A Philosophy of Evil.*
PIOTR SZEWC, *Annihilation.*
GONÇALO M. TAVARES, *Jerusalem.*
  *Joseph Walser's Machine.*
  *Learning to Pray in the Age of*
    *Technique.*
LUCIAN DAN TEODOROVICI,
  *Our Circus Presents . . .*
NIKANOR TERATOLOGEN, *Assisted Living.*
STEFAN THEMERSON, *Hobson's Island.*
  *The Mystery of the Sardine.*
  *Tom Harris.*
TAEKO TOMIOKA, *Building Waves.*

JOHN TOOMEY, *Sleepwalker.*
JEAN-PHILIPPE TOUSSAINT, *The Bathroom.*
  *Camera.*
  *Monsieur.*
  *Reticence.*
  *Running Away.*
  *Self-Portrait Abroad.*
  *Television.*
  *The Truth about Marie.*
DUMITRU TSEPENEAG, *Hotel Europa.*
  *The Necessary Marriage.*
  *Pigeon Post.*
  *Vain Art of the Fugue.*
ESTHER TUSQUETS, *Stranded.*
DUBRAVKA UGRESIC, *Lend Me Your*
  *Character.*
  *Thank You for Not Reading.*
TOR ULVEN, *Replacement.*
MATI UNT, *Brecht at Night.*
  *Diary of a Blood Donor.*
  *Things in the Night.*
ÁLVARO URIBE AND OLIVIA SEARS, EDS.,
  *Best of Contemporary Mexican Fiction.*
ELOY URROZ, *Friction.*
  *The Obstacles.*
LUISA VALENZUELA, *Dark Desires and*
  *the Others.*
  *He Who Searches.*
PAUL VERHAEGHEN, *Omega Minor.*
AGLAJA VETERANYI, *Why the Child Is*
  *Cooking in the Polenta.*
BORIS VIAN, *Heartsnatcher.*
LLORENÇ VILLALONGA, *The Dolls' Room.*
TOOMAS VINT, *An Unending Landscape.*
ORNELA VORPSI, *The Country Where No*
  *One Ever Dies.*
AUSTRYN WAINHOUSE, *Hedyphagetica.*
CURTIS WHITE, *America's Magic Mountain.*
  *The Idea of Home.*
  *Memories of My Father Watching TV.*
  *Requiem.*
DIANE WILLIAMS, *Excitability:*
  *Selected Stories.*
  *Romancer Erector.*
DOUGLAS WOOLF, *Wall to Wall.*
  *Ya! & John-Juan.*
JAY WRIGHT, *Polynomials and Pollen.*
  *The Presentable Art of Reading*
    *Absence.*
PHILIP WYLIE, *Generation of Vipers.*
MARGUERITE YOUNG, *Angel in the Forest.*
  *Miss MacIntosh, My Darling.*
REYOUNG, *Unbabbling.*
VLADO ŽABOT, *The Succubus.*
ZORAN ŽIVKOVIĆ, *Hidden Camera.*
LOUIS ZUKOFSKY, *Collected Fiction.*
VITOMIL ZUPAN, *Minuet for Guitar.*
SCOTT ZWIREN, *God Head.*